The Daughter Gambit

JUSTIN ROBINSON

League of Magi
BOOK TWO

CAPTAIN
SUPERMARKET
PRESS

Captain Supermarket Press
info@captainsupermarket.com

First Printing, 2016
ISBN 978-0-9892781-3-3
eISBN 978-0-9892781-4-0

Cover art by Yoly Cortez

Book layout and composition by Lauri Veverka
Typefaces: Gill Sans MT, Adobe Garamond Pro

www.captainsupermarket.com

For Lauri,
who makes everything
possible.

The League of Magi

CONTENTS

The Daughter Gambit

THE CONDOR'S NEST WAS PERCHED on a hidden plateau just south of the four Huandoy peaks in the Peruvian Andes. Mist enshrouded it on most days, like the thick smoke of a hundred campfires. The few paths to it were steep and rocky, making it almost impossible to reach from land. And since it was not the highest peak around, it made an unattractive destination for thrill seekers.

When the Priestess chose the location for her home over two thousand years ago, she had chosen well.

It had changed over time, although the specifics were guesswork. The Priestess kept no written records in her early days, and there were only a few bas-reliefs on the inner walls that showed somewhere that might have been the Condor's Nest before the Europeans came. To a layman, it might have appeared like any village from any Pre-Columbian civilization, but that was deceiving. The Condor's Nest took elements from every one of the great civilizations, marking itself as not one of them but rather born from and superior to all of them.

Step pyramids stood at the northern and southern ends of the plateau. They were almost perfect twins of El Castillo at Chichén Itzá, each with eighteen terraces and ninety-one steps, referencing the Mayan calendar. Despite the apparent age, the stones showed no sign of wear, each maintained the same sharp edges it had when it had first been built. The staircases were bordered with exquisitely crafted sculptures. The northern one had Kukulcan, the feathered serpent, and in the diffuse light of dusk each side appeared to slither down the stairs. The southern had ants marching up and down the sides, a far more powerful if less well-known symbol. The boxy temples at the top bore the symbol of the sun.

Between the pyramids was a wide field of impossible, emerald green. This was broken by the pale red lines depicting stylized ants walking north to south in the fashion of the Nazca Lines. Bordering the field were colossal stone heads in the Olmec style, brooding inward at one another. Around them were squat one-story buildings making up the living quarters of those in the organization who called the Nest home.

The apparent newness of every structure was due to the fact that the Priestess had kept a Physurgist Apprentice to maintain the Condor's Nest since the first building had been constructed. She kept a good relationship with the Lion, and the Crone before him, for this reason. The black shape perched on one of the Olmec heads was probably the current Apprentice, Kisin. Like all Physurgists trained for the Priestess, he specialized in earth and stone. Kisin was not the Priestess's heir, and the only Magus he threatened was the Lion, someone with whom the Priestess had few problems, and thus Kisin lacked political importance. This is why he drew all of the difficult jobs. One look in his eyes and it was obvious it wore on him.

Teotl looked down at the Nest from the helicopter as it broke through the mist, the rotors spinning it away in smokey whorls. It bore toward the central ant in the field, ready to set down in the middle of its thorax.

Teotl had no intention of waiting that long. Without warning the pilot, she stood up from her seat and opened the door. The chill wind cut right through her jacket, whipping her long black hair around her face. She jumped from the helicopter, falling twenty meters to earth, a grin splitting her face the whole way. Even knowing the fall was harmless, her blood still sang with it. A cheap, harmless thrill, one of the benefits of being a Familiar.

She hit the ground with a thump that sounded as though the earth were inhaling. The energy from the impact flooded into her tissues, an electric hum threatening to explode out of her. She could have held it in, felt the constant jangle of the power seeking a way out and finding none. Instead, she let it go, focusing the blast outward with her arms, targeting one of the Olmec heads. The energy swept out of her, slamming into the rock and knocking a good chunk off the brow.

She knew from experience she could hold the charge for a couple hours if she had to, but it got uncomfortable after the first. It required constant concentration, the clenching of muscles she hadn't known she'd had until the Priestess had flooded her with raw power. The gift had turned Teotl into a conduit, and energy wanted to move through her more or less freely, to be redirected instantly. Fighting the flow was unpleasant.

The figure on top of the Olmec head stood up. It was Kisin, his long brown coat flapping around his lean body in the propeller wash from the helicopter. He muttered something as he moved, and stone stairs burst from the ground in time to meet his feet. With another word, they sank into the earth, the dirt closing up over the top, erasing the steps from existence.

Teotl smiled as they met each other by the head.

"You know I have to fix that," Kisin said. He spoke Olmec, despite the fact that both of them were native Spanish speakers. Olmec was the language of the Priestess's organization, peppered with loan words from Spanish, Nahuatl, Portuguese, and even English. All learned to speak it soon after initiation, and soon it became more natural than their native tongue.

"Not hard for you," she said.

"I suppose not."

They had not seen each other since San Francisco, a little over three years before. The Twins had gotten their Familiar and killed one of the Priestess's in the process. It had been a bad defeat. More than that, it was a failure. Teotl had failed *her*. Teotl returned to her home in Tumaco to stew in shame and waited for a call that only came the previous day.

"How are you?" she asked Kisin.

They started walking to the southern pyramid, nicknamed El Hormiguero by the organization for the relentless ant motif. The symbol of the Priestess's Art, ants could be found incorporated into every sculpture and bas-relief in the Condor's Nest.

"I've been better," Kisin said. "She has not mentioned San Francisco. She summoned me last week and will not see me."

Teotl shook her head. "We knew this was bad."

"Sometimes I wonder how she got the story at all."

"One of your men maybe? One of mine?"

"My men would have informed me. Those that survived."

"I hardly see mine."

Kisin chuckled. "You Familiars. Your bodyguards are a luxury rather than a necessity."

"Anything that can kill me can kill them more effectively."

"True, but that buys you time to escape."

Teotl was quiet as Kisin's words sunk in. She knew he was callous, especially when it came to mortal lives, but the casual way he tossed that off chilled her. Her men weren't a necessity, but she still liked to look after them. Their lives weren't something to be thrown away. They were to be spent, like precious stones, and their sacrifice honored.

"I don't think my men were summoned," she said finally, to keep things from being too awkward.

"Huracan's men, then? One or two lived."

She nodded. "That would seem most likely. They had to be reassigned anyway."

They climbed the steps of El Hormiguero to the Temple of the Sun at the top. The mist twined around the verdant peaks of the Andes. In the bracing air, Teotl felt alive the way she did nowhere else on earth. The Condor's Nest was an enchanted place. Even to those who knew about the real world, it was almost mythical. Only members of the Priestess's organization had the chance to see it, and then only a select few ever actually did. It was a rare privilege.

One Teotl had treated disrespectfully when she had failed.

They entered the temple at the top. The sculptures waiting there were in the style of the old gods, but they were of the real gods of this place: the Priestess and her Apprentices. The mistress of Sorcery stood in the center of the temple, arms outstretched toward Sorcery's source, the sun. All around her, the sculpted ants formed the base of her power. The other three stood around her, Itzcoatl by her side, looking up at the same sun, though not quite touching it. Kisin's representation was on the right, wearing a skull mask with his necklace of eyes. His bracers were etched with flies. Santa Orisha was on the left in her robes, a dragonfly perched on her outstretched hand, a jaguar crouching at her feet.

A stone staircase led down into the guts of the temple. Kisin and Teotl followed it. Inside the temple, lights were spaced evenly along the ceiling. They were the exact color of the sun, and shed a pleasant heat. There were no cords, just veins of crystal reaching into the rock.

"I've been meaning to ask," Teotl said, the stone swallowing her voice. "About what happened." The name was on her tongue, but wouldn't come free. "The Familiar?"

"Coldheart?" Kisin asked.

Coldheart, standing over her. His starved blue-gray flesh desiccated, his hand, like a claw, outstretched. He held her with the freezing storm. The wind and ice wrapped around her body extracting warmth, life. Effortlessly, ready to end her.

She shuddered in the sudden chill, turning it into a nod.

"Reports of him in Montreal and New York," Kisin said. "They're probably keeping him in reserve for the time being. It's unwise to use a new Familiar, even one so powerful, as an assassin before they're fully ready."

"True."

"Looking for a rematch?"

"He nearly killed me the first time."

They stopped at a heavy stone door, etched with ants worshiping the sun.

"Nearly doesn't count," Kisin said. "Good luck in there."

"Take care of yourself," she said to him.

They weren't friends, not exactly. It was difficult for Apprentices and Familiars of the Priestess to be friends. Maybe in other organizations, but hierarchy was important to the Priestess and thus to her servants. Apprentices had more autonomy, and had larger responsibilities, but Familiars were linked directly to the ruler of Cemanahuatl. They were killers and bodyguards, yet had a shard of the divine in each of them. A glowing heart of pure magic, turning them into conduits of her power. When she bled, they died; they were the same spirit, the same flesh.

Teotl touched the sun carving, and expelled a tiny bit of energy she had held over from her fall. With a heavy, grinding sound, the door slid aside.

The Priestess waited on the other side. It was a long moment before Teotl could perceive anything else. The Magus was simply more present, more real. She was the sun on earth, a fount of raw power. Her features were some kind of South American Native, an exemplar of a standard long extinct. Her skin was smooth and red-brown, her hair long and glossy black. Her nearly black eyes were slanted over cheekbones that were high and sharp. She was beautiful, but it was an antediluvian beauty, something not seen anywhere else on earth for thousands of years. Sky blue robes clung to her curves, and large golden disks hung from her ears. A high headdress of gold, decorated with multicolored feathers, added to her regal appearance. Resting over her breasts was another golden disk, this one carved with the symbols of Sorcery: the sun and the ant. Because the Priestess had ruled Cemanahuatl and had occupied the seat of Sorcery since the inception of the League, those symbols had become her own.

Only then did Teotl register the presence of others in the rounded stone room. Standing at the Priestess's shoulder was Itzcoatl, her heir and one of the oldest Apprentices still living anywhere on earth. He had been born an Aztec priest, and he carried turquoise plugs in his nose and labrum. His sense of fashion had evolved, and he wore a pinstriped Armani tailored to his diminutive stature. His features were craggy and rough, his body compact.

The room was lined with the Priestess's Servitors, Los Luminosos. They appeared human, but shed a golden light from their flesh. They wore loincloths and blindfolds, a sunburst embroidered on both. All were young and beautiful. As with every time she saw them, Teotl had a brief moment of wondering: had she been a half step slower, a little weaker, or even slightly less stubborn, she would have been among their number.

"Welcome," the Priestess said. Her voice was full and powerful, a murmur carrying like a shout.

Teotl dropped to one knee and bowed her head. "Mistress." To stand in front of the Mistress of Sorcery was to be at arm's length from an atom bomb.

"Rise, my child."

Teotl looked up to meet the Priestess's depthless eyes. No one knew exactly how old the Priestess was. Older than the League certainly. One of the oldest beings on the planet, accumulating power with every passing year, and losing her humanity at the same pace. But then, what use did a goddess have for humanity? Teotl loved the woman for all she had done, and hated herself for the failure that put disappointment in those eyes.

The Priestess gestured, and Itzcoatl produced a scroll. With a lazy wave of the Priestess's hand, the scroll floated across the room to Teotl. The Priestess no longer needed to speak for the simplest uses of magic; they were mere reflex to her. "I have a task for you."

Teotl reverently accepted the scroll from the air, and the Priestess's buzzing force vanished from it. Teotl felt a little of the residual energy leaking into her; later she would fire it off into the air. She unfurled the scroll and held it up, reading by the light of the glowing people.

It was a dossier for one of the Butterfly's Apprentices, the Prophet Wei Lai. He wore red Triad robes, trimmed in white. He was lean and handsome, but what was most striking about him was that his eyes were sewn shut. The writing on the scroll detailed what little biographical information was known, some speculation that he was once a gambler working for the Triads in Hong Kong in the 1930s, and the various places he had been sighted.

"I want you to kill him," the Priestess said.

It was unnecessary to say. Getting a dossier like this, on a member of another organization, there was really only one possible order. Teotl had done it before, though not so many times that she didn't have a slight pause as she thought that a normal person might ask why.

"When and where?" Teotl asked.

The Priestess stood up from her throne. Every step seemed to carry her the equivalent of two or three, a smooth and graceful progression to Teotl. The Priestess laid a hand on the cheek of her Familiar. Though Teotl knew it wasn't flesh and hadn't been for many centuries, she still closed her eyes and felt comforted at the touch.

"Good girl," the Priestess said. And answered her Familiar's questions.

The touch stayed with Teotl on the flight to Lima. It was only the second time the Priestess had ever laid a hand on her.

The hand passed right through Teotl's flesh, only she was still Esperanza then, her name out there for all to hear. The touch felt like pure electricity, grabbing, shuddering, pulling her nerves into a new place, beyond pleasure and pain. And inside, something was beginning to form, the core of a bright new star, spoken into being by the arcane litany tumbling from the Magus's lips.

Teotl knew she had to make herself worthy of that touch. There had finally been forgiveness after the failure in San Francisco, offered without acknowledgment. Redemption was hers to take, and all she had to do was put one Apprentice in the ground. Wei Lai was as good as dead. She called the leader of her bodyguard detail, Rodrigo Sanchez, from the air to have him meet her at the airport with the rest of the men.

The private jet landed at Jorge Chavez International, taxiing down a side runway. The men waited with their gear in the shadow of a fuel truck. Teotl smiled in spite of herself. Though she never used them for their intended purpose as bodyguards, it was always good to see them. They were her soldiers, her assistants, her boys. The plane rolled to a stop, and she was already up and heading for the door.

She came out into the late evening as mechanics affixed the fuel hose to the plane. She briefly wondered who they thought she and her men were. Some rich lady and her bodyguards, probably. It was a piece of the truth.

Her men were dressed simply, in gray cargo pants and tight t-shirts. None wore their weapons in the open; those would be packed in the bags and cases around their feet for the most part, though all would have at least a concealed pistol on them. Some had jackets on, others kept those in their packs. The jackets had patches on either shoulder, on the left, the Priestess's sunburst. On the right, was the symbol they had given to Teotl: the silhouette of a woman on a field of blue, golden light coming from a point in her chest. She had nothing to do with its design when it had appeared a little over twenty years ago on the shoulder of Rodrigo Sanchez, at the time a young soldier in her unit.

"What is this?" she asked him.

"Your symbol," he said, looking more than a little terrified but proud all the same.

"My what?"

"Your symbol. So people know we're your men. The other squads all have them, except those who don't belong to an Apprentice or Familiar."

"And where did it come from?"

The blush was vivid, turning his pale cheeks bright red. Sanchez could blush like no one she had ever seen. "I made it," he mumbled.

It started to appear on patches, on tattoos drawn into their skin, and once as a crude version shaved into a man's hair. It embarrassed her, but the men seemed to like it. They were asked to trade their lives for hers. A little embarrassment wasn't much of a price to pay. They only wanted to honor her.

They straightened as she stepped out onto the tarmac. Every one of them was taller and broader than she was, recruited from military and police forces around Central and South America. Sanchez smiled as he set eyes on her. It was tough to reconcile him now with the boy who made the patch. Age and battle had cut lines into his face and dusted his hair with gray. He was still a formidable man, but he was far closer to the end of his career than the beginning.

"Miss me?" he asked in Spanish as she approached.

"Not even a little," she said with a smile. "Get the men loaded up and I'll brief you."

He nodded, turning around. "What are you ladies waiting for? Move your lazy asses!" The men responded instantly, grabbing their gear and filing into the jet. Sanchez continued to bark at them whenever they didn't quite move fast enough for his liking, and in minutes, the ten men were on the jet, their bags stowed.

Teotl smirked at the reflexive sexism of calling the men "ladies." They served a woman who served another woman. But that kind of thing was ingrained so deeply, they never bothered to correct it. Even with a full, long career ending in retirement, the men came and went so quickly.

Teotl and Sanchez got onto the plane last, taking seats just behind the cockpit. The men had settled, some were reading, others had earbuds in. A card game had already broken out in the back between four of them. Teotl buckled her seat belt, not because she was worried, but if they were to crash her practically invulnerable body could smash someone to pulp.

Sanchez handed Teotl a manila folder from his pack. "Here's the file you asked for."

"Thanks," she said, turning away so he didn't see her face as she put the file under her seat.

"You don't think we're going to run into him, do you?"

"Not in Shi Jie. We're going to China. I wanted the file because I thought he might be the target after this one."

If Sanchez noticed the lie, he didn't comment. "So it's a hit."

She nodded. "We'll get it done quick and you'll be back in the arms of that cow you married."

"Jealous?"

"Sorry, Drigo. I like men with their original hair color."

"That's a low blow, love."

She waited until the plane was over the Pacific, the windows black with night, to stand up. The men immediately went silent, putting away books, removing earbuds, setting cards face down on tray tables.

"Good evening, gentlemen. Tomorrow morning, we will set down in China. Our target is Wei Lai, Apprentice to the Butterfly." She handed out a picture of the man. Each soldier took it, memorized it, and passed it on. When it hit the hands of the youngest member of the team, he shuddered.

"He is a Prophet," Teotl said. "That explains the eyes. He will be up in the Changbai Mountains, and that is where we will hit him. There should not be much resistance, plan for his standard complement of bodyguards. We'll have the element of surprise."

The young soldier was plainly nervous, his hand slowly rising.

"Yes?" Teotl said.

"If he's a Prophet, ma'am, doesn't that mean he knows we're coming?"

"I'll spare you the metaphysics of Prophecy, Mr..."

"Rinc... er... Morales," he said, finally remembering the false name the organization had given him.

"Mr. *Morales*," she said, driving the name home. "The short answer to your question is maybe. Think of Prophets this way: they see time the way we see space, so he can see the pathways available, and often the risks on each one, but not necessarily how everything fits together. There's a chance that he hasn't seen us, or that whatever he is doing is worth the risk, or he might know we're going to fail." She broke into a grin and swept her boys with her gaze. "I know it's not the last one."

"*Susordenes, Jefe*," they said in unison, making jittery Morales return her smile.

"That's what I thought. Moves sharp and eyes clear, gentlemen. Let's do this and get home."

She sat down. She heard the boys relax behind her, start to joke, and return to what they were doing. The cards snapped and the coins clinked.

"Are you all right?" Sanchez murmured, quietly enough so the other men wouldn't hear.

"I'm fine. Why?"

"You're tense. Don't try to pretend you're not. Is this about San Francisco?"

"I'm not tense."

"We walked away. Soldiers died, but that's what soldiers do."

"I nearly died."

Sanchez blanched. "I'm sorry. I was on the other side of the street. They had one of their demons in my midst and it was shredding the men. I should have been there for you."

"Then you would be dead."

"At least I wouldn't feel so guilty."

He grinned, and the lines in his face disappeared and he was young again and...

A dingy hotel somewhere in Damascus. Rodrigo's mouth was on her, hands divesting her of clothes. The need in both of them was overpowering, the feeling they physically could not exist for a second longer without being together. Death was still close, but it only spurred them on.

...he was the same man, but he was older now. Different. Over twenty years together, a relationship gone through all the paces. Military, romantic, and now friends. Sanchez was the most loyal person she had ever met, the only one she knew that would die for her without hesitation or regret.

"San Francisco was a catastrophe," she said.

"You couldn't fight it forever. The files said the Twins had tried before, and we stopped them. Kisin was even there that first time. You want to blame someone, blame him."

"You shouldn't talk like that."

"Oh, come now. We both know he's broken. He looks like a man and talks like a man, but there's nothing in him anymore."

Teotl fell silent, but couldn't help nod. "Still."

"You're right, of course. But talking to you and talking to anyone else are still very different things."

"Yes. Yes, they are."

"I understand how the kid is feeling," he said, nodding in the direction of young Morales. "Lot of new blood in the squad for one thing."

"They're talking about San Francisco, aren't they? About the men they replaced. I failed. They died."

"No one thinks that. I don't know if you know this, but shooting at Familiars and Magi isn't really the recipe for a long life. All right, maybe we don't know exactly what that means until it happens for the first time, but before that we were in some group where getting shot at is part of the job description. When a mission fails, it's the fault of the other side. And that's their job."

"Easy for you to say. We've been together since..."

"The raid on the Serpent's facility in the Black Forest."

Facility was an odd term. It was a grove of wych elms in the middle of the forest, human-sized cocoons hanging from the branches. Six-foot caterpillars crawled along the brown surfaces, tending the precious flesh within. Some of the cocoons bled, others burned. Corpses of these monstrous caterpillars, cut apart by gunfire, lay sprawled on the forest floor. Some of Teotl's men lay with them, bleeding from hideous lacerations or burned black by fire. They fought between the trees, firing up at the author of their destruction, Sotek, one of the Serpent's Familiars. She dodged in and out of the canopy, her leathery wings beating the air, landing long enough to rip a man to pieces with her talons, or char him with her fiery breath. Teotl was trying to pin Sotek down, but the hobgoblin was too fast. A bullet tore through the side of a cocoon, and the pasty white form of a man slumped out, featureless and hairless, dripping thick white mucous and blood from his nerveless hand.

"We lost a lot of men that night too," Sanchez said.

"But we accomplished our task. Burned that grove to the ground."

He sighed. "I can see I'm not going to pull you from this self-flagellation. I suppose I'll just have to succeed tomorrow and stay alive."

She allowed herself a small smile. "That might do it."

"Then I'm going to need some sleep." Sanchez folded his arms tightly and shut his eyes. In moments, his breathing had slowed and his face had relaxed. Just like a foot soldier to be able to sleep instantly and completely as soon as there was any time to do so.

Teotl could not sleep, and so took the file from under her seat and studied it. It was not just the failure that kept her awake, though in the week that immediately followed San Francisco, she had not slept. It was the fear of doing it all again. Of failing again, and getting more of her men killed in the process. She couldn't even consider the possibility, but it was there, whispering in her ear.

Her, little Esperanza, seven years old, cowering on the floor, the sounds of machetes on meat in the other room.

Her, fourteen, holding Michaela's body, her adoptive mother cut down by gunfire, looking up into the Priestess's depthless eyes.

The memories ran in her head throughout the flight. When the wheels touched down, it jolted her from a state almost like sleep, and she focused, her attention clear and bright in the sharp morning. She stepped out into the bracing wind, the airstrip in the middle of nowhere. The Changbai Mountains rose out of the earth on the horizon. The truck, a small and beat-up cargo model, was waiting on the edge of the tarmac by the road to the highway. It looked shabby, but Teotl knew it would be in top shape. The driver was a man named Wu, the operator of the Priestess's local safe house, known to the League as lighthouses. Teotl nodded to him as she and her men piled into the back. Wu was heavyset, and had probably been an impressive specimen in his youth. Now, muscle was turning to fat, black hair to gray.

Wu was an unpleasant reminder of an essential truth: a Magus's organization continued far beyond their borders. There were agents, sleepers, doctors, and many others. Cemanahautl was overrun, the same as any other, but it was easy to forget when not looking directly at evidence to the contrary. These personnel were scattered throughout the world in enemy territory because they were needed there. The fact that most Magi deliberately ignored was this: their organizations would collapse without these mostly invisible humans.

By the time Teotl pulled herself into the back of the truck, her men were already assembling their PARAFAL assault rifles in quick, clacking motions. Two of the men carried M3 shotguns, and one was putting together a German sniper rifle. Every man also carried at least one pistol and one combat knife. She knew they had the safeties on all their weapons, but it was for their benefit, not for hers. It had been almost forty years since guns were any danger to her. Her brain had even rewired itself, now registering a gun in the hands of an assailant as a funny joke. She took a position at the head of the trailer, her back resting against the cool metal wall. Her men stretched out on either side, five on each.

The truck rattled the whole way up into the mountains. She spent the entire ride trying to affect the serenity she didn't feel.

She hoped that as long as she looked calm and in control, her boys wouldn't be afraid. The thoughts returned, and with each bump and rattle she saw a new way to disappoint her mistress.

The truck pulling over was a relief. She waited until the back opened and the door slid upward. The men hopped out, weapons ready. Teotl followed. It was afternoon, but the heat from the sun didn't do much for her up in the mountains. She shivered.

The freezing air pulling around her, a living thing, the gray-blue monster holding her life in his claws.

There would never be a cold as deep as what she had felt in San Francisco. This slight chill was nothing, though she knew after that moment, dying in front of Coldheart, she would never feel truly warm again.

Wu set about faking a flat tire while Teotl gathered her boys around her. Wu would wait here until they returned to smuggle them back to the airport. The faces of her men were set, though Morales, the youngest one, was merely putting on a brave front. They had their rifles slung.

"All right," Teotl said to them. "Charge me."

"Pistols," Sanchez said. As one, the ten men unholstered their sidearms. "Silencers." They screwed the long cylinders to the end of the barrels. "Aim." In a line, the men leveled their guns at Teotl. "Fire."

The silenced nine millimeters snapped. Teotl closed her eyes, feeling each individual impact in her torso, in her outstretched arm, in her face. She imagined them as a burst of light, sudden, bright yellow-white, then bleeding outward, and fading, each hit making her glow just a little brighter. The force wormed inward from each point, igniting a warm path, like the burn of good bourbon. Each separate path joined in the center of her, right next to her heart. The bright impacts spreading with a web of cracks that united, glowed, pouring more of the energy into her. The force fed itself, building and building, joining and joining, until it was a burning, humming, shining star, demanding to be let out. And she knew she could, in bits or all at once. She was power.

The bullets, robbed of their kinetic energy, tinkled to the ground at her feet.

She opened her eyes and smiled, the hum of the bullets putting her hair on edge. "Let's go."

They hiked into the woods. Sanchez put his scouts on point, and the rest stayed in staggered formation. Sunlight dappled the ground, and a breeze snaked through the trees. Teotl had gone into many of the remote places in each Magus's fief on her assignments. Apprentices and Familiars generally lived in cities, though there were exceptions to that rule. There was more protection there, and it was less likely to have assassins come in and start throwing around magic where mortals could see it. But the real business of the League was done in the wilderness, away from the eyes of the populace. A single human was not dangerous, but humans traveled in swarms. The history of the League was littered with Familiars, Apprentices, and even Magi who forgot that and died for it.

It remained to be seen what Wei Lai was doing.

She stopped dead as Sanchez held up a fist. Up ahead, one of the scouts lowered a dead man into some bushes. They moved on, and as Teotl passed the corpse, she regarded him. A young man in a paramilitary uniform, probably recruited from the People's Liberation Army of China originally. His throat had been cut ear-to-ear, and he stared up, glassy-eyed, into the sun. Teotl wondered if Wei Lai would feel for this man, or if he had known the particulars of this death before the man himself. Did a Prophet grieve for someone they knew was already lost?

The energy hummed within her. It wanted to be let out. She

fought it, and for the time being, it was a pleasant sensation.

The scouts killed three more men as they continued through the woods. It seemed like too many. Why would Wei Lai keep that many troops so far from him? It wasn't worth worrying about. If the worst thing that happened on the mission was that they killed more of the Butterfly's soldiers than they thought, they could call it a resounding success, and Teotl would never have to see disappointment in her mistress's face again.

Sanchez made another signal, then turned to Teotl, murmuring, "They've found it."

She nodded, approaching quietly, hunched over and hidden, Sanchez by her side. The scout was just ahead, flat on his belly and peering through some bushes. She dropped to her belly next to the man, and looked through.

They were on top of a small rise, overlooking a dell. On the clear ground, circles had been made out of human bones. No, not circles. Clocks. The borders were done with vertebrae, the hours were marked with skulls, and the hands were constructed from femurs adorned with the metatarsals of the feet and the metacarpals of the hand. They were set at the cardinal directions, and thus did not line up precisely with the shape of the clearing, but looked to be exactly equidistant from one another and arrayed about a central point that was unmarked in any way.

Wei Lai stood in the clock at the north, about twenty meters from Teotl. He wore his red Triad robes, his head freshly shaved and gleaming. His eyes were sewn shut, but even at that distance, she could see the eyeballs moving around under the lids, as though he were dreaming. He was toying with a mahjongg tile, his undulating knuckles making the piece walk over them. Whatever ritual he was conducting had not begun yet, or was in the midst of a lull. At his feet was a man who looked like he had been a farmer. He lay face up, staring up at the sky with sightless eyes, a bullet hole in his forehead. Five other men stood with him in a loose ring, armed and uniformed. Soldiers.

In the southern circle, a tall and pale woman was perfectly still, arms at her side. She looked to be Chinese, her skin stark white, her hair kept long. She was dressed simply in a utilitarian garb of black canvas pants, boots, and a sleeveless gray shirt, showing off her skinny white arms. She looked frail, but Teotl knew there was enough strength in those arms to rip iron apart. This was Jiangshi, one of the Butterfly's Familiars. She too had soldiers with her, though she hardly needed their protection.

The eastern and western circles had five more men each. More soldiers to watch over whatever was happening. They all had the grizzled look of veterans, and judging by the military precision of their uniforms and movements, they were recruits from the People's Liberation Army, the same as the dead boy in the woods.

Lastly, a nude shape crawled on all fours between the circles. The figure was roughly masculine, though he had no body hair and no genitalia. His ivory flesh was entirely smooth, broken up by jet black hair and eyes. He moved like an animal, his teeth chattering compulsively. It was a ghost, one of the Butterfly's most dangerous Servitors.

The intelligence had been wrong. Very wrong. This wasn't a small force. This was an Apprentice, a Familiar, a Servitor, and twenty men, plus any who were still out in the woods guarding the other directions. This was stiff opposition, and Teotl had every justification for leaving at that moment and blaming a failure of intelligence.

She took a deep breath and focused. That would be almost worse than San Francisco. She wouldn't even be trying, and that was not something she wanted to return to tell the Priestess. Instead, she took stock. If she wasn't going to retreat, she needed to assess the threat.

First, the soldiers. Their guns couldn't do much more than charge her. They would kill themselves with every shot they fired. They could target her boys, but they were elevated and in cover. It was a good position for an ambush.

Wei Lai had very few offensive powers. Prophets were dangerous enemies until you cornered them, and then they were the most helpless of any Apprentice. Even her boys could take the Prophet, if they weren't dodging lead from the men who outnumbered them two to one. She would kill him herself, as per the orders, her only fear that he might get away in the general chaos.

Jiangshi next. She was inhumanly strong and nearly indestructible. Dangerous to some, almost helpless against Teotl. She had tangled with the walking corpse before, and it was a minor miracle Jiangshi had managed to escape.

It was the Amazon, Jiangshi and Teotl on the opposite sides. She sent Jiangshi sprawling through the trees with a single backhand, stored from who knew how many of the undead woman's punches.

The ghost was the truly dangerous one there. That thing would be wearing the first man who fell as a suit. Depending on its power and age, it might have other abilities. It would be completely immune to the kind of physical force Teotl or her boys could bring to bear. Watch it, try to keep it out of any of her men, and evade it on the way back to the truck.

Teotl watched Wei Lai, wondering when the ritual was going to commence. It was always best to attack an Apprentice when their attention was divided. As vulnerable as they were, they were far more versatile than any Familiar. She watched him fidget with the mahjongg tile, his blind attention apparently focused on the point in the middle of the ritual rings. He wasn't talking. This wasn't even a ritual.

He was waiting.

"We're attacking now!" Teotl whispered. "Concentrate fire on the soldiers and fall back as soon as the target is dead." The men nodded, their weapons coming up as they lay flat on the short ridge. "When I break cover, you fire."

Teotl leapt out of the bushes. She didn't bother sliding down the ridge, letting the minor impact of her feet on the earth flood into her for a little extra power. The guns chattered from above and behind her, spitting smoke and death into the clearing.

Teotl heard a man shout, "Now!" in Mandarin, and the soldiers in the clearing opened fire onto the ridge. She prayed her men were safe, but had no time to check.

She felt a few bullets impact her, probably from someone unfamiliar with her powers. She flung her arms out, directing pinpoints of force toward the Prophet. She relaxed her grip on the force just enough to release the tiniest bit, one gunshot each, like pinching off a drop of water from a full spigot. Soldiers jumped between the force and Wei Lai, their chests shredded in favor of their master. Like they knew the phantom bullets were coming even before she released them.

Wei Lai stood serene in the gunsmoke, the tile walking over his knuckles.

Teotl dug her feet into the earth to run at him.

She felt it first. A bass thrum, almost silent, yet heavy enough to vibrate her teeth and bones. She staggered, focusing on the center of the clearing. The source of the apocalyptic note burned into her eyes. It was a point no bigger than a pea, glowing the opposite of light: somehow shining, though it ate the day around it. A point so dark it was brighter than the sun. It seemed to be there forever, the world freezing around it as the pure strength of the tiny object pulled everything into its onyx depths, warping the very world around it. It had the staggering presence of a planet materializing in front of her.

And then, the flash.

Blinding white light, and a thudding wall of force slammed into Teotl. There was no sound, or at least none she could hear. Maybe it was like the light, the opposite of sound, a wall of deafness that consumed every noise around in a great, aching void. There was only the agony of the energy flooding into her cells, expanding, pulling them apart. She had never felt anything so powerful, not even the touch of the Priestess when the sun had been ignited inside Teotl's chest. Every atom of her body was overloading, and she could only hold on, and find a way to remain herself in the face of overwhelming power. Keep her body from flying apart into dust. Hold herself together by sheer force of will.

In that single moment, she could feel the Priestess through the link they shared. A link that was normally invisible, functioning on a purely instinctual level. Magus and Familiar, forever shackled with magic. The agony bled through the link, and Teotl knew that though the Priestess was only feeling a fraction of it, it was still too much. Even then, the pain through every fiber of her, threatening to tear her apart, she wanted to spare her mistress any discomfort. And if the Familiar could have taken the anguish away, she would have, even if it meant oblivion for herself.

The light grew brighter and brighter. The energy was never ending, and would continue to soak into her until she died. It flooded and tore, her cells separating by new rivers of raw power. She fought to ride it, to redirect it even as it came into her, but she could not. She could only take more and more of it, until her vision was consumed in white, her hearing in the rush of static, her screams in a blank tone. She had no idea how long she spent in agony, the explosion forcing itself into her tissues. Centuries or seconds were all the same in the heart of a star.

Finally she could take no more and tumbled into the brightness, her final coherent thoughts a prayer to the Priestess to forgive.

The next thing she remembered was black. Maybe it was because the light had burned out her ability to see anything at all. She wasn't even certain she still had eyes, or if they had been scorched from her skull. She was being jostled, over and over. She could scarcely feel anything over the insistent energy buzzing through her body, and it made her teeth ache trying to keep it in.

The world resolved in a haze of vein blue. She hadn't gone blind. Some good news at least. Her face was bumping against something wet that smelled like rare meat. The sky was brown. No, that was the ground. She was upside-down. Being carried over someone's shoulder like a sack of grain.

As the realization pushed into her scrambled mind, the person carrying her let out an exhausted grunt and fell to one knee. He lost his grip on her, and she tumbled to the ground. The impact succeeded only in awakening the power coursing through her, making it probe her defenses for an escape. Her entire body was alive with electric spiders. She winced, putting her arm out, and relaxed to release the hideous pressure, but the power stayed in her. Humming. Maybe she was too hurt. Maybe it was too much. She turned instead to her rescuer. Strange to have one of those after thirty-eight years of not needing one.

Sanchez had been carrying her. His uniform was shredded, burned, and stained with blood. Where his flesh was visible, it was a livid ruin. One eye had been closed, the bulk of his hair burned to ash on his scalp. Teotl glanced back the way they came, and saw trees blasted down, some burning, others black.

"Drigo!" she said, taking him in her arms.

He collapsed onto the earth. "You're alive."

She looked at herself. Her clothes were a little dirty, but that was all. There was only the oddness of the energy in her body. She should be able to release it, but she was still frazzled by whatever had happened in that clearing. Whatever it had been was more than she'd ever experienced. "What happened?"

"Explosion," Sanchez gasped. "The Butterfly's people… those circles of bone protected them somehow. All of ours were killed."

"How did you survive?"

"I was running down to join you. I think you absorbed some of the blast. You saved my life."

She looked into his remaining eye, the white turned blood red, the lid burned black. "Just returning the favor," she said, her words breaking off as she swallowed the sob threatening to come out.

"Let me rest for a minute, all right?"

She nodded.

"I'll be fine," Sanchez said. "In a minute."

His remaining eye closed. His breathing slowed. Stopped.

Teotl stood up, setting him gently on the ground, the tears cutting through the grime on her face.

"I have her. Fifty meters south-southwest of the site. All on my position," said a voice in Mandarin.

Teotl looked up into the face of a wiry thirty-year-old soldier. He was dressed in a paramilitary uniform, a mahjongg tile hanging around his neck where another man might wear dog tags. He was standing five meters away and was pointing a Chinese-made assault rifle at Teotl's heart. He didn't have a cruel face. It would have been easier if he had. Teotl tried to focus on him, but he kept going all wobbly and vanishing into pure color.

He switched from Mandarin to halting Spanish. "I don't want to hurt you. You don't want me to hurt you. Surrender and you will be treated well. All right?"

The energy from the explosion sang through Teotl's body. Her mind was calm enough now. She could focus and let some out. There was enough in there to turn the soldier into atoms many times over. And when that was done, she could go back for his friends, and then the Prophet. For Sanchez, she told herself. They would bleed for what they did to Sanchez.

She raised an arm, pointing at the man's chest.

"Please don't do this," he said.

She stopped fighting. The energy wanted to come out, wanted to wreak its destruction, only prevented by the power the Priestess had granted. She exhaled, relaxing her body. Teotl felt it, a tornado of locusts roaring and hissing through her belly, chest, legs, and arms. It should have flooded out of her arm and into the soldier. It should have found the conduit easily, tracing the path of her arm to be set free to do its terrible work.

It didn't.

"I don't know what you're trying to do, but stop."

She concentrated, trying to push it up and out of her. It would not move. There was so much within her, it should have been gratefully released.

Contact then? Something to jolt the power into functioning? The explosion had scrambled her worse than she thought maybe, and it just needed a bit of guidance.

At that distance, the assault rifle would hit her several times. A little more power wouldn't hurt, not after what she had absorbed. It would be some tiny drops of energy released into the hapless soldier. She ran at him.

"Bad idea," he said. The rifle barked.

She felt the bullet impact her shoulder. It spun her around, flinging her bodily onto the ground, sending her rolling down the hill. She crashed into a tree down the slope. Instead of the comforting feel of power worming into her core, she felt only the hot agony of the bullet's path. Her cells still buzzed with unreleased energy, and now, blood was blooming across her shirt and jacket.

Looking up, she saw the soldier, his rifle still leveled at her, but she was much farther away from him. She looked at her shoulder again, unable to understand how the bullet had hurt her. It was only a bullet. It should have been nothing.

"Stay right there!" the soldier shouted.

She would do nothing of the kind. She needed to get away. The truck was past the soldier and the clearing, so her only option was down the slope and to the lighthouse. But first she needed to get away from the suddenly dangerous man with a gun.

Maybe she would live long enough to learn why her powers were gone.

- 2 -

The explosion was the constant. Wei Lai saw it first, when the tiles tumbled into place, laying out the story that was to come. It sprang to life in his mind, a constant that no amount of manipulation on his part would change. He approached it, the situation clarifying, details flowering as though they had always been there but were suddenly visible.

And it was the first step on the long path to revenge.

It had become so familiar to him that when it actually happened, when the quintessence appeared and reacted, he was silent and still. The circles blocked the wash of heat and force, though he could feel it in memory, on the paths in which he did not prepare the circles. He felt his body stripped away into atoms, reduced to a shadow on the ground. He felt the ghostly itch of pain as the unimaginable force tore through the forest around him. It touched him only in the faint wash of wind and a faraway clap.

The gunfire had started moments earlier. Wei regretted the sacrifice of his men in the forest, but they had to be there. On the other pathways, when there was no one, Teotl grew cautious and arrived late, which resulted in anything from sixteen dead men, to Jiangshi torn apart, to the end of the path for Wei himself. He could not die yet. Not for a little more time. He had to draw Teotl in, and from there, the path branched in ways he could not quite control. There were too many of them, webbing outward, intersecting, turning back on one another. In many, she died. In a few, she did not.

She was very important. Not to the world at large, but to him. They had never spoken, but she was the only one with the potential to give him the most beautiful gift of all.

Wei ordered his men to return fire with a clipped, "Now," knowing he needed only to pin them down on the ridge. The quintessence would do the rest.

As the explosion passed, it would be a memory to all the men present. To Wei, it had been a memory before it had happened, and he possessed memories of several different scenarios. He still felt the the sudden agony and the darkness. He could see that path terminated, and as it disappeared behind to be usurped by the hundreds of thousands of new choices, perhaps he would forget it.

He stood at a wheel, with spokes going off in every direction, more than any wheel would ever need. An inexperienced Prophet would have been paralyzed by the choices, but Wei had seen them up ahead. He had mapped them with his tiles, and he was ready to track them. They all led to the same place.

All paths did. Eventually.

The explosion was gone. The clearing had been expanded. There was now a crater in the center, and dirt, the little that hadn't been instantly vaporized, would be raining around the forest over the blackened and fallen trees for miles. He didn't see it with his eyes, he had them sewn shut in a fit of mania during his Apprenticeship. He had never regretted the decision, as with it came the clarity of power. Kabur had teased him, and he smiled at the memory, telling her he would not need eyes to see anymore.

"Captain Zhu?" he said to the head of his bodyguards. "Find the intruder and kill her."

Wei could see the frown creasing Zhu's craggy face in a hundred memories focused into a single point before frilling outward. "Sir, the explosion likely did the job."

"That was Teotl," Wei said. "If anyone could survive that, it is her. And in point of fact, she did."

Zhu saluted and barked orders at his men. Wei might have been concerned at remaining relatively unprotected—though he still had a Familiar and a Servitor by his side—but there were no paths that led Teotl back to the clearing. None where she killed him in this time and place.

Zhu and his men disappeared down the slope after Teotl, the men in a single, irregular line. They'd beat her from hiding and drive her in front of them like fox hunters. Wei could not be certain they would catch her, but he could be certain that this would keep her away.

"Kaeru, if you would be kind enough to get the quintessence before it reacts again?" Secondary explosions loomed down several of the pathways, great flashes of light and thunder, eclipsing the horizons of time.

The ghost, in response to his name, chattered his teeth. *Tiktiktiktiktiktik.* The only sound the poor devil could make when not encased in flesh. He crawled along the ground on his hands and feet like an animal, to the corpse of the man they had brought for this purpose. Kaeru crouched over the body, pressing his white hands against the bullet hole, his body dissolving into something not quite smoke and not quite milk, and flowing into the wound. Soon, the ghost was gone.

The corpse sat up. The man had been a farmer, with a wide, honest face, and a body that was more sinew than muscle or bone.

He had seemed half-witted to Wei, and one of the reasons they chose him. Now, the corpse's face was set in a knowing smirk, the mark of any body possessed by Kaeru.

"I hate it when they're not fresh," the corpse said.

"He was killed two hours ago."

"That's long enough for things to get soft." The corpse stood up, and stumbled before he got his balance. Kaeru tried a few steps in his rotting suit. "All right, I'm ready."

"The container," Wei said, producing a Ch'ing Dynasty coin with the square hole through the center. He flipped it to the corpse, who caught it with practiced ease.

Kaeru left the protection of the circles for the crater. Nothing would have gotten Wei to follow. There were too many pathways when he did and distracted the ghost, giving the quintessence time to explode again. Despite his distractibility, Wei liked Kaeru. They were both gamblers.

"This reminds me of a joke I used to love in my breathing days."

Wei had already heard it many times, though Kaeru had not yet told him.

"These scientists decided they were as good as God, so they challenged Him." The corpse's fingers picked up the tiny spot of quintessence from the center of the crater. Where the sallow flesh touched the stuff, skin, muscle, and bone dissolved. First it was the pads of the fingers, then the meat underneath, and soon bone was turning into smoke. Too long, and it would react, the dead body proving enough of an accelerant for a second explosion. If Wei spoke, that would be long enough, so it was best to let Kaeru do what he was doing.

"So, God came down—because this is a joke, and God does that sort of thing—and said to the scientists, 'I made life from dirt, so if you're my equal, you can do the same.'" The corpse held up the quintessence and peered at it with one milky eye.

"The scientists said, 'Easy,' and started scooping up some dirt." The corpse's right hand was almost completely gone. It fit the quintessence into the hole in the center of the coin, forcing it in with the exposed bones of its ruined hand.

"'No no no,' said God." The corpse held up the coin. The quintessence was in the middle, spinning like a tiny planet, never touching any part of the coin itself.

"'Get your own dirt.'" The corpse turned, revealing that the damage had not been confined to its hands. Its face was horribly burned, exposing the blackened bone of tooth and jaw. It seemed to be grinning, and it was, as no one liked Kaeru's jokes more than he did. The corpse flipped the coin back to Wei, who plucked it right from the air and put it in the pocket of his sleeve.

"Thank you, Kaeru."

The corpse regarded Wei, and the Prophet was tempted to just answer the question and save the trouble of speaking it. Manners being what they were, he waited.

"What would have happened if that stuff had appeared in a populated area?"

"Then you, my friend, would have become very, very redundant."

It was strange to see a corpse shiver, but that was exactly what happened.

Wei had to smile. Not a Necromancer himself, he was nonetheless an integral part of a Necromancer's organization—the Necromancer, really. He never had the Apprenticeship to learn to create, control, and communicate with the undead. His revulsion had to be tamed naturally, and over time he had begun to understand and appreciate them. Still, it pleased him whenever they were the ones disturbed by something. "Now that the quintessence is in my hand, I would like the two of you to assist Captain Zhu."

Jiangshi turned. Unlike the stuttering movements of the ghost, she seemed to operate on a preternatural level of grace, every motion part of a slow and subtle dance. "Sir?"

He waved her concern away. "I am quite safe." He knelt, and cast a handful of his mahjongg tiles across the earth, whispering a few words as he did so. The pathways opened up along the tumbling tiles, and he followed them, watching the players navigate a maze whose shape they could never see. "Find Captain Zhu at the waterfall. Our quarry will be there in half an hour." He cocked his head, his sightless eyes apparently seeing something in the tiles. "Go that way," he pointed. "You'll find something that might be useful."

* * *

Teotl ran, or as close to it as she could come. In reality, it was closer to an exhausted stagger, a series of falls only broken when she put one wobbly leg out to stop her plowing face-first into the earth. She clutched the wound in her shoulder, feeling her flesh somehow torn open, a sensation she barely remembered and was certain she would never feel again. The bullet had punched through her skin, which now sported a peeling hole that burned with pale fire. Her blood was a sticky mass turgidly pushing through her fingers. She felt more warmth on her back that rapidly turned to streaks of cold. Her own steps jarred and jostled it, pushing fresh spikes from the wound into the rest of her body.

She knew it wasn't a bad wound as these things went. A single hit, and it had punched clean through. Some basic medical care and she would be fine. But then, any wound could be life threatening. This one was slowing her steps. She could hear the soldiers coming through the trees up the slope. Less than an hour ago she would have laughed at the idea of men with guns trying to kill her. She might have even given them quick deaths as a mercy for their stupidity. But now, now they were the most dangerous enemy she had ever seen.

It was almost funny. When she won the Prize, the Priestess had told her she would live forever. That was the deal every Familiar got. Even then, it wasn't a sure thing. Familiars would never die of natural causes. They could never get sick, never grow old. Compared to a human being, they scarcely needed to eat, drink, breathe, or sleep, the tiny god-shard of the Magus's power being more than enough to power their bodies. Yet they could be killed, and the history of the League, and the chaos that came before it, was littered with the corpses of Familiars. They were the fists of their masters, and the easiest way to hurt one of the living deities of the League was to cut a Familiar down.

Yet the Priestess told Teotl she would live forever. And Teotl, though she still used her True Name then, believed her. She didn't truly understand what the Priestess meant, but even then, she knew the Priestess was divine, and a divine being could not lie.

Teotl stumbled against a tree. Her hand came away from her shoulder and pushed off from the bark.

She hadn't really believed it until she watched the soldiers who had been young when she joined, grew old and retired. It wasn't many of them, as the soldiers of any organization had lifespans that were measured in eye blinks, but those few who did made her believe. She saw men that she had met as smooth-skinned boys retire as scarred men with deep wrinkles and graying hair. She could even describe how they had gotten each scar, those men closest to her, and as they were worn down and diminished, she was still the same woman preserved in beautiful youth. She believed it then. She was going to live forever.

That was only a quarter of a century into her immortality. She was still young by League standards, still existing in the span of a single human life, but she felt it. That's when she got reckless. She took stupid risks. She thought that just because she was literally bulletproof, that extended to other things, forgetting that the creatures of the League had so many ways to kill. Older now, though not by too much, she had seen this same progression in others. They truly understand they have forever, and they forget about those things that could take it away. That was when most Familiars died, in that period between the moment they thought they understood eternity, and the moment they really did. That usually came when they passed the threshold of a life. Beyond that, time really did become precious. Even as they hoarded it, they always wanted more.

Those Familiars, the ones who understood, they could still be killed. They had lifetimes of experience, incredible powers, and a keen desire to live, but that didn't always matter. When it finally happened, when eternity shrunk to a moment, when a thousand years became five seconds, Teotl thought they probably felt the way she did, fleeing through the rugged slopes of the Changbai Mountains.

All she wanted was one more breath.

* * *

The corpse staggered drunkenly next to Jiangshi. Kaeru was having a hell of a time moving the thing around. Two hours dead wasn't so bad, and in the chilly weather, it was almost as good as new. Still, he wished Wei Lai had thought to bring a cooler. *Well, then I'd be complaining about how stiff the joints were*, the ghost thought to himself, pleased he could do that through the body's softening brain. He let out a little chuckle, which, due to the corpse's partly-dissolved tongue, sounded like a series of pops. That made him laugh, and the sound was truly chilling.

The only one around to hear was Jiangshi, and she could not be disturbed by anything. She couldn't be much of anything, really. It was disappointing to Kaeru, as the woman was still quite attractive despite being dead.

She did turn at the outburst, though no expression creased her face. She had the most exquisite features. Apparently she had been some kind of Chinese aristocrat in her breathing days, and that showed in her porcelain beauty. "What? Did you see something?"

"Oh no, just thinking."

"Oh." There was no disappointment in her tone, but Kaeru supplied it anyway.

"Just thinking," he said, choosing to ignore the disappointment he might have invented. "You're dead. I'm dead."

"If we were not, we would not be here."

"Right, yeah. I don't know what it's like being a walking corpse."

"You're *in* a walking corpse."

"Yeah, but I don't know what he thinks about it. He's a dead guy. His soul's gone. If I weren't here, his brain would be completely worthless."

"I don't follow your point."

"You're a walking corpse. You know what it feels like."

"I have no other frame of reference beyond mortality, and that was too long ago."

Kaeru, rambled on, barely hearing what Jiangshi had to say. When he first met her, he was in awe of her. In awe of all the Familiars, but she had become a known quantity. And she was a terrible conversationalist. "When I came back... or was brought back," he couldn't remember, and it didn't really matter anyway, "I didn't think I would miss my body. Why would you when you can go anywhere? Walk through walls, be invisible if you want to be, and the other little tricks you can do? But you miss it."

"I wouldn't know," she said.

"No, you wouldn't. But it's things you never even consider. You can't think properly without a body. Not like you remember thinking anyway. The thoughts get... muddled. And don't even try speaking. The words come out wrong. All wrong." Kaeru shook his borrowed head. The initial horror at what he had become had faded and now it was just a fact of life, even though it had only been a couple years. The Butterfly's servants had a strange lot in the League, suspended between life and death, two states they had previously believed to be absolutes.

"There," Jiangshi said, pointing one delicate finger. She didn't care about the state they were in. No, she was only concerned with the here and now. A body without a soul could hardly be faulted for not having any desires, but it could be frustrating.

She was pointing to a corpse. It was in even worse shape than the skin Kaeru was wearing currently. This one looked badly damaged by the explosion, its flesh melted off the bone in a few spots, its paramilitary uniform in tatters. Apparently, the man who used to belong to the body had walked here and collapsed. With the wounds on him, that was an impressive feat.

Kaeru moved the farmer's feet in the slow, shambling steps toward the fallen man. He began to smile as he recognized the corpse. Not as an individual, but enough to know that this was indeed that useful something Wei Lai had mentioned. Kaeru smiled, showing even more teeth on the corpse than those revealed by the melted lips. "This will make things more fun."

* * *

"Sir, I have a handprint here!" The voice belonged to Corporal Wang Pingtou, who had another name when Captain Zhu Baolin first met him in the People's Liberation Army. Wang was an excellent soldier—that was why Zhu recruited him into the Butterfly's organization in the first place—even if he didn't have the best sense of decorum. He was keeping his jokes to himself at the moment, as they all knew hunting a Familiar was a dangerous game. He stood by a tree, and as Zhu approached, he could see there was indeed a small handprint—Teotl was a small woman; 5'2" and barely a hundred pounds when she wasn't filled with kinetic energy—the blood growing sappy on the bark. Several ants were stuck in the browning blood, their struggles frantic and futile.

Wang touched the stain, and held up a finger. "She's close. It's still wet."

The men were still in their loose line, searching for evidence of Teotl's presence. They were all excellent soldiers, and Zhu had brought each and every one of them into the organization. They had all served under him in their mortal days, and when he was tapped to lead Wei Lai's bodyguards, Zhu insisted on creating the team from scratch. Wei had smiled and given Zhu full authority to do just that. Zhu knew all of these men, trusted all of them with the most sacred duty there was. He had never been part of a finer fighting force.

Now the keen-eyed Wang had found what they were after. Zhu called the men in, looking at each of their faces while he rattled off orders he knew would be followed to the best of their abilities. They could focus, then spread out, like a series of flowers until they found the next sign. And again, and again until they had her cornered. "Remember, men. She's wounded, she's lost, she's far from home. She is also a Familiar. The instant you forget that, you will be dead."

The men nodded, murmuring, "Yes, sir." Only Wang hardly seemed to be paying attention. He was grimacing at the blood on his index finger. "Hang onto this for me, will you?" he said to the man next to him, and wiped the blood on his sleeve.

Zhu allowed himself the barest hint of a smile, and did Wang the courtesy of not noticing the breach in discipline. When they had Teotl, then Wang would become the cold professional that had so impressed Zhu when they'd first met. Based on that handprint, the time was soon, and there were only so many places the Familiar could hide.

Zhu gestured, and his men moved down the slope, peering into the dappled shade, their weapons at their shoulders.

A branch snapped behind him. His conscious mind barely registered the recrimination—had he managed to walk right past the hiding Familiar? Had she walked them directly into an ambush baited with blood? Later, he would scold himself for allowing anything to sneak up on him, but as he whirled and saw Jiangshi approaching, his limbs loosened, and the barrel of his weapon dropped.

A badly-burned man stood next to Jiangshi, and since she was not presently tearing him into pieces, Zhu could safely assume it was just the ghost trying on some new flesh. From the looks of it, this was one of Teotl's men. A good choice.

"Status report," intoned Jiangshi.

"Teotl is badly wounded. Corporal Wang wounded her and she is losing blood. The falls are just ahead, and we believe we have her trapped against the river. In her present state, swimming will be difficult."

"When we find her, keep your men back. I will finish her off."

"Ma'am, I understand Mr. Wei's orders, but we should take her alive."

"Wei stated—"

"Yes, ma'am, I understand that. But we have a chance to capture one of the Priestess's Familiars alive. There is unprecedented leverage to be gained here, to say nothing of whatever information she may give up in interrogation."

"Wei stated that we kill her," Jiangshi said.

"I understand that, ma'am, but I believe it is in the Butterfly's best interests if we take Teotl alive."

"Killing her doesn't preclude talking to her," the ghost said inside his stolen flesh. "Before, after, or during."

"Ma'am, I..."

"She dies," Jiangshi said. Though she never raised her voice, Zhu thought he could detect some kind of anger in the monotone. "She dies not because Wei ordered it. She dies because every death weakens *them* and strengthens *us*."

Zhu snapped to attention, the authority in her voice plucking the strings military life had installed. "Yes, ma'am."

"If I may," Kaeru said, "I believe I have a plan."

* * *

Teotl stood on the shore of the river, her back pressed against the trunk of a pine tree, the bullet hole throbbing in her shoulder. Right ahead, the river was a churning mass of white, tumbling over falls that were thirty meters high. The shore was broken in two, a cliff falling the same distance. She would have to backtrack up the slope to find another way down the cliff, or upriver to find a calmer spot to cross. She knew her pursuers were close, even if their footsteps were eaten by the angry roar of the river.

"Teotl!" She knew the voice. Even warped now by the hideous wounds on throat and mouth, she knew that voice. She shut her eyes against the tears filling them. They left cold streaks down her face.

"Teotl!"

It was Rodrigo Sanchez, or more accurately, his body. The fucking ghost had taken it. No matter how much she wanted to pretend her friend was alive, that somehow he had recovered from the shattering explosion, she knew the truth. The force within her churned with as much rage as the river in front of her, and she wanted to let it out. To obliterate Drigo's body. It was not the hero's burial he deserved, but it would at least deny the Necromancers their plaything. It would let him rest. But the Butterfly never let anyone rest.

Rodrigo, telling her about the woman he met. Teotl, smiling, giving her blessing. Behind the smile, there was real happiness, but also regret, a tiny shard to worry away in her heart. She would never have a family of her own. Not in the human sense.

"It's me!" the ghost called in Rodrigo's battered voice. "You can come out! It's safe!"

She wished she could stand and fight them. She couldn't hurt the ghost, but she could punish the rest of them for it. They wouldn't live long enough to regret the day they faced Teotl, the fist of the Priestess.

She couldn't. If she did, with her powers refusing to listen to her, she would die. And then Drigo's sacrifice would have been for nothing. They wouldn't honor him, but she would.

She sprinted for the water. There were only six meters of wet, rocky riverbank between her and the churning river. Her pounding steps tore into the bullet wound, sending jagged stripes from her shoulder into her body. It wouldn't be the worst thing she would feel. In a moment, there would be blinding agony, but she couldn't let that stop her.

"There! She's there!" the ghost screamed.

The chatter of automatic weapons started. She never braced for a hit, as that might slow her down. Even a half-step might be fatal. She dove into the white waters. The current ripped at her shoulder, and she cried out, but it came in the form of fat bubbles that were instantly shredded. She tumbled end over end. She felt like her arm was being torn off at the root. The agony put white screens in front of her eyes, a roar in her ears, and a fist on her heart.

And then she was in air, breathing, but not without sucking water in every mouthful. She was falling, falling. Forever it seemed. She gained only glimpses, when the pain receded enough to give her a snapshot. When her overheated brain managed to focus on something for an instant.

She saw the sky, as she fell amongst dots of white water glittering like jewels. She saw the white water below bleeding out into the slate gray of the pool. The slick, throat-like surface of the rocks behind the waterfall.

Then she hit the water and her mind disappeared into a shriek.

* * *

Alone in the clearing, Wei Lai walked into one of his ritual circles and paused. He removed the quintessence from the pocket of his sleeve. Now that he was alone, he felt comfortable in doing so. It was a silly thought, either Jiangshi or Kaeru, no matter the ghost's deficiencies of character, stealing the pea-sized bit. They were loyal servants of the Butterfly both. Yet Wei could not escape the sensation that the quintessence was his only temporarily.

It was difficult to track through the webs of time. Not because it was particularly hard to find, but because its presence was physically painful to look upon. It bored into Wei's head and planted a knife between his eyes. So wherever it settled on a nexus of decisions, it obscured the exact moves it would make as it advanced on to the next. He saw it find a home in the vaults of the Butterfly. He saw it stolen by an agent of the Twins to be used in their never-ending war with the Serpent. He saw it consumed and destroyed by Teotl herself. There were more fates than that for it. There always were. Those were merely the ones that had many pathways.

He walked the coin over his knuckles. Though the quintessence was shielded in its prison of magic, he still felt it whenever the flat of the coin collided with his fingers: a faint buzzing reaching into his bones. Even locked away, the strange prime matter wanted to eat away at everything in the universe.

He flipped the coin into one hand and closed his fingers around it. He began his incantation, focusing on both places and times, and stacking them one on top of the other. These invocations never felt as real, as instinctive as his walks through probability. The Hermit had spent much time teaching Wei these skills, and he was still not certain he truly grasped them. He understood them well enough to work, yet without the true understanding of a master.

Time and space were merely different ways to understand location, and once one realized they were but points on a graph, one could change them. It took effort. Will. The proper words to focus the mind and sharpen the desire. It would drain him almost completely, and he would have to return to one of his sites to recharge, but it could be done. There was very little difference between the ritual clearing in the Changbai Mountains and his home on a tiny island off the coast of Hong Kong.

For a moment, he was simultaneously in both places. He could be seen, interacted with, and even touched, if there were anyone in either location to do so, and they would never see that he had stacked two times and places on top of one another. He could have watched them walk through walls and each other that were only there for him.

He used it to travel. There was no pathway; he created one, and then he erased it behind him. He felt both the cool piney breeze of the forest as he did the salt tang of the air through the open windows of his tower. Gradually, the forest faded away, its sounds and smells diminishing until there was nothing but the comfortable open space of his office, at the top floor of Fantan Tower, his home.

Though his eyes were sewn shut, he could see his office, both in his present reality as well as any number of future and past incarnations. Only those in which he was dead—a disturbing number of those—did the office fade away. He could trace the pathways for some distance, and it was this way that he saw his revenge in the gloom of the future. He'd heard of this during his tutelage, the increasing number of dead futures. Manipulation of the future was the Prophet's stock in trade, and what made them so valuable to their masters despite being almost useless in direct confrontation. Yet this manipulation could prove the Prophet's undoing. Close off too many potential futures, and sooner or later, none of them would include you.

Wei had closed off a great many in his seventy years in service to the Butterfly, and it was still not enough. There were many in which she was dead. Permanently dead. And he had yet to close the door on most of them.

He had learned early on that when the chance came to close off a truly unacceptable future came, he would take it. Had he accepted this lesson earlier, perhaps Kabur would still speak to him. Perhaps Jun would still be alive.

He had the quintessence. That was enough, for now. He had bypassed some of the futures that involved his mistress's death. Not enough, but one at a time. He was not entirely certain there was a future that contained both his mistress and the fruits of vengeance. Sometimes he wondered, if forced to make the decision, which he would choose.

He was ready to die, but was he willing to sacrifice his mistress too?

Clutching the coin in hand, he made his way to his desk, picking up his phone just as it rang. "Captain Zhu," he said by way of greeting. "She got away."

"Yes, sir. She jumped into the waterfall before we could stop her. Is she still alive?"

"I'm afraid so." Wei walked down the staircase that emerged from the floor of his room. The floor directly below his office was a ritual space. A clock had been painted onto the floor, the numbers replaced with runes. His magic was much easier here, where the work had already partially been done. He drew his tiles from his pockets, felt the comforting rattle in his hands, and cast them into the clock. Wei was impressed with Zhu's discipline, remaining silent while the Apprentice worked his Art. Zhu was important in the days to come, though the man himself did not know it.

Wei looked at the tiles, and they were constant across every conceivable path. Each one opened up the webs, sending red-gold light racing through the pathways.

"She will be at Yingkou Port in twelve hours," Wei said, and hung up the phone.

He had to let the men follow her. The more he interfered, the more likely the future would kill his mistress. He was playing the most dangerous game a Prophet could: trying to win on two fronts without losing on a third.

* * *

It was night when Teotl hauled herself out of the river. Her right arm, under the perforated shoulder, hung limp. Whenever she tried to move it, shards of agony ripped through her. She felt as though it had frozen over entirely in the icy mountain water, and in cracking the sheet of ice, she exposed the red pain underneath. She wasn't even certain how she could still be bleeding. In her mind, her veins would be empty, replacing what she'd lost with filthy river water. She imagined herself to look like Jiangshi, the Butterfly's zombie, with blue-gray skin and hair hanging like lank clumps of seaweed.

She was alive. That was what mattered. She didn't know how. Maybe the energy that still swarmed through her tissues like angry bees was the only thing keeping her alive. She would have expected it to lessen somehow as her body leeched on it to stay alive, but it was as strong as ever.

Dead. Something she hadn't had to think of in many years.

She was running. Running from that awful thing she had seen in that house, clutching her stuffed dog to her chest. She could barely see through the tears. She was only seven, and she had some vague sense that she had seen someone that no one ever should, let alone a child. At that moment, there was only the sick sensation of fear. That any moment the men with the machetes would come out of her house. They would see her. And that would be all.

Now, half-drowned, half-frozen, half-dead, she stumbled across the countryside. She knew where to head. Had she been anywhere in the world, she would know the closest lighthouse. Here, it was the one Wu operated. She never thought she would need one, but she kept them memorized for her men. All of whom were rotting up on that mountain somewhere.

Yingkou would be the closest one, and from there, she could get smuggled out of Shi Jie. She hoped Wu had returned from the mountains when they missed the rendezvous time. She hoped he hadn't been captured and broken for the information in his head.

Would being caught be so bad? At least she would not have to explain her failure. Maybe the Priestess would forgive her. Again. All Teotl could do would be to beg to get her powers fixed, and promise to try again. She shook her head, fighting off the frustrated tears. The Priestess had taken her in, given her power, given her eternity, and this was the price of that trust.

Michaela was the first. Teotl—no, she was Esperanza then—had been on the street for five years at that time. Her stuffed dog was ripped and soiled, but she kept him as a reminder. Michaela had reached out to the girl, smiling. Esperanza had never seen such a beautiful smile.

It was dawn when she knocked on the door to the lighthouse. She had spent time walking, running, and had even stolen a sputtering old car to get her to Yingkou. She knew how much she stood out. Her dark *indígena* features were common enough back home, but in China, she might as well carry a sign screaming "Outsider!" She kept her head down, her wound concealed under a jacket she'd stolen from the seat of that same car, her face hidden behind her long black hair.

She had never been to this particular lighthouse, and even as she knocked, she felt the niggling doubt. Had she remembered properly? Had she studied every friendly location enough to be used when she needed it? Or was she about to wake and scare some poor family who had no idea who she was?

The door opened, revealing Wu, wrapped in a bathrobe, which showed that his left leg ended mid-calf. He was getting around with a simple prosthetic and a cane. She couldn't imagine his lighthouse was used very often, and he had been awakened to the surprise of his life.

Wu blinked. "Mistress? I— Come in, come in!" He swept the tiny woman inside and closed the door behind her. "Were you followed?"

She shook her head.

"Good. Are you hurt?"

She gingerly removed the coat, showing the weeping bullet wound in her arm.

"I'll tend to that first. Please, sit down in here."

The house was not large, but it was well-furnished. Everything in it looked to be the best available of whatever it was, from the stainless steel kettle he put on the stove, to the classic art he hung on his walls. Teotl barely spoke to Wu, barely knew him, but she knew why he served the Priestess. It wasn't idealism or even power. No, his reward was money and comfort, the surest way to insure loyalty.

He cut the shirt off her body to get at the wound. She might have felt self-conscious at this, but Wu showed no interest in her beyond the professional. He asked her what had happened, and she gave him the broad strokes. He listened carefully, nodding along, and speaking in a halting version of the Olmec patois used by the Priestess's servants.

He checked her wound, cleaned it, and stitched it up on both sides. "You're lucky," he said. "It's stopped bleeding. Other than the infection you probably picked up from the river. A shot or two and you'll be fine."

He didn't ask why the needle was able to penetrate her flesh all of a sudden, and she didn't tell him. He took her stained clothing and pointed to the back of the house. "There's a room back there, with some clothes in the closet that should fit you. I will contact our mistress for an extraction. In the meantime, get some rest. I'll bring you some food in a little while."

"Thank you," she said.

The Priestess saw to it that this crippled old man would never suffer. He'd live out his days in comfort, and he likely would never have to do anything else in his life to deserve it. He needed only to have this lighthouse available on the off chance anyone would need it. The price was high, if invisible: if the Butterfly's people ever detected him, they would kill him. People like this man died across the globe every day.

That was the difference between Familiars and mortals. A thousand of them could die, and their mistress would never feel a thing. When a Familiar bled, the mistress bled with them. If only a little.

She found herself, crouching by the closet, crying tears she had not cried since she was seven years old. Fighting only made it worse, so she cried until she could stand again. Wiping at her stubborn tears, she stripped out of the rest of her clothing, stiff from the river.

She poked through the closet and found what Wu had promised. She stripped out of the rest, and replaced it with clean underwear, then jeans and a tank top, a work shirt over that, and finally a new leather jacket. She winced as she pulled the shirt over her wounded arm, but Wu had done a good job. She was bandaged tight. There were even boots in her size and nice, heavy socks. Looking at the line-up of boots, she figured that of the ten pairs, there were eight that precisely fit every Apprentice and Familiar in the organization.

Dressed, she lay down on the bed. Sleep was coming to her on big dark wings, and she wanted to let it. Wu could wake her up when he had the extraction planned. Until then, she needed rest, and if the force soaking her tissues would allow it, she was going to take it.

There was a knock at the door. "Ma'am?"

"What is it? I want to sleep."

The door burst open. Her reflexes saved her. She was rolling aside, off the bed, as the bullets tore into the pillow and mattress, yanking out gauzy towers of stuffing. Wu was in the doorway, holding a silenced pistol, and firing where she had been moments before.

She was fast, though. That was what had won her the Prize to begin with. When she was little, she had used that speed to get out of the way of harm. In the nearly forty years she'd had of her gift, she had used it to eat up punishment, to get into harm's way. Now, she had to remember her old reflexes, the ones she'd had as a child on the streets of Medellín.

"I'm sorry," Wu said.

She fell into a crouch and rushed the door, slamming it shut onto the operator. He yelped in surprise, the pistol going off two more times.

That sound, that muffled clack, as her men fired bullet after bullet into her. Their pre-combat ritual. All dead now.

She pulled the door open and kicked Wu in the groin. He took it, sinking in as the blow wormed its insidious way into his guts. Now he was low enough to reach, and she punched him on the jaw with her left hand. It was the kind of blow that should have knocked him out, one she'd perfected in her younger days. She could lay out a boy twice her size back then, and did often. The punch staggered Wu, but he did not go down. And one more false move meant that gun was coming up.

She grabbed it with both hands, crying out as fresh spikes pressed into her shoulder. She threw another knee into his groin, feeling something crunch under the blow. He grunted, and his hands wanted to drop to protect his balls. She threw another knee, forcing the gun down, and leveling it at Wu's good foot.

It went off.

With a howl, Wu fell into the hall. He lost the gun, and now Teotl had it. She let her right arm hang; her left held the gun, pointed at the operator's forehead. He stared at her, his face contorted with agony, fat tears welling up in his eyes and falling down his cheeks.

"Please. Do it quickly." In his anguish, he'd reverted to Mandarin.

"Why did you come after me?" she responded in kind.

He didn't know what to cradle, his crushed testicles or the foot leaking blood over his hardwood floor. "Orders. Please, I'm sorry."

"Orders? Whose orders?" Who wanted her dead? Other than the Priestess, only an Apprentice could order that. Not Kisin; as odd as he was, they were often allies. Santa Orisha didn't care for anything beyond her own skin. Itzcoatl. It had to be Itzcoatl. The weeping man wouldn't answer. Teotl thumbed the hammer back. "Whose orders?"

"Our mistress! She gave me the order! She said to kill you!"

"Why? Why did she give you that order?"

"I didn't ask."

She looked into the man's eyes. She would not have asked either. The Priestess ordered someone killed, and Teotl killed them. There was no difference.

"Please, kill me quickly," said the operator.

"No," Teotl said, unscrewing the silencer and putting both that and the gun into her pocket. "You get to tell her why you failed." She patted the man down, took his extra clip and his keys, and walked for the door.

She left Wu to bleed in the lighthouse, and went out into the late morning. The way out would be the port. She could stow away on one of the numerous cargo ships that plowed into Liaodong Bay daily. As for a final destination, that was far murkier. She didn't want to believe the operator, but there was no lie in him. The Priestess had ordered Teotl's murder. It was difficult to concentrate on precisely why. Though her shoulder no longer burned, a persistent ache had settled into her flesh and bone. The energy in her body was still buzzing about, and holding it in had become both impossible and inevitable. And even though she needed less food and rest than a human might, she still needed some, and hunger was beginning to gnaw at her.

Shi Jie was not safe. The Butterfly would still be hunting her, and with Wei Lai coordinating the search, Teotl fully expected to be found. She wondered if it mattered that the Priestess seemed to want her dead as well. Was it her death they wanted, or something else? With the Mistress of Necromancy, it was a good idea to leave that as a mystery.

Teotl reduced her larger problem into smaller ones. She could solve those, and with each one behind her, the overarching dilemma would grow smaller. Eventually, it would become something she could handle. Or she could die. She smiled at that; it was the kind of glib fatalism Drigo would have enjoyed. The first step was getting to the port. Wu had a boxy van parked in a carport next to the house. Teotl quickly searched it, finding a billfold full of cash, a basic first aid kit, a .32 automatic pistol, and a flashlight.

She looked at the two pistols she had acquired, turning first one, then the other over in her hands. She hadn't used one of those in a long time.

Michaela had been shot through the chest. It made a sucking sound every time she breathed, crimson bubbles forming on her chest and popping. Esperanza held the woman who had been her mother for two years, and sobbing, picked up the gun. It was so big, so heavy. She fired and kept firing at the men who had shot her mother. She would fight until there were no bullets left. And then she would fight some more.

Everything she found went into her pockets. Satisfied she had everything, she started the van and rolled out.

Teotl tried to concentrate on the nuts and bolts of saving her life, but it all circled back to one thing: forgiveness. She had thought this mission meant that she had been forgiven for the failure in San Francisco. She wanted to take responsibility for all of that, for allowing Coldheart, the Familiar that had the League shaking in its collective boots, to be created. She didn't know what else they could have done: they killed every last possible host, except for that strange, scared man in the Ruiz house. No one knew he had been consecrated. No one could have known.

But it was her fault. A Familiar had been killed—that chilled her more than anything. Coldheart had just been born, and he killed an experienced Familiar like Huracan effortlessly. He nearly did the same to Teotl, but he had stopped. He had shown her mercy.

Was that her sin? That she lived?

And did she really have a right to the forgiveness she craved?

She failed in San Francisco, and now she failed in the Changbai Mountains. Wei Lai and Coldheart lived. That she failed was an indisputable fact, but did she deserve an ignominious death in a lighthouse?

How could the Priestess even order such a thing? After a Familiar was given her gift, she became part of her Magus. It was not exactly like a body part, as a Magus only experienced far lesser versions of the pain or pleasure her Familiars did. Teotl's murder would hurt the Priestess. It was therefore worth that amount of discomfort to insure Teotl's death.

The money in the billfold became a bribe to the guards at the gate. They let her through, and she left the van in a parking lot. She headed into the maze of cargo containers in the direction of the cranes. Yingkou Port was like any other: long asphalt roads divided up into stacks of faded containers. The only difference was all the words were in Mandarin. There were several container ships in the harbor, and one was even being loaded at that moment, the crane lifting from one stack to set it down on another, like some robotic child playing with blocks. Teotl picked up the pace, jogging in the direction of the loading area. The odds were that they would be heading for Pemhakamik. It was as good a place as any.

She stayed alert. The Butterfly's people would know that the port was the way out of Shi Jie. She expected them to come around the steel corners of one of the dull red containers, armed and ready to kill. She kept her left hand on the gun in her jacket pocket, ready to draw and fire as soon as she saw one of them.

She paused at the bottom of a stack. The crane was above her, plucking the crates one at a time while longshoremen secured the hooks in place. This would have to do. She found the padlock on the container. If she had some tools, she could have picked it easily.

Her nine-year-old hands snapping open a rusted padlock into the back of a restaurant. She was going to stuff herself that night.

She would have to improvise.

"Concentrate your search around the ship." The voice belonged to Jiangshi, and it was close, carrying over the persistent hum of the cargo cranes. Teotl had suddenly run out of time.

She shrugged out of her jacket, then the work shirt. She screwed the silencer back into place, then wrapped the gun and the lock in the shirt as best she could. She could hear the low murmur of men approaching. They could not be more than one row away. The energy caromed through her body, trying to drown out her thinking. She wouldn't let it.

She put the barrel of the gun against the lock and fired. The shirt smothered some of the sound, but there was the distinct snap of the gun and the metal bite of the lock.

"Did you hear that?" It was Jiangshi. Closer now.

Teotl unwrapped the shirt, and the lock came free. She caught it without thinking, and opened up the container. There was barely a creak as the door opened, and Teotl crammed herself inside.

"This way," Jiangshi said.

Teotl shut the door behind her. She stayed by the door, the silenced pistol in hand, ear pressed to the steel skin of the container.

"There's nothing here, ma'am." Teotl recognized that voice too. She could never forget it, even though she would never know the man's name. He was the one who put a bullet through her shoulder, and the sound of his voice made the wound ache.

"I can see that, Corporal," Jiangshi said.

Teotl heard footsteps on the top of the container, then the snap of hooks going into place. She was going to be loaded on a ship. The container shifted, and Teotl stumbled. She clicked on the flashlight and played it about the room, hoping to find that she had somehow stumbled into the one container that was shipping a bunch of protein bars, bottled water, and a bed. What she found instead were stacks and stacks of cardboard boxes.

Curious, she opened one of them up. They were filled with small, plastic toys, each one wrapped up in plastic. It looked like the kind of thing from a Happy Meal. She didn't recognize the character: some white-furred monster with a goofy look on his face. She rolled her eyes and thanked the universe for the joke. She almost threw it back when she noticed something important: the writing on the wrapper was in English. She pocketed the toy. It was apparently good luck.

There was a little space in the front. She could sit, not quite lay down. It would be comfortable enough to ride out at least part of the trip. There was a thunderous clang as the container set down on the ship. In the stuffy container, sleep returned to her in fluttering fits. A little while later, she felt the unmistakable sway of the sea. There wasn't much of it, just enough to know she was away from land. She moved her wounded arm just enough to provoke a bolt of pain to wake her.

The first problem was over. She should be out to sea in a few hours, and though parts of the Pacific were technically Shi Jie, in practice most Magi did not police their aquatic borders very well. It would be only a matter of time before the Butterfly's people figured out that she had slipped through the net at the port, and they would come after her. Out to sea, there was nowhere else to run. She was going to have to prepare for the inevitable.

Her mind—fogged with pain, fatigue, hunger, and the incessant hum of the energy that refused to leave her—gave her a solution. It wasn't so much a solution as a near certain suicide, but she couldn't think of anything else. She would have to admit that this was in the back of her mind, and had been for some time. She might as well. And besides, the toy had to have been a sign.

She dialed the number on her phone.

"Hello?" He was confused. No doubt he had never seen the number calling him.

"Do you know who this is?" The question hung in the air between them. Her stomach tied itself into buzzing knots while she waited for the word she needed to hear.

Finally: "Yes."

"I'm being chased by the Butterfly. My own people are trying to have me killed. I'm on a freighter, heading your way. I'm sorry to call you, but there's no one else, and I need help. Please."

She had never had to beg anyone in a long time. She hated to do it, and if she had any other option, she wouldn't have. That was just it. This was the only thing she could do, and she was banking on the sympathy of an enemy.

"I'm on my way. Try to hold out."

- 3 -

Teotl had no idea how long she was in that steel box. It seemed like days. The ache from the bullet wound had diminished while the pain in her belly intensified. It was like there was a certain amount of hurt in her body and the two places were trading it between each other, but as one bled into another, both seemed to get stronger. Her body had room for as much pain as she put in.

One bit of comfort gleaned from the experience was that whatever was blocking her power was not interfering with the other benefits of her immortality. A human would be suffering from dehydration already with the beginning of starvation close behind, Teotl felt these only as small annoyances. She eventually could die from lack of water and food, but it would take much longer than a mere trip across the Pacific. Her efficient body, drawing upon the renewable magic within her, was keeping her alive just fine.

She slept, though for how long it was impossible to say. She closed her eyes, and it might be a blink, or she might sink into a dreamless sleep, only to awaken with a fresh twinge. She found herself dissecting what she had done in San Francisco, and in the Changbai Mountains, and at Michaela's death, and in the mimic grove of the Serpent, and in a thousand other places. She located her mistakes and flogged herself for each one. Before long, it wasn't incredible that the Priestess ordered her murder, it was remarkable she had waited so long.

Yet Teotl was not so far gone that she did not want to live. She prayed to hear the sounds of men on the top of the container, or the crates beginning to be offloaded, of English thrown back and forth between the stevedores. She wouldn't be safe at her destination, but at least she would be unexpected. All she heard from the outside was the faint rush of wind, the crash of water off the bow, and the occasional muffled conversation of crewmen passing by the stacks where she hid. The idea that she would hear cranes was a foolish one; either the Butterfly's people or her cavalry would arrive long before the container ship saw the shores of Pemhakamik.

The klaxon answered her question about which. It roused her from the semi-daze she had been in since the first hour of the voyage. The crew of the container ship probably thought they were dealing with pirates. Teotl wished it were pirates.

She opened the door to her container, and was hit in the face with a blast of salt wind. That brought her all the way out of her trance, even if she had to shade her eyes from a sun that seemed brighter than was possible. As her vision returned, the first thing she saw was a gull, surfing along the air currents, at about eye level. She looked down, and found that she was at the top of the container stack.

The ship was in open water. Motorboats were buzzing in, the

shapes too small to make out any features. Teotl knew she would recognize the men on board them: the same ones who had pursued her in the Changbai Mountains. She briefly considered coming out. Waiting until the men had been emptied onto the ship, and then stealing one of their boats. It was a flashy move, but also foolish. They'd see her on the open water even easier. No, she had to hide and cling to the hope that help was coming.

Until she looked down. A motorboat had pulled up right next to the ship. The crew of the container ship were frantically attending the automated water cannons while the soldiers in the boat peppered them with assault rifle fire. One of the men on the boats was not firing. He was looking directly at Teotl from her position in the door of the container. She knew that man. He had shot her.

She could read the man's lips, even if she didn't have to. "There!" he was shouting. "She's there!"

"Shit," Teotl muttered. She was going to have to move. While she could have defended the container from men, Jiangshi was on that vessel, and the zombie wasn't going to fall with the bullets Teotl had in her guns.

She popped out of the container and lowered herself down. The rest would be a jump. She hit the deck and fell into a crouch. The force from the landing tried to flood into her body, but it was met by the energy bounding around and already filling her. It repelled the force, and Teotl winced with the sudden flare up of pain in her feet. She should have remembered after the tumble off the waterfall, but falls hurting were still a strange new experience.

She stayed low, running down the line of containers, away from the motorboat. She could hear the crew shouting, the deafening rush of the water cannons, sounding almost exactly like the falls, and the chatter and spang of the assault rifles bouncing bullets off the ship's hull. There were other sounds, louder clangs of metal. Grappling hooks. The ladders were coming up and the Butterfly's men would be on the ship.

She made it to the corner and paused, peeking around to see the corridor she'd just vacated. A soldier pulled himself up over the side and landed in a crouch at the other end. He saw her immediately, shouting "Here!" in Mandarin before his face was blocked by the muzzle flash of his rifle. Teotl ducked around the side while the bullets ricocheted off the containers.

She cursed again. They had her.

* * *

Captain Zhu made it onto the deck of the ship moments after the first burst had been fired. It was Private Lung who had fired, a good soldier it had been Zhu's privilege to recruit. The young man had taken up position by a corridor formed by cargo containers, his rifle pointed down the end.

"I saw her, sir. She was at the other end."

"Good job, soldier."

Zhu's men piled over the railing beside him. Some were taking the crew into custody to be locked in one of the cabins. Others were forming up around him, following the orders he issued on the boat. They were crouched, low, having been warned by Wei Lai that Teotl would have a gun. Jiangshi was the only one of them standing on the deck unafraid.

The soldiers hustled the frightened crew off the deck. "Wang, take three men on that side. Chu, three men on the other. We're going to hem her in and…"

His breath was coming out in a fog. It was chilly, but not that cold. Or, at least it hadn't been, even in the teeth of the wind. He exhaled again, and the fog was thicker. He found he was shivering. He looked at Wang, and saw that the other man's lips were turning blue. Zhu felt something, old and hungry, staring down at him. He whirled.

The creature standing on the deck five meters away was not human. It was almost twice the size of a man, hunched over, the points of its spine stretching its thin bluish flesh. Its face was deformed, its jaw too big yet somehow not big enough for all of its sharp teeth jostling for position. Its nose was sunken into the center of its face, giving it the look of a skull. Its deeply-pitted eyes were a bright animal yellow, and as it focused on Zhu, the old soldier knew fear.

Its body seemed ragged at the edges, swirling in on gusts of icy wind, only to disappear moments later. It was hard to see the entire creature at once, and even trying made Zhu wince from an abrupt throbbing in the back of his head. What were clear were the creature's arms, far too long for its body, and its massive, splayed hands, tipped with curved yellow-gray claws.

Zhu knew what he was looking at, only because of a file with a single poor-quality picture. This was Coldheart, the Twins' newest Familiar. He was supposed to be one of the more powerful creatures in existence. And suddenly he was here.

"Men! Fall back!"

Coldheart seemed to wash away from where he stood, his body reforming on a spit of wind. He was right next to Lung, who barely had time to scream before the Familiar sunk his claws into Lung's chest, and tore the man open. The soldier was dead before the partially frozen remains hit the deck.

"Fire!" The assault rifles chattered into the impossibly thin corpse man. A few tore holes in the bloodless flesh, looking like rips in paper. Most of the bullets passed harmlessly into air as the wendigo disappeared into ribbons of swirling snow. "Pull back, pull back!"

He grabbed one of his men—Gao, a hard-nosed soldier from Sichuan—and had to physically shove him away, down the deck.

Coldheart re-emerged from the snow to plunge an icy hand into the chest of Ran, the youngest of the recruits. Zhu put his rifle to his shoulder, a snarl rippling his lip, and fired round after round into Coldheart. The wendigo was most solid when he attacked. Maybe, just maybe, one bullet would hurt the creature. Even in this moment, with rage consuming Zhu's mind, he was thinking clearly: *How best can I hurt this enemy? How can I put him down? How can I save my men?*

The bullets tore into Coldheart's chest and skull, but the wendigo was gone, shoveling a heart now freshly encrusted in ice into his dripping maw. Ran fell, his chest a gaping frozen hole. Zhu grabbed Ma and nearly threw him down the deck. "Retreat, soldier!" Ma, ever the berserker, had to pause before obeying.

They were not moving quick enough. The Familiar was too fast, and he was killing each man with a single swipe of his claws. Zhu shepherded them ahead, knowing if a single one fell behind him, that man would die.

Then his men stopped dead. They looked behind Zhu with dawning horror eclipsing their features. Zhu knew what it was, and he turned, ready to go down fighting. He briefly saw the claws as they raked down his face, but he did not remember them.

* * *

Wang watched his captain fall to the deck, his face a mask of crimson. The wendigo paused, raising one skeletal arm to plunge it into Zhu's back and take another grisly trophy. Wang screamed in rage and fired. The squad followed suit. It was worthless, and maybe they knew it, but that didn't stop them. Coldheart looked up, his claws never falling into the unconscious Zhu. The Familiar seemed genuinely confused as the bullets punched through him.

Finally, he held his arms out as though welcoming a hug. A wind kicked up behind the squad. It yanked Wang off his feet, and it was pure reflex that caused him to grab the ship's railing. The other soldiers weren't so lucky; Wang saw them sliding across the deck toward Coldheart, then heard the wet cracks and crunches, the shrill screams torn off in the middle.

The wind died as abruptly as it began, and Wang fell to the deck, barking both knees and chin on the rough but spongy sole. He rolled over, hand groping for his pistol, hoping to put a few rounds in the face of the monster. He wished he'd run.

Coldheart stood in a growing pool of blood and viscera. Parts were frozen over into hillocks of gore, others were slopping around on the deck, and falling over the side. There were recognizable parts too, and that was the worst. The stark white face of He, locked in the final terror of seeing his monstrous murderer, a forearm and hand that belonged to Li only identifiable from the brand-new watch on the wrist, a knee that could have belonged to anyone, even Wang himself. Some of the men were still alive, opened up to the frigid air, and trying to crawl away. Their mouths worked soundlessly, their lungs having been obliterated. There was nothing Wang could do.

Coldheart held Yuan up with one hand while the man fired pointlessly, the wendigo's claws sinking into his chest and cracking bone. With the other, he was digging into Shen's freezing chest.

Wang's mind stopped working. He saw, he heard, he smelled, but he could no longer make sense of what he was experiencing.

"Coldheart!" Jiangshi strode over Wang's prostrate body, stopping in the spreading pool of blood.

Coldheart paused, casting the mortally wounded Yuan over the side of the ship. His other hand emerged, gory to the elbow, and in it he held Shen's freezing heart. The yellow eyes narrowed as he watched Jiangshi, but he did not attack.

"This is none of your concern. Leave now, and the Butterfly will forget you were here." Jiangshi spoke English.

The wendigo smiled. Wang thought he had passed through fear and found the terrible emptiness that was on the other side. He was wrong. Seeing amusement in those eyes, on that face splattered with the blood of his friends, coming in sticky drool through those terrible teeth, to freeze into stalactites, that was the most horrible of all. Before, Coldheart had been a force of nature. Merciless and terrible, certainly, but impersonal. Now, he was capable of mirth.

"Is the Butterfly on this ship? I haven't had a chance to meet her." Coldheart's voice was high and reedy, the howl of a storm harnessed into understanding.

Jiangshi took another few steps into the blood. The men at Coldheart's feet had stopped moving. A tiny mercy. "I am here, and I speak with her voice."

"How nice for you. Well, I speak with the voice of the Twins, and you get the same deal."

Jiangshi was within two meters of the monster. She was quiet, staring up at the wendigo looming over her. Wang could not see her face, but it would be as expressionless as it always was. Coldheart opened his mouth to speak again, and that's when Jiangshi lashed out. She was quicker than a snake, her fist impacting the monster's now-solid jaw. The crack was louder than an assault rifle. Coldheart staggered backward, his lower half disappearing into swirling winds.

He touched his jaw in a peculiarly human gesture. Blood, his blood, leaked through the teeth now, bluish and crusted with ice. Amusement crinkled his eyes. "That was my fault for underestimating you." He brought his hands up, and bolts of wind enfolded Jiangshi, lifting her off the ground. The blood at her feet sprouted ice crystals. Her skin turned blue. The wind spawned snowflakes. It might even have been beautiful.

Wang felt strength return. He wanted to run, needed to run,

but he could not. He lunged forward, past the swirling vortex imprisoning Jiangshi, and into the blood and gore at the wendigo's feet. He grabbed the unconscious Zhu and dragged him out, away from the fight, and around a stack of containers. There he stopped, unable to move anymore, even as he knew that once Coldheart was done with the zombie, he would finish off the only two surviving men.

* * *

Teotl heard the carnage first. She moved toward it, never running, and came around the corner to see horror. The creature who had once been the scared young man in that house in San Francisco had ruthlessly butchered the Butterfly's men. Pieces of their bodies were scattered over the immediate environs. And now, he had Jiangshi suspended in the air, freezing her solid.

He almost did the same to Teotl back in San Francisco. She felt the icy grip of the wind. She felt her body shutting down, unable to absorb this new and strange energy. He would have killed her. Except... he didn't. He let her go.

And now he was here.

"You came," she said.

Coldheart turned. The wind died, dropping Jiangshi to the deck. The Familiar was frozen solid, trapped in the same agonized pose she had been in while off the ground. She had been defeated and now she was forgotten.

"I ca—" the monster started to speak, but cut himself off. He shook his horrible, bloodstained head. The voice changed, becoming a little deeper, a little more steady. "I guess I did," he said.

"We should go."

The wendigo held out one of his claws to Teotl, but she wasn't ready to take it. She used one of the ladders the Butterfly's men had used, the ones hooked onto the railings of the container ship. The cannons were off now. She climbed down into one of the motorboats, bobbing by the side of the ship. It was about fifteen meters long, and included an indoor cabin. Coldheart materialized on the deck a moment later in a swirl of frigid wind.

He stank of blood, and the weight of his gaze caused her to shrink away. She went about starting the boat, and soon they were out into open water, leaving the container ship behind. As she drove, she heard a faint howl, and the stench of blood went away. She turned and found the man she remembered. More or less.

His hair was still short, but where it had been a dirty blond, it had faded to almost silver. His eyes were the same feral yellow as the creature's; the Twins' Familiars always betrayed their inhumanity in the eyes. When she first met him, when he had been human, he was impossibly fragile. Now that had changed. The fear was gone, replaced by an easy confidence as he stood on the deck of the boat. The tailored suit, all in white, didn't hurt matters either. He had been cute before, like a wounded puppy. In his transformation, he had become handsome.

"Teotl, right?"

His pronunciation was terrible. She nodded and took his hand anyway. It was cold, though not icy. "Right."

Even though she felt no threat in his posture or in his genuine smile, there was something in those feral amber eyes of his. Some part of him that wanted her dead.

"Can you drive?" she asked. "I want to see what we have to eat."

"Yeah, of course." He took the wheel, and she went into the back, checking in the compartments under the seats. Shortly, she found cereal bars with Chinese labels and some bottled water and tore into them, settling back into one of the seats as she did so. It was as comfortable as she remembered being. Coldheart sat at the wheel, guiding the boat through open ocean. He let her eat and drink in silence, and she emptied several bottles and a full box before she was done. It wasn't the best meal she'd ever had, but it would do, especially after the privation of the last day or two.

"You're bleeding," Coldheart said.

"What?"

"I'm sorry. I... I smell it." The words broke off at the end.

"It's all right. I am. I was shot."

"I thought you couldn't be shot."

"Me too," she said.

Coldheart was silent again. The slump of his shoulders returned. The violence done, he was back to himself, and probably didn't want to speak for fear of sounding stupid.

"I should probably explain." She did. She told the story of the explosion, of her powers being gone, and of the attempted hit at the lighthouse. She never hesitated about revealing the loss of her powers, either. He had proven at his creation that he could kill her even if she was at full strength, but more to the point, she didn't feel he wanted to. Whatever part of him that hated her was deep inside, and the boy he had been was controlling it. Besides, he had come when she called him.

He absorbed the story while driving the boat. "I'm sorry," he said finally.

"I suppose that's all there is to say."

"It's all I could think of."

"Where are we going?"

"You tell me."

"I have nowhere to go."

"Is Seattle all right? I have a house near there."

"Seattle? You moved?"

Coldheart glanced over his shoulder. "How did you know that?"

"Your file." She sighed, covering up the blush. Yes, she had been researching him. Yes, she had asked Drigo to bring Coldheart's file.

"Your creation was a big blow to the Priestess. They stopped it a hundred years ago, even. Kisin could tell you stories about that first time."

He shook his head. "Tough to wrap my brain around that. It's one thing to share a soul with a monster. It's another thing to think about the same people fighting for centuries."

"You'll get used to it."

"My file said I was in New York, right? Probably mentioned that thing with the Lion's people. I admit, I was not prepared for them. I figured that we were the weird ones." His voice turned excited. "Did you know they have a person who is actually a miniature sun?"

The trees were all on fire. Oorun strode down the center of the street, leaving molten footprints. The shape of a woman could be seen within the incandescent yellow of the flame. Darker spots outlined her shape periodically, drifting over her and vanishing. She was the sun, and all Teotl could do was fling the energy of the car accident in the Familiar's face.

Teotl broke into a smile, even as the memory of fighting Oorun surfaced. "Yes, I know. She has a file too."

"You're making fun of me," Coldheart said, the amusement clear in his voice as well.

"No, it's just that you don't hear many of us expressing wonder. Oorun is someone to fight, not something to marvel over."

"Well, I fought her too, if that helps." And he laughed.

She knew that part as well. Oorun had been the one Familiar thus far to challenge Coldheart, and he had nearly killed her as well. The file said that he was protecting the Twins' heir Ash Wednesday at the time. That had apparently ended. It was common for an Apprentice to have a favorite Familiar that they often worked with, but the detachments were far from permanent, and the pairings were sometimes mixed and matched. Whatever had happened, now Coldheart had the time to rescue an enemy in the middle of the Pacific.

"Thank you," Teotl said.

She heard him take a breath, and knew the glib response was *For what?* But he knew what she was thanking him for. He seemed to be chewing over an answer, and she appreciated that. "You're welcome," he said finally.

* * *

Zhu regained consciousness on the deck of one of the motorboats. The agony in his face was unbearable; it felt like his head was on fire. He reached up to touch it and found bandages.

"Sir, don't move." Wang was above him now, the face half eaten by the light.

"Let me sit up," Zhu murmured.

"You've been hurt pretty badly and—"

"That was an order, Corporal."

Wang sighed and helped Zhu up, moving him over to the seats. Zhu rested against those, his legs trailing out over the deck. He looked around. It was just him and Wang, while Jiangshi drove the boat. He knew immediately what had happened, and the crushing sense of loss made him long for the oblivion he had just emerged from.

Wang saw it on his face, the little bit that was not covered by bandages. "I'm sorry, sir."

"You followed my orders. You fought when I said to fight and you retreated when I said to fall back. You did everything you could have done."

"No, sir. No, I didn't. When that monster was killing the men, I ran. I hid."

"Following my orders," Zhu said, punctuating the words with a poke to the soldier's chest. "If you want to blame someone, blame

Coldheart. Better yet, blame me. I was the one who recruited them. They would never have been on that ship but for me."

"You recruited me too. Do you remember what you said?"

Of course Zhu had. He'd said the same thing to every man he brought into the Butterfly's service. "I said that you would be fighting for something more important than even China herself."

"And you were right. The men who died, who you recruited… it's a testament to them that they were willing to die for the Butterfly."

Zhu started to shake his head, but the fresh blaze of agony through his ruined face stopped him. "No. No, they deserved better than to die on some ship filled with cheap plastic shit. They were China's best."

* * *

Teotl opened her eyes. It was dark, and for a moment, she thought she was back in the Condor's Nest, sleeping in her chambers. The wind kissing her face was not the thin, clean air of the Andes. It was heavy, savory. She sat up and found she had been sleeping on the cushioned bench of the motorboat. Coldheart, his back to her, was guiding them into a harbor. She could see the lights of other boats through the windshield, like stars that were too near the earth.

Coldheart slid the boat into an open slip, and turned, seeing she was awake. "Thought I was going to have to wake you."

She stood up, head still muzzy. The buzz of sleep joined with the energies in her body. She knew it was still trapped. Her shoulder, though, was feeling much better. The magic that animated Familiars, that shielded them from age and disease, also healed them faster. Even if her powers were blocked, at least that wasn't. Otherwise she would have aged thirty-eight years in a night or two or collapsed of thirst in that container.

Coldheart hopped from the boat to the pier, and held out a hand, helping Teotl do the same. She glanced around the deck and shivered in the air. Coldheart removed his white jacket and offered it to her. "Please, take this," he said.

"No, I'm fine."

"Please. I don't get cold anymore."

She accepted it. As she pulled it on, she expected some residual warmth from his body heat, but there was none. "Why wear it then?"

He shrugged. "To remind me of when I did get cold."

They walked up the pier, between the gently bobbing ships. A wall of fog was coming in from off the ocean, and would envelop the sleeping city soon. Everything was green, but it was a different green than she was used to. Starker here.

"Are you going to tell the Twins I'm here?" she said. The only sound was the clunk of their footsteps on the wooden docks, and the gentle wash of the tides against the boat hulls.

"I hadn't planned on it."

"Thanks."

It was a strange feeling for her. He was an enemy, a servant of the Twins. All the other Magi were technically enemies, but the proximity of the Twins made them the most bitter. She saw the beast within the man, and felt the creature's cold hatred. But she knew that there was no way the young man who shared the monster's body would ever hurt her. She felt safe.

He led her up some stairs in the shadow of pine trees, and out into a parking lot. As soon as she laid eyes on it, she knew where they were headed. It was a motorcycle. A simple standard model, with a white gas tank and little else to mark it as property of a Familiar. Coldheart took the white helmet from the back and handed it to Teotl. Only then did he notice the smile.

"What?"

"I didn't think you would drive this."

"I used to, you know, before. Never one this nice, though."

"The life has its privileges." She accepted the helmet, feeling silly when she slipped it on. How many cars had she rammed into walls to charge up?

San Francisco, the blizzard closing in, she was going into the house where she would meet a frightened young man. She needed a charge, and she rammed a stolen car into a lamppost. She had used the charge to fling a frightened young man across a room.

The same man whose waist she now wrapped her arms around as his motorcycle streaked out of the lot and into the dark streets. She pillowed her head into his back. The vibration of the engine underneath her joined the persistent buzz inside of her. The buzz that wanted to expel the force of the explosion in a single hyper-destructive blast, but was stuck like a cork in a bottle.

Coldheart took a freeway a short distance north, then kept turning onto smaller and smaller side roads. Soon they were amongst the pines, the night sky utterly eclipsed by the natural spires. He finally stopped on a lonely road. A large wooden house was barely visible from the winding, one-lane street. As Coldheart cut the engine down the steep driveway, the house revealed itself. It was huge, spread out over the slope of a hill, and peeking through the trees at the bottom, Teotl could see the glassy calm of open water. The house was unpainted, the wood stained a rich red-orange. It looked like a cabin owned by someone who had no intention of ever leaving creature comforts behind.

A small garage opened up ahead. It was nearly empty. Of course, he had been a Familiar for a little over three years. He had barely just moved in. They got off the bike, and he wheeled it inside, and rejoined her. A wooden walkway that was half stairs and half deck led up to the front door.

"Did you want to get some sleep?" he asked.

"I've had enough sleep. What's down there?"

"The lake. Do you want to see it?" Even if she hadn't, the childlike eagerness in his voice would have made her say yes.

She nodded.

As he turned, his eyes caught the faint moonlight, and they disappeared into amber orbs, like the eyes of a dog when hit with the beam of a flashlight. But then the light was gone, and he was a normal man again. He led her down a series of staircases, all punctuated with landings and platforms.

"Are your men here?" she asked.

"Scouting me for a hit?" There was humor in his voice, but it was a serious question. This would have been some kind of odd fishing trip to kill a threat. It wasn't the kind of subtlety the Priestess was known for, yet the worry was there.

"As if your soldiers could do something you couldn't."

"That was a strange feeling when Rose assigned them to me." He was talking about Rose Cross, the Twins' Spymaster and unofficial commander of the entire organization. She made Teotl's skin crawl. All Theurgists did. "'Here you go! These guys will all die for you, no questions asked!'"

"She actually used those words?"

"Oh no. She had a much more flowery way of putting it. She talks like a grandmother."

"To us she's terrifying. Able to crawl around in our heads... makes our power seem useless."

"I'm sure we get the same stories about you. 'Saltamontes could be anywhere! Keep an eye out for Saltamontes!'" he said, referring to the Priestess's teleporting Familiar.

"Anywhere with a whorehouse," she said.

Coldheart broke out laughing. Teotl was momentarily shocked at what she'd let slip, but then joined in with him.

"They're people to us. To you, they're monsters."

"You especially," she said.

"Oh, they're right about me."

She was about to deny it, correct him, tell him that he was at least a little heroic. She'd seen him nearly sacrifice himself to rescue the woman that should have been Coldheart, and when Teotl called for help, he'd responded. The denial was too big to voice in the still air, and while she was still trying to form it into words, they arrived at the bottom of the slope.

"Here it is."

A deck had been built into the side of the shallow hill, reaching out into the water. A single pier extended from there, a small boat moored to it. The lake was bigger than she had imagined, and she could barely see other houses peeking from the foliage on the distant shore. Near Coldheart, there were trunks poking from the water itself, like jagged teeth.

"It's beautiful," she said.

"Four years ago I was living in a crappy apartment, barely scraping by on disability. I never could have dreamed of living in a place like this."

"I know what you mean. I grew up on the streets before they found me."

That pulled his attention to her. "I didn't know that. It's not in the file."

"So, you looked me up," she said.

"Yeah, well, know your enemy," he said, turning away.

"Strange life we've found for ourselves. It's easy to forget that."

"I was thinking, I might know someone who we could ask about what happened to you."

"Rose Cross? No, Coldheart, any of the Twins' people would have me killed immediately, and that's if I were lucky."

"No, nothing like that. Believe me, I won't trust them with your life any more than you would. There's a Prodigal I know in the area. Part of my job is keeping an eye on him, although he tends to do a better job of that than I ever could."

"A Prodigal? You haven't killed him?"

"Why would I do that? He's not hurting anyone."

"But he's draining your resources. He could cause trouble."

Coldheart waved that off. "As I understand it, there's more than enough for everyone. And if he caused trouble, yeah, they'd probably send me. But in the meantime, he can make himself useful."

She shook her head. "And every organization has different ways of doing things."

"I'm still muddling my way along."

They stayed out there for a little while longer before Teotl made a noise in her throat, and Coldheart took the hint and invited her inside. The interior of the house didn't seem exactly like him either. It felt like it had come furnished, in a wealthy catalogue Native American sort of way, with only a few flourishes that actually belonged to him. The bookcase, with its battered paperbacks felt like him. The jigsaw puzzle on the coffee table likewise. But Coldheart still seemed to be living in someone else's house.

"I didn't know that Magi could kill their Familiars," he said. "I mean, I knew they'd survive it, but I didn't think they would."

She paused. The words pinned her to the spot. "I didn't know either."

"I'm sorry. I shouldn't have said anything. But this is still new to me, and I didn't know. And I'm sorry."

"It's okay," she said. But it wasn't. She had thought the same thing. How could the Priestess want to kill her? While a blood enemy was acting like the best friend she'd ever had.

"I'm sorry," he said again. He shook his head, knowing he couldn't fix what he'd said, partially because he had been right.

So he changed the subject. "There's a bedroom down that hall, and a bathroom right next to it. There's a lock on both, so don't worry."

She didn't mention that a locked door would mean precisely nothing to him physically. It seemed like it would mean everything to him psychologically, and that was more than enough.

"Thank you, Coldheart."

He nodded, and she went down the hall. The room he directed her to matched the rest of the house. There were self-consciously "Native" paintings on the wall, throw blankets on the bed and chairs, and everything in earth tones. She undressed, hanging her pants and jacket over the chair. She stared at the bed, but she wasn't tired. A few hours was more than enough, even wounded. Besides, a shower sounded good.

She found the bathroom where Coldheart said, and there were clean towels and even toothbrushes still in the packaging. Cleaning up felt heavenly, even if the pounding spray from the shower felt odd as her body repelled the kinetic energy trying to sink into her body. The wound in her shoulder had closed. The flesh was raw, and a blue-black bruise spread from the impact. She dried herself off, wrung out her long hair, and proceeded to comb it into a long and damp curtain. She still felt full with the force inside her, but it had settled into a pleasant discomfort, a pressure that would only build until a sudden and violent release.

She pulled on her shirt and underwear, and thought she might grab a book from the living room to help pass the time. She walked into the living room and found Coldheart reading. He didn't have a reading lamp on, his bright yellow eyes easily tracking across the page.

"Oh," she said, and put her hands in front of herself, suddenly very conscious she was in her underwear. "Couldn't sleep?"

"You should talk." He looked up, and she watched his eyes

dip to her hips and legs, and go back to his book. He stared hard at the words, clearly doing his best not to look at her. "I... uh... I don't really sleep anymore."

"I was a little hungry," she lied.

"There should be some apple pie in the fridge," he said, gesturing toward the kitchen and resolutely not looking up.

She thought of going back into the bedroom and putting her pants on, but this was kind of fun. Teotl went into the kitchen through a wide doorway just off the living room. Windows looked out onto the docks and the lake. A slice of moonlight glimmered across the still water. She opened up the refrigerator.

She wasn't certain why what she found surprised her. Coldheart was a carnivore, after all. It was raw meat, top to bottom. Cuts of it, wrapped in plastic. It was equal parts horror and thrill as she wondered, *How much of this is human?* Scolded herself for the thought, but it kept returning with the same fascination. The only thing that wasn't meat was a box, and sure enough, she found an apple pie inside.

"You like apple pie?" she called through the doorway, taking the box out, and setting about getting herself a generous slice.

"I used to. Now, I only like raw meat."

"Then why—"

"Shahmeran gets them for me. She thinks it's funny."

"You two still don't get along?"

San Francisco. Coldheart had been incarnated, an avatar of winter and hate. The first thing he did was attack the snake goddess, leaping on her back and tearing into her with his talons.

"I took her eye."

"When?" Teotl put the pie back. She could see him through the doorway, conjuring the memory with a smirk.

Coldheart put the book down, carefully marking the page. "I put a letter opener through it. I was still human at the time."

Teotl chuckled, coming back into the room. "Wish I could have seen that."

"She's hard enough to take as an ally. I can't imagine what you must think of her if you're not on the same side."

She settled down on his sofa, holding a small plate of pie and a fork. She sat up straight, crossing her legs, and began to eat. "At least she gets you good pie."

"I'll let her know. Oh, don't worry," he said to the sudden frightened expression that must have flashed over her features. "I'll just call you a guest."

"Have a lot of guests, do you?"

"Nope."

She covered the grin with another forkful of pie.

"I don't know how long you'll be here," he said, "but if there's something else you need, let me know. I can pick things up tomorrow."

"Something beyond raw meat and apple pie might be nice."

"I have a stove."

"And no spices, from the looks of things."

"I was never much of a cook."

"So who is this Prodigal of yours?"

"His name is Rahsan Ashar. He eats breakfast at the same place, same time, same thing, every day. He... he can't help it."

* * *

That place was a battered silvery diner on a lonely road. A gravel parking lot was the only gray except for the narrow strip of highway disappearing into the fields of green in either direction. Pines grew in groups of twos and threes out of the irregular terrain, and all around rose into the blue hills and then mountains. This diner, an hour's ride from Coldheart's home, felt as remote as it was possible to be.

Teotl watched the land go by as she hugged the skinny Familiar around his waist, her head tucked against his back as though she were listening to his heartbeat. The tinted visor of the helmet dyed everything a dark blue. Out here, it was easy to, if not forget, at least ignore the war they were both fighting. It looked like peace.

The only odd thing she saw was a flash of movement by a treeline that looked to be at the edge of a small dip. At first, it was a black mark, but as she got closer, she saw that it looked like a group of three dogs. It was difficult to tell, but they looked fairly large. Their coats were russet and black, their heads large and blunt, their chests wide and muscular. They looked like watchdogs, but they were at the edge of nowhere with nothing to watch over.

The motorcycle turned and pulled into the gravel driveway. There was no sign other than the big red DINER at the top. It rose out of the green, with longer stems of grass hugging the side as though the fields were trying to reclaim it. Through the wide windows, Teotl could see groups of men, women, and children enjoying big American breakfasts. She knew instantly who they were looking for.

The man who sat at the corner booth was small and skinny. His brownish skin was dry and flaky, and his small, nervous eyes were behind a circular pair of glasses. His beard was short and scraggly. He was wearing an old tweed suit, a bowtie knotted around his throat.

Coldheart entered the diner, and a wash of cooked grease flooded over them. The diner was a pleasant cacophony, with clinking silverware and dishes, conversations, patter from the waitresses, and the hiss of the grill all warred for attention. The staff looked like they'd been there forever; none were under fifty, the women pulled into short uniforms, the squat men behind the grill in greasy aprons. Coldheart gestured at the man Teotl had picked out before. "That's him."

He saw them as soon as they were through the door, the ringing bell pulling his attention up. Teotl saw recognition and it seemed some genuine pleasure at the sight of Coldheart, but there was also fear. It was impossible to know Coldheart in any capacity and not be a little frightened.

"Coldheart!" Ashar said as they got close.

"Hello, Rahsan," Coldheart said, sliding into the booth across from him. Teotl slid in next to Coldheart.

Ashar was in the process of eating a huge breakfast. He was only a few centimeters taller than Teotl, and didn't look to weigh much more either, but if this is what he ate every day, she didn't see how he was so skinny. He had a plate, half-finished, of eggs, hash browns, toast, and bacon, and a mug of coffee the color of balsa wood.

"They're not ranging as far these days," Coldheart said, nodding out the window. Teotl saw that the gesture was in the direction of the three dogs she clocked when they were driving in.

"No," Ashar agreed. "I'm allowed less and less play... There are *things* out there, you know."

"Yeah, I do."

"What can I do for you?" The tone was that of a kid, eager to please his big brother.

"I need your expertise. My friend saw something we need you to identify."

Ashar blinked and looked over at Teotl. He started, as though this was the first he'd seen of her. "Hello. What thing did you see? Be specific."

"It looked to be a stone, maybe the size of a pea?"

"Color?"

"Hard to describe. I want to say gray, but it was white at times, and black. And sometimes it was another color... a non-color. Something I've never seen before."

A smile spread over Ashar's chapped lips. "Yes? Yes? And what did it do? Where did you find it?"

"It appeared out of nowhere, and when it did, there was an explosion like nothing I've ever seen. You know what I'm talking about, don't you?"

"Oh yes, of course I do."

"Can I get you something?" The waitress sidled up, refilling Ashar's coffee mug.

"Coffee," Coldheart said.

Teotl nodded, and the waitress plunked two mugs down, filled them up, and moved off into the diner.

"What is it?" Teotl asked.

"The explosion came from nothing, yes?"

"Yes."

"No. *No.* The explosion came from *everything*." Ashar leaned back in his seat, a proud grin plastered over his face.

"I don't understand."

"You saw quintessence. You saw *prime matter.*"

"I don't know what that is." She glanced at Coldheart, and he shook his head.

"Walk us through this, Rahsan."

"Oh. Oh, okay. Yes. All right, it's like this. When quintessence touches normal matter… by which I mean anything you see around you. In the diner, out there—well, not them, obviously," he said this about the dogs, and moved on before Teotl could ask for elaboration on that point, "almost anything you would see in your life is normal matter. When quintessence touches it, there's a reaction. Boom."

"It's like anti-matter?" Coldheart asked.

"No! No. It's the opposite. If anything, this," and he rapped on the table, "is the *anti*-matter. Quintessence is far more solid than anything in this universe. What you saw as an explosion was the reaction of the normal matter; the quintessence itself didn't expend anything. Couldn't." He shook his head. "I can't imagine a piece so large finding its way here."

"Where does it come from?"

He shrugged. "Another time? Another place? Some think that's where the universe comes from—our universe—the first case of the prime matter coming in and exploding. And we get... everything. Of course, in that case, it would have been a much larger amount. Say, the size of a golf ball."

"What about the energy?" Teotl's excitement forced her to lean forward. "You said it doesn't expend energy in the explosion."

"It couldn't!" Ashar matched her enthusiasm. "Energy, matter, they're the same thing. And it can't be created or destroyed. This is super-matter. *Prime* matter. There's nothing solid enough to take the energy from an explosion like that. There would be no way to bleed it back into the world. Isn't that wonderful?"

It was, in a horrible way. Teotl had the key to the problem of her powers, and the likely solution to it. It opened up a host more problems, but at the very least there was some hope. "Thank you, Mr. Ashar, you've been a great help."

"You're tracking it, aren't you?" he said.

"Stay safe, Rahsan," Coldheart said.

"Good luck finding your Tunguska," Ashar said.

* * *

Kaeru's replacement body had finally thawed out. He picked up a new one from one of the Butterfly's local freezers because he was tired of his thoughts coming in an unbroken stream of gibberish. The Magus claimed the unclaimed, and when that wasn't enough, she merely bribed crematoria for fresh ones and let the bereaved take home a vase of wood ash. It was all the same to them, anyway, once the soul was gone. This one had been a young man, killed with a single gunshot wound to the heart. Kaeru felt his power reanimating the meat around him, forcing the destroyed heart to pump the body's new plasm.

He stood with Jiangshi in a penthouse suite in Hong Kong. They were still recovering from the defeat on the ship. Captain Zhu was in one of the Butterfly's facilities, his face getting stitched up. He'd lost his left eye, but considering the carnage Coldheart had wreaked on his men, one eye wasn't so bad. Wang, the only other survivor, was gathering up another squad of men, armed with the dossiers Wei Lai had provided for their selection.

Kaeru and Jiangshi were left to try to salvage some kind of victory from what had happened. It felt to Kaeru like it was over, and they had lost. If Teotl had been taken by Coldheart, she was either food or she was having her mind stripped layer by layer by Rose Cross. Whenever he thought of Theurgists, Kaeru was pleased that, technically speaking, he had no mind anymore.

He stood with the Familiar, facing a window that should have looked out over the neon night of Hong Kong, but opened into the top of Fantan Tower, the lair of Wei Lai. The Apprentice sat across from them, his ritual circle between. He seemed to regard them through his stitched up eyes. Kaeru swallowed the laugh: *He and Zhu had something in common now.* He wondered if Zhu would appreciate the joke.

Jiangshi delivered the report. She said exactly what had happened, never editorializing, never embellishing. She was completely honest with the Apprentice, totally unconcerned with how it made her look, even when Coldheart had mercilessly thrashed her. Kaeru had watched the whole thing happen from the other side. He waited for a body to spring into, but Coldheart had made a ruin of them. There was scarcely any meat in a large enough piece to be a good host. Instead, Kaeru was forced to watch the ghosts appear in front of him in that little gray space in the middle of the cold black of Diyu, the underworld. Each one, swirling into form like milk dropped in water, their eyes black, their skin stark white, being torn to pieces by a phantom attacker. Some fell into the depths, while others tried to flee along the thin pathways of the upper levels, only to find that they were bound to the place of dying.

The truth was, against Coldheart, they had been helpless. This was Jiangshi's point, and Kaeru could not argue it. At least it was only soldiers who had died. Wei had probably seen that, and judged it a reasonable expenditure. It was scarcely a loss for the Butterfly; any number of those men could be brought back as ghosts to continue their service.

"They fled west. There has been no report of either individual in the week since."

"They will return," Wei said. A mahjongg tile walked over his knuckles. "And when they do, we will have to be ready."

"How?" Another Familiar might have sounded angry, but Jiangshi was beyond emotion.

"The Familiars of the Twins are fragmented souls," Wei said, popping the tile off his hand, palming it, and casting it across the circle.

Kaeru grinned. He didn't need the power to read the future. "You want someone to fragment that soul further."

"Exactly," Wei said. "A Necromancer."

"Tōriki Satoru."

"I will tell him to expect you both."

- 4 -

Teotl had lived in the house of her mortal enemy for nearly a month. The rest had done her good, and the energy in her body had become a constant hum under her muscles that she could almost ignore. The first day, he had gotten some more variety for food. She wouldn't need much, but she wanted more than raw meat and apple pie. She had enough to read, and the house was remote enough that she felt safe.

She grieved for her men. There were sleepless nights at first—closed eyes meant seeing Drigo's dying face. She would never be completely healed from his death, and she didn't want to be. She wanted to carry some amount of pain with her, because that pain was a memory. As long as the pain survived, so would he.

The loss of the other men was not quite as personal. Some she had known for a good deal of time, and others were new. They were all hers. Her boys, ready to kill or die as needed. It was not the first time she had lost a man in the field—far from it—but it was the only time they had been wiped out to a man. What stung was that they were dead because of her. There had to have been some way to have saved them. Maybe not all, but some. Instead, they were all gone. She saw them too when she closed her eyes, though their faces merged with all of those others she had lost in her decades serving the Priestess. Humans weren't built for this shadow war between gods, but they were just useful enough to serve, and that was their doom.

The wound of his loss grew less raw over that month, much more slowly than the bullet hole which faded to near invisibility after two weeks. Though the forces buzzed and hummed, making her muscles twitch and her heart pound, she could be more or less comfortable. She spent a lot of her days out on Coldheart's deck, looking out over the lake with a detective paperback in her hands, reading or just contemplating this peaceful place.

Coldheart left her alone, though he was rarely far. The first time he left her alone, to get supplies, she was half convinced he would return with Rose Cross. She saw the albino Theurgist getting off the back of Coldheart's motorcycle, her red eyes boring into Teotl, then everything she knew would belong to the Twins. Though she shouldn't have so much loyalty to the Priestess after the lighthouse betrayal, the core of Teotl rebelled against the idea.

The secrets had been given by a betrayer, but they had been given to Teotl, who had kept them in good faith, and would continue to do so. When Coldheart returned with grocery bags rather than the Spymaster, Teotl nearly laughed.

He continued to treat her respectfully. He left her alone, but he could be sought out, and he was always willing to talk. She still had that impression, of that part of him that wanted her dead. She felt it in him, and in the dense woods around the lake. She saw it in the moon looking down on her, and felt it in the bite of the wind. The wendigo could be bound to a man, yet it could not entirely be contained. It was there, and it hated her.

The man, however, was gentle. From the stories, and what she had seen on that container ship, she might be the only person safe from him. Of this, she had no doubts. He never visited her at night either, even when she left the door open a crack.

Coldheart was spending some of his time locating Wei Lai, who should be holding onto the quintessence. If anyone in that organization was studying it, it would be the Prophet. The problem was, Coldheart was new, and had not had the hundreds of years to build up the web of contacts any other Familiar might have. Teotl hesitated to approach any of hers, after the incident at the lighthouse, and the last thing she wanted was anything to blow back on Coldheart, the one person who was helping. So they were left with his only resource, the one person Teotl most feared: the Spymaster of the Twins, Rose Cross.

"She'll know," Teotl said.

"No. She can't read me." Coldheart seemed almost ashamed of this revelation.

"Because of the wendigo?"

He shook his head. "Because... because there's something wrong with me. Always has been."

"Something wrong."

"I'm… My brain chemistry is off. Or it was. I don't know. I used to take medicine for it, but now I don't need it anymore. The wendigo, or the Twins, or something has stabilized me, but whatever it is is still there, and Rose has a hard time reading me. It's painful for her, so she doesn't."

She wondered if he realized he just spilled a big secret to the Twins' organization to an ostensible enemy. Did he think of her as an enemy? Was she anymore? She didn't know, so how could he? "I wonder if it's just her or all Theurgists?"

"I don't know. We haven't had any trouble with the Wolf yet."

"All right. I trust you."

She sat quietly when he called Rose Cross. Coldheart paced from the expansive living room and into the kitchen while he spoke. Teotl spent the conversation looking up at the rafters, and the railing of the second floor that overlooked the living room. There was the head of a deer hanging on the wall, and she stared into its glassy eyes as she heard Coldheart's side of the conversation.

His voice was odd with Rose Cross. It was slightly higher, a touch more childish. When he was silent, presumably listening, it was raptly. When he spoke, everything was a polite request. When he called her "Rose," it sounded like he wanted to say "Miss Cross," and had to stop himself, having already been asked to be more familiar. The conversation started with banalities, and Teotl heard him lie to Rose Cross several times. The lies were as obvious as hand grenades to Teotl, and she winced inwardly whenever Coldheart said something. Cross had to hear them. There was no way the Twins' Spymaster was buying Coldheart's story.

"Thank you," he said finally. "Goodbye."

He ended the call, and turned to Teotl, smiling. "She said she'll send us the file tomorrow."

Relief flooded into her, but she could never completely relax. Not with the power still bounding around inside her. "Good."

* * *

Rose Cross turned her phone off, and held it up over her shoulder. Her man Barnes plucked it from her hand, and promptly disappeared off into the edges of the party. She was lost in thought, staring through the people in their evening wear, twirling over the outdoor dance floor to the sounds of the string quartet. She stood on a terrace of perfectly manicured grass behind one of the great manor houses of South Carolina. A creek bubbled sluggishly at the bottom of these terraces. Willow trees gave the place a touch of lovely melancholy that was native to the area. Charleston was one of her favorite places in the world. Not in the least because she had been born so close by.

Rose was wondering why Coldheart was lying to her. He hadn't had the smoothest recruitment into the organization, that much was true. Rose had spent much of her time, in that first year when she was tutoring him, getting him to form some positive attachments. The poor boy seemed to have been broken even when he was mortal, and the death of Sarah Strauss had not helped him. It was up to Rose to glue him back together in some useful form. She found, to her surprise, that she liked him, or as close as affectionate pity got to that emotion.

No matter what she did, he still hated Shahmeran and distrusted the Twins. He respected Rose, and all of the others in the organization had at least been cordial to him. She wanted him in the Pacific Northwest, as close to the sweet-natured Blackthorn as possible, but Ash Wednesday had other ideas. After the skirmish with the Lion's people—far too early in Rose's opinion, though the young Familiar had acquitted himself admirably—she had insisted Coldheart get time to himself. As the Twins barely seemed to notice their organization when they didn't directly need it, Rose's commands were generally seen as orders from the Magi.

And now he was lying to her. He wanted information on Wei

Lai, the Prophet Apprentice of the Butterfly. A dangerous man, to be certain. Any Prophet was. Hard to corner, but once that was done, easy to kill. Was he trying to take out an enemy of the Twins on his own initiative? That seemed unlikely. Coldheart was a killer, but he had not come to enjoy it.

Or was he hoping that the Prophet's command of time would be enough to somehow pluck Sarah Strauss—the woman he had loved in his mortal days, who had been killed during his gifting—from the past? That seemed more likely, but that would result in disappointment. The only Prophet who might possess an ability so powerful would be the Hermit. Wei seemed an odd choice, but it wasn't as though there was a Prophet in the Twins' organization. Of all those in the world, Coldheart might see Wei, quite reasonably, as the one most willing to help.

She was still woolgathering when the flute of champagne appeared in her eyeline. She turned to find Shahmeran offering her one with one eyebrow arched. The wyrm was dressed in, for her, a very conservative white minidress, her purple and orange hair pinned back. "What was that all about?" she asked.

Rose accepted the champagne in one red-gloved hand. "Coldheart." She explained what he wanted, though not her speculation behind it. She was curious to see where the suspicious Shahmeran would take it.

"You think he's going rogue?" the wyrm asked, sipping her champagne.

"I don't think so."

"If you do, you need to tell our mistresses."

Rose smiled indulgently at her frequent companion. They had made a good team over the years, with Shahmeran as the body and Rose as the mind. "Oh, I will. I don't doubt his capacity for loyalty, assuming we can nurture it. Looking the other way, at least for now, is the best way to do that."

"And what if he does the worst?"

"What is the worst? A trap, baited with Wei Lai, for one of ours. You and I would be sent in as a rescue, or else the Machinist and Blackthorn, it barely matters who precisely. And do you know the kind of damage we could do? And after that, we will have bought the loyalty of Coldheart with a rescue. I couldn't design a better outcome, and that is our worst case scenario."

"I don't like it."

"I know, and I understand. It's important to remember that he is young." Rose finished her champagne and set it on the tray of a passing waiter. "As he grows into his rider, he will become what we need him to be. Until then, let him enjoy himself. We should do the same." She placed Shahmeran's hand on the small of her back, and took the other hand, and the two of them danced to the liquid strains of Vivaldi.

* * *

Teotl came out of her room, dressed in the new clothes Coldheart had purchased. The new ones were black: boots, jeans, undershirt, shirt, and leather jacket. She liked the feel of them: sensible and functional. She tied her hair back with a simple band. He was waiting in the front, and as she entered, he put his book aside.

"What do you think?" she asked.

"Everything fits?"

"Yes. Thank you."

"Well, we have..."

The knock on the door cut him off. He was on his feet quickly, and Teotl retreated to the corner. The energy buzzed angrily, begging to be released. She knew it was pointless. If the Prodigal was right, it was stuck in her because there was nothing solid enough to project it into. Nothing except the source itself.

Coldheart went to the door and opened it. Teotl could not see who was beyond it, but she knew the voice, and after a moment, recognized the perfume. Shahmeran. With her powers, that would have been a fight. Without, Shahmeran could have killed her without thinking, and considering the wyrm's opinion on enemy Familiars, without hesitation.

"Hello, Coldheart." Shahmeran's tone was smug. It was nearly always smug.

"I see it's grown back. Depth perception must be a pleasant change."

"Cute. Here's the information you wanted."

"Thank—"

"Rose might trust you with it, but I don't. If you try something, if you betray the Twins, you'll answer to me."

"One tip. When threatening someone, you should make sure it's someone who can't kill you quite so easily."

He shut the door and turned, holding up a manila folder. Teotl peeked out the window and saw Shahmeran stalking back to her car on those impossibly long legs. She climbed into the sleek Porsche, and sped off into the trees, leaving Coldheart behind.

He offered the folder to Teotl. "I suppose we should get reading."

* * *

Zhu's face still hurt. Coldheart had torn the left eye from Zhu's head, and left three ragged claw marks down it. The flesh was closed, though still bubbly and raw, the stitches long gone. The patch over the empty socket irritated his skin. The scars would soon toughen, the skin would form callouses, and there would come a time when he forgot what it was like to have two eyes at all.

The important thing was that the Butterfly's doctors had done well. They couldn't address the nightmares, when Coldheart emerged from the sudden winter, slaughtered his men, and came for him. They couldn't address the nightmares because Zhu never told them. He could not. If they knew that a soldier was having such foolish dreams, terrified of a mere Familiar, he would be relieved of duty. Then who would replace him? Better nightmares he could control than someone else given the task of guarding Wei Lai.

He had finished his recuperation in Fantan Tower at Wei's insistence. Much of the lower floors of the pagoda, and several of the outbuildings, were entirely given over to Wei's soldier and servitor bodyguards. In addition to the men Zhu directly commanded, Wei kept Kaeru the ghost and a number of deathless shock troops. It seemed light to Zhu, especially to protect a Prophet.

Now Zhu was ready to continue his duties. Wei had insisted he rest, reassuring Zhu that he had the time. Zhu could stand it no longer. He had to feel useful. Otherwise, it would be another day in bed, another day dreading the moment his eye shut. When the darkness closed in, and the wind picked up, carrying a bite and a howl, he'd see those yellow eyes, and the mouth spilling over with carnivorous teeth. And then the screaming of his men.

He knotted the tie on his suit, checked the Chinese-made automatic pistol in his shoulder holster, and left his small apartment. Wang was waiting for him in the hall, and the younger man instantly saluted as he had back when they both served a human army. Zhu returned the courtesy.

"Good to see you, sir. You look well."

"I look like hell. And it's good to see you, Corporal."

Zhu started down the hall and Wang fell into step beside him. He watched Wang's body language relax, the little joke about his appearance had done its work. "I found eight more men to your specifications. All former People's Liberation Army, all well-trained."

"Where did you pull them from?"

"One was on Oni's protection detail and two were from Jiangshi's, but you know Familiars. They don't care who's bodyguarding them. The other five came from the general pool."

"Good. Experience?"

"Varies. The bulk are relatively green. Based on the reports Wei has been giving, I would guess that will change soon enough."

"An attack?"

"'All but inevitable,' I think were his exact words."

Zhu came out into an open room, and the eight men all snapped to attention. Like Zhu and Wang, they were in unimpressive suits, and had the bearing of good army men. They were all armed, with pistols under their arms and knives at their belts. Their rifles wouldn't be far. They stared straight ahead, while Zhu walked back and forth, looking them over.

They were young. He could not escape that thought. They looked like children to him. Children playing at dress-up, who had somehow obtained loaded guns. They could pretend to be soldiers. They had even been trained by one of the finest fighting forces on the planet, yet they would not be prepared. Not for what the League had to show them. And Zhu knew it would not be long before he would bury every one of them.

He would have to find a way to accept that.

* * *

Kaeru had chosen a new body out of the freezers for his trip to Tokyo. Like any sensible ghost, he had made the trip from Hong Kong to Tokyo through Diyu, surfacing through the site of a particularly gruesome double murder—a man had hacked his parents apart with a prop sword—and met Jiangshi at the airport.

Kaeru wanted a pleasant experience, so he chose a young man who apparently died of suicide. Poison, if Kaeru had to guess, based on the way the blood vessels felt oddly crispy as he tried to move around. The body was fresh, the freezers having done their jobs well, but by the time he had taken a car from the motor pool, picked Jiangshi up, and started the drive to the lair of the Butterfly's heir, he was already irked.

It was the corpse's ass. He had been sitting on it the whole way—he was driving, after all, and it wasn't like there was another way to do that—and he felt the fluids settling. Even the ectoplasm he pumped through it didn't do much more than stir the muddy mix at the bottom. He felt like he was sitting on a slowly rotting cushion, which, of course, was exactly what he was doing.

He hadn't even been aware he was talking until Jiangshi said, "Mr. Kaeru, if you would focus?"

"You never think about soap when you're breathing. Oh, you think about it, just in that if you don't use it you smell more like yourself. I don't use it and I start smelling like rotten meat."

"Mr. Tōriki is quite used to rotten meat."

"Well, yes, I suppose that would be an integral part of the job, wouldn't it."

He wound the car into the rich Roppongi district, looking for a place to park. He finally found an elevator lot, and dropped the car off there.

"You shouldn't complain. You don't rot," he said to Jiangshi. She didn't have anything to say about that.

It was nighttime, when Tokyo was given over to the fluorescent subcultures of youth. Kaeru hadn't been dead for more than a couple years, and it already seemed alien to him. He had run with a rougher crowd—that had been what did him in—and he sometimes wished he'd chosen a more colorful but less dangerous association. He might have lived to enjoy more of his life. But then, being a ghost could be a great deal of fun.

Jiangshi led the way into the club where Tōriki spent a good deal of his time. Not hard to see why once the bouncer—one of Tōriki's bodyguards—waved them past. Everyone in the place looked like Victorian vampires. Floor-length black gowns, pancake makeup accented by black lipstick and eyeliner, and hair dyed all the colors of the rainbow regardless of gender. Others were dressed as Victorian gentlemen on the way to funerals, or else large and living dolls, done up in black lace and garters.

"I'm a ghost wearing a dead guy, and I don't think I'm dark enough for this crowd," Kaeru said.

If Jiangshi heard him, she made no sign, slithering through as the ghoulish assemblage danced to the wailing of electric guitars. Kaeru was beginning to regret bringing a body at all, but he was the one who was going to have to do most of the talking. Tōriki agreed to see them only reluctantly, and Jiangshi couldn't be trusted to do any negotiations. She'd just thump the Necromancer over the head and carry him off. Not the best way to promote good relations amongst Apprentices.

And the atmosphere in here, so many people sweating off layers of makeup and perfume. Kaeru felt it sticking to his dead flesh, as though it would eat the stuff away and leave him obviously rotting. "Soap," he muttered.

Jiangshi turned, and the slightest frown creased her porcelain face.

Kaeru took that as an invitation. "Soap. I could wash myself, right? But the last time I took a shower, I ended up washing half the body's fluids all down the drain. I felt like I was turning into one of those mummies. You ever see that movie?"

She turned away and kept walking through the crowd, occasionally relocating someone who didn't have the sense to get out of her way.

"It's about this guy who finds one of those lost cities in the Egyptian desert. Cities of the dead. You know, like the ones the Crocodile supposedly scattered all over Khem. Come to think of it, you ever wonder if those movies are actually about the Crocodile? Like someone in Hollywood knew about him this whole time? Some of those movies are weirdly accurate. It's enough to make a man suspicious. Like the Twins aren't doing their part to keep this whole thing of ours nice and hush-hush."

Jiangshi pushed open a door at the other end of the club where another one of Tōriki's bodyguards waited. Like the last one, he was a big man with a shaved head, his black suit making him look like a funeral director. He stood aside at Jiangshi's approach and let Servitor and Familiar through the door. They went down a flight of stairs, and the music grew muffled above them, bleeding away to the quick heartbeat of the drums and the thin blood-rush of feedback.

They emerged into a hall, at the end of which was a heavy, metal door, decorated with inlaid runes and sigils. Two beautiful young women stood on either side of the door, dressed like Victorian dolls. They were both dead, and Kaeru knew they would be better security than either of the men upstairs. Kaeru's gaze lingered over each of them, snagging on the thin expanse of thigh between their black stockings and frilly dresses.

"I need a new body," he said.

"Welcome, honored one," the two dead girls said in unison, addressing Jiangshi.

Jiangshi did not acknowledge the greeting, and the girls never waited for one. One stood aside while the other opened the door. It sounded like the portal to a submarine.

The smell hit Kaeru first. It was the bite of decay. "Is that me?"

"Some of it," said Jiangshi.

Both of them had served the Butterfly long enough to no longer be bothered by that particular smell. In fact, it was often a feature of home, where they were safest. Still, when Kaeru stepped over the threshold, a shudder worked its way through his borrowed skin, pulling at the fibers of his pale form. "What... what is that?"

"Wards," said a voice from within. "Wards to trap disobedient spirits. Fortunately, this does not include you."

The room was a Victorian parlor filled with antiques. As the door closed behind them, the music cut off. The sound was now from an old phonograph, playing a scratchy record of a child singing in a language Kaeru didn't recognize. Jiangshi stepped through the living room and through the doorway beyond, toward the source of the voice. Kaeru forced himself to follow, the whole time wincing and flinching from the screeching discord of the wards.

He flinched again when he entered the next room, though it was for an entirely different reason.

It looked like the room of a doll maker's shop, with limbs, and heads, and gowns, all hanging from the walls. But the dolls were corpses, or else pieces of them. There were several assembled ones, looking like the dead girls at the door, and they were busy sewing together another of their number, who lay half-assembled on a long table. One dead girl was carefully attaching an arm, her stitchwork precise. Another was selecting a dress for the dead girl to wear, comparing her peaceful face and washed-out skin to a variety of different cloths. Another was picking out the proper pair of legs.

Kaeru could barely fit this into his attention because of the man who turned to address them as they entered. He was not especially tall, though he countered that with his top hat and high-heeled boots. He wore an elegant topcoat over an embroidered waistcoat, matching cravat, black pants, and a pressed black shirt. Kaeru's eyes were drawn to the glint of the silver watch chain hanging from one button of the waistcoat to a pocket. Charms dangled from it, tinkling like windchimes: a skull, an eye, and a hand. He watched his dead girls putting the new one together.

He smiled, and the persistent chill worming its way through Kaeru began to thrash.

"Now, what can I do for you?" asked Tōriki Satoru, Heir to the Butterfly.

- 5 -

Teotl stood with Coldheart on the railing of a cruise ship. She had convinced him that this was the best way back to Shi Jie, the one place the Butterfly's people would be least likely to watch. It was a factual statement, but not a truthful one. The truth was that she chose this route because it was slow, and she was afraid.

Her powers were broken. A bullet had hurt her badly, and another could quite easily kill her. There was no shortage of Familiars who had been taken down by something as simple as a man with a gun. The enemy knew they were coming, and he would be prepared.

Yet, it was not just this that frightened her. She was worried that this effort would come to nothing. She had never tested it. There was no way to know for certain, and she was basing everything on the rambling of a Prodigal. That would be the worst, to weather the storm of Wei Lai's forces, to survive it all, and get her hands on the quintessence only to find that her powers remained gone. And then what? Live forever until the Priestess sent an assassin to reclaim the little bit of her soul that resided in Teotl. In the worst of ironies, the Priestess would likely pick Kisin for the job. She could watch another tiny bit of her ally die as he smothered her in stone.

She tried to convince herself of her plan by convincing Coldheart. He was a Diabolist's Familiar and thus understood extradimensional entities, but the raw energy of magic seemed to be something of a mystery to the wendigo. "It comes down to what Ashar said. If there is a finite amount of energy within the quintessence, my absorbing of some of it could have produced a vacuum."

"It sounded to me like that stuff is infinite," Coldheart said.

"If it were truly infinite, there wouldn't be different sizes. Remember, he said the amount that had created the universe would have been bigger than the amount I saw. That says that the size is at least somewhat tied to the amount of energy inside."

"So you're planning to get close enough and hope that what's in you returns to the quintessence?"

"That's it."

Coldheart nodded. She saw a thought pass over his face, and for a moment, he choked on it. But he gave it voice. It seemed as though he had to. When he spoke, his words were small and broken, barely audible over the brisk salt wind and the waves crashing against the hull. "Or more of the stuff floods into you and you explode."

She saw it, not in her eyes, but with her mind. She saw herself, a silhouette of purest black against the blinding white of the explosion. Even using those absolute terms, "black" and "white" were inadequate. They were far more different than something so prosaic. There was only the quintessence, and everything else, the not-quintessence.

"I... I think that was the intent all along."

"What do you mean?"

"Sorcery is the Art of magic at its base. Everything comes from it. That's why we use the symbol of the sun—it's the source of all things. But it's not really. The real source is quintessence. Sorcery is all about prime energy, and it sounds like quintessence is prime matter. Matter and energy are one and the same, and so quintessence *is* Sorcery. The knowledge of how that worked would be priceless to my mistress."

"She'd let you die for a little knowledge."

"Not for a little. But for this?"

Coldheart put his hand on the railing closer to hers. She put a hand on top of his. It was icy cold, but she kept hold of it. He was still so young. He had no idea of just how far from human the Magi really had risen. Teotl, though, saw it all. Once she learned the value of the quintessence, the motive of her mistress became horrifyingly clear.

"She wanted me to get caught in that blast," Teotl said.

"How can you be sure?" He didn't want her to be certain. He wanted to believe that the loyalty he felt was reciprocated. While the Twins might value their Familiars, or even love them, it was closer to the love of a master and a dog. Losing a pet hurt, but there would always be others.

"The intelligence," was what she said. "It was very specific, and often correct. The ways it was wrong... they were also specific, and too damning to be coincidental. She gave me the right place, but a false estimate of the opposition."

"Maybe she didn't know enough. Maybe her spies couldn't get the precise details."

"It doesn't matter. She told me I was there to kill Wei. What would it have mattered had Jiangshi been there too? That would have only made my job easier. One of her punches would take Wei's head clean off. No. She lied."

"You can't be sure of that."

She met his eyes. They were soft, the predatory amber dark from the shade of the deck. She wanted to comfort him for this realization. She had known they were capable of this kind of thing, but she had never thought she would fall victim to it. Now, the illusion stripped away, she could see things as they were. He was getting his lesson earlier than most.

"They feel what we do, though it's the smallest reflection of it.

She would have learned so much in that moment, and afterwards, she could measure what it did to me by what it was doing to her." She shook her head. "I wish it weren't true, believe me—"

The Priestess brushed Teotl's face, only the second time in existence the Magus had touched her Familiar. At the time, it had been the sweet caress of mother to daughter, but now in her memories, she saw the hint of sadness, of regret, on the ageless face of the Magus.

"—but it is."

She turned away, unable to bear more of Coldheart making excuses for a woman he had never met, and would try to kill if they ever somehow ended up in the same place. He had nothing else to say either, already spinning away into his own mind about what he meant to his mistresses. Teotl left him on the deck and returned to her cabin. It was small, but comfortable. As a child, she never would have imagined such luxury, now as a Familiar she could barely tolerate it.

She stretched out on the bed and wondered what the hell she was going to do next. It was a silly thing to plan for, as she was likely marching into a trap and would be dead in a day or two, yet she could not stop her mind from working. The thought she kept turning back to was the Priestess, and before that, the woman who had chosen to be her mother.

Michaela, hugging her. The first happy year Esperanza had in a long time, her thirteenth. Thirteen was supposed to be a time of misery and change, while her body steadily betrayed her, yet with Michaela raising the girl as her own, in that big house, Esperanza knew the peace of a full belly, of clean clothes, and most importantly of love. Michaela had given everything, and in return, Esperanza had done the same.

The knock at the cabin door broke Teotl from her spiraling thoughts. Michaela and those who had died before, Drigo and those who had died after, were still dead. Teotl had no intention of joining them. As much as she treasured her memories of both of them, she welcomed the interruption. She sat up in the bed. "Come in, Coldheart."

The Familiar entered, grinning sheepishly at being identified. Teotl still had a hard time reconciling those halves of him: the sweet young man and the murderous monster. "I'm still not used to the name," he said. "There's a part of me that wants to correct you every time you use it."

"That feeling never goes away. I haven't heard my name spoken out loud in about forty years. There's something to it, the real name your mother," and here her voice stuttered for just a moment, "gave you has power. It's linked to you."

Coldheart sat down on the bed next to her. He was close. Half of her wanted to scoot toward him. The other half was afraid. The fear itself was thrilling, and Teotl savored it. "Rose gave me that lecture. 'Don't tell anyone your name, or you'll be easier to control.'"

Teotl smiled. His impression of Rose Cross was terrible.

He went on: "It's weird. As much power as we all have, and we're terrified of something as simple as our names."

Terrified of someone calling her name. Her real name, the one she hadn't heard for so many years. Then it was her only name. She was only seven, and she was sure they were going to call her next. They were going to know she was there, out in the alley behind her house, clutching her stuffed dog. Hiding under the stinking garbage. While inside the bad men hacked her family apart with their machetes. And now, the bloody blade was her name.

"I know what you mean," she said.

"I wish I could say something. Do something."

"You're already doing it."

"What about when this is over? Are you going back to the Priestess? Or are you staying out in the cold?"

She moved a little closer. "The cold's not so bad." Teotl could feel the other side of him, gazing through the flesh at her hungrily.

She liked knowing it was there. The knowledge sent chilled fingers up and down her spine.

"It can kill you." Yet he didn't move away, and didn't look like he could move at all. There was hunger in his eyes too, but it was a different one than the creature inside. She knew there was the same look in hers. His breath was cold, picking out gooseflesh on her face. And it smelled, ever so slightly, of blood.

"I know," she whispered into his mouth. She kissed him, and he took hold of her gratefully. His lips and tongue were like ice, and they seemed to stir the energy of the explosion through her body, moving it now in great leaps from her belly to her heart and back again. Through the kiss, she could feel the wendigo. It wanted to devour her whole. The kiss was the merest reflection, at turns tender, then at the edge of terrifying need. Teotl moved into his lap, held him as close as she could, lost in this man that should be her enemy. His mouth was at her neck, the frigid wind of his breath tickling her skin.

The creature inside him ate the heart of her friend. She saw the blood dripping from his claws, his mouth, his jagged teeth. The amber eyes said that more would suffer to quell a hunger that could never be sated.

His flesh against hers, warmth against cold. The instinct was to recoil, both from danger and the cold itself. She found she liked it, and tried to cover every inch of herself in him.

His flesh was barely there. It was howling wind and driving snow: nothing more. When he made it look solid, it was an illusion. The bullets told her that, impacting things like skin and muscle and bone, punching holes into them, and yet there was no blood, and the wendigo was gone, ready to reappear and tear into his victims. No matter how many helpless bullets they pumped into him.

She needed him. All of him. And when they were finally together, and her vision once again went white, she felt three individuals in that room. There was her. The young man. And the monster.

It killed—he killed. With no remorse. Those men on the boat were torn to bloody ribbons, and he would only ever want more.

In the quiet afterwards, they lay under the covers of her bed. Coldheart was nearly dozing, and she was pillowed in his arms. His skin remained as cold has it had been, and she started to move away. He opened his eyes.

"Sorry. Your skin is freezing."

"Oh. Sorry."

"No, it was nice during, but I need to warm up."

She moved to the other side of the bed, wrapping the covers around herself. She still felt him on her, in her, in the slowly-warming pathways of her body. Coldheart watched her cocoon her body. "The wendigo changed me in some strange ways. There's the body temperature. And other things."

Teotl felt the warmth creep back into her. It was pleasant, but she regretted losing the closeness she'd just had. The question that bubbled up into her mind was something she'd been curious about since they'd met again, and probably should have asked before. "How much influence does it have over you?"

"It's the human soul—my soul—that's in charge, but the wendigo has desires of its own. I have to let it indulge from time to time or I'll lose control. It's why the Twins have kept me so busy."

"And it speaks to you."

"All the time. It hates anyone I'm close to."

"Are there a lot of those?"

"No." He paused. "I think, in a weird way, it wants to protect me."

"We don't get voices. We just get power."

After winning the Prize, and being escorted into the Temple of the Sun at the top of El Hormiguero, the woman who would soon be Teotl was in front of her mistress. The power was blinding, flooding into every part of her. She felt the change, but she felt it as the all-

encompassing blaze of a new star being born within her. She promised herself she would not scream. She broke that promise in less than an instant.

"How old are you?" He blanched. "I'm sorry."

"I was born in 1943."

"Oh god."

"I could be your mother."

He laughed. "Let's not go into that."

"You asked," she teased.

He leaned partially over, and she finished the trip, kissing him lightly on the mouth.

"We should get some sleep. Big day tomorrow."

"Good idea."

He started to get up.

"Where do you think you're going?" she said.

"Back to my cabin. To sleep?"

"You can sleep here."

His face lit up. "Okay. I can sleep here."

And he did, shortly thereafter. Teotl watched him, the energy still buzzing inside her, though now it felt like the individual particles were snow, chilling whatever they touched. This might be the most vulnerable she would ever see Coldheart. The only chance anyone in the Priestess's organization would ever have to kill him. After her failure in San Francisco, she practically owed it to her mistress.

She leaned over and brushed a kiss over his cold forehead, then rolled over and went to sleep.

* * *

Kaeru could not believe his ears. Well, they weren't his ears, technically. They belonged to one of the Butterfly's soldiers who had eaten a bullet at the behest of Koshmar, one of the Wolf's

Familiars. They worked fine, and what with the putty work on the back of the head, it was almost impossible to tell that a bullet had shattered the back half of the skull. Kaeru was impressed there were enough brains at all to think through, but the corpse wouldn't have wound up in the freezer if there hadn't been. What Jiangshi said, though, beggared belief.

They were in one of the living rooms in Fantan Tower, mostly just waiting, and Kaeru didn't want to spend his time with the frightened soldiers. As boring as Jiangshi was, at least she was fun to look at. And occasionally, she would say things that were so insane, they gave Kaeru hours of material to wax poetic about.

"You have to miss it a little," he said, still unable to formulate a proper response.

Jiangshi reclined on a gold couch, patiently waiting either Wei or Tōriki to call her to action. "I don't."

"But this is sex we're talking about. I understand, you're a soulless monster who exists only to inflict pain on the enemy—"

"Follow the wishes of the Butterfly or those expressed by her Apprentices."

"—or that. And I know you don't care for fine dining, or games of chance, or liquor, or music, or anything else that gives one's life meaning."

"We're dead."

"Fine. Gives one's *death* meaning."

"The Butterfly gives us—"

"Oh god, enough with that. Yes, I know the Butterfly is incredible, and I serve her, and I love her in that platonic, admiring way that is good and decent and not at all gross. I'm there. I'm totally there. But there are times of the day, sometimes days or even weeks or months where no one needs me. I get to do whatever. And yes, I'm a lowly Servitor, and there are a million of me, and you're a mighty Familiar, and there are only five of you, but you still get time off."

"I spend it contemplating the majesty of our mistress in this world and the next."

Kaeru collapsed. "I give up. No. No, I don't. Because then the forces of boring win, and I will not have that. Do you hear me?"

"I trust that question is rhetorical and you just enjoy shouting."

"Sex, you remorseless statue. It's the whole reason we have all that other stuff. Everything comes down to sex, mostly because without it, we wouldn't have a race to transcend in the first place."

Jiangshi was silent, and Kaeru sat up, wondering if he'd finally made a dent. She looked like she might just be considering what he said. Finally: "I never liked it much. Even when I was alive."

"That sounds to me like you never had the right partner," he said getting up and crossing over to her. "I would be more than happy to show you what you were missing. There should be enough blood left in this body for what I have in—"

The proposition ended with a bone-cracking crunch. As Kaeru flooded out of the now unsuitable flesh, he saw Jiangshi lifting her palm out of the corpse's head, which she had slammed into the floor. The wood had splintered, and the skull, already weakened by the hole in the back, had been completely flattened.

Kaeru tried to complain, but he couldn't form a coherent thought, much less transfer it to his voice. Instead, he clicked his teeth, and wandered off in search of another body.

* * *

On the top floor of Fantan Tower, Wei Lai continued his contemplation of the quintessence. It was even more fascinating than he had hoped it would be. He could not claim to understand it, but he now knew what it was that he did not understand. He would not get a chance to finish his study; one way or another, he was losing the precious treasure, so he wanted to wring every last secret he could.

Even as his fate was bearing down on him.

He kept seeing Jun's little face in his mind, back along the pathways that were receding into darkness. He walked them far too often. But Jun was dead, and nothing would bring her back. All that was left was revenge.

Tōriki Satoru paced in the room, his high-heeled boots clicking on the wooden floor. He had arrived not long ago with a contingent of men and a few of his elite stitched-together dead girls. He needn't have done it. Either his presence alone would keep Wei alive, or it wouldn't. The twenty men downstairs would only be more gristle for the mill.

"Thank you for coming," Wei said for what was probably the hundredth time.

"It's no bother."

"With Coldheart on his way, you really are the only one with a prayer of stopping him. And with him, Teotl has an excellent chance of killing me."

"Why not move?"

"I'm afraid it makes my chances worse. We'll be fighting a weakened Teotl and an inexperienced Coldheart. It is the best we can do." He didn't mention that moving would put the pathway of his revenge forever out of reach. While Tōriki might understand that, he would not understand that moving also gave the Butterfly a better chance of survival. The choice had arrived, and Wei made it. His vengeance was more important than his mistress.

"It sounds like we don't have much of a chance."

"*We* don't. *You* do."

Tōriki grinned. "It has been some time since I've tangled with one of the Twins' demons."

"You should be very pleased in about twelve hours. One way or the other." Wei paused, unsure if he wanted to place the suggestion of defeat in Tōriki's mind. What Wei needed to say was too important to be left out. "One thing. If I should die, promise me: Captain Zhu Baolin should be made head of the Butterfly's personal guard."

"Your man?"

Wei nodded.

"His job is to protect you, and if he fails, you want me to promote him?"

"He has very few ways to affect the outcome here. And trust me."

"All right," Tōriki said. He watched Wei watching the quintessence. "What is so interesting about that little piece of dirt?"

"Everything."

"So interesting that you tell me Teotl has a good chance of murdering you, and you can't look away."

Wei did look away, or at least he appeared to. His eyes were stitched up, and he wasn't seeing the light reflected from Tōriki, he was seeing the time and probability of it. Every copy of the Butterfly's heir had tiny differences, but they added up to the single most probable version of the man, and this was what Wei chose to interpret as Tōriki's true appearance. "Do you know how many times I have seen my death? Because I don't. I've lost count. There are only so many things one can do to prevent such a thing, and once they are done, worrying further helps no one. Your presence gives me my best chance of survival. You are here. So now I am choosing to use my time to plumb the mysteries of this 'little piece of dirt' as you call it."

"Fine, fine. You've made your point."

No. He hadn't. Because the point itself was treason. Jun had been a Scion, and as such her existence had been illegal. Kabur had been too frightened to keep her, and it had been up to Wei to keep their little girl safe. But the choice came, protect the girl or protect the mistress. There had been only a tiny chance that Kisin would find the baby, and Wei was a gambler. He took those odds.

He had been wrong.

And he had spent the last sixty years putting his plan into place. Kisin died in so many futures it was barely necessary to bring them about. The Priestess, though. She was difficult to kill.

Though not impossible.

* * *

The fog was icy. The cloying moisture collected on Teotl's hair, crystallized, then melted into chilled rivulets that trickled down the neckline of her clothes. She shivered, gazing out into the expanse of white. She and Coldheart piloted the stolen boat toward Wei Lai's island. She could not see it, trusting instead that Coldheart could navigate through the fog he'd called off the ocean.

Wei's men had to know what was coming. The fog practically announced Coldheart's arrival. But it was that or come in entirely exposed and while he treated bullets as an inconvenience, she no longer did. The boat itself was nearly silent, the sails fat with the wind Coldheart summoned. Teotl walked from the cabin out onto the deck, and the shivering increased tenfold. The fog had only been isolated tendrils snaking into the cabin; now it was all around, clutching with dead man's fingers.

"We had an agent drive us to our last mission site," she said.

Coldheart chuckled. It was a chilling sound. "An agent might report your presence to the Twins."

"Oh I know. I'm glad it's just us."

"It is a little sobering to think how many enemy agents are around us when we think we're safe."

"Probably best not to think about it."

"Easier said than done." He flashed her a smile, and he might have intended it to be the winsome grin he gave when he was human, this had shades of the feral monster on the deck of the container ship. The more he used the powers, the closer he got to killing time, the more the wendigo took control. She couldn't stop herself from taking a step back. He barely seemed to notice her, instead closing his eyes to steer the boat with gusts of freezing wind.

He opened his eyes as a dock emerged from the white. Figures moved around on the wood, walking their routes.

"I have to change now," he said.

"I'll see you when we're finished."

She felt the chill wind, heard the distant howl, and smelled the freshly spilled blood. The gusts gathered around him, shot through with snow, whirling and changing. It left behind bits of itself, and as Coldheart's human silhouette grew gray and indistinct, it was replaced with the looming figure of the wendigo. Three meters of cold-starved flesh, grasping claws, and ancient hunger. The wendigo turned is head, as though to catch Teotl in his view, but the neck stopped halfway. Then the creature uttered a sepulchral chuckle and said, "Have it your way." She got the impression he was talking to himself.

The wind whipped past, taking strips of the wendigo with it, until the creature was gone, invisible on the snowy gusts. She thought she saw his eyes, cruel and feral, in the fog ahead, but that could have been in her mind. She heard him, though, the high-pitched cackle in the storm. As the boat drifted ahead and she took the wheel, she saw Coldheart appear on the docks behind one of the men. The claws flashed, and the man fell to the docks. One by one, the Familiar vanished and reappeared, sending soldier after soldier crumpling into broken heaps.

At the last one, the monster knelt and began to eat.

Teotl guided the boat into the slip, tied up, and hopped onto the dock. Coldheart looked up, the gore dripping from his distended jaws. For a fraction of a second, Teotl saw the shame in his eyes, but then it was gone, replaced by animalistic fury. He reached into the body and with a wet pop, yanked the heart from the chest. Frost spread over the surface of the still organ.

"I'll open the way," Coldheart said.

She nodded.

He crammed the frozen heart into his mouth, and once again, he turned to wind. A path snaked up a short hill. She could see the dim shape of Fantan Tower looming from the fog, but not enough to make out details. The pagoda had taken on a Victorian appearance, the points of the rooftops looking like gargoyles. Ahead, she could make out the sound of falling bodies, of flesh being torn, of blood spilling then freezing. It came to her from every direction, the fog baffling and redirecting the sounds. The hair on her neck was standing straight up, and she had to force herself to go up that path and into the fog. There was a monster in there. Her monster, but only just barely. She would never be able to control him. She wondered if anyone really could.

She went up the path, paved with gray stones wet from the surf and smoothed by many feet. Now and again, she would pass one of Wei's soldiers, killed and mutilated in the tall emerald grass by the side. They all had a look of locked surprise on their faces. Coldheart had dealt with them quickly, leaving behind a mostly intact and half-frozen body. It was the kindest fate any of them could have hoped for.

Teotl emerged from the fog at the lip of an incline. The path here dipped down into the flat clearing where Fantan Tower sat, behind a wooden gate and its expansive Chinese garden. The gate now stood open, painted in blood, two more guards torn to ribbons at the base. Their blood flowed, uniting in a stream dripping into a pond of koi. The fish gave the spreading stain a wide berth.

Up ahead, Teotl heard the first scream.

* * *

The scream came from outside. It was shrill with terror, and sliced off as suddenly as it had started. The men were in the pagoda's front hall. These were Wei's security force; all the others had been assigned to outdoor duty. From the sound of the scream, the enemy had arrived.

Zhu held his left hand up, keeping his men from firing. His right hand was closed around the grip of his assault rifle. The others bristled with their weapons, all trained on the big double doors at the entryway. Jiangshi stood close by, her impassive expression calming the men. She would take the fore in the coming battle.

"That's the alarm," muttered Wang at the scream.

"Corporal, fetch Mr. Tōriki, please," Jiangshi said.

Wang sprinted upstairs. There were others that might mistake his speed for cowardice, but there were none that Zhu trusted more. The young man had thought he'd broken at the sight of Coldheart. To Zhu, it was rational fear, and even in the midst of that, Wang had saved his life.

The doors exploded inward on a powerful gust of snowy wind. The cold curdled Zhu's remaining eye and blistered his face. Outside, he could only dimly see the front garden, covered now in a layer of frost. A figure strode out of the fog. At first, it looked human, but as it approached, it was soon clear it was anything but. It was far too tall and thin, its arms too long, its back too hunched. And before the details of its thin blue flesh could be seen, there were the eyes, glowing yellow with hate.

Coldheart stepped into the threshold and looked over the assembled soldiers. "Nice of you to prepare a feast for me."

As the firing started, the wendigo was already wind.

* * *

Teotl watched Coldheart descend onto the soldiers. She felt a momentary pang of pity for them. They had shot her, hunted her, and slaughtered her men, but to unleash Coldheart upon them just seemed cruel. The gunfire was chaotic, at first passing through the doorway, to zip past her and chew up clumps of small pines and bushes in the gardens. As the wendigo shifted from solid to wind, the firing went in every direction.

She sneaked forward along a bridge spanning a pond that had frozen over. She climbed the stairs to the front hall and peeked inside. Coldheart had already killed half the men. Only a grizzled soldier in an eyepatch, half his face covered in hideous scars, seemed to have kept his composure, moving around the room away from the gusts of wind, and firing only when Coldheart took flesh. Jiangshi was by a corner, poised to leap.

When Coldheart solidified to kill the eyepatched man, Jiangshi pounced. She landed on Coldheart's back, where the points of his spine threatened to poke through his crepe-thin flesh. "Captain Zhu! Fall back to Wei!" Jiangshi shouted.

"Ma'am!"

The eyepatched man ran for the stairs, pausing for a moment to watch the wendigo and the zombie wrestle, and went up. Coldheart vanished into wind, causing Jiangshi to fall through him, he materialized across the room, grinning.

Teotl knew she could not stay and watch. She had to find Wei and the quintessence. She followed Zhu, the man in the eyepatch, upstairs.

* * *

Kaeru watched as the bodies appeared in the underworld. At first, the room in Fantan Tower was poorly defined. The dim lights revealed a generic floor and some plain walls. The doorways were there, but they led only to the pervasive gloom of Diyu. And then, the first of the bodies appeared on the floor. The man was maggot-white and nude, his chest opening up in horrific gashes.

Then it ran backward and forward, like a film, the man coming back together and onto his feet, then ripped open and left to fall.

As he appeared, the walls grew slightly more detailed; there was the hint of a tapestry on one, the grain of wood on another. One of the doors revealed stairs that stopped after the third step and went nowhere.

The second body appeared. The cause of death was similar, though this time the phantom attacker had torn open the man's throat. His head bobbled and fell backward on a ragged and bloodless strip of flesh. Then he was in one piece, and for a moment, in a firing pose, yet he was far too weak an apparition to actually produce his weapon. Then he was dead again.

And the room sharpened.

It went like this, the bodies falling, every one of them ripped, torn, eaten. And with each death, this place strengthened its connection to Diyu, and wrote its fate upon the surface of the underworld. After four deaths, the attacker started to become visible. First as a nebulous white shape, tall and skinny, with spidery hands. The deaths sharpened him as well. Kaeru soon recognized Coldheart the Familiar, though the shape that appeared in Diyu was not exactly accurate. What the underworld was taking was the feelings of the victims, the rage of the killer, and crafting an identity for him, a shadow that would continue his murders for decades to come. Somehow, the death-reflection of Coldheart managed to be so much worse. Kaeru knew this was not the only place that would have it. There would soon be legions of ghostly Coldhearts all over Diyu, shredding armies of hapless men.

Kaeru was far more interested in finding a body. It looked like the wendigo wasn't planning on leaving anything that would be pleasant to inhabit, but a couple looked like they might still move. Kaeru crossed over, easy now that the room had become so sharp. The walls and floors barely changed, only the light, from

dim lamps in the other room, and the electric light overhead, was
blinding for a moment.

He clicked his teeth in annoyance.

A crash drew his attention. Coldheart was battling Jiangshi
now, but they were not truly fighting. Coldheart was playing with
her. He had stripped the flesh of her right shoulder to the bone
and now the arm hung by her side, useless. He had torn her face
nearly off her skull, the papery skin flapping in the wind. The
way she was limping said she had several broken bones.

Kaeru cast around for a body to possess, wondering what he
could to do help. The thoughts were a useless slurry, an array of
images, of scents, of sounds, that made no sense. He knew only
that he needed flesh, and one of these fallen men had to have
enough on him to help.

"Oh, he has been busy."

Kaeru turned. Tōriki Satoru was on the stairs, flanked by Zhu,
Wang, and two of his dead girls. The Necromancer had a smile on
his face as his left hand toyed with the charms on his watch chain.
As the tiny metal objects tinkled together, Kaeru flinched, crawling
away from this raw power. He could swear that within the clinking
metal, he heard screams.

Coldheart paused, and Jiangshi did not press the attack. She
sagged backward, her body trying to fold in on itself.

"Coldheart," Tōriki said.

"Who are you?"

"Does it really matter?"

"I suppose not."

Coldheart lunged at the Necromancer, but Tōriki held out his
right hand as though asking for something and began to speak.
Kaeru could not have understood those words even if he had
a body and a brain to think them through. They were power,
insidious, hissing power. They pulled at the ghost, even as they

were not directed at him. They were like Coldheart's wind: chilling and everywhere.

The wendigo stopped in his attack, dropping to his spindly knees. His outline grew less and less solid, the wind whipping away sections of his body only to bring back another, different piece. He tried to cover his hideous face with long-fingered hands.

Tōriki kept speaking those horrible words. Kaeru clapped his hands to his head, even though he had no ears, and even if he had, that would not block the words out. The Necromancer was addressing the soul itself, and compelling it to do his bidding. Kaeru saw it, the wispy form of something almost like smoke and almost like milk, freeing itself from the kneeling monster. There was a face in that smoke, and hands, and arms, but the human features vanished and reappeared so quickly it seemed like imagination. The soul moved to the Necromancer's hand, and, still speaking, he touched his watch chain. There, a silver heart crusted with frost, appeared next to the other charms.

Only then did Tōriki Satoru fall silent.

The wendigo got to his feet. This was not the ponderous act of a human being, but the effortless motion of a monster. The wind returned, washing away the kneeling figure like sand, and then brought the creature back, standing. It loomed over Tōriki and the others, but its attention was entirely on the Necromancer. Tōriki never quailed, merely looking up at the ancient beast with interest.

"You freed me," said the wendigo.

"I did."

"Then I'll kill you last."

Tōriki stood aside as once again the wendigo disappeared into wind and flowed upstairs.

"Sir?" Zhu said. "Mr. Wei is upstairs and..."

"He's assured me that Coldheart won't kill him. If you can't trust a Prophet..." He finished the sentence with a shrug.

Kaeru found a body and flowed into it. It was missing a heart, but the rest was intact. He could fashion one out of ectoplasm, but it wouldn't last long. Long enough for whatever was happening now. As he was getting up from the floor, he saw Wang catch a faltering Jiangshi.

"Thank you, Corporal. I need to heal. If you can just help me to the couch." She leaned on Wang on the way to the other room.

Kaeru stood up.

"We'll wait down here for the time being," Tōriki said. "Except you, Kaeru. I have an assignment for you."

The ghost smiled with his borrowed lips.

* * *

Teotl was several floors up, hunting for the staircase for the next one. She had the impression that Wei Lai would be on the top floor of his tower, calmly waiting for his fate, if indeed it was within her power to bring that. Now she was in a darkened hall, with doorways on either side of her. She knew she had to move quickly. Coldheart was powerful, not invincible.

"Teoooooooooootl." The sound drifted up the stairs behind her, soaring on the cold breeze that followed it. It was Coldheart, and he was close. That was not the voice of an ally. That was the voice of the monster. The name sounded like the wind howling.

"You can't hide from me, Teotl. I know your scent."

She glanced at the hallway behind here where some of the light, dimmed by space, still bled upward. There was the skinny shadow thrown against the wall, then gone just as quickly, leaving only his mournful menacing voice behind.

"It's all over me still. There were three of us in that room, you know. While he was in you, I was in him."

She ducked into the nearest room just as the wendigo materialized in the hall. She could hear him outside, his bare feet on the rug, his long claws playing off the wooden walls. His big body, hunched over to fit in the hall, brought the chill of winter with him. She was in a bedroom, and she slinked down and away from the door, cramming herself into the narrow space between a bed and the wall.

"It probably seems cruel to kill you. But it's not out of cruelty. I don't hate you. Those two whores shackled me, and I'll be damned if I let anyone else get their hooks into us."

He was getting closer. There were gusts of wind now, probing the darkness for prey. They swished about invisibly, only heralded by the deep chill they brought. Seeking her like icy eels.

"You have to die."

The wendigo was close now. She could see his shadow through the doorway, a massive dark blob against the back hall. Could he smell her? Or did the rivers of spilled blood downstairs drown her scent? The claws continued their rending along the wall.

"For his own good."

The wendigo stalked past. She heard the massive shape in the hall, the momentary interruption of his claws over the doorway. She felt him, cold and hungry and murderous. The attention forced her deeper into that ball—

Men with machetes in the other room. Don't make a sound, no matter what you hear. No matter what they did to mama and papa.

—and wait. Hope. Pray this creature born from the nightmares of starving men, did not sense her to add to his bloody tally of corpses. To know that this was the desperate pleading of all his prey, and so few would ever have their prayers answered.

And then he had passed. She stood soundlessly and opened the door behind her, slinking through it and shutting it behind. The room was absolutely dark. She could hear the wendigo out in the hall, still talking to her with that wind-voice. The man she had been with was gone. She didn't know how, maybe the slaughter downstairs had suppressed him completely. Maybe he never had control of the creature. Maybe it wanted him to think he did. Or maybe he just wanted to kill her.

A month, a month of care, of stolen looks, of honest being there. *He came to the container ship. He saved her. He helped her when everything said he shouldn't. If the young man in the Familiar wanted her dead, she would already be with Rose Cross.*

The light clicked on. A dead man sat in a chair across from her. He was one of the soldiers from downstairs, though he no longer carried his gun. His chest had been torn open, and was crusted in frost. The suit he was wearing was more or less ruined, though a gory tie still hung over the ragged hole. Inside, she saw a pumping heart, made from some pearly white substance. It turned her stomach.

"There you are," whispered the dead man.

"Stay where you are," she whispered back, pulling the pistol from its holster. It was the gun she'd stolen from the operator of the lighthouse. The holster had been a gift from Coldheart.

He looked at the hole in his chest and moved the tie aside mournfully. "It's been a long while since I've been shot. I'm tempted to have you pull the trigger, but if you do, you die." He nodded to the hallway. "Besides, you and I need to talk."

"Talk about what?"

"A way to save your life."

She barely paused. The dead man was lying. He had to be. She went to the door of the office and peered through the crack in the hall. Coldheart was still talking out there, but she was scarcely paying attention.

"Firstly, my name is Kaeru. You're Teotl. I'm pleased to formally meet you. You're probably wondering why that pet out there has decided to murder you. Funny story. We took his human soul away. Well, not 'we.' Tōriki Satoru is downstairs, and you know how he is. Anyway, we can return the soul to the monster, and you can get him to go away. I mean, we don't really mind him here, since all he's doing is making the raw material for ghosts and zombies and we love that sort of thing, but he's scratching up Wei's walls, and do you know how hard it is to get a good contractor out here?"

Kaeru swiveled the chair around and leaned back. It creaked, and Teotl winced at the sudden sound.

"Teooooooootl," said Coldheart. "Don't hide from me."

"All we would ask in return is a little information. About your organization. Well, your former organization, that is. We both know that if you were on good terms with them, they might be backing you up instead of one of the Twins' monsters."

"I'll make it quick, I promise," Coldheart said.

"A little information. Nothing serious, just what you want to give us."

"You won't feel a thing."

"So," said the dead man, "which one of us will you respond to?"

- 6 -

Teotl stared into the eyes of the dead man, already growing filmy. Outside the room the wendigo stalked back along the hallway, his claws playing against the walls, the tendrils of wind reaching around corners and washing through the dark. She could only think of Kaeru's words.

Betray the Priestess.

It was a good deal. Teotl had already been betrayed. This would be repaying treachery with treachery. The Priestess hadn't even wanted revenge; she had used Teotl for a little bit of knowledge. A lab rat. Thrown her into the experiment just to see what would happen, and when the enemy didn't clear up the mess, she ordered her own people to do it.

"So what do you say?" Kaeru whispered. "Do we make nice or do I make noise?"

She thought she might feel fear. Of her former ally. Of the fact that she was effectively powerless and surrounded. Of those in this tower who had the power to kill her with a word. But she was utterly at peace. There was no doubt in her. "I say no."

"I'm sorry to hear that," the dead man said. And then he opened his mouth and let out a long, keening shriek. A single, unbroken vowel that tore into the still air of the pagoda. The wendigo would be on them in seconds.

* * *

Kaeru was disappointed when Teotl said no. She seemed like a decent sort, and after her waterfall escape, he had come to admire her a little bit. She was crazy, that was obvious, but it was an action hero crazy he could really get behind. She would have been a fun ally to have, and then once she was dead, he could have shown her the ropes of being a ghost. They could have had a wonderful time.

But she said no. Her loss.

Coldheart was a frigid shadow in the doorway. Kaeru felt the baleful yellow gaze on him and would have shuddered had the body still possessed that capacity. He looked up into the face of the wendigo, who had a quizzical expression on his hideous, gory face.

"I already killed you," the wendigo said.

"I get that a lot."

"Where is she?"

The dead man pointed to the doorway Teotl had arrived through. "That way."

"Thank you," said Coldheart, casually ripping the corpse in half and spilling its ghostly cargo across the floor.

* * *

Teotl's legs burned. The energy inside of her collected in her abdomen, thighs, and calves, wanting to explode out of her in a series of leaps up the stairs. It wouldn't. It butted against the open air, but like that cork wedged in a bottle, it refused.

She could hear Coldheart downstairs now. He was moving deliberately through the pagoda. Whether it was to make sure she hadn't doubled back or just to season her flesh with fear, she didn't know. And she didn't care. She had business at the top of the tower, and he wasn't going to stop her. The gun was slick in her hand, the long barrel with its silencer unwieldy as she swung it with every step.

Her breath was acid, her veins heavy, as she burst into the room at the top of the tower. She wanted to double over, try to put air into her aching lungs, but she wouldn't. Wei Lai was in the room, standing within a ritual circle as though waiting for her. The room itself looked something like the inner chambers she had seen belonging to other Apprentices: a place to work their magic that was safe, familiar, and prepared. He stood in his flowing Triad robes, seeming to look right at her, despite his eyes being sewn shut.

The quintessence, locked in the coin, walked over Wei's knuckles. The sight of it burned her eyes and wormed into the holes of her face. Instead, she watched the man. The pistol was pointed at the floor.

"Welcome, Teotl."

"You seem calm, considering what I'm here to do."

"I've already taken every step I can to prevent this," he said. She could see there was something else in him. Something he was holding back.

"You want something," she said.

"We all want something."

"Something that can only be gained by your death."

He smiled. "You won't begrudge me that."

She started to ask him what it was, but she stopped herself. "No. No, I won't."

"Thank you. There is a part of me that's screaming, though. The part that wants to cling to eternity for just a little bit longer."

"I know exactly how you feel."

"I suppose you do. I regret that I won't be alive to see you take your revenge."

"Revenge?"

"Against she who wronged you."

"The Priestess." For the first time, she spoke the name like a curse. It hit her then. So obvious, it was a wonder she had not even asked the question before the answer appeared before her. "You told the Priestess where the quintessence would be."

The smile widened. "Not directly. I made certain her spies heard what they needed to."

"My revenge is your revenge."

"A question of daughters." She could tell the statement had great meaning to him, and she saw, or at least thought she saw, what it meant to her, she did not know what it did to him. Courtesy, and respect for what he was sacrificing, kept her from asking. He went on: "Sometimes you succeed, sometimes you fail. There is, unfortunately, nothing I can do to help either way after this moment. The roads to both are winding and branch many times, but there is one constant. The seed has already been sown."

Teotl looked at the mahjongg tiles spread over the ritual circle. They told a story, but only for those with eyes sewn shut.

"Thank you, Mr. Wei."

"What's a little advice between soldiers?"

She raised the pistol and took a few steps toward the Prophet. He flinched, so slightly she would not have noticed had her world still contained anyone else. She raised the pistol, pointing it between the man's stitched-up eyes. The bullet cut him down.

The coin rolled from his knuckles, away from the bloodstain now enveloping the ritual circle and engulfing the fallen tiles. It went end-over-end into a circle and hit the blood, falling flat. Teotl plucked it out of the gore, and she could feel the energy humming on her fingertips, collecting there, straining for the quintessence. She palmed the coin—

The explosion flooding her with all of its energy, no, all of the energy ever. There could be none left in the world after this moment. Every cell screaming as it was inflated past its threshold, and ready to explode, yet somehow unable. Only something she had felt—

The Priestess touched Esperanza's—no, she was Teotl, at that moment and all beyond, she was Teotl—bare chest, just over her heart. The energy then entering every fiber of her, altering her body, making her no longer human. Now her cells hungered for it. They ate the force of anything around, but did not consume. They held onto it for her to use and now—

—it was happening again. Her body expelled the force in a shuddering wave, leaving her gasping and shivering. It was agony, yet it was also bliss, a single moment of pure, profound relief.

She opened her eyes. Nothing buzzed within her. The quintessence sat in her palm protected in its coin. She put it in her pocket.

She felt normal. For the first time since the explosion, she felt perfectly fine. A floor or so down, she could hear Coldheart coming up the stairs. If he caught her, she'd be dead. The only way down was with her powers. She looked at the gun, unscrewed the silencer and dropped it on the floor. Suicide either way.

Wei's words echoed in the room like the gunshot. *Clinging onto eternity for a little bit longer.* She was never supposed to live even this long. She should have died at seven. She should have died during her years on the street. She should have died with Michaela. There were so many places, so many paths that she had avoided that ended in her death. Wei would have seen them, but Wei was dead, and she was a piece on his game board.

Death was coming up the stairs. She held death in her hand.

If she died now, then the Priestess had all she ever wanted. She got her information, she even killed a rival Apprentice. Teotl would die on the soil of Shi Jie, far away from home. The mess cleaned up. *The perfect crime*—words from one of Coldheart's detective novels.

The thought burned with the sullen heat of the wendigo's winter. The Priestess had to be called to account. For what she had done to Teotl. For whatever she had visited on Wei. Teotl owed the Apprentice that, after taking his life. There was only one thing left to do. She had to know if her powers were truly back.

She put the barrel to her head.

Coldheart was just outside, howling like the angry wind. His claws ripped along the walls. The murderous winter, coming to kill her.

The gun was safer.

She pulled the trigger.

The bullet slammed into her and crumpled, the energy hitting her temple and webbing outward through her tissues. After containing the explosion it was like nothing. She could have kept that little gunshot, like a bee, held comfortably between her fingers forever.

The bullet fell to the floor, followed by its casing.

She was fine.

She grinned. Time to charge up, she thought, firing the gun into her right thigh as she walked toward the window. The casings and the bullets tinked against the floor as she moved.

And then, it was time to get Coldheart back.

She leapt from the window in a perfect swan dive, the ground hurtling up to meet her. The smile on her face was wide and brilliant. She hit the ground, and exulted as the impact spouted up into her body to take its buzzing place inside. She stood and turned, now facing Fantan Tower. The front doors had been blown from their hinges; one now hung drunkenly to the side. The entrance hall spilled amber light onto the porch, and inside the carnage from Coldheart's rampage was coagulating.

There were five figures all standing in a loose circle, four around one. The five were a badly-wounded Jiangshi, two men with guns—Teotl recognized both the man in the eyepatch and the man who shot her in the Changbai Mountains—and two of the strange dead doll girls. The man in the middle was Tōriki Satoru, the Butterfly's heir. Their attention was mostly focused on the stairway up. Easy to guess why after what they had released there.

Teotl walked up the front steps. "Hello," she said.

The two soldiers whirled and fired off bursts of their assault rifles. The bullets clattered off her chest, and she shut her eyes in pleasure as the force webbed and pulsed into her. She opened her eyes to find that the soldiers were trying their best not to be intimidated, but they knew she was death. The man behind them, in his frock coat and top hat, grinned in naked amusement.

"You should have run when you had the chance," Tōriki said.

"I couldn't leave without making sure you released Coldheart."

"I did. Didn't you see him upstairs? That's the real Coldheart, with none of that weak human in the way. I wonder what would happen if I stripped the human from you?"

"Won't work. My soul's not fragmented."

"Good thing I have other tricks." He spoke a word then, a slithering syllable, and it stretched out through the room. Even after he had fallen silent, Teotl was certain she could hear it, continuing its shivering pass over the floor. It was not directed at her, but rather the corpses all around. They started to move, using whatever power Coldheart had left them when he tore them apart. Some dragged themselves along on their hands, others could stand up with gaping holes in their chests betraying the atrocity that had been visited on them. Their eyes were milky, their skin like the belly of a fish. Their dry lips peeled back over teeth that somehow seemed whiter, and they lunged at her.

Teotl welcomed the attack. The energy sang through her body. She wanted to use it.

She gave them the fall from the top of Fantan Tower first. She flung her arm out, directing bits of it to each one, story by story. Each one hit went sprawling. One stayed still on the floor.

Tōriki and his personal guard backed off, and it was a wise move. Teotl sprayed the bullets that had been put into her, chewing up the rising corpses in a hail of phantom gunfire. She was about to turn on the Necromancer, a taunting quip on her lips, when she saw all of those who Coldheart killed on the way in coming through the door. She put the force of the bullets into them, but there wasn't enough. They kept coming.

She whirled, spotting a pistol on the floor, dropped by one of the men Coldheart had killed. She jumped for it, hoping to empty the clip into herself.

Tōriki spoke another word. Teotl instinctively winced, as the word itself bled into her and turned something inside cold and black. Again, she was not the target. As she rolled over, the gun in her hand and pressed to her forearm, the onrush of zombies was upon her. She readied herself to eat the force of their punches and throw them right back.

But they did not strike her. Tōriki's order had been smart. The corpses rolled over her like a wave, holding her down, but not hitting her. More and more added to the pile, bleeding all manner of foul liquids over her body. Their ragged flesh was over her face, and as she tried to breathe all that came was their rotting ichor.

Was this what Wei had intended? Somehow, he saw no escape

for himself, but at least this would mean he would get his revenge. Teotl fought, trying to throw the dead men off of her, but there was nothing to throw. They were too torn up, too soft to really get a handle on. And they kept adding to the pile, another weight on her chest crushing the air out of her.

Then the temperature dropped twenty degrees.

"There you are." Coldheart. He was somewhere just above her. His voice sounded miles away, but it carried to the bottom of the pile.

She had lost the gun as she tried to push the corpses off her, and she groped for it now, not knowing where it was.

The pile started getting lighter. One of the corpses was ripped from on top of her, and she saw Coldheart looming over the heap of dead. His amber eyes lit up when he saw her. "So glad you're still alive. You are mine to kill."

The wendigo pulled more bodies off the heap, throwing them aside like garbage, eagerly staring down at his victim. Teotl's hands scrabbled through the heap of gore and viscera that covered her, trying to find that pistol. It had to be somewhere close. There was nowhere else for it to go!

The last body was torn away, most of its insides raining out on the floor. The pistol came free as well, clattering to the floor. Teotl lunged for it, her hands closing over the grip.

Coldheart laughed. "Didn't you see? Bullets are useless."

Teotl pressed the gun to her chest. "Not entirely."

She fired.

Coldheart's claws closed around her neck and yanked her up. Her toes brushed the floor as he held her. She reached out a hand, felt the hard nub of energy from the gunshot, and forced it through her limbs. It streaked from one finger toward its path. Frost spread like a plague from Coldheart's hand, bringing with it a web of agony. She hoped her aim was good.

The force hit one specific charm on Tōriki's watch chain. It could only be that one; Teotl had clocked it as soon as she saw the Necromancer. The heart covered in ice. The force tore through the clip connecting the charm to the chain and lanced into Tōriki's side. The Necromancer grunted in pain, clutching at the bleeding wound.

The ice heart fell, but before it hit the floor, it unfolded. She saw the young man, ethereal and beautiful in this form, shifting, changing. He sank into the wendigo, the strands of white flowing into the skull-like nostrils, the distended mouth, the amber eyes. The monster howled in rage, dropping Teotl. She fell into a heap, absorbing that negligible bit of force, while she clutched at her throat, desperately massaging warmth back into the ravaged skin.

She saw the group of Tōriki and his men hustling away from the pagoda, keeping up a cordon around the wounded man. All of them, save the dead girls, looked to be in bad shape. Teotl ignored them. She could have forced it, pursued, and maybe killed one or all, but she had no stomach for it. Not after the way Wei had gone to his reward with such grace. She could honor him in that way.

Instead, she moved to the monster, that had fallen to his knees in front of her. It was still the shape of the beast that had hunted her through the pagoda. Yet this pose, fallen, defeated, shoulders slumped, seemed far too human. She wanted to believe it was Coldheart, and a tiny part added *her Coldheart*. She touched the cold and skinny shoulder. "Coldheart? Are you there?"

The monster looked up, and its features began to dissolve. The gusts of wind blew the dead, starving flesh away, revealing the familiar face underneath. "I'm sorry," he said.

"It wasn't you." She held him, and he held her back.

"Thank you," he said, the words muffled by her neck.

"You did the same for me."

She got to her feet and helped him to his, refusing to let go of his hand. He seemed just as reluctant, his cold fingers interlacing with hers. They walked out into the night hand in hand, and did not speak. She tried not to notice the streaks of blood and flattened grass where the zombies had made their path up to the pagoda, or the evidence of their original butchering. Teotl and Coldheart stopped on the docks. It was time to separate. Both knew it, but neither wanted to let the moment end. Teotl knew it was a silly dream, the two of them. He had to know what she was going to say. She also knew she had to say it.

"I'm going back," she said.

"You don't have to. We could find a way. Somehow."

"You know that's not true."

"I can still wish it were."

"She tried to have me killed."

"I know."

"I need to find a way to turn it back on her. I'm going to get my revenge, but I'm going to live to enjoy it. I don't know how. Somehow. But I know the first step is to make her need me again. Trust me. Love me. Then, I don't know. I'll see her dead."

Coldheart nodded, and the look in his eyes was so tender, she thought that if he asked again, she just might say yes. But he didn't ask. "Good luck, Teotl."

She took his hands. Her voice was breaking when she spoke again. She was never supposed to say it, not even a fragment of the truth, but she couldn't stop herself. She didn't want to. She needed him to know. "Esperanza. My name is Esperanza."

He kissed her with cold lips. "I'm Chris. It's nice to meet you."

She heard the truth in his voice as much as he heard the truth in hers. She smiled into his lips, kissing him again, and breathing in the cold mist of his breath. They held each other, not wanting to let go. "Good luck, Esperanza," Chris whispered to her, and she felt him turning to wind under her fingertips and blowing away.

Then she was alone by the docks, the boat bobbing in the tides. She felt a momentary pang of regret, but that was quickly consumed by the simple pleasure of someone knowing her. Not someone— Chris. It mattered it was him. They had seen each other at their most helpless, and they had not turned away. They had saved one another. And she knew that if she called him on her quest for revenge, he would come.

Teotl would not let him strike the killing blow. No. As Chris's dark half would say, the Priestess was hers to kill.

- 7 -

Teotl walked back into the Condor's Nest two months after killing Wei Lai. Even though she knew where she was going, the journey was a difficult one, and she could not rely on the resources of her organization. She was left to sail across the Pacific, landing in Peru, then hiking into the Huandoy peaks on her own. It had been some time since she had tried this route, not since 1960 with all the others vying for the Prize. After those two months, she was well aware of the other secret she carried.

As she emerged onto the plateau with the Condor's Nest stretched out in front of her, the stone temples glinting in the sun, she smiled. This place might be the abode of her enemy, but nothing could rob it of its beauty. There were so many wonderful places in the world, it was nice to soak it in from time to time. The soldiers on duty saw her, but none approached.

She walked across the central field, over the ant hieroglyphs in the soil, up El Hormiguero, and into the Temple of the Sun. She found the Priestess on her throne, instructing a young Middle Eastern man in the arts of Sorcery. A new Apprentice, and from the looks of him, for the Artisan. Teotl briefly wondered what this new treaty might mean for the organization as a whole, but pushed that aside. She had more important things to think about.

The Priestess looked up and while there was no surprise in her face, there seemed to be a bit of wonder. Her mere attention felt a bit like the quintessence, a persistent buzzing that Teotl's cells reached out for and longed to hold within. Was that the genesis of her previous loyalty? Was it something so venal?

"Jibreel, leave us," the Priestess said.

The young man looked from his teacher to Teotl, rose from his kneeling position, nodded, and left. When he was gone and the stone door closed behind him, the Priestess spoke again.

"Welcome home, Teotl. It is good to see you well."

Teotl wanted to give a derisive snort. Instead, she said, "Wei Lai is dead as you commanded. I apologize for the delay. I also acquired this." She flipped the quintessence, still in its coin, to the Magus.

The Priestess spoke a powerful syllable, one that rattled the walls around her, and the coin stopped in midair. A smile appeared over the ageless Magus's face, though Teotl knew that even that expression was an affectation. There wasn't enough left of the Priestess to smile. "You have exceeded my expectations."

"Had I known that's what you wanted from the beginning it might not have taken me so long."

The Priestess might have started, had she been younger. Instead, she merely turned, fixing Teotl with her depthless gaze while the quintessence revolved in front of her. "And yet here it is, and here you are." She smiled again, and it looked exactly like the first, the magical energy executing one of its standard routines. "You deserve a reward. Six months—"

"I want one year."

The Priestess stopped, watching Teotl, baffled at the impertinence. Finally, she said, "One year. I will not call upon you."

"Thank you."

Teotl left the Condor's Nest in favor of her small island off the coast of Colombia, Santa Rosa de Lima, choosing that over her more accessible home in Tumaco. She spent her days swimming in the crystal blue ocean, reading in the sun, and occasionally getting reports from Kisin or one of the spies she was friendly with. She would only speak with them on the phone, refusing any visitors. She would not even meet her new bodyguards. She let the organization believe whatever it liked, but she did it out of a sense of self-preservation.

After a few months, the changes couldn't be ignored.

At first, it was just her appetite. She was hungrier than she had ever been, and the only thing that helped was raw, read meat. Then the meat had to be chilled. Now frozen was better.

Before her belly grew too big to hide, she found a doctor and paid him a great deal of money. He was on call now, living in her guest house now that the nine months were nearly up. As soon as she was ready, he would put her under and deliver the child that now incubated within her, feeling like a rather large ice cube she had swallowed. Delivered painlessly, so the Priestess would not know. She smiled, cradling the baby within her. And knew.

It had not happened yet, and maybe it would never. But it was at the end of one of the many pathways branching from that moment in the ship's cabin. Teotl stood with her daughter—Catalina Ochoa, but there were none who knew that name, and Teotl only ever called her Invierno—on top of the Temple of the Sun. The girl looked twelve, but she was already much older than that. Scions aged so slowly. Her hair was long and brown, with blonde highlights from her father. Her skin was olive, brown freckles over her cheeks and nose. Her eyes were bright amber, but there was no word for the parent that gave her those. She held her mother's hand, and the blood that was coating Invierno's arm up to the elbow had flowed onto Teotl, and was even now drying between them. In front of them lay the little bit of the

Priestess that was left after thousands of years handling raw magic, and that had been destroyed, the false life still in those few bones torn away when the girl ripped away the Magus's heart. Revenge had been Teotl's.

As Wei Lai had said, the seed had already been sown.

Children of the Snake

HE HAD TOLD HIS FOLLOWERS that he was communing with the Goddess and was not to be disturbed. That had been a lie. He had really just wanted to read this Richard Matheson collection in peace. He reclined in his private chambers, on the circular white bed, and read the story of the last man on earth amongst vampires. It spoke to him. After all, he was the only one of his kind as well.

The lie was not complete. Had he wanted to commune with the Goddess, she was but a phone call away. For the time being, he was content to be alone, free of the demands of his followers. And there were always demands, even if they were phrased as requests. *Intercede with the Goddess, ask her special for me, I've been loyal.* He had heard all of it so many times he had his responses ready. *She has heard your prayers, she has a plan, she loves you.* What his followers never understood, what they could never know, was that the Goddess was entirely more physical than most deities. She was, most assuredly, quite real.

The knock was timid. "Father Typhon?" The voice belonged to Roger Carroway, the first of Typhon's converts, the only one of the faithful who had seen the face of the Goddess when she entrusted Typhon to him. Typhon knew who it was before the voice, plucking the scent of the man's flinty aftershave from the air with the lazy flick of his tongue.

Typhon put the book face down on his chest. He was in a loose linen shirt, open over his slender chest, and matching pants. Snow white and diaphanous, it proudly displayed the vibrant colors of his scales beneath. "Yes?"

"May I come in?"

Typhon sighed. He smelled the worry on Roger, stronger even than the aftershave. It was probably important. Matheson would have to wait. Typhon set the book aside and rose, padding over to his meditation circle, marked with a few arcane symbols. Most were meaningless, but a few, like the dragonfly at the westernmost point, meant something. Typhon settled down into the circle, affected a pose of interrupted meditation and said, "Come in."

The door opened, and Roger Carroway came in. He was dressed much like Typhon, though he revealed only human flesh beginning to go to seed. His hair was rapidly fading to gray, and he blinked myopically through his thick horn-rimmed glasses. Roger might not seem it, but he was a powerful man in Hollywood, an agent to more than a few stars. More importantly, Roger and his wife Muriel had built and maintained the temple in which Typhon made his home. They had been surrogate parents of a sort for many years.

"Father Typhon, we had a visitor." It was odd calling him "Father." Though Typhon was much older than he looked, he appeared to be only about sixteen or seventeen years old, while Roger was pushing fifty. Roger and Muriel had been taking care of him for nearly two decades, and though he never called Roger "Father," there were times Typhon thought he felt something akin to that for the old man.

"Go on," Typhon said, lying down in the circle, and coiling his body just enough so as not to touch the edges. It was a serpentine gesture, one that came quite naturally to him.

"Well, Father, myself and a few of the other faithful were going about our duties and a detective just barged in the front door and started asking questions."

If Typhon had eyebrows, he might have raised one. "Detective?"

"He said his name was Banks. Martin Banks."

"What did he want?"

"He was asking about Betty van de Kamp."

The fear slithered off Roger in waves, and Typhon resolutely kept his mouth shut so he wouldn't have to taste another red tendril of it. "Asking? Asking how?"

"Her parents hired him to find her. Someone told him she knew Ellen Davies, and that led him here."

Anger or frustration must have flashed over Typhon's face because Roger flinched. Typhon was glad his mouth was shut, or more of that fear-stink would have wormed into his mind, though he felt mildly guilty over scaring the old man. "And you told him…?"

"Nothing! I told him Ellen didn't live here, that she came here once or twice and we haven't seen her and that we've never heard of Betty van de Kamp."

"Good," Typhon said. "That is what I would have told you to do."

Roger sighed in relief.

"And if he should come back, come fetch me. Even if I am at prayer."

"Of course, Father."

Typhon didn't have to wave Roger away, the older man vanished on his own, disappearing up the stairs to the rest of the complex. The eventual presence of this Banks fellow, or some other gumshoe just like him, was likely inevitable. Still, it worried Typhon more than he wanted to let on. He left the solitude of his room for the central chamber.

It was circular and quite large. Like everything, it was furnished in white, with thick white carpets and white couches and pillows scattered all around. Lights like crystal teardrops hung irregularly from the ceiling, bathing everything in a crisp glow. There were only a few girls in there now, all almost as young as he appeared. They were all at leisure, as was their right. As he entered the room, they sat up straight, tracking him as he made his way across. They did not relax even when it was obvious he hadn't emerged for any of them. He opened the rounded door on the far side, revealing a stone staircase descending even deeper into the earth.

The stairs led into an ovoid chamber, lit with the deep amber of candlelight. It was warmer, though not because it was closer to the center of the earth. The source was far more mundane: industrial heaters keeping the air just below ninety degrees. As he descended, the dais at the center of the chamber came into view. Five eggs, the size of leathery footballs, were clustered at the center, nestled amongst the broken shards of two more. Typhon had to resist the urge to scamper excitedly to them, to caress the dimpled surfaces and to feel the life moving within. He had to display a certain amount of decorum.

"Father Typhon?" He turned. He had been so enchanted by the sight of the eggs—*his* eggs—that he hadn't noticed the scent of his most trusted aide right next to him. Ellen Davies stood beside him, smiling radiantly even as the heat plastered her blonde hair to her forehead. He reached out and caressed her pale skin, and she leaned into his palm. His hand, covered in minute, jewel-like scales, brushed over her cheek.

"Ellen. How are you feeling?"

"Very well! I believe I am expecting again."

A grin exploded over Typhon's face. Ellen had once found that sight unnerving; now she echoed it with her own. "That is wonderful news," he said, placing a hand over her belly. Her hands folded over his. "Where is John now?"

"With Edith and her mother." Ellen said the name *Edith*, the name of Typhon's first daughter and second child, with reverence. *Mother*, she said with barely concealed contempt. He might have scolded her on another day, reminded her that they were all one under the Goddess, but that day he had more important things to do.

"And Betty?"

"Resting. You know how the last month is."

He only had a bit of experience with it, with Betty being the eighth now. He knew it was five months before the laying, then five more until the hatching. All the mothers had trouble just before they laid. Most could barely keep awake.

True to this, Betty van de Kamp lay on one of the couches that ringed the room, dozing. She was beautiful, and though Ellen was jealous, it never stopped her from finding the most lovely young women to bring to him. She was small and delicate, like a bird, with glossy black hair and bright blue eyes. She cradled her belly, now great with the egg growing inside her. Typhon knelt beside her, and the girl's face lit up.

"Typhon," she said, the smile spreading over her sleepy face.

"Hello, Betty. How are you?"

"Wonderful," she said, reflexively cradling her belly. "Muriel said two more weeks until I can lay."

He brushed his scaled lips over her forehead. Her scent was bright and happy, and that pleased him. He could not blame her for that detective. She had come from Wisconsin to be in pictures. Change the name of the state, and that was the story of all of Typhon's brides. They would never achieve that. It took luck, and connections, and a willing to debase oneself, and these girls were of too high a character. They would be doomed to some other fate, but they had been rescued, and brought to the worship of the Goddess. Now they knew peace and love.

Her sleepy gaze wandered over him, along with the light caress of her fingers. His scales were a pale purple, with designs picked out in subtle orange. It was these patterns she followed along his face, then his neck, chest, forearm, and hand. She was still fascinated by his blatant inhumanity, and he loved that she could take such joy in him.

"Betty, I have to ask you something."

"What?"

"Are you happy here?"

"More than you could know."

"After you lay... would you want to return home?"

Her blue eyes widened in terror. "Are you sending me away?"

"No! No, Goddess, no. I want you to stay here with me forever and a day. But if you wanted to leave... I would not keep you here against your will."

Her hand found his cheek. He knew his scales were cool and dry. His brides often compared them to pebbles smoothed in a river. "You have brought me to the love of the Goddess. I would never leave you."

His hand closed over hers. He was careful not to squeeze—with his strength, he could break her bones like matchsticks. "And you will never have to. Rest, my love, and let our child grow strong within you." He leaned in and kissed her, his tongue flickering once. The scents coming from inside said she was healthy and the baby was doing well. When they parted, he smiled once more. "Our son," he said.

She brightened. "A boy?"

He nodded. The scent of the child was quite clear. "Let the Goddess give you a name in your dreams, and that's what we'll call him."

Even as he spoke, she was drifting off. It was no magic. Between the strains on her body of incubating the egg and the heat of the room, anything other than sleep was unnatural. He rose and spoke to Ellen. "Make certain she is eating enough."

Ellen nodded. "Of course." He kissed her, his first bride, and she held him. He let her hold onto him longer than he might like. Though he could show no favoritism, Ellen needed the reassurance, so he let her take it. He touched her belly and said, "I am so pleased," and left her with the other young mothers.

* * *

It was perhaps a week later, when Typhon was in the nursery, playing with John and Edith. They were both infants, unable to yet move themselves. Their mothers stood beside one another, watching him with the babies, their personal animosity momentarily forgotten. Ellen even reached out to take Theresa's hand, and Theresa squeezed it back, even though each of them despised the other.

Edith was more obviously inhuman than John. Both had scales, though Edith had them all over her body, including on her bald head. Typhon wondered if she would ever grow hair up there, or would be like him, and remain entirely hairless. John's scales were in patches, on the expanses of skin between his joints. The scales were even smaller than Typhon's, and an even paler purple. Both had human eyes, John with the lambent green of his father—and his grandmother, though he would never meet her—while Edith had the chocolate brown eyes of her mother. Other than that, they appeared human and would be able to pass with minimal disguise.

Typhon could not have been more pleased with either one of them. He was still amazed he could make anything so beautiful, and remained grateful to Ellen and Theresa. He could have played with the babies for hours, and was so happy that soon both would have more brothers and sisters like them, filled with the blood of the Goddess.

"Come in." Typhon sighed at the first frightened knock. He smelled Muriel's fear even over the thunderous scent of his children.

Muriel Carroway opened the door. Typhon was already standing, reluctantly leaving his two infants to roll around on the carpeted floor. Ellen and Theresa each picked their baby up. As much as Typhon tried to impress upon them that all were children of the Goddess, Ellen invariably took up John and Theresa Edith.

"He's back. The detective. Banks."

Typhon hadn't needed the clarification. It could be no one else. "Take me to him." He kissed both babies and both mothers on his way out the door, affecting a calm attitude to help assuage the fears in Ellen and Theresa.

Muriel scampered through the front room, leading him toward the door that led up to the rest of the property. Typhon sauntered, acutely aware of the frightened looks the girls in the central chamber were giving him. Muriel opened the door at the top of the stairs soundlessly, and Typhon emerged onto the ground level of their Hollywood estate. The light hit like a physical blow, and he had to squint, navigating through the scents on the air. There were the familiar ones—Roger, Muriel, some of the others devoted to the Goddess—and one that was not. The aftershave was all wrong, and soaked a core of whiskey and cigarettes. Far more troubling was the sting of gun oil. The detective was armed.

Typhon's eyes slowly adjusted to the light streaming in through the big picture windows. Los Angeles spread out below the house, nestled in one of the dun-colored folds of the hills. A few of his children were out working in the gardens. The new wing of the house, added to from the donations of new converts, was barely more than a skeleton of uncovered wood. Soon the compound would stretch all over the hills. The murmur of conversation came from the living room, and he made his way to the secret door in the kitchen. One of his followers gave him a nervous glance—probably had not seen him since the initiation ceremony—as Typhon disappeared into the small compartment.

The room was the size of a small closet. Typhon removed the plug and peered through the peephole. Roger was facing him, sitting primly on one of the fat white sofas in the living room. The detective was standing, his back to Typhon. The man was in a rumpled blue suit, his dark hair liberally dusted with gray. His body was short, compact, powerful. "...the Cult of Set," Banks said, his voice creaky, as though it resented being used at all.

Muriel came back in with a silver tray holding a short glass with some kind of cocktail. It rattled as he spoke "Cult of Set," and Muriel tried to cover up her surprise. "Your drink?"

Banks accepted the glass off the tray and Muriel withered under his scrutiny, the suspicion wafting from him in sour waves. "Thank you, ma'am." He had a fighter's face. Squashed nose, a scar bisecting an eyebrow. Typhon reflected that had he been human, Banks might have intimidated him.

"Cult of Set?" Roger said, faking amusement, and not very well. "I'm sorry, Mr. Banks, I don't know where you got your information but—"

"Does that matter?"

"I should say so, if they plan to slander us."

"You deny it then?"

"Mr. Banks, we are a social club. Hollywood is a dangerous place, especially for new arrivals. We provide a little security, a little friendliness, a little taste of home for—"

"Betty van de Kamp, then. What kind of taste of home did she get?"

"I told you, we never—"

"Yeah, yeah."

Banks was interrupting, keeping Roger off balance, and he was doing very well. Roger's frustration was a singing yellow. Typhon wondered if Banks could smell it; the man was certainly acting like he could.

"So this isn't a cult in any way."

"Cult? No!"

"Religion?"

"N-no," Roger stammered.

"Right," said Banks, sipping at his cocktail. Smelled like an Old Fashioned to Typhon, Muriel's specialty. Banks must have agreed, as he raised the glass to Muriel, now quailing beside her husband. "You mix a good drink, Mrs. Carroway."

"Thank you," she muttered.

"Now about this Cult of Set."

"Detective," Roger said, "You are being very rude! I told you, there is no cult, no religion—"

"And all those snake statues... the ones in the garden, the ones on the shelf behind me, and the little designs over the door, those are what... decoration?"

"Yes! What's wrong with snakes?"

Banks shrugged. "This is the second time I've been here, Mr. Carroway. In my experience, if I end up at the same place following two different sets of leads, whoever is there knows something. You're telling me you've never even heard of Betty van de Kamp. That's your story."

"That's the truth."

"I don't think so, and neither do you. You know where she's gotten off to. All I want to do is let her folks know she's all right. Can you do that for me?"

"Mr. Banks, I wish I could help you but—"

"But you're sticking to your story." Banks downed the last of the drink and set it aside. "Good day to you both."

Muriel rose to escort him out.

"It's all right, ma'am. I know the way. Getting pretty familiar with this place."

Typhon waited until the door shut to come out of the spying

room. Roger and Muriel were running into the room, and a few more of his followers were gathering around. He did not need his powerful sense of smell to detect the sickly fear bleeding from each of them.

"He came back!" Roger said uselessly, as though Typhon hadn't just watched the entire interview.

"Father Typhon, we have to do something," Muriel said.

"Kill him!"

"Follow him to his office and—"

Typhon cut them off with a wave of his hand. "He was only here to try to panic us. We have nothing to fear from that man. Does he think he'll find Betty? No, she is completely safe from the likes of him, and none of us would betray the family. Return to your tasks and think of it no longer."

His followers murmured and nodded along, as the fear vanished into the comforting embrace of conformity. Typhon wished he felt a fraction of it. He had to get away from the followers who thought he knew the answers simply because of his blood. He needed to talk to the one who did. He needed the Goddess.

* * *

The phone call had been made, and the meeting arranged. They could speak in shorthand to one another, so that any happening to listen in would not have any idea where they were meeting or even who they were. He told the Carroways he was not to be disturbed, and opened up the passageway in his chambers. The bed shifted aside on its moveable platform, revealing a spiral stairway plunging into the earth.

Typhon descended into the cool darkness without hesitation, his sense of smell taking over for his eyes. The shaft dropped into the meat of the hill before opening up into a gently sloping tunnel. It had been built relatively recently, though most of his followers had naturally assumed it to be some kind of escape hatch. The laborers were under the impression that it was a fallout shelter, just coming into vogue amongst the wealthier denizens of the city. The irony was even Roger and Muriel Carroway, on whose property it was built, did not really know what it was for. They did not question their High Priest when he wanted it constructed. Typhon knew he could not tell them, as it might negatively impact their faith. What sort of priest needed a tunnel to commune with the godhead?

He was not thinking of Roger or Muriel, the most important of his followers, and the humans who had nurtured him for the past twenty years. Martin Banks consumed his thoughts. The simple solution, of allowing Betty van de Kamp to surface, was no solution at all. She was hugely pregnant, and even the most ignorant knew there hadn't been enough time for her to be so far along. And when she delivered, it would be a soft, oblong, ivory egg. Had Betty wanted to leave, there might have been some negotiation on that front, but she didn't. She wanted to stay with Typhon and the rest of his followers.

So how dare Martin Banks terrorize an innocent girl?

"The Cult of Set." Even that was an insult. Probably what the few people who had heard of the new church in Hollywood called them. The Cult of Set and their Snake Goddess. It was insulting. Derogatory. Coming into Typhon's own home to frighten one of Typhon's brides and threaten an old man? The thought of murder was a pleasant one, and while Typhon certainly had the ability to kill a human being, he had learned the hard way that this was not always the best method of problem solving.

He made his way down the tunnel, following the switchbacks as it dug deeper and deeper. Finally, the busy tang of an underground river invaded his senses. He paused, finding the lantern hanging on the wall by the scent of burning whale oil, and lit it. He plucked it off the wall and the handle squeaked as he carried it into the chamber beyond. The room was plainly artificial, a false shore around a rushing subterranean river. The chamber opened up into a massive tunnel on either side, as though this was just a train station for some colossal beast heading toward the sea.

Typhon waited. When he was at rest, he was totally motionless. Perhaps it was the reptile part of him, if that's truly what it was. He would have seemed a statue, though a statue that grew more inhuman the closer one got. He tried to cultivate the serenity he extolled amongst his followers while he waited, but he could not. Every time he thought of a calm sea, or the sun, or a flower, he saw Martin Banks. Banks, Banks, Banks. Bedeviling him.

Roger had failed to put the man off, but that was hardly Roger's fault. Banks was too clever by half. Too clever for his own good. He was the one who made this necessary. Disturbing the Goddess. Typhon should kill the man just for that.

He smelled the Goddess before he heard her. In some ways, it was a more powerful version of his own scent, something he did not consciously recognize until another source drew attention to it. It was clean and reptilian, with a hint of more exotic spices, and a clear touch of burning brush and the sting of chemical venom. Yet the Goddess also brought with her the perfume of a summer meadow, and no matter how much Typhon wished he could be as pure, he was not.

He heard the Goddess before he saw her. The scrape of scales along concrete and stone, as well as the muffled splashing of a body far too big for the river. Her breath came in a sepulchral hiss that rattled the very earth. It was a sound that filled him with dread, even as he knew he had nothing to fear. The strangest was the absence of sound as her massive body abruptly cut off sections of tunnel, sounding like a gargantuan hand stifling a yawn for moments at a time. She brought with her the sense of size, a rapidly approaching eclipse.

Until she did not. He knew she was taking her human form, which she preferred for interaction. He understood why—she was beautiful beyond the inadequacy of that simple word, and she tended not to make people flee in terror as she would in her other form. *Her true form*, he thought, even though he knew that was not technically correct. He wished he could assume a perfectly human form, to walk amongst them and not be recognized. His power came with a price. He supposed he should be grateful: the only ones who interacted with him were those for whom such prosaic matters as appearance didn't matter.

Except for Martin Banks.

He was in the midst of another round of plotting bloody revenge when the Goddess came around the corner. Yes, beautiful hardly described her. She was tall and slender, though far from boyish. In the dim light of the underground, her green eyes seemed to glow, while the flickering gold played off her olive skin. Her hair was purple and orange, the same vibrant colors as her scales. Her features were strong, making her appear as a queen from old, whose beauty broke prevailing standards and replaced them with something too lovely to be contained. She smiled as she saw him, holding out her arms. She took his face in her hands and stared at him with pure, rapt love. She was Shahmeran, the Snake Goddess.

"Reza. How are you, my handsome boy?"

Reza. His name. The real one. Only she knew it, and only she would speak it. Even his father, who had given him a last name, never knew of his existence and had died nearly thirty years before. Shahmeran had shown her child some of the man's films, telling Typhon that the silent movie star was his father.

"Hello, mother."

She embraced him, and though she had the strength to crush mountains, she was gentle with her only son. "I missed you so much. I wish I could talk to you more." She parted, her hands brushing over the scales of his forehead. "What's wrong? What can I do?"

Typhon told her the story of Betty van de Kamp and Martin Banks. She listened, always keeping one hand on her son, and nodding at each of his points.

"She's pregnant?" she asked finally.

"Yes, mother."

"Good boy. That is what is truly important." She paused, and he could tell she was trying to say something difficult. Something he might not understand. "I am a Goddess," she said, without any hint of irony. He nodded eagerly, provoking an indulgent smile. "But you know that even Goddesses have Goddesses of their own?"

She had spoken of her faith only once before. Typhon knew of it in broad strokes, that his mother worshiped a single Goddess who somehow existed in two forms, in two planes entirely. He would have liked to know more, if only to share the faith of his mother. She was happier with his position of High Priest of her church, though, and if this was what she wanted, this is who he would be.

"Children are very important to my Goddesses," Shahmeran said. "Your children."

"They know of us?"

"Oh no," she said, smiling. "Their attention is often focused on larger matters. It is up to their servants to work in their best interests. Do you understand?"

"Of course." He almost did, and he thought it was close enough.

"Your children and your children's children, and so on, could be very important in the future. They are who you need to protect. And this Betsy..."

"Betty."

She smiled again. "Such a good boy. This *Betty* is carrying your egg, she is what matters. This Banks fellow needs to let it alone."

"I don't think he will, mother. He's said as much he's coming back."

Shahmeran sighed. "If he is so foolish, kill him."

"What if he told others where he was searching? What if others come after him?"

"I have resources, my love. Let me cover your tracks. You just see that he's dead."

"Yes, mother."

She hugged him again. "Now that's out of the way, tell me more about this Betty. She sounds lovely."

* * *

Betty squatted on the top of the birthing dais, wrestling the egg from her body. One of her bare feet was pressed into the hardened and broken shells of the egg that had given Edith. One day, the mothers wouldn't be able to step into the room without treading on the history of all Typhon's children. The thought, and the sight of Betty's tiny toes turning as white as the shards of shell, made him smile.

The entire family was in the birthing chamber for this most sacred of events. Betty was not alone on the dais, Ellen and Theresa held her arms to keep her standing. Typhon stood between Roger and Muriel, and the rest of the room was lined with devotees and his brides, some swollen with the eggs within, while others gazed enviously up at the sweating and exhausted girl in the center of the room. Even the babies were in the room, though they were being cared for, not by the women who laid their eggs, but by those whose children would hatch in the next several months from the oblong shapes Betty squatted amongst.

Betty herself was white. Her gown and legs were stained with streaks of blood. Nothing to be alarmed about, and Typhon was pleased that thus far all of his brides had shown admirable fortitude. Her black hair hung lank around her face, a swatch glued to her clammy forehead. Her face was contorted with agony, yet he could smell the joy radiating from her as she brought the newest one of his children into the world.

Those around the room were holding hands—except for Judith and Anne, who held John and Edith so gently—and singing the hymn of the Goddess, lending their strength to the girl on the dais. Typhon never felt the love within his family more than he did during the laying ceremony. They all came together as one, if he could not tear his eyes from Betty, fierce and gorgeous in her heroic struggle, he would have embraced each of them.

The egg emerged from her by inches. It seemed much too large, and would split her in two. When Ellen first laid, Typhon had nearly panicked, and threw poor Roger across the egg chamber before calming. Now, with the eighth egg coming from a human body, he knew she would be all right. The ivory surface was streaked with blood and bile, evidence that though a human *could* carry it, the body was not designed for it. Betty would be spending the next month resting and healing from the ordeal. Ellen and Theresa whispered to her, brushed the hair from her eyes, and extolled her to push when the time came. Typhon had never been more proud of his family.

"Everyone hold it right there."

Martin Banks stood at the bottom of the staircase, an automatic pistol in his fleshy mitt. He had it lazily pointed at the room at large, not at any one person in particular. The group fell silent, first near him, then the song dying in waves through the room. Betty only noticed the detective when Theresa and Ellen stood straight up and stopped talking. She turned, but was immediately crippled with another contraction, her body wringing the egg out another few inches.

"Betty?" Banks asked. "What the hell have they done to you?"

"Get out!" she screamed at him. "Get out! You don't get to see this!"

Her command was enough, not to move Banks, but to move her family. Jimmy, one of the youngest members, lunged at Banks, but the squat man was fast. He put a single bullet into the boy's chest, who crumpled into a heap. Muriel screamed.

"Who the hell is in charge here?" Banks still hadn't seen Typhon.

Roger stepped forward, shielding his High Priest from the murderous detective.

"Ah, Mr. Carroway. Should have known. This what you do? Kidnap sweet little girls fresh off the bus from Sheboygan?"

"It's not what it appears, detective."

"Tell it to the marines, you old lech. Miss van de Kamp's parents hired me to bring her daughter back, and that's what I'm going to do." He momentarily wiggled the gun in front of Roger to emphasize it. "And I got seven reasons in here why you're going to let me."

Betty ripped the standoff in two with a shriek of agony. Banks jumped, turning his head to look at the girl. His eyes fell to the hem of her gown, where the egg was just beginning to appear between her bloody thighs. Only then did he really seem to understand. "What the hell...?"

It was enough distraction for Roger. Later, Typhon would regret not restraining his friend and surrogate father, but he was pinioned to the spot. He could not comprehend an outsider in this most sacred of spaces, and yet it made perfect sense. Everyone had come in for the laying, leaving a clean passage in for Banks. No telling how much he had wandered about before finding the staircase leading into the sublevels. And now he could threaten Typhon's brides, his eggs, his *children*.

For a moment, it looked like Roger might reach Banks. The detective was distracted and horrified, and the old man had a spurt of vigor that would have been the envy of a teenager. It showed how much Roger Carroway loved his new family. But Banks turned in time to see him, and the detective was as fast as a boxer. Roger took two slugs through the chest and fell, the last thing he heard would be Muriel's shrill screams merging with those of the girl on the dais.

Roger falling shocked Typhon from his stillness. Shahmeran, the Goddess Herself, commanded her son to kill Banks should he ever return. This would be it.

Typhon began to move. Banks saw him coming out of the corner of his eye, and whirled. He stopped when he saw the inhuman shape step into the light.

"What the hell are you?"

"My name is Father Typhon. These are my children."

"I'm the ghost of Christmas—"

But he was tackled. Ellen and Theresa had let Betty go—Typhon would learn later that Betty had begged them to do it—and leapt from the dais onto the detective. The gun went off, and half the family ducked as the bullet whined off one of the walls. He was already struggling free, punching Theresa in her nose, and kicking Ellen off of him, but it was too late.

Typhon's scaled hand wrapped around the gun and twisted it from the man's grasp. He was brutally pleased when he heard the bones snap like sticks in a fire. Banks grunted, and released his hold on the gun. Typhon let it clatter to the floor and pulled Banks in close. From the floor, Ellen comforted Theresa, who was cradling her badly bleeding nose.

"You should not have come here," Typhon whispered.

Banks struggled, and he was strong—for a human. Typhon wrapped him up in his arms, snaking a forearm over the man's throat, bracing it with his body and arm. And squeezed. Banks thrashed, landing a few blows that did not much more than bounce off Typhon's scales. Each hit was softer, as the strength bled from Banks. Typhon's forearm was up under the detective's fleshy neck, cutting off air, blood, energy, thought. Banks's vision would be irising closed, like the end of one of those silent pictures Typhon's father had starred in. His thoughts would become muddier, dying in the barren field of his mind. Typhon could have squeezed all day, but he would only need six minutes. Perhaps it was the serpent in him, but there was nothing more natural than wringing the breath of his prey. Banks seemed to be moving underwater. His mouth made little sucking sounds, each one quieter than the last. Typhon smelled the insidious gray scent of death enter the detective's body, even before the man's bowels loosened. When Typhon finally dropped the corpse at his feet, Betty lay exhausted by her newly laid egg, perfect and radiant. The High Priest smiled. As his newest child entered the next phase of his existence, so too had Martin Banks ended his.

Typhon touched the faces of Ellen and Theresa on his way up onto the dais, and whisked Betty gently into his arms. She opened her eyes and smiled wearily at him. "You're all right," she said.

"Don't think about me. You're the truly brave one." He kissed her clammy forehead and carried her from the chamber. She slept peacefully for the next day.

* * *

Roger Carroway and Jimmy O'Hara were given honorable burials. Typhon himself, flanked by his eight birthing brides, spoke with reverence of both men, praising their bravery and sacrifice. Muriel was given an exalted place in the family, and she helped raise the next generation. When Betty's baby was hatched, she named him Roger.

Typhon called the Goddess and placed the corpse of Martin Banks in the tunnel. After that, he never saw it again.

Playback

THERE WAS NOT A SINGLE lightbulb in all of Ezcalli. Antonio Vilar had checked during his first weeks. He still hadn't been to the entire complex, even eight years later, but every place he had been, it was the same story. Five hundred feet beneath the streets of Mexico City, and not a single lightbulb. No outlets either, and this was a place filled with some of the most expensive computer equipment on the planet.

This is not to say Ezcalli was dark. There were shadows, of course, collecting in plentiful corners like spills of velvet. The lights shone bright gold from crystals in the seams of the great stone bricks that made the underground temple facility. The crystals existed in veins of a quartzlike material, only shining when they collected into nodules. Anything that needed to be plugged in, from the sophisticated computers to the refrigerators in the cafeteria, were mated to these glassy arteries. The crystals descended another few hundred feet into the depths of Ezcalli, where the nexus chamber was located. Antonio had been to that place—the powerplant at the heart—only one time, and he was unnerved at the people who tended the glowing star in the great stone room: teams of near naked and blindfolded people with glowing skin. He had no reason to descend again, and was glad for it.

It was his understanding that Ezcalli was around six hundred years old. It should have been flooded, as Tenochtitlan and later

Mexico City were prone to. That was the benefit of being built by a Sorcerer: magic had solved what it took technology half a millennium to do. He had only seen Ezcalli from the outside one time, a great inverted pyramid extending from the cave's ceiling to rest on a single island in the middle of a black underground lake. He had been there with a few of the other agents, the Quetzalcoatls wanting to give them an idea of the enormity of their new lives. Antonio stood on the shore of the lake, while the water lapped up against the black mud and pale pink creatures slithered just out of sight. Every word had echoed through the gloom to vanish in the distance. He shivered then, understanding the true meaning of power. He went back into Ezcalli, resolving never to see the exterior again. On all other days, he entered and left it the way most of the 400 Sons did, through a nondescript office building and a secret elevator.

Ezcalli housed more than the offices of the Centzonhuiznahua, known more commonly as the 400 Sons, the intelligence apparatus of the Priestess's organization. Itzcoatl, the Sorcerer who built it and held back the waters, made his home there as well, albeit in another wing. Viracocha, one of the oldest Familiars alive, often stayed there as well, protecting the Priestess's heir. Each of them brought their elite bodyguards, though in practice the nearly invulnerable Viracocha tasked his men to the protection of Itzcoatl. Beyond that, there were a large number of conventional troops—most came from the local cartels, which Antonio found foolish at best—and a sizable contingent of the shapeshifting bakru. Itzcoatl, whom the men referred to with some affection as El Viejo, was the undisputed lord of everything within Ezcalli, and Antonio was just one of his servants.

The wing of Ezcalli that housed the 400 Sons was a single large room, filled with computers, and surrounded by nine smaller rooms like the spokes of a wheel, or more accurately, like the Aztec calendar itself. Antonio worked in the room marked with the dragonfly, the one collating the intelligence coming in from the Twins. In many ways, this was the most important of the rooms. Proximity had forced the two organizations into constant conflict, while all others were an ocean away. The Twins and the Priestess were either preparing for war or at war, and the intelligence that came through the dragonfly room was the first ingredient of victory.

Of the nine rooms, eight were dedicated to the enemy. The ninth was the one Antonio feared. The one marked with an ant.

There were ten analysts in each room, led by their Tlamacazqui, a fancy name for a department head. Antonio's understanding was that it was an Aztec word for "priest," but the position was nothing so spiritual. His Tlamacazqui was a woman named Alejandra Rios, though he knew, like his own name, this was not one she was born with. She was in her forties, and spoke in a soft Honduran accent, only beginning to cave beneath the harsh pressure of Mexico City's hard consonants. Nine of the analysts were responsible primarily for one of the nine immortals in the organization, either Magus, Apprentice, or Familiar, and all of those directly in support of that individual. The tenth tracked those mortal personnel whose purpose wasn't immediately apparent.

Those who worked in the 400 Sons did so when they were called. The immortals at the top of the League often acted with agonizing slowness, and there were times when Antonio was called that the intelligence he was there to organize and catalogue, ostensibly new, was already weeks or even months out of date. This did not render it worthless; even constructing a timeline for one of the Familiars or Apprentices could be valuable if a pattern emerged. That was what he was doing today, getting together the latest reports on Rose Cross, and trying to see if he could predict her movements.

When he found the pattern—and there always was one in the endless cycles of the immortals—he would write up a detailed report and place it in the dead drop. A day or two later, he would prepare a second report, leave out one piece of crucial information, and turn that in to Rios.

Antonio would do this because he was a traitor.

Double agent was the technical term, and he was that. He no longer bothered to justify it to himself. He had been caught in a classic honeytrap, a buxom white girl told him she was on spring break and let him do things to her that no woman ever had. Once she had him wrapped up in her, she dropped it on him. She was an agent of the Twins, and he now belonged to her. To *them*, really, and she said it with certainty of a fanatic. He almost found it funny. If she was an agent, that meant she ultimately reported to Rose Cross, the woman he was charged with tracking. He wondered if Cross even knew she had ensnared so specific a prize or if she was merely after an analyst and got very lucky.

Antonio's new handler set up a dead drop, really nothing more than an alcove beneath a bridge in the Tepito neighborhood of Mexico City. She instructed him to wrap whatever information he had in a waterproof bag and slip it up under the rim where the steel skeleton of the bridge was laid bare. Then he was to put an empty Coke bottle next to the garbage. That was all.

At the time, he had been appalled at himself for falling for something so transparent. He knew that he could never get a woman this beautiful. She said her name was Candy, and she giggled when she said it. At the time, he thought it was adorable— sweet as candy. He had a sweet tooth. He figured she was drunk enough to take him home, and he wasn't going to argue the point with her. It wasn't until later, when she finally revealed her identity did he realize he had been so effortlessly played. At least there was money involved.

In some ways, he felt like he was being paid to fuck the most beautiful woman who'd ever said his name. He wasn't much to look at, short, acne-pocked, and with a beer pudge he couldn't lose and never cared to try, but he had a good mind. He knew that for a fact. It's why he had a career in the Centro de Investigación y Seguridad Nacional before Alejandra Rios recruited him for a more important job. The fact that the Twins wanted him too, well that just proved what he had known all along. Now he proved that every day he went into the 400 Sons, took sensitive information out the door, right under the noses of excellent spies. Their lofty opinion of him was correct, even if their trust was foolish.

Candy was more than willing to keep the physical part of the relationship up, in those rare times they met face-to-face, usually in some sweaty hole-in-the-wall closer to the border. She was still the most athletic and adventurous woman he'd ever had, and no request had ever so much as fazed her. For their rendezvous, they stayed away from border towns like Juarez or Rosarito. Those belonged to the Twins as much as they did to the Priestess, and would have been a red flag to anyone looking into Antonio. It was important to avoid even the appearance of impropriety, while giving the enemy everything she wanted.

He was getting everything he wanted too. More than just excellent sex; there was money. Lots of it. The bulk of the cash went into an account in a Grand Caymans bank under the same false name on his flight papers. The account got fatter and fatter as the payments increased. Every payment was bigger than the last, drawing Antonio farther and farther along the trail. It was insidious. Any pang of conscience was erased upon the sight of some new deposit, and at the same time, the increasing money encouraged him to stay the course. The longer he stayed as a creature of the Twins, the more money he would ultimately have, with no real idea of what the ceiling might be. Or even if there was one. He knew Rose Cross, the woman he was presently stalking through a field of paper, was responsible for this golden leash. Brilliant really.

He was going to stay as long as he possibly could. He had his eye on a ranch in Saskatchewan, nice and far from Ezcalli. He loved the name: Saskatchewan. It sounded so deliciously exotic to him. A place where it was always nice and cool, and he could wear a jacket every day if he wanted to. Spend his time with horses and cows out in the sun and never have to worry about a thing. He didn't have enough for that ranch. Not yet. But in a little while, he would, and then he could vanish into his promised life.

He was at his desk, a sheaf of reports, receipts, a few grainy photographs spread out over it, and he was attempting to put them in some kind of order. He wasn't even certain all of them pertained to Rose Cross. Anything with an albino got sent to his desk, and more than once ended up tracking some hapless woman across the United States before realizing she was unimportant. He wondered if Carlos Galindo, who usually tracked the Machinist, got everything that mentioned a woman with tattoos. It would explain his usual indifference to his workload.

Antonio had been at it for hours. His mind was trying to wander, and he was doing his best to rein it in. His eyes were beginning to cross as he held up a Denny's receipt, wondering which idiot of a spy thought Rose Cross would eat anywhere with even a second location. He could rattle off her favorite restaurant in half a dozen cities, and none of them had menus with pictures. He put the receipt down, looking for another receipt that was a far more likely location for Cross to have dined at. It had been lost in the white wasteland of paper. He groaned. Finding anything could take hours, and then there was the attempt to place it in context, if it even could be. He couldn't face it right then.

He stood up, right at the same time Demian Reyes and Carlos Galindo did as well. All three men looked at one another and chuckled, the gallows laugh of men who reached a breaking point at the same time. The fatigue on the faces of Reyes and Galindo was echoed in Antonio's own heavy lids and sagging cheeks. The spies had sent in everything at once, and now the whole office was suffering the consequences.

Reyes was a gaunt man with perpetually droopy eyes and a mustache to match. Galindo was a moon-faced man with small, active hands. None of them would get a second glance on the streets of the city above. Yet another reason they were valuable.

The three of them went out the door to the central room with a single goal in mind, never even having to give it voice.

"I don't know why they bother," Reyes said as they walked. "Ghostwalker is nowhere. Until he's somewhere. Then someone dies and he disappears again."

"Yeah, well, you have to figure out how to make that stop happening," Galindo said.

"Easy for you to say. You just let Rincon track Blackthorn and then say the Machinist has to be in the same spot."

Galindo shrugged. "Worked so far!"

It was that kind of thing that made Antonio feel better. Galindo was lazy to a fault, and he was still getting paid by the Priestess. Antonio actually did his work. For two different employers, but the work got done. He chuckled at Galindo's joke, so the other man wouldn't think anything was wrong. It could be tiring keeping up appearances.

As they reached the coffeepot in one of the outer rings of the center room, the elevator door swished open. Everyone's attention was instantly on the door. Any visitor to Ezcalli was cause for interest. A severe-looking woman stepped out. She was compact, her brown hair pulled into a tight bun, looking like it wanted to yank her hair out by the roots. Her skin was fair, though her wide face and sharp cheekbones said she had some *Indio* in her. She was dressed in a conservative gray suit, a leather briefcase hanging from a strap from one of her shoulders. Her quick steps and ramrod posture screamed military. That was not what concerned Antonio.

What worried him was that she went into the room marked with an ant.

"Who's she?" Antonio asked, hoping he didn't sound as brittle as he feared.

"No idea," Galindo said, pouring a cup.

"Huh," Reyes said thoughtfully.

"What? You know?" Antonio heard the hysteria creeping into his voice, and tried to keep it from his face.

"I heard someone was going to come in. Guess that's her."

"Her who?"

"Supposedly there's a leak somewhere."

A leak. That said it all. A leak called Antonio Vilar. And they brought a spyhunter in. Antonio forced himself to pour the coffee, but he knew nothing would make it into his gut. It was tied up far too tight.

***

Cervantes arrived at Ezcalli at precisely nine o'clock, showed her identification to the men in the building above. After they vetted her, she got into the elevator and began the descent. When the door opened, she never looked directly at the men and women watching her. She took each of them in with her peripheral vision, marking in her mind who was the most interested in her arrival, and walked directly toward the office of the Priestess.

She went through the door marked with an ant, and past the desks of the agents. These people were doing the same thing that the agents were in the other rooms, only these were collating the intelligence gained from people in the Priestess's own organization. She walked through it, noting only that the men and women in this room were far more calm about her presence than the fearful men getting coffee outside, then moved through a door and into another staircase.

She descended into the office of the Quetzalcoatls, a smaller mirror of the arrangement in the top. The difference came in that the central room was occupied only by soldiers and bakru wearing human form. Instead of nine rooms, there were only three, and she went into the middle of these, which was marked with a sun, finding a stone table and a comfortable chair. She sat, removing files from her briefcase, and waited.

The insistent stench of the marshy waters penetrated the stone walls. The men outside resumed murmuring, the conversation having cut off as she strode through. She was sitting in what looked to be a conference room of some kind, but the only art on the walls was the bas-reliefs etched into the stone itself. Aztec warriors beheading one another, speaking with feathered serpents. If Cervantes noticed the art, she gave no sign.

A few minutes later, the two people she had been waiting for arrived. The first was a young woman who was a few inches taller than Cervantes. She was dressed in a suit, but she moved with the grace of a killer. Her face was scarred, including a deep furrow over her cheek that the reports said came from a bullet that barely missed taking the back of her skull off. Her skin was middling brown, and her eyes were nearly black, emotionless doll's eyes. Cervantes knew this woman as La Luna, a former assassin who worked for the vigilante group La Sombra Negra.

The second was an old man leaning heavily on a cane. He looked almost caucasian, his skin such a pale olive it was barely worth the name. His hair was snow white, and he kept a neat mustache and van dyke. His wrinkled skin gave him the appearance of kindness, but his green eyes showed only the vague interest of a predator. His designer suit had the whiff of old world glamor. He was a veteran of the Dirección de Inteligencia Nacional, more famous as the brutal secret police of the Pinochet regime. He was known as El Conejo.

El Conejo y La Luna, the Quetzalcoatls of the 400 Sons, the two who reported directly to Itzcoatl. Cervantes rose respectfully as they entered, and saw La Luna's hand twitch slightly, an old reflex from when she was hunting Mara Salvatrucha through El Salvador.

"Miss Cervantes, good morning," El Conejo said with the same old world charm as his suit. "Please have a seat."

Cervantes nodded, taking her chair as the two Quetzalcoatls did. "Thank you for seeing me."

"We didn't have a choice," La Luna said.

"Excuse my colleague. We wanted to thank you for coming. You've been out in the cold for a long time."

"I have. I would not be here today if I had not found this disturbing evidence."

"Show us," La Luna said.

Cervantes opened the briefcase and drew out the specific reports she needed without looking, so precise was her organization. The two Quetzalcoatls could have cut themselves on the razor-sharp corners. "What emerges here is a pattern. A systematic failure of our operations against the Twins in the last five years, beginning with the disaster in San Francisco."

El Conejo nodded sadly. "It has been most disappointing."

"Most of our operations fail against any of the others. Just as most of theirs fail against us," La Luna said. "It's the nature of the war."

"Correct. Yet we're failing at an increased rate." Cervantes pointed to the relevant paragraphs. El Conejo removed a pair of wire-framed spectacles from his jacket and blinked at the reports.

"This says the failure rate is only off by a few percentage points," La Luna said. El Conejo dropped the paper he was looking at to get a glimpse of the figure.

"True. It is far from conclusive, but I believe that this number indicates a traitor in our midst. Specifically here."

"How do you know the failure doesn't have to do with the spies in the field? They're weak. Easy to turn. Eager, even."

"That was my first impulse, but it looks like the failure encompasses too many spies. Either there is nothing, and our spies are just not performing up to task in this one area, or the error stems from this office. Those are the only two possibilities."

El Conejo looked to La Luna. "Galindo," he said, and she nodded.

"Carlos Galindo is on my list of suspects, but would you care to elaborate?"

"The man is a disgrace," La Luna said.

"My colleague is correct. Lazy, shiftless... we've considered removing him, and replacing him with someone from the other offices. We can be shorthanded when it comes to the Artisan or the Serpent, but it's suicide to be so against the Twins."

"Understandable."

"How many suspects do you have?"

"Five, all in the Twins' room. Carlos Galindo, Demian Reyes, Rosa Fox, Antonio Vilar, and Cristina Alvaro."

"You'll find that it's Galindo," El Conejo said. "The man's laziness would be a perfect cover."

"I am certain that will be the case. In the meantime, I would like access to their personnel files for research."

"You have it. They will be brought to you, and for the duration of this investigation, this room is yours."

"Thank you, Quetzalcoatls. Your cooperation has been invaluable."

"What are your orders?" La Luna asked. This was the first time she seemed the slightest bit worried.

"Find the mole in question and execute him. If I am unable, inform Itzcoatl at the first opportunity."

"Good," El Conejo said, smiling. Cervantes caught the tension in his eyes. Even the Quetzalcoatls feared the spyhunters.

They left her, and a few minutes later, a soldier arrived with the files. Cervantes thanked him, and was unsurprised to find that the files were only the ones she asked for. Nothing extra would be provided. No matter, the traitor was one of the five analysts whose files were now arrayed in front of her. The files were complete, with only the real names of the agents redacted. They contained biographical information, though not enough to identify them by their old life, their countries of origin, and the organization they had been recruited out of. All of them were impressive in their way, even Carlos Galindo. Beyond that, their service record to the Priestess unspooled. Here, the details grew more detailed. The elder agents, like Fox, had almost complete novels, while the younger, like Reyes, had nearly nothing. Cervantes took the service records and matched them against the failed operations, slowly eliminating the possible traitors. One by one, three folders were put to the side as Cervantes found to her satisfaction that they were innocent.

Two folders remained in front of her: the ones belonging to Demian Reyes and Antonio Vilar. The former was in charge of tracking Ghostwalker, but beyond that he had a shocking amount of freedom. In monitoring the most elusive of all the major players in the Twins' organization, Reyes could get nearly any piece of intelligence, claiming it was relating to the subject of his investigation. It looked like he exercised this ability often.

The other was Antonio Vilar. The fact that he was the one monitoring Rose Cross was the most damning evidence of all. Operations involving her specifically had taken the biggest hit in the all-around decline. Granted, Cross was the wiliest of the Twins' servants, a woman who had turned herself into one of the best spymasters in the world. She was almost impossible to track, capable of modifying memories as she saw fit, and those hunting her had to make do with imagines from cameras, or know the myriad names she used for credit cards.

Vilar and Reyes, Reyes and Vilar. Cervantes was positive one of them was responsible.

She set the files aside, straightened up her area and went to the door. "Soldier?"

Several men turned. She pointed to the nearest. "Would you please inform Carlos Galindo that I wish to see him down here? You will find him in the office of the Twins."

"Ma'am," the soldier said, disappearing upstairs.

Cervantes sat across the room and waited. A few moments later, a visibly sweating Galindo came in, flanked by the soldier. She nodded to the soldier, and he returned to his post.

"You wanted to see me, ma'am?" Galindo stuttered. He was already on the verge of falling apart. She had a lot of tricks to get people to tell her what she wanted to know, but knew she wouldn't need them on this man.

"Close the door and sit," she said.

He obeyed so quickly, it looked like he was scared his legs were about to give out. "I'm not him!"

She raised an eyebrow and cocked her head slightly. She did not speak.

"I'm not the spy. I'm not the mole. I'm not the... whoever it is!"

"Who said I was looking for a mole?"

"Reyes! Reyes told me this morning. Said you were here looking for a traitor in the Sons."

"And what do you think of that?"

The sweat rolled over Galindo's cheeks in fat, milky drops. "It's important to catch him! Very important! But I'm not him."

"Who said you were?"

"That's what you're here to ask me, right? That's why you called me?"

"Mr. Galindo, I looked through your file. You know what I found? A history of sloppy work. Lazy work. I saw a man who let several very good operations slide right past him because he didn't see the importance in what he was doing. If the Machinist were here now, she should personally thank you for saving her life." Cervantes watched Galindo sweat for a few beats. "But I don't think you are disloyal."

Galindo let out a long breath. It stank of coffee.

"Your record could use some improvement, obviously. How would you like to help me track the spy?"

"I'm sorry?"

"Do you want to assist this investigation, Mr. Galindo? Perhaps prove that the prevailing opinion of you as a useless analyst is incorrect?"

"Okay! All right!" Galindo nodded, terrified.

Cervantes smiled. Galindo flinched. "Now, what can you tell me about Antonio Vilar and Demian Reyes?"

***

Antonio watched as one of the Quetzalcoatls' bodyguards came into the room, and said, "Carlos Galindo?"

Galindo was sweating as soon as he saw the man coming through the stone doorway. Antonio's guts were twisting up, and he was positive the man was there for him. The submachine gun clipped to the soldier's uniform would come down and draw its black hole over Antonio's forehead. Instead, the soldier asked for Galindo, and the moon-faced man let out an audible groan. Antonio was glad to see that; Galindo's lack of composure should help put the spotlight on him.

As Galindo went out of the room, dripping sweat, his rounded shoulders slumped, Antonio's mind raced. He considered running. Galindo was innocent, after all. They would find that out eventually, probably. If Antonio ran at that moment, he might make it. Might not. Ezcalli was on heightened alert just because of the presence of the spyhunter. Running now would be a sign of guilt.

And then there was the element of money. Antonio had some cash, it was true. He could probably get a house somewhere in Pemhakamik, but it wouldn't be the ranch, the one in Saskatchewan he had his eye on. The one he had promised himself as the prize for all this treachery. He couldn't leave without that ranch. Not when it was already so close.

His mind spun in another direction. Fleeing wasn't an option. What else was? What if Galindo was the traitor? Antonio nearly giggled, realized it was nerves, and clamped down on it. It was possible Galindo was a spy. No one said Antonio was the only one. More to the point, Galindo could very easily be made to look like the spy, especially acting the way he was. Galindo's reputation was already bad in the office, it was clear neither Rios nor either of the Quetzalcoatls had much use for him. He was the one no one in the office particularly liked, and he might actually be a traitor for all Antonio knew. He might be doing everyone a favor.

Antonio put the information on Rose Cross in front of his face, capped with a badly pixellated photo of her on the security camera in front of a nightclub. *I work for you,* he thought at her, *and we will never meet.* The photo was barely good enough to qualify as evidence. He was fairly certain it was in fact her, as she was getting out of a BMW that looked a lot like the one she had been seen in before, but who knew? All of intelligence was like this. Suppositions and bad guesses based on incomplete information. He smiled. That was it, right there. This spyhunter had nothing. Just a few stabs in the dark, and there was no way she would connect with anything.

Antonio settled back into his chair and shuffled the information again. Sightings of Rose Cross in Charleston, Seattle, Las Vegas, and Juarez. Juarez. Antonio took that report, delivered from a spy who ran a small establishment that was sometimes used for the exact kinds of rendezvous he could not be caught at. If Cross were there…

…then Galindo could be too. Antonio made a mental note of the date. A few dummied receipts, nothing in Juarez, but along the way and he could put Galindo on track for a meeting with the Spymaster of the Twins. The knot in Antonio's belly loosened.

The realization of the plan must have summoned Galindo. He came back in looking like he had just finished a long tango with death. His skin was pale and clammy, the sweat only starting to dry. His breaths were stuttered and shallow. Antonio glanced around. The others had all made a note of it as well. He waited for Galindo to get to his desk and lean heavily on it before heading over. When he put a hand on Galindo, the other man jumped. "How are you doing?" Antonio asked him.

"Not… not bad," Galindo stuttered.

"Come on, let's get some air."

Galindo barked a short and hysterical laugh. "We're five hundred feet underground. There's no fresh air here." He still followed Antonio out of the room. Galindo was on the shaky edge, and probably had a disastrous interrogation with the spyhunter. He was very fragile.

So Antonio would do his best to break him.

Antonio didn't speak until they through the door, once again heading for the coffee station. The walls of the room were a dark, greenish gray stone. Points of gold, like stars too close to earth, threw light and shadows across them. It was easy to see recognizable shapes in the fingers of the shadows, but it was all the product of the mind. Antonio looked at these shapes now, letting them focus and sharpen him.

"So, what happened?"

"Um… nothing. Nothing happened."

"She thinks it's you."

"What? No!"

"I'm sorry. I should have seen it coming. I mean, obviously it's you."

"But it's not!"

"I know that. Anyone who knows you knows you're an innocent man. If she asks me about you, that's exactly what I'm going to say, too. Problem is, she doesn't know you."

"What's that supposed to mean?"

"Come on, Carlos. You know. Your work? Not really up to the standards of the Sons."

Galindo laughed, and it came out sounding like a burp of hilarity. "Actually, she doesn't think it's me. She thinks it's either Reyes or, um, Fox."

Antonio didn't like the final lie in that sentence. How did this man get to be an analyst? *By never having to be in the field.* Right. A facility for deception was actually a bad thing in this line of work. All Galindo had to do was sort intelligence. He didn't have to find any himself. Antonio knew that the spyhunter never mentioned Fox. Galindo had summoned the name desperately to fend off the name she did use. Which had to be his.

Antonio hoped the string of curses he uttered in his mind could not be seen in the bland smile he plastered over his face. "Reyes and Fox, huh? I don't think so. Of course, if she did suspect you, you don't think she would tell you that, do you?"

Galindo blinked, and Antonio could almost see the information worming into the other man's heart, binding him up and making him sick. "I guess…"

"The only thing you can do is hope to pawn off suspicion on someone else."

"Someone else?"

"She wants Reyes, you should give her Reyes. I'll even help you."

"You will?"

"Of course I will. I'm not going to let a good man die for some witch hunt."

"Die?"

"You didn't think she was going to make you dinner, did—"

"Antonio Vilar?"

The soldier had approached silently, and Antonio had to fight not to jump out of his skin. The man spoke with a Brazilian accent. Probably one of those recruited from the urban warfare specialists of BOPE. "Yes?" Antonio said, trying to ignore the assault rifle across the soldier's chest.

"Agent Cervantes would like to see you."

"Of course." Antonio shot Galindo a reassuring smile and followed the heavily armed young man down the stairs to the second level of the 400 Sons. He seldom went down there, only going for infrequent agency-wide briefings. The soldier led him into a conference room, where Cervantes was sitting behind the table. She looked up when he came in. Her eyes were the tawny brown of a bird of prey. There was nothing else behind them. No emotion, no memory, no humanity. He thought of those as spy's eyes, that sucked in information and yet gave nothing back.

"Antonio Vilar," she said. It was not a question. "Sit down."

She gestured at the seat directly opposite her. Antonio considered sitting in the one next to it, in hopes that might throw her off, but dismissed it. That would also show an unwillingness to cooperate, and he wanted her to believe he was a loyal company man, up and down the line. He sat down and put on a slightly confused smile.

"I will ask you some questions, and you will answer them honestly."

"Of course. What's this about?"

"You work collating in the room dedicated to the Twins, correct?"

"Yes."

Cervantes watched him as he spoke, her eyes still as empty as a smoggy night sky. "Your desk tracks Rose Cross, correct?"

"Yes. And, well, some others. Rose Cross is my major responsibility, but I also try to stay on top of her non-immortal personnel. Bodyguards, Servitors, silver bearers, and so on."

"Rose Cross is your primary responsibility, correct?"

"Correct." Antonio paused slightly before each question, even though there were none yet he would have to lie about. He did this because he knew that when he would be forced to lie, he needed the pause to sound no different than his normal procedure in answering questions. He would use the time to come up with his answer and force himself to believe it. In his mind, he would be telling her the truth, and so she wouldn't read the lie.

She continued in the vein of questioning, pinning him down to his true job within the 400 Sons. He was fine with this, as she could confirm the information elsewhere. Deception here would sink him before he could even begin.

The first question he was truly wary of came after a numbing line of inquiry, probably intended to lull him. He had kept up his pauses, but it had been difficult. He wanted to move along and had to resist the urge to snap off quick responses. "On May 26, 1996, Rose Cross was in New York." He remembered that date, not because it had been four years earlier, but because it had been one of the times he had blocked the stream of intelligence flowing to the Priestess.

"Yes. We believe this had to do with Coldheart's deployment there. It was less than a year since his creation then."

"Rose Cross's presence had absolutely nothing to do with Coldheart's."

She was correct. According to the reports, Cross didn't seem to have interacted with any of the immortals. "That does appear to be right."

"Your report came three days too late to plan an assassination. Why?"

The pause here was a little longer than the others he had taken. The real answer was that if Rose Cross was killed, he was officially at sea, a target for the Twins and the Priestess. The real answer was that the money would stop coming. "Human error, I'm afraid. I had not pinpointed Cross's position reliably until it was too late."

"Difficult to track an albino fashion plate, Mr. Vilar?"

"One who is an expert in tradecraft with over a century of experience? Who can erase memories of her presence? Yes, ma'am, it's very difficult." He hoped be put the right amount of wounded pride into the response.

"What specifically was difficult for you?"

"Cross operates under a good many aliases, and a lot of her interaction with mundanes is through proxies." He smiled. "The Red Lady of the Twins doesn't talk with peasants."

"Specifics, Mr. Vilar."

"I was not certain which hotel she was staying in. She books more than one room, and she's quite capable of giving staff false memories of an albino woman. I was tracking her through financials, specifically the credit account linked to one of her silver bearers."

"And this silver bearer is still in play?"

"Yes. He's an heir to a timber fortune. Makes hiding the money in his accounts easy. We could kill him if we wanted to, but it wouldn't do much more than inconvenience her. His accounts have the latest security on them, and even he has several proxies and aliases. It's like trying to pull a mouse out of a thornbush."

"September 5, 1998. Cross was in Seattle."

He stuttered, "Uh... yes, yes, that's right." It wasn't an act. She was getting under his skin.

"Alone. Her most consistent companion is the snake goddess, who, according to eyewitness reports, was fighting our own people in El Paso."

"Yes, her most consistent companion is Shahmeran, but she has been sighted with several others, and Seattle is close to where we believe Blackthorn has a home."

"Was she seen with Blackthorn?"

Antonio conjured a photo in his mind, one that did not exist and never had, and around it placed more false intelligence. Yes, Rose Cross and Blackthorn had been together on some errand or another. "Yes, ma'am. Two separate, reliable reports."

Cervantes was surprised for the first time. "Really?"

"Yes, ma'am." He could see the reports clearly in his mind. They were as real as the table. As real as the spyhunter.

"The timeline in your service record did not reflect this. Why not?"

"I don't include everything in the timeline. If I did, it would rapidly become unreadable. I prepare the reports ultimately for Itzcoatl himself, and he comes from another time. He likes simplicity and accuracy without extraneous embellishment." Antonio smiled. "His words."

"If I requested this information, I would find it in the archives?"

The archives were another floor down, a massive stone basement filled haphazardly with records dating so far back some were inscribed in stone. "I would never assure anyone they could find anything in the archives, ma'am. But I did file it properly."

"January 18, 1997."

"I'm sorry?"

"Another sighting, another probable solo sighting, and you were late in reporting."

He knew he had to switch the lie, but even thinking of it that way was wrong. It wasn't a lie. It was the truth, but it was a different truth than before. "Late? I wasn't late. I requested an operation be put together."

"And why was none ordered?"

"I wouldn't know. I can only recommend action after I finish a timeline. In that case, I recommended Rose Cross be tracked to… I believe she was in Montreal, and killed."

"This is also not in your service record."

"Why would it be?"

"I'm sorry?"

He inwardly exulted. It was the first time he put her even slightly on the defensive. "If a low-level agent asks for an operation that is not taken, and it later proves that this operation would have eliminated someone as powerful as Rose Cross, wouldn't it make more sense to hide?"

"You're accusing your Tlamacazqui of this?"

"I'm not accusing anyone, ma'am. I'm merely pointing out that it makes good sense."

It was smooth from there. He dodged her questions, parried her insinuations, and blocked her accusations. She had nothing. He knew this going in and was gratified to find he was correct. She had suspicions, true ones, but suspicions were smoke. He knew enough not to mention Galindo. He would let her come to that suspicion herself, as he systematically broke the other man down. It was not about being innocent or even appearing that way. It was about appearing the least guilty.

When Cervantes dismissed him, it took willpower not to flash a triumphant smirk at her. She'd been beaten. As scary as she was, she was only human. She wasn't as good as he was. He wanted to laugh in her face, tell her that he was the traitor, and there was no way she would ever catch him, but this was more satisfying. In a couple years, when he was safe on his ranch in Saskatchewan, she could look back and see the moment she had lost the traitor to the Priestess and wonder how many good operations he had destroyed.

He left the room and went back upstairs, escorted the whole way by the same stern soldier who had brought him downstairs. Antonio put a serious, though not sad or fearful, expression on his face. This was serious business. He returned to his desk, meeting Galindo's terrified gaze for a moment, before returning to his job. He worked hard that day, putting a detailed timeline together for Rose Cross, doing some of the best work of his career. He'd warn his handler with ample time to save Cross, but for the time being it had to look real.

He left late, and returned home well after dark. He owned a modest house in a nice suburb, outside of the basin of Mexico City. It was furnished pleasantly, if generically. He took a frozen meal from his freezer and stuck it in his oven, going into the other room to watch the football game. He was barely thinking about the spyhunter when the knock sounded on his door. He figured it was one of the neighbors on their pleasantly misguided attempts to meet the quiet bachelor who worked long hours. He opened up the door and found a terrified Galindo on his porch.

"Vilar! Vilar, you have to let me in!"

Antonio stood aside, and Galindo hustled inside. The sour stench of sweat and fear billowed off the moon-faced man. "What the hell is it?" Antonio demanded. In the background, on TV, Las Chivas scored. Antonio barely noticed, concentrating on his terrified co-worker.

"You were right, Antonio. You were right about everything. She thinks it's me. She fucking thinks it's me!"

"Why do you say that?"

"She interrogated everyone. Everyone. I'm the only one she called back again."

"She started with you. She'll probably call everyone else back tomorrow."

"No, you don't understand. The first interrogation was nice. Pleasant even. This time, she was grilling me. She wasn't taking no for an answer!"

"What does she have on you?"

"Nothing! There's nothing to have!"

Antonio could not quite believe his plan was going so well, and he had barely started it. He figured he only had to throw a little more gasoline on this particular fire before it was raging out of control. "She probably figures that any traitor smart enough to operate in the 400 Sons would also be smart enough to destroy physical evidence."

"Oh god. Oh *god!*"

"We need to figure out what to do."

"Should I run? Maybe I should run!"

"Are you ready to run?"

"No. Yes. A little. I mean, you always think—"

"You are?" For a moment, Antonio wondered if Galindo really was a traitor and Cervantes actually was there to hunt him. Wouldn't that be funny?

That hope was dashed when the front door swung inward, and Cervantes stepped onto the adobe tiles of the foyer. She was raising a sleek black pistol, the long silencer obscene at the end of the barrel. She was already shutting the door behind her when Galindo turned and moaned in terror.

"Good news, gentlemen. I've found the traitor."

∗∗∗

Cervantes looked from Vilar to Galindo, satisfied that both men were too stunned to go for a weapon. Vilar appeared to have been interrupted in a quiet evening: beer in hand, football on the television, the smells of a meal wafting from the kitchen. Galindo was a wreck. He looked like he'd lost ten pounds since that morning, his flesh hanging off his frame like shredded sheets. She raised the gun, not pointing it at either man just yet.

"The traitor is you, Mr. Vilar."

Vilar's eyes went wide, and the bottle slipped from his hand to shatter on the tiled floor. The pungent scent of beer filled the room. Galindo turned to the other man, frowning in confusion. He had that same look on his face when Cervantes put a bullet through his temple. She stepped forward and put two more rounds into his chest, insuring he was, in fact, dead.

"You work for me now, Mr. Vilar, or your true allegiance will be brought to the attention of your employers."

"Who are you?" he breathed.

She leveled the gun at him. "Doesn't matter. Do you understand what I am telling you?"

He stared at the barrel, probably imagining the bullet that would end his life, lurking just inside of the shadows. "Yes. Yes, I do."

"Very good. I will instruct you in your new dead drop. You will give me information before it goes to either the Twins or the Priestess. Your first assignment is Mr. Galindo. Dispose of his body for me."

He nodded.

"Good night, Mr. Vilar." She glanced at the television. "I hope your team wins." With that, she was gone. The next day she appeared in headquarters and requested a meeting with El Conejo and La Luna. She glanced into the office of the Twins and found Vilar. Only his eyes were twitchy, meeting hers, then glancing away. He was used to duplicity. He only had to get used to one new master, not the whole concept of betrayal. He would do fine.

El Conejo and La Luna met Cervantes in the conference room. "I merely wanted to let the both of you know that the traitor was who you believed."

"Carlos Galindo," La Luna said.

Cervantes nodded.

"And he has been dealt with?" El Conejo asked.

"Personally, sir."

"We appreciate your speed and discretion, Miss Cervantes."

"Thank you, sir. Ma'am."

They dismissed her, and Cervantes was able to return home. It was not her true home, just an apartment she had rented for the duration of her present assignment. The only furniture was a bare bed. The place had begun to stink. She checked the bathroom. The corpse of Josefina Cervantes was turning to greenish gray sludge in the bathroom. She looked at it for a moment, realizing it was almost the same shade as the stones of Ezcalli. The stench of rot was strong, and would have turned her stomach if that kind of thing bothered her anymore. The air fresheners she had hung around the room were not doing much. No matter. The job was finished, and the body could be safely disposed of.

Cervantes went to the kitchen and removed a pen and what looked like a bill from the phone company from one of the drawers. She added a few details to it. To most people in the world, it would look like a paid bill. To the right eyes, it would say, "Mission accomplished," signed with her codename, Barone. She sealed it in an envelope. As she thought of the envelope's destination, her features ran like wax before they solidified again into the perfect copy of the face of Josefina Cervantes.

Forever
for a
Moment

ROSE CROSS COULD HAVE STAYED in the bath for hours. Though hot baths had long ago lost their novelty, that simple fact didn't make them any less wonderful. She lay back in the large tub, the water as milky white as her skin, the delicious scent of lavender boiling off her. She had to rouse herself, as she had important plans for her day. And the rest of the preparation, to say nothing of the goal in mind, would be at least as pleasant.

She rose from the water and lifted a towel from the rack. It felt like angora against her skin as she dabbed herself dry. She hung the towel neatly on the rack and stretched. Her muscles, loosened from the water, buzzed with sleepy intoxication. She left the bathroom for the suite's bedroom. Floor-to-ceiling windows looked out over Fifth Avenue, and she paused, gazing down on the tiny people below. Though it had always been Ash Wednesday's home, she loved New York almost as much as he. It could be a cacophony, especially if she opened herself up to the clattering minds all around, but it was lovely in its way.

On the narrow ledge outside the penthouse suite windows, she caught the barest hint of a shimmer. It was one of the vree-ka-vree Ash loaned her to bolster her forces while in town. The five boroughs were crawling with the creatures, making New York one of the more dangerous places on earth for anyone not loyal to the Twins. The city ghost was somehow perched on a ledge barely a few inches wide. Its camouflage was nearly perfect, its elastic body all but undetectable. Rose placed a hand on the window, and could just feel the teeth of autumn beyond. A portion of the window blurred: the vree-ka-vree shifting and acknowledging her presence.

She had laid out her clothing in advance. The underwear was silk, as she would never accept a lesser substitute. It was divine, slick and smooth, brushing over skin still tingling from the bath. She rolled her black stockings over her legs, and stood. She stepped into her red dress, and after shifting it to reach the zipper, zipped it up to her neck. It was sleeveless, showing off her long, flour-white arms.

In her youth, she had been ashamed of her skin, of her red eyes, of her silver hair. She had long since left those feelings behind. Not because she had seen into enough minds to know she was considered lovely, but because the skin, the hair, the eyes, they were her. They had helped shape her, made her an outsider in her youth, and helped bring her to magic. Had she been born like her sisters, she would likely be as dead as they. Now the name of Rose Cross was a feared one to a powerful subculture, and her albinism had become a dangerous signpost to her enemies.

She checked her hair in a mirror, noticing the Thraxian hiding within shifting away so as not to be seen. She smiled at her guardian: Zeryss, a good and faithful Servitor. The Thraxian shyly smiled back—she had been practicing human expressions with the soldiers, and had gotten rather good at them—and vanished beneath the bed in the mirror.

Rose turned her attention from the creature to her own reflection. She had had her hair done earlier in the day, pinning it up with a few curled strands falling free to elegantly frame her face. The bath had not caused it to come undone. Her makeup was quick, done to enhance her odd appearance rather than hide it. She then affixed a silver broach shaped like an earwig just above her breast. It might seem an odd choice of symbol, but those with the eyes to recognize the power would accord it the proper respect. It was the only item of jewelry she would wear that day that would come from her regular collection.

She looked her best, and more importantly felt her best. She was ready for the last part.

A chest, like the elegant jewelry box of a starlet from Hollywood's Golden Age, sat on the table. Rose put it in front of her and opened it up. The box was deeper than it appeared to be, holding a series of interlocking shelves on either side. A gift from the Machinist, Rose had been surprised by such a thoughtful present. Pieces of jewelry, all different, all gorgeous, were nestled in each compartment of the box. She smiled as she brushed her hands over the pieces within, moving the shelves aside to touch each one. A necklace with a cameo. A pair of emerald stud earrings. A bracelet of silver knots. She went over each story in her mind as she touched the object, sending a kiss down the strands of time to the giver.

She closed the box and set it aside, putting another series of boxes on the table. There were no mystery to these. They had come from Tiffany's on the previous day. The clerks had been politely shocked at how much Rose spent, but money was money, and they wrapped up the purchases without comment.

These she put on. A silver necklace around her delicate throat. A collection of bracelets on her graceful wrists. Rings, earrings, an anklet. She was dripping with precious metal and stones by the time she was finished. It was a little gauche, but necessary. At least the individual pieces were all tasteful. In particular, she liked the drop earrings, the rubies glittering like her eyes. Black, white, and red, the three colors of Rose Cross. She thought sometimes she might want to take another color or too, but then, she was too old to go expanding her palette too much. Let Shahmeran wear the rainbow.

She put on her long black coat, belted it, and went to the door. She was ready. On the other side of the door were four of her men, waiting in the suite's living room. Alert against any threat, they straightened subtly as she entered. The man closest to the door was Michael Barnes, her loyal protector for... Rose did not know for certain. A long enough time that Barnes had the kiss of familiarity about him, the simple comfort of home to his mere presence. She could imagine life without him, but she would not want to. He nodded to her as she came in, and she offered him a smile. He loved her, even if she hadn't had the power to poke through minds, she would have known that. She loved him too, as a favorite son and steadfast companion.

The other three men in the room, Corso, Bennett, and MacDonald, had not been with her quite as long. These were not their real names, but aliases assigned to them when they joined the organization. Rose could not even pluck their names from their minds had she wanted to. It was the one thing Theurgy could never do: the mind guarded its skeleton key too closely. If she wanted to know, there were always the files, under heavy guard in Northwind, Chevalier Tower, Bellamente, and the Machine Shop.

"Mr. Barnes, if you would have Mr. Righetti bring my car around?"

The way he blanched, she knew she had made a mistake. A moment later, she realized it. Righetti had to be dead. She tried to remember when that happened and found she could not.

"I'll have Mr. Diaz bring your car, Miss Cross," he said in that way that kept him from correcting her. He didn't even emphasize the new man's name. She was grateful for the little ways Barnes spared her feelings.

"Thank you, Michael."

Zeryss the Thraxian appeared momentarily in the mirror of the suite, and then was gone. She had traveled from Rose's room, to there, then likely to the mirror Barnes kept on him at all times. That would be a nasty surprise for an unwary attacker. Two more of her men—Tomko and Washington, she thought, but she was worried about making another mistake, and so did not greet them by name—joined them in the hall. They formed a loose cordon around her, and although none of the men were visibly armed, she knew they could produce pistols from their jackets in the blink of an eye.

She realized she was likely nervous. It was a silly thing for someone so old, doing something she he had done many times before, but there it was. A pleasant tingle in her belly threatening to expand outward along the paths blazed first by warm water, then by the caress of her clothing, and finally by the errand itself.

They went down to the lobby of Langham Place, Fifth Avenue, where Rose's armored BMW waited. She climbed into it along with Barnes and Corso. "The Metropolitan Museum of Art, please, Mr. Diaz."

"Right away, Miss Cross."

Two more armored BMWs followed them, carrying the rest of the team. The vree-ka-vree would be up above, their cries to one another heard as the wail of traffic. The car pulled up at the museum, and she, Barnes, and Corso got out. The other cars stopped as well, disgorging five more of her men. They fanned out, fading into the crowd as much as they could, always with one eye on her. Barnes and Corso, the leader of her men and their medic, stayed the closest to her, but all gave her ample room. With a whispered word, she could sense the alien minds of the vree-ka-vree close by, slinking along the rooftops. It was a shame such precautions needed to be taken. She was not expecting an attack. Yet there was a word for Apprentices that took less than every precaution: dead.

Rose entered the museum and donated lavishly as she always did, before surrounding herself with beauty. She loved the artwork, specifically the Met's collection of sculpture by the European masters, but she was more interested in the people around. The art was a mere backdrop to the faces she picked out in the crowd. She moved through them, doing her best to edit out the faces of her men, and pretend she was alone amongst humanity.

She searched, waiting for someone to catch her eye. Someone always would. It just took a little seeking.

She saw him browsing through the mummies in the extensive Egyptian section. Rose herself always loved art of the dead. The mind was gone, and Rose's power over it was too, but the beauty produced was for the living. Rose wondered if the young man had the same idea.

He was small and slight, dressed in tight tweed and wool. He wore thick glasses, and his stubble was a day or two from being able to be called a beard. He was good looking, but better than that, he looked nice. Someone who would be sweet, who would hold her hand, who would write her little romantic notes.

She settled in next to him and whispered a single word. The power left her lips on the wings of that word, snaking into the man's mind. It flashed behind her eyes, a maelstrom of spinning thoughts, memories, feelings, desires, and sensations, all too jumbled to make sense of. She teased out the problems one at a time, as her master, the Monk, had taught her to over a hundred and fifty years before. It had become second nature, an ability she scarcely had to think to perform. The young man's mind was no more busy than average, and soon she had separated him into discrete strands to be woven into an intelligible narrative.

Rose was irritated to find that the story was sour. The boy was from money, old money, which he flaunted and hid in turns, depending on the power he could reap from the social situation. He was not contemplating the mysteries of the dead, but idly wondering how much each corpse was worth, and in turn how much his body would be worth when he died. He was beginning to think of a business selling bits of the dead, dried and treated, to people looking for a souvenir. As noxious as this plan was to Rose, the worst part was that he abandoned the thought as soon as he contemplated how much work would be involved. Why work when the money came for free? A hundred and fifty years ago, and several hundred miles to the south, and he would have been a perfect planter's son. She'd had enough of those in her first lifetime.

He turned to speak to her, and she was already drifting away.

She moved down the halls, looking for someone else. She found her staring at framed samples of Chinese calligraphy, apparently enthralled in their elegant lines. She was small and dark, with bronze skin that was nearly red. Her black hair was done up in one of the more elaborate modern styles, and her dress was short and tight. She looked like fun to Rose, someone who would encourage her to suck the marrow from life. Go out, have fun, try new things and truly enjoy eternity.

Rose settled in next to her and with a whisper, was in the woman's mind. No, the Theurgist was utterly wrong. As she wove thoughts, memories, and feelings into a form she could observe, she did find a fun person, but that was all. There was no second layer to this woman. She was obsessed with looks, and hers most of all. She had noticed Rose, and was already cutting her admittedly strange appearance apart. The implicit reaction bothered Rose far less than the fact that this young woman seemed to be half a person, with no understanding of the pinnacles of human achievement all around her. She was not appreciating the bold lines of the calligraphy in front of her, she was looking for another tattoo. She had two of them, both characters that meant nothing, and wanted a third that was equally meaningless. Rose herself could not understand the younger generation's fascination with ritual scarification, but at least the Machinist, who was covered in tattoos, could explain the meaning and significance behind each one. This woman could not even fathom a tattoo as having meaning.

Rose moved on.

She found him standing in front of a Rodin sculpture, one of her favorites. In white marble it depicted a man on a throne holding a woman one armed and kissing her. The ambiguity of the scene—the woman's pose in particular was open for interpretation—always fascinated Rose, as there was no mystery of human interaction she could not solve with a few words.

The man was considering it thoughtfully, and Rose hoped he truly was analyzing the statue or at the very least appreciating it. Older than the other two, he might have a little more wisdom. Nothing compared to hers, of course, but he would be beyond the rank shallowness of youth. He wore a simple suit displaying frugal, but impeccable taste. His skin was a chestnut brown, and he kept his head shaved to conceal a receding hairline. His short beard had a few spots of white in it. But it was his eyes, a deep chocolate, that entranced her. She hoped he would be the right one.

She whispered a word, and the vista of his mind was laid out for her. She wove together his story, placing memory, thought, and desire into the proper places. She smiled when she saw what was he was thinking: he was wondering about the pose of the woman. He was wondering if the excitement he was experiencing was proper, or if it was something to be ashamed of. He was appreciating the precision of the sculpture, the way that, though it was stone, it managed to capture an irresistible sense of movement.

Rose whispered another word, and that thought bloomed like a flower. The associations, connections to other places, spilled outward. In her youth, she would have panicked, thinking the information would be lost. Now, she serenely took its petals one by one. This intersection of excitement and shame was nothing new to this man. He wrestled with it constantly. He had been raised by a very religious grandmother in Brooklyn. He accepted the morality of the faith, in particular prohibitions against killing and theft and so on, but had trouble with the supernatural. He probably would not be pleased by the revelation that there was not one god but several, and all—or at least most—had been human at one time. The morality was far more important to her. Rose saw great value in loyalty. She followed his moral code, and found it unshakable. It differed from hers, but it did so in ways she could understand. He was not fighting her war. He was living in what he thought of as the normal world. This was a good man haunted by the fear that he might not be good, and it was this doubt that spurred him.

She saw him and her, together, hand in hand. It was the end of a date, the streets fragrant with a recent summer rain, and though he desperately wanted to come into her home, he would not. He would give her a kiss, the kind she would think about for the next few days, and return home.

Doubt. The word enchanted her, because it was so rare. In her life, she knew so many clear-eyed fanatics, yet the idea that a man might not know what was right, might not know what he thought or felt, was intoxicating.

She followed the sullen gray doubt through his psyche, finding its roots like a parasitic vine throughout him. In many ways, he could be defined by that one simple word. It was easiest to find in his religious upbringing, as that was the most obvious to both word and character, but it was in other places as well. He was instilled with faith, but it never sat easily with him. He could not reconcile a loving god with the evil and injustice he saw around him. The doubt crept beyond that, as once it found root, it could flourish. He doubted the claims of news and politicians. He doubted his friends when they made promises. He doubted the world's intentions toward him. He doubted himself for doubting all these things. And yet, as his doubt increased, so too did his mind sharpen. The more he doubted, the more he researched, read, verified. He was no genius, but he was an intelligent man growing smarter with every claim he checked for himself. Of course, he doubted his own intelligence, believing that others accepted easily, and thus so too should he.

She saw herself, comforting him. She would be the missing part in him, the part that could give him the faith he missed in himself, and in others. She could hold him, stroke his head, and tell him all the things he needed to hear. He would grow stronger, knowing that his doubt was his greatest strength, but there were certain things he never had to examine.

He was not a man who loved easily, though once he did, once the doubt was stripped away, he would love completely. It had not happened to him yet, but that was a matter of time. Rose saw the strings already, where a mate could carefully unravel the armor he had woven around him. When this was done, he would give of himself, all of himself, to her. He would not try to change her, though force or manipulation, he would accept her, cherish her, and give her a solid foundation.

She saw them together, growing old, dying, hand in hand.

With a few words, spoken with her insidious power, he would be hers, for all time. She could have him likely without the assistance of her magic, but it would hang between them, a string begging to be plucked.

"Hi," he said.

She blinked, and realized he was looking up over the statue at her. She recognized the look in his eyes. She had seen it already in his mind. The strands quivered, and Rose could see just where they were weakest. Everything in her wanted to do just that, to take what she had learned, and use it.

"Hello," she said, and moved on.

She left that perfect man to wonder what he did, to doubt, really, that he had seen something within her. She headed for the front of the museum, and her men joined her, one by one. Barnes summoned the cars before they were outside, and as the group was making its way down the stairs, the BMW and the SUV pulled up in front. All eight of them piled in.

"Back to the hotel, please, Mr. Diaz," she said.

"Right away."

The cars took her back, and her men peeled away one at a time until they were back to their original group. At the door to her room, she smiled at Barnes. "Thank you for coming today, Michael."

"My pleasure as always, Miss Cross."

She returned to the bedroom, and took off the jewelry, one piece at a time, setting each piece in its original wrapping. She would have one of her men return all of it. All except one piece. The last she removed was the anklet. She almost hadn't bought it. It had seemed almost silly to her at the time, the little silver chain. Yet that is the piece the sweet man would have bought her. She could see him, wrapping around her ankle, and pressing a kiss onto the arch of her foot as he did so. She saw it with new eyes, with his eyes, and because it was from him, she would love it.

She unclipped it with reverence and gave it a single, sweet kiss, before opening up her jewelry box. The box, so much bigger on the inside than the outside, unfolded its shelves for her. As always, she found an empty container, one that had not been there before, and laid the anklet inside. With one final brush, she closed the box.

He would be with her forever, the gift given.

Conservation
of Light

IT WASN'T QUITE A HUT, nor was it quite a house. It stood on a muddy dirt track that went from nowhere and to nowhere. Follow it far enough south and it would eventually lead to another road, to another, and another, and finally to Lake Petén Itzá. Follow the road north, though the dense green foliage, and the ruins of Tikal would rise from the jungle. Its location was only distinct in its proximity to these places, otherwise it wasn't even a speck on the map.

The hut had wooden walls. The gaps in the slats were wide enough so that it wasn't so much drafty as actually windy, though its sole occupant was seldom bothered. The roof was corrugated aluminum. Spots of rust dotted it like islands in a white sea, but there were no holes. It was as watertight as a drum, the plentiful rains sluicing off into a garden plot that produced the kind of vegetables that would win contests were there any of those in this segment of the world.

The front door was along the side of the structure. A visitor would have to leave the road for a rough path leading downward, which in turn led to the rickety wooden stairs terminating at the door. Though the path was often slicked down by wet grass and there wasn't a stone step to be found, no one ever slipped on its reddish mud. Everyone, from toddler to the oldest man, was as sure-footed as a mountain goat on the way to this particular home.

Knock at the door—and no one in the village would have dreamed of doing anything less—and the occupant would open it wide, greet the visitor by name and invite them in. Unless she was out in the fields, on the slope of the hill descending to the tiny trickle of a creek that had carved it. She could be tending her garden plot, or else wandering the area on her frequent walks, looking for specific animals and herbs. She could be found, for those that looked hard enough, or else they would wait. When home, she was always happy to have visitors, even if they always came with requests.

Those animals and herbs she gathered were on display inside the little building. They were on shelves, in glass and clay containers. Some were forged in the kiln down the road, like the clay pots that wafted the dense scents of the jungle throughout the room. Others were refuse, like the Coke bottle containing the tiny green ambush bug or the cloudy cave water. Others were odder shapes, like the fat glass bottles holding the mantis, or the grove of speckled mushrooms, or the colony of brightly-colored frogs. These were everywhere, and each one had a specific purpose.

The other furniture consisted of her bed, hidden behind a curtain of woven blankets, a knit rug, her rocking chair and a simple stool for guests. The scents in the room, both from the shelves of jars and from the pervasive tobacco smoke and the frequently wet dog, were so overpowering that many people went nose-blind. Their olfactory sense just shut down rather than attempt to process all of it. And yet, the combined smell wasn't bad necessarily, just too many competing aromas to properly catalogue. Most of the people in the village associated that overpowering odor, however their addled brains processed it, as comforting. The place it came from was a house of healing.

It was the home of Olga Pineda and of Benito, her dappled mutt. Olga was the *bruja*—witch—of their tiny village of Santa

Januaria. It was a term of respect. Witch she was, but she was their doctor, their leader, their mother, their counselor. Nothing in the village was undertaken without her blessing, and she often lent assistance wherever she could. Without Olga, Santa Januaria would be nothing, and she was given every bit of respect her lofty position deserved. She never had to demand it. Not once it had been earned. Her age alone meant she was due at least a little.

It was not every woman who reached one hundred and sixty.

On this particular morning, she rose slowly. Benito was on his feet, wagging his tail, and ready to eat. Her joints ached, every one of them, like a bubble was balanced in the exact middle, and wherever it touched, dull pain. She knew what that meant. It was time.

She moved to the edge of her bed, grabbing the cane leaning against the wall nearby. It was black wood, carved by Reynaldo Flores in thanks for settling his stomach. The poor man was sick to his core. The thing in his belly was eating him whole, and it would only be so long before it spread to the rest of him. A little tea put him right, and he was healthy as an ox now. It took so much out of her to brew, she had to return to her place two years early. Still, it was better to heal the man than let his daughters grow up fatherless.

She pushed herself to her feet, her knees instantly throbbing under her. Benito scrambled up from the floor, gazing at her with hope radiating from his blunt head to his shaggy tail. It would be a walk, but it would be worth it. She picked her pipe off the shelf, checked her pocket for her tobacco, and satisfied at her supply, opened the front door.

Benito, who had been ready to bolt through the front like a fuzzy missile, came to a stop so sudden his claws raked across the wooden floor. Jairo, who lived down the road and had thoughtfully made the very pipe that was tucked into Olga's belt, was there. His fist was raised to knock, and his wide, honest face was filled with the kind of fear that could only mean one thing.

"What's happened to Carlos?" Olga asked.

Jairo blinked, then recovered. The village would chalk this up to her powers, but the only reason Jairo would look like that would be a threat to his son. "He was bitten by a snake, Doña Pineda."

"What kind of snake?"

"*Coralillo.*"

She nodded, returning to her shelf, selecting a few of the pots, and pouring the contents into an empty beer bottle. "How big?"

"Large, Doña. I didn't see it, but my boy said as long as his arm."

Olga measured a mental picture of Carlos. About two feet. A big snake was cause for some relief. They generally bit animals too large to eat as a warning to stay away. It was the babies who had no idea what they could fit in their mouths that were a danger. They injected every last drop of poison, while the adults usually only used a little. Even that little would be enough to kill a boy, though at least only once over. For Olga, these degrees mattered, especially with her meager reserves of power.

She shook the bottle and peered in, judging it to be enough. She reached into a larger bottle and removed an eagle feather. "All right, now get out of my way."

Jairo hopped down the stairs and climbed the slope up to the muddy road. Olga followed. She was slower than she would have been on another day, and her knees protested every inch of that track. It was days like these she wished she'd embedded stones in the mud, but that would have been admitting that she needed them. That would puncture the illusion she'd worked the last century to build. So she suffered the climb, even swatting his hand when Jairo tried to help her up. When she gained the road, she barely let herself pause for a breath, even though it was coming quicker and rougher than it should have been. She hobbled off down the road as quickly as she was able.

Jairo walked next to her, obviously wanting to jog but knowing the Witch of Santa Januaria never moved any quicker than she was presently going. She would arrive in time. She knew it, and he did too, even if his instinct as a father was to sprint. Jairo's house was just down the road, right past a bend that had claimed more than one truck during the rainy season. Stand at the road's elbow and look down the slope, and there were the rusted remains of two cars poking from the tall grass. There were others beneath those, far older, being swallowed in the reddish clay at the foot of the hill. Olga imagined there were more under that: wooden carts dating back to the arrival of the Europeans, and before that the bones of those who had slipped and fallen, steadily ground to dust over the march of eons. She had been alive to see those cars when they had newly been deposited there, and had tended the wounds of the living that had been pulled out.

Jairo was one of the descendants of that wreck, the blue beetle that was turning red with rust and clay. His mother had been in the car with her boyfriend at the time. She had survived; he had not. Without that wreck, Jairo would not exist. Carlos would not exist either. And so forth, and so on. She would save Carlos's life today, and she would get to know his children, his grandchildren, his great-grandchildren. She'd save them too, and they would know her as their local witch, their godmother, their protector.

Jairo's house was as much of a patchwork as hers. He built it on a brick foundation, and his roof was aluminum. The walls were covered in plaster, and except for a sizable hole near the southwestern eave, was in good shape. When the building was in sight, Jairo could no longer fight the urge and broke into a run. Olga couldn't have followed if she had wanted to. When she was freshly returned from her place she could run like a little girl, though she never did. The illusion of her frailty was more important to maintain than the reality of her power. A witch required a certain image, and she would play the role.

She hobbled up the front steps of Jairo's place and into the house beyond. The boy was on the bed, doing his level best not to cry. He must have been in agony. He wore shorts, and his bare left leg was swollen to three times its normal size. The wounds were livid, drooling a bit of clear liquid along with the blood, looking like ink suspended in oil. Jairo stepped away from the boy, gesturing at a chair by the bedside. Olga sat and inspected the wound.

It was bad. Carlos would lose his leg if not his life. To cure it, she'd have to use the last of her reserves. She mentally shrugged. She had been planning to extract power today anyway. Might as well use the rest to good effect.

"Hold still, boy," she said. "I am here now."

She watched the relief flood over his face, even as it warred with the obvious pain. He started to whisper his thanks, but she cut him off.

"Save your strength."

She shook the bottle again, tapping out a bit of the ingredients into her hand. These she popped in her mouth and chewed. The acrid taste made her wince, and lingered even after she spat the paste onto her fingers. She rubbed this onto the wound, and it began to sizzle. The smoke smelled of burned sugar. She drew the feather across the wound, focusing the energy stored in her body through it and into the boy's leg. Her body felt heavier, though something was leaving it. The aches grew to pains grew to agony. Her vision dimmed. Her breath caught as she fought the wind in and out of her lungs. She felt what it was to die.

The boy's leg was smaller now. The blood running from the wounds had been turned mostly to venom, flowing from him in thick streams. The flesh was no longer angry. Carlos would live.

He would even walk in a day or so. In a week, it would be like it never happened at all, save for two small scars to remind him to stay away from serpents.

"Clean his leg," Olga said as she struggled to rise. She momentarily reflected that it actually was as difficult to move as she usually pretended it was. It would almost be funny if it didn't remind her the price of her longevity. "And let him rest."

Mother and father fell over each other to thank her while Benito inspected first the boy's leg, then allowed himself to be petted by the recovering patient. Olga waved the thanks off, and hobbled outside onto the road. In her present state, the walk would be too long. She walked a few more houses down to the Flores place. He had a pickup truck, an ancient thing that looked like it should be collected at the bottom of the hill with the other wrecks. He kept the machine running through sheer force of will, and on that day, she was grateful. She knocked on the door to his house and when he opened it, he was shocked to find her.

"Doña Pineda? I didn't… Is something wrong?"

"Calm down, Reynaldo. I would like a ride."

"Of course! Let me get my keys."

A moment later and she was in the cab of the truck with Reynaldo next to her. Benito was in the flatbed, watching the green hills rush by. Reynaldo never asked where she was going or how long it would take. Olga asked for a favor and she got it without hesitation. Reynaldo was a good boy. Never forgot what she had done for him.

She gave him directions, and he followed them, going from dirt road to dirt road, directly away from what an outsider might call civilization. There were more important things than big buildings and air conditioning. There was community. And there was power. When used as they were meant to be, these two things fed one another. As her power waxed, her community grew strong. In many ways, she was Santa Januaria, though she always recognized the importance of every last soul in her care. They were all of a place, but she was the only one out of time.

"Here," she said.

The road continued on, running along the edge of the trees. It was scarcely a road at this point, and many areas would have been impassible to a smaller vehicle. It was barely wide enough for Reynaldo's truck. There was a footpath, big enough for one person at a time, snaking into the dense jungle.

Reynaldo pulled over without question and Olga got out, Benito bounding from the truck bed. He knew where they were going, and would have happily run off into the trees had not he known instinctively to stay by her side. She was grateful for this. While she was unlikely to meet anyone on the road at all, let alone someone who would trouble an old woman, the same didn't hold true for the wildlife. A dog would make them think twice, and when it came to animals, that was often enough.

"Would you wait here for me?" she said.

"I didn't think you were going to walk home," he said.

"Don't get wise," she said, but smiled anyway. A good boy.

She hobbled onto the track and as the trees folded in around her and ate the path behind, she thought of the first time she had walked this way. It was around a hundred years ago, give or take. She never knew the precise date she was born, and it didn't really matter. Her age was completely arrested when she was fully charged, but as she used the energy in her body, the years began to trickle by, albeit slowly. She had aged another twenty years over the last century, and was probably doing even more damage to herself today. Nothing to be done for it. She wasn't going to let Carlos die of a snakebite just to spare herself a wrinkle or two.

She had been out walking when she found the path originally. She hadn't noticed getting lost—no one ever did. Being lost was something that happened gradually but was only ever noticed all at once. One moment, she was a little distant from her home, on a pleasant walk to help digest her dinner, and the next she was in this place and night had fallen. The trees loomed over her, and the wind going between the trunks made it sound like the jungle itself were breathing.

When she saw the light ahead of her, she assumed she must have somehow found her way back home. She left the path and moved into the jungle itself. She was younger then, but it was still a trial getting over the fallen logs, the uneven ground, and half-buried stones. She expected that at any moment, the jungle would open up and she would find Santa Januaria waiting for her through this section of trees she had never before seen.

It wasn't until she saw the source of the light that she knew.

The light itself was gold, much like a lantern whose glass had been washed almost to transparency. Each separate point had a tiny flare, and from that sections of rainbow, but the light itself was the kind of clean gold that was always imagined but seldom seen. These lights seemed to sway back and forth behind the trees, and Olga pictured the people she knew moving around on errands. It was a lot for it being night, but they were guiding her home, so she could scarcely complain.

As she got closer, she saw that the lights were not behind the trees—they were among them. They danced between the trunks on random paths, never crossing, just going on endless circuits in the gloom of the jungle.

Even closer, and she saw that was all they were: lights. Orbs of golden light that moved without any source or carrier. They even appeared intelligent as they seemed to be chasing one another through the trees. Fairies. Sprites. As the light touched her face, it found a wondering smile. She moved deeper into the jungle, needing to find the source of these fairy lights.

Soon the wisps were all about her. They never touched, zigging and zagging away as she got nearer. They closed around her, and as she moved through the trees, there were more and more of the eldritch lamps lighting her way.

She had no idea how long she walked once she left the path. Time was a concept of the outer world, and here was a place of magic. She could not have known how correct she was in that knee-jerk assumption. It felt right, an idea sprung fully-formed and with the weight of knowledge behind it. The trees did finally thin out, and she could see the beginning and the end of the wisps. They formed up ahead, in the jungle clearing, zipped through the trees, some on long tours of the dark, others only in quick jaunts, to return to this place.

It looked to be a ruin. Later, she would find that it bore the closest resemblance to an Olmec site. The large stone heads, all with the same saturnine expression, in concentric rows marked it as that. The werejaguar statues, perched atop the heads and standing at the borders of crumbling staircases, were also a strong sign. It looked a bit like an amphitheater carved into the earth, the stairways running between heads and werejaguars, yet at the middle, they were looking at nothing.

She knew what they would be looking at. And without any hesitation, she followed the closest stairway and took her place at the center of the amphitheater. The wisps no longer shied from her. They were born of the stone, flitted through the jungle, and ended with her, plunging into her body and suffusing her form with light.

As the first touched her, she felt something that could not be described. Sex was close, though it was orders of magnitude lesser. The sudden understanding of something new and wonderful was just as close, though it failed to account for the vitality in her body. The connection to her home was almost there, yet she never knew the roads and houses of her town like she knew this place she had never been.

There was power. Her body was light. The aches and pains of age were gone. She felt twenty years old again, yet even at twenty she had never felt like this. In later years, she would compare it to the feeling an Olympic athlete might have, yet there were no Olympics then to draw the reference. She felt like she could run for miles, lift the rock heads all around her, jump onto rooftops, or shrug off a gunshot. She knew, even then, that this wasn't quite the same power flooding into her; it was different. It was more. It was so unlike anything a human had experienced, there was no way to truly understand it in the moment that it entered her, and she was forced to use the rough physical comparisons that even then she knew were hollow.

There was knowledge. The energy came from the land, and the air, and the water, and every living thing. It flowed in streams, invisible to the naked eye, to collect in great whirlpools of power. This was one of those whirlpools. She could see it now, shining in a way that would shame the sun. She felt the energy reaching out in every direction, and this collection was a discrete section of space. She glimpsed it in stutters: the place all around her that made the blood that now flowed in her. It was never more than a flash before her eyes, gone almost before she had a chance to consciously register it.

The connection flowed from this. She was the land, and the land was her. This was how kings felt, though their stewardship was a pale reflection of what she felt now. The land was both exalted and diminished by the power she siphoned from it and into her body.

She knew the way home to her village intuitively. It would be a quick walk overland, and with how light and powerful she felt, she would get there well before morning. The thought of her prosaic home unplugged her from the streams of energy. Her body was hers once again, and she had somehow been moved from the center of the amphitheater to the base of one of the stairs. All around her, the great heads watched her, and though their faces were locked in the famous Olmec scowl, she felt their blessings upon her.

She went home, knowing that she would return to this place often, to get a taste of the majesty reclaimed from within. The walk home was quick. She could have run, each breath coming clean and fresh as one drawn during a leisurely walk. She took her time, looking at the trees, the birds, the soil, with fresh eyes. She knew what it truly was now: the prime energy of the world given solid form, and it had a soul the same as a human being. A soul that traveled along great invisible rivers.

It wasn't long before she realized she no longer aged like the other people in her village. It was the drought that changed things. She soon learned that she had some modicum of power. It was little things at first. If there was something she wanted to eat, someone inevitably had extra and invited her to take some. If she was cold, the flames of her lantern burned brighter. The world seemed to reorganize itself to subtly cater to her desires. The rains showed her it lacked scale.

They were in the middle of a drought several years after she had returned from the ceremonial site. She prayed for rain. The Blessed Virgin had likely guided Olga's steps to that place, and would possibly hear Olga's prayer and take it before God. That site, that magical site, was clear evidence of God's Hand upon earth, and her finding it had to be some kind of sign. The torrent that followed said that not only had the prayer been heard, it had been answered to a degree that suggested it offended. The rain loosened the mud higher up in the hills, and a wave of red barreled down into the village, killing several and destroying more. After that, Olga dedicated herself to learning to use the power that now thrummed in her tissues.

She was more cautious, learning the limits of what she could do. No longer did she level destructive prayers at the heavens and hope for the best. She was measured in her requests, careful in her desires. The townsfolk were soon aware of her power, and frightened at first. After dark, they came to her. Make my crops grow, they asked. Help me conceive a child. Take the pain away. And she did. With every miracle, the power ebbed from her. She felt the aches returning, and from time to time when she was really low, she could see a new wrinkle form on her skin. She returned to the ceremonial site and drew more energy into her body, once again reveling in the power, the knowledge, and the connection of the prime.

The people of her youth died, and a new generation took over the village. Olga Pineda was the one constant. Over time the elders came to her for advice as it became clear who was really in charge. Olga never lorded her authority over anyone. She behaved more like a servant than a master, curing pains and bringing prosperity.

She was a witch now, a *bruja*. She had heard the stories since her youth, but hadn't believed them until she truly came to terms with it. She reasoned that there must be more of them out there. She had to find them, so she left her village to search.

She charged herself fully before leaving home. It was around the turn of the century by this time, and Central and South America was undergoing a period of modernization. The old ways were in open conflict in places, and it was this tension that helped outline those who were the focus of her search. Yet every single person she found was a fake. Some were very good fakes, but it wasn't long before she saw the strings.

There was one who was not.

She had heard the rumors very soon after beginning her search. There was a man, living on the shore of the Nezahualcoyotl, who sounded different. The stories called him a Nahual—a shapeshifter —and though she initially guessed he had some kind of trained jaguar which he released only after hiding from view, she began to suspect there was more to it. More than one person claimed to see him change. They described it in such a way that it sounded real. She wanted to believe it, but couldn't bring herself to, not after so many fakes. She would see it with her own eyes.

He was a hermit, the story went, living alone in a broken shack and living off the land. He hunted as a jaguar, or a coyote, or a hawk. He left the locals alone, being treated as more of a curiosity than anything else, though he was cordial enough to any he ran across. Armed with this, Olga went to Lake Nezahualcoyotl, and began the long trek around it.

As she closed in on the shack and the home of the shapeshifter, the frequency of the stories increased. At first, they were the tales of friends of friends. Then they were the reports of relatives. Soon, they were memories. People had seen the Nahual, whom they called Domingo Rey. They had seen him take the forms of animals. They had seen him close wounds with the pass of his hands. They had seen him call wind and rain with a few words.

And soon, Olga Pineda saw him as well.

The shack stood at the edge of the woods. Unless someone was searching, it would be easily missed. The trees grew close to its wooden walls, and the copious leaves shaded it from inquisitive eyes. Most of the day, shadows would swallow it utterly, but Olga saw it instantly. She had seen the energy permeating it, and could still perceive the golden residue on an object so used.

She moved up the beach cautiously. She didn't know how Rey might react, but any man who would hide his home away wasn't necessarily one who appreciated the odd visitor. He was supposed to be pleasant, but that was to the powerless. Olga was a witch and might be considered a threat. Her steps were still light, still charged from her last trip to the Olmec amphitheater. As she approached the hidden house, she felt something she hadn't felt in a long while: fear. If he was real, unlike all the others, he would be the one person who might be able to hurt her.

The shack appeared, at a distance, to be slapped together between several trees. She saw that it was in fact made from the trees themselves, grown out of the living wood. There were concessions to camouflage it as something made by human hands: skillfully-sculpted boards, but that's all they were. There wasn't a nail in the entire structure. The house was part of the living tree, sculpted by the hands of a *brujo*. The trunks supported it about a foot off the ground. The stairs leading to the door on the forest side were made of roots.

Olga watched the cabin for a while, wondering how she would approach this man. Would he know others? Would she find some kind of connection? Or would she find a misanthrope who wanted nothing to do with his kind?

The snarl behind her cut the thought short. The wolf was big, though not unnaturally so. Its shaggy coat was a mix of brown, gray, and white. Its eyes were wrong: they were the eyes of a man, staring from the furry face of the wolf.

"Domingo Rey?" she said.

The wolf padded to the left, beginning to circle her, keeping his man's eyes trained on her. It wasn't how she wanted to introduce herself, but a century on earth had taught her that one could seldom choose the method of anything.

"I was looking for you. I'm like you."

The wolf stopped. He didn't pant like a normal animal. He kept his mouth closed, though whenever his lips rippled in another barely-voiced growl, she caught sight of canines as big as her little finger. The wolf stopped his padding around and settled onto the sand. The message behind the eyes was clear. A challenge.

She looked up at the clear blue sky, then back at the wolf, and nodded to the unspoken request. An hour later, and the sky was gray. Two more hours and the rain was falling in great, fat drops.

As the first of the water hit his shaggy face, the wolf stood on his hind legs, the fur folding up beneath his skin. His snout was swallowed into a human mouth. Now Domingo Rey stood before her, his long black hair streaked in gray, his reddish-brown skin nearly entirely smooth. He was small, looking like one of the *Indios* so common in the wilder places of Chiapas. His body was compact and muscular, his face handsome and angular. "You're the first one who could do that," he said.

"I could say the same to you."

He smiled. "Welcome then."

"I'm..."

"Don't tell me your name. Names are power, *señora*."

She frowned, and said nothing, following him up and into his shack. It was larger than it first appeared, stretching off into the cool darkness at the edge of the jungle. It looked old and drafty, but the openings were well-placed, keeping the structure aerated and comfortable rather than cold. Domingo excused himself after inviting her to sit, and returned quickly, dressed in old worn pants and a peasant shirt. He was still barefoot.

"You found a ritual site, didn't you?" he said.

She nodded. "Many years ago."

"Once you find a spot like that, it can keep you young. I don't know how long, but it's been several hundred years, and I've scarcely aged a decade."

"Several hundred years?"

"I'm not certain how long exactly. We were still using the old calendars when I was born."

"And you have a place?"

"I do. You'll understand if I don't reveal the location. It's old, all ruined and strange."

"And there are lights?"

"Oh, yes. When I found it, it was already old, but since I've been there, it hasn't aged any further. It's as though my regular visits are keeping it in the same shape it had been. Just like me. Perhaps it's like a cow, needing regular milking to stay healthy." He shrugged. "Then again, it's possible I'm just not noticing the decay."

"How did you learn to change?"

"How did you learn to make it rain? It seemed the natural thing to do. I'd grown up with legends of the Nahual, so once the power was in me, it was the next step." He smiled. His teeth were white and even: evidence of the magic that kept him alive for so many years. "Don't you love the feeling when the power gets into you?"

She returned the smile. "I felt like I could run forever."

"You probably could! Physical action will drain you, but not as much as magic. Transforming a thought into solid form is what takes the most."

They continued the conversation into the night, and Domingo invited her to stay. She settled into a hammock and scolded herself. Domingo was handsome, but he was several hundred years older than her and looked several decades younger. Romantic feelings were fine, even inevitable. She'd keep them to herself, instead valuing the new friend.

The next morning, she'd gone out to gather some firewood. When she was returning and saw the house through the trees, she knew something was wrong. She paused, taking cover about thirty feet away. The door opened, and Domingo came stumbling out. He was shirtless, his chest covered in bleeding scratches.

The man following him out put a booted foot into Domingo's back and shoved, sending the small Nahual stumbling to his knees. The man was tall, and pale as a Spaniard. His black hair was long, and his brown eyes were soft like a woman's. He wore a long brown coat over a fancy suit that was decidedly out of place this deep in the jungle.

"Leave me in peace," Domingo said. Each word came with blood.

"I can't. When you take what's not yours, you have to die."

"No one was using it!"

"I don't see how that matters."

The man marched Domingo to the beach of the lake. The bloody Nahual fell to his knees, his shoulders slumping. The man looked up at the sky. "How long have you been stealing from the Priestess?"

"Centuries."

"Then call this a mercy," said the man. He bent down and scooped up a handful of sand, brought it to his lips and whispered to it. It came off in a dust devil, picking up more and more from the beach. Soon, it was the size of a man. Then, with a word from the brown-coated *brujo*, which Olga did not hear but felt in her bones, the sand changed directions and slammed through Domingo. It shredded him from head to foot, and what fell onto the beach in a bloody heap didn't look human anymore.

The sad-eyed man stared at what he'd wrought, and shook his head, perhaps in sadness or regret. He muttered something to himself, and this Olga could neither hear nor feel. The man then turned and walked back up the beach, his head down, his shoulders slumped. Olga was frozen in her hiding spot. Nothing could have brought her out.

Olga returned home. She never forgot what happened to Domingo. He had been sweet, hurting no one, and the sad-eyed man had killed him without hesitation or remorse. She often awoke from a nightmare, either seeing Domingo's shattered corpse start to move and beg her for help, or else she saw his executioner stalking her through the dark, ready to give her a similar fate. She awoke from these covered in sweat, and would not sleep for the rest of the night. They didn't feel like dreams; they felt like memories that hadn't happened yet.

She never looked for another *brujo*. She never escaped the nagging sensation that her calling that rainstorm had been what called the sad-eyed man either. Not finding them was safer: with no calls for proof, there would be no way to summon the sad-eyed man. So she'd lived for more days than anyone had a right to, in peace. She never forgot Domingo, and on that day, returning to Reynaldo's truck with light steps, she thought of him again. She vowed to use her power well and subtly, and never catch the sight of the sad-eyed man. He was still out there, somewhere. He was like her, and thus ageless.

She petted Benito, taking comfort from the way the dog responded with simple bliss. He was still a puppy, and the sum of his life was the blink of an eye to her. Still, he was a good friend in the time he had, and she treasured it.

She returned home, lost in thought. Reynaldo took her to her front door, and she left the road to navigate the short path to her stairs. She opened the door and would have gone inside had not Benito paused at the door and growled.

"Doña Pineda?" She knew the voice that hailed her from inside. She had heard it in her dreams for many years. "Please, come in."

She looked down at the snarling face of her dog. "Benito. Stay." The dog looked up in confusion. He knew the threat inside, and he wanted to protect his mistress. She repeated the command, doing her best to keep the tears out of her voice.

Benito stayed, even though his whole body was shaking with the strain of not charging the man inside. Olga went in and shut the door, keeping the dog out.

The sad-eyed man sat on her stool. He looked exactly the same, though his hair was a bit shorter, and his suit was modern. His coat was no longer a Colonial cut. "Thank you," he said. "You could have run. Or you could have set the dog on me."

"You would chase me down and kill my dog."

"As I said, thank you."

He regarded her. He had the face of an angel, albeit one in perpetual mourning. She looked into those deep brown eyes and she thought she saw more despair in them, more than she had seen that morning on the shore of the Nezahualcoyotl. More ghosts of murders past. She wanted to talk to him. Convince him that she wasn't worth killing, that she was in fact helping the people of this small corner of the world. She had felt the stewardship implicit in the harvesting of the energy and had accepted it. She was no threat; in fact her continued life was enriching those to whom she had a sacred responsibility.

"Please," was all she said.

"I know what you're going to say. I've heard it before, many, many times. If it were my decision, I'd recruit you to the cause. I'd tell you never to go to your nexus again. I'd leave you in peace to live out whatever days you have left. The worst of it is this: it's not my decision. My mistress sent me here to deal with a thief, and to the Priestess, the wages of theft are always death."

She felt the tears on her cheeks, flowing down the ruts carved by her wrinkles.

"There was a time when I would have seen those tears and flinched," he said. "I miss those days. I'll promise you this, Doña Pineda. It will be quick. One moment alive, the next... gone."

"Why?"

"You're stealing."

"But no one has ever used my site. No one in a hundred years."

"And no one will use it when you're gone."

"What?"

"She has nexii underground—places like your ritual site, but they're artificial ones. She can build them with her magic, and they become self-sufficient, drawing energy to them just like a natural point. We use those… these surface ones go to waste."

"Then why are you here?"

He stared into her eyes. "Because she told me to be here."

She never felt the spear of rock that came from the earth and impaled her heart. One moment, she was alive, and the next gone, just as the sad-eyed man promised. To those she had served, her death was assumed to be the fault of the freak mudslide that had taken her house and smashed it to bits at the bottom of the little ravine. Reynaldo Flores and Jairo Carrillo pulled Olga Pineda's body from the wreckage, and her funeral was the largest Santa Januaria had ever seen.

After killing her, Kisin never thought of her again.

Wooden Faith

THE AMAZON JUNGLE WAS PURE cacophony. In other places, this would have meant the persistent buzz of industrial logging equipment, the constant chatter of the clear-cutters, and the sepulchral coughing of diesel engines. The Hounfour was so deep that these noises were entirely absent. Instead there was the trill of birds and insects, the call of monkeys, and the rush of water. The only human sounds came from the Hounfour itself, and they were always muted. Even casual conversation was kept to a minimal volume, as unnecessary shouting carried with it a severe punishment. A human could pass within thirty meters of the compound and never know it was there, which was the entire point.

Arcadio had not expected that when he crossed over to serve. He had expected a fortress standing bold and unafraid. A mountaintop somewhere, proclaiming this the sovereign home of a goddess, populated by an elite guard more there for ceremony. The goddess herself could easily dispatch any threat.

He had not expected to be living as a mouse.

He padded through the undergrowth beneath the curtain of rustling foliage. He had not expected that either. He had heard stories and felt the sculptures of those who had returned, but there was nothing that could really prepare anyone for the stark difference between his home in Tawa and this strange part of

Axalik. In particular, the trees were bizarre. They were curiously static and vertical, the trunks rough and pitted, and the leaves, everywhere the leaves. They were scarcely recognizable as the plants he had been familiar with back home.

The animals were of baffling variety as well, and all confined to a single shape. The mere fact that animals and plants were two separate categories (and one soldier informed him of at least two *other* categories—the very thought!), was in itself hard to grasp. He knew the fauna of this place was soft and easily killed, even when one was not intending violence. The blistering wash of feathers, the smoothness of scales, or the warmth of fur was entirely alien. Each creature had its own covering, and it was precisely that: a covering, a discrete part of its body as distinct from the central mass.

As fascinating as the fauna was, he was alert for only specific kinds. Humans of all types, as any could be representatives of the other eight clans that stood against the goddess and her patron, the Priestess. In particular, he was alert for those who came from the clan of the Twins, the archenemies of his goddess. These were who his goddess feared most. Back home, they were known as the Sisters, and though the theology was clear on the state of antagonism between the Sisters and the goddess, he had not been aware that the religious war burned quite so hot. Because of this, their Familiars and Apprentices, and the creatures that made up their Servitors were all readily identifiable to any of those serving in the Hounfour. He had already known of some, recognized as demons and demigods by his people. Here, there were samples of scales, swatches of skin, catches of scent, and of course the endless descriptions in the files written in the raised pictograms of his native tongue, making those demons unsettlingly real.

This is why Arcadio was out in the northwestern sector of the surrounding jungle, the alternate kiss of dry warmth and moist cool along his flesh. He was hunting for the inevitable attacking force from the Twins. He was waiting for something that would never come.

He wore his jaguar form. He was a large specimen, at almost three meters from tip of the nose to twitching tail, though not unnaturally so. He had never seen his coat, but was told it was black, and in a touch of verisimilitude, spots could be seen when he stood in the sun. An expert would be surprised to find that close up, the spots appeared more like knots in wood. He looked to weigh a little over two hundred pounds, but was in fact closer to four, and though his muscles seemed to bunch and shift under a loose coat of fur, actually touching the surface would reveal it to be hard and a single piece. If he bared his teeth or extended his claws, they would not be revealed, but newly formed from the central mass of his body, ready for their bloody business.

Not that he was expecting any violence. As Arcadio stalked through the trees, occasionally scaling one easily where he would concentrate on the jungle brushing against his skin, he knew he was waiting for a threat that was simply not there. He was hunting the goddess's madness.

He had been raised in the Orisha faith from birth. In some ways it was luck of the draw. There were other religions: the Cult of the Sisters, the Neithites, and many others. The Orishans were the largest of all of these, and the only one that spread all through Tawa. This was partly because the other deities were far more distant and strange, visiting only rarely if at all. When the Sisters required something of his people, it was demanded and assumed. This was uncommon, as the Sisters—called the Twins here—had their own loyal races: the deadly thraxians, the city-ghost vree-ka-vree, and the powerful orrerites among many others.

Santa Orisha distinguished herself by coming to Tawa often, as well as pledging herself to the bakru people, and displaying a deeper relationship than the other gods ever did. Her first visit had been a century and a half ago, when she entered into a contract with the bakru. She outlined her responsibilities to them, and them to her, on the wood of one of the spiraling elder trees. A copy existed on the sanctuary tree of every church, available to read for any who wished to know how a goddess, a real one, trusted her Servitors. Arcadio had first felt it when he was still a sapling and used a different name. He had been amazed at the idea a goddess could have obligations to those she ruled. As he grew capable of understanding such things, he began to see the importance of the other side of the equation.

The inductees gathered in the central plaza of the town every three years. All were voluntary, and there were always more than were needed. Only the best of the Cult ever crossed over to Axalik to serve the goddess, and only the best of those became her personal bodyguard. Arcadio stood at the borders of the plaza, feeling the wind displaced by the bakru chosen to cross over, he smelled the pride in their posture, and knew he would be one of them one day. He worked toward nothing else for the duration of his life, and when the time came for him to stand in the plaza, to await the few returning veterans—who having grown too cracked, warped, and wild to exist on the other side—Arcadio was there.

The training had been long and difficult. It proceeded in degrees, first requiring only the basic skills to exist on an alien world, then imparting the lessons on how to be useful.

He had refined his shapes. First, the human. This was the most important for any bakru to live on Axalik. He spent countless hours getting the limbs right, learning the proper tint to give his flesh, perfecting the odd task of creating eyes. The elders had vast reserves of bodies, preserved in various states by a coating of resin, along the walls of the Shifting Temple. He learned the skeleton, then layered organs, muscles, fat, and skin. They did not function; they were all part of the same mass of wood, a texture useful only for mimicry. The bakru who wanted to cross over would be found there, perfecting the shape of the body, before one of the human adherents could coach them through the alien task of applying "color" to the skin.

Arcadio worked hard at mimicking the body stage by stage. He had to appear natural to those who spent their entire lives seeing creatures like this and never questioning they were anything but what they appeared. The elders tested him. Keeping the human shape was initially an effort, though the grain of his flesh now knew it so well, it was natural. He couldn't take another human's form, but this would be enough. When he first gained the skill, a sudden shock could get him to lose control, to change into something between human and bakru. Now he could be in a plane crash and he would appear perfectly human.

The second shape he learned was the jaguar. He never knew why this was the preferred combat form for the bakru; it simply was. There were so many other predators on earth that would have been more effective. And it wasn't as though the bakru were confined to creatures that already existed. It was easier to mimic, but Arcadio knew that more was possible. They could have combined the shapes of any number of beasts to create a perfect killer. In any case, the Orishan Document stipulated jaguar, and there were numerous preserved specimens in the same state as the humans to practice from.

Then he learned to fight. The bakru had an advantage over all the creatures in Axalik: their wooden flesh. An injury that would kill or cripple an Axaliko would do little more than inconvenience a bakru, and given time and light, they would recover from all but the most grievous wounds. As long as the heartwood stayed intact, so would they.

The elders, many of whom had served on the other side, had brought back a collection of Axaliko weapons. Like everything from Axalik, it was a dizzying variety, and Arcadio at first could not imagine a people needing so many different kinds. Once he came over and saw the similar variety of creature, he understood. Some weapons, specifically those that belched nightmarish gouts of flame, were there mostly to show what mobile death looked like. Others, the clubs and blades, were nearly useless against him. They had a few humans, some there willingly, others prisoners, who fought the bakru and sharpened Arcadio's skills. After learning as a human, he learned again as a jaguar and found it was even easier. His claws tore right through skin and his bite could crush bone.

He was suitable as a warrior, one of the many elite soldiers commanded by Santa Orisha in service to her titan patron. He would not be satisfied until he was more than that.

Stealth came next. He learned to use both shapes to the utmost, and to mix in his natural abilities to become invisible in the wild. For these, he was brought to the Garden Temple, where the central chamber was converted into a jungle much like the one he would eventually find in Brazil, this one was powered by a miniature sun that blazed near the stone ceiling. Other bakru would hunt him through this jungle and he was forced to hide and evade. Any confrontation was a failure. Soon he was able to avoid them for days at a time, convincing the elders he was in fact cheating.

Last came education. Others regarded this as a waste, but he did not. His goddess was one of many on the other side, and whenever there were deities about, it was a good idea to learn about them. A few of these were friendly. Most were not. Some were creatures straight from nightmare. Arcadio had not been able to sleep when he learned of Oorun, one of the Lion's Familiars, a being that could kill not only Arcadio but every bakru with not much more than a stray thought. The concentration, though, was on the servants of the Sisters and their false faith. Back on Tawa, he had often wondered why any bakru would willingly serve them when the Sisters offered nothing in return. It struck him as a religion of fear, as though without the worship, the Sisters would raze the entirety of Tawa. After learning of the beasts they kept at their beck and call, he was beginning to think the Cultists of the Sisters were correct. The Axaliko branch of the Cult of the Sisters was different in shape, if not in motive.

The most dangerous was Ash Wednesday, known on Tawa as the Thousand Man, the demigod and son of the Sisters. He had been conceived in their flesh, and given life in their words. On Tawa, he was understood to be the personification of their malign will: the Sisters wanted something gone, and it was the Thousand Man who killed it. Arcadio learned that Wednesday was actually closer to an heir. Santa Orisha feared him over all others, even the Twins themselves, though he seemed to be some kind of sibling to her in a way Arcadio could not understand. The Thousand Man would be the one who would ultimately come for Santa Orisha, and he would bring with him one of the other monsters: the massive serpent Shahmeran, the white bear Winterhide, or the hound Ghostwalker. Arcadio learned everything he could about them, knowing one day he would have to face one or all of them in combat.

He passed every test set before him and was marked as one of Orisha's bodyguards. The day he stood in the plaza under the three cool suns of Tawa with all the others going over was the proudest of his life. He was going to serve the goddess directly. The gateway opened, and the few veterans, those who had survived their long service on Axalik, stepped through. They shivered in the chillier air, their practiced shapes beginning to fade. As the assembled bakru greeted the returning heroes, the new crop went to the other side, knowing that for most of them, that would be the last time they set foot on Tawa.

They emerged in the courtyard of the Hounfour. Though Arcadio had felt the models of human architecture, it was still odd to touch the currents up close. The compound was deep in the Amazon (and later, Arcadio learned what this meant), built around a natural clearing, and then partially expanded. Trees still grew from the wet soil within the walls, the canopy shielding the collection of buildings from the sky. The main building was the church, recognizable even to Arcadio, though it was not in the bakru style. He learned later that this would be referred to as "Spanish Colonial," though he knew them more by the shape of the air currents coming off the buildings and bringing scents and sounds. The only thing with instant familiarity was the latticed gate symbol of Santa Orisha above the double doors. The individual tines were picked out in crosses, skulls, dragonflies, and other markers that were as legible as any heraldry. It marked this place as devoted to the goddess, and he felt an instant surge of comfort. This was home.

The other buildings were in similar styles, though the church was the tallest. The bunkhouse for the humans spread out, connected to their mess hall and arsenal. The entire place was surrounded in a ten foot wall of stone; later Arcadio would learn that a trench surrounded all sides, making the wall even taller. It extended down into the bedrock, and had no distinct bricks or mortar; it was a solid chunk of rock. Guard towers stood at the corners of the walls, and a guardhouse was at the front gate. The only access on land was that gate, leading out onto a footpath that wound into the verdant jungle. The only other exit from the compound was on the opposite site to the bunkhouse, and was a rocky cave sinking into the earth. Arcadio had identified it instantly as the entrance into *el Labertino*, the most important place in the Hounfour.

When he arrived with the others, all thirty of them, the church doors had been shut. The central compound was arrayed with Santa Orisha's bodyguard. Twenty armed men smelling of sweat and gun oil. The bakru outnumbered the humans and stood in places of honor, most notably on both sides of the church's double doors. They smelled of home, though the scent was subtly marked by their time on Axalik. They had changed in the service of the goddess, but they were still bakru. It was a statement, *We are honored here*, that, at the time, had made Arcadio's fibers swell even further with pride.

As the new recruits stepped from the portal, the bakru opened the doors wide, revealing the interior of the church. There were cages of insects whirring in circles lining the wall. The pews were wood, sculpted out of whole trees, honored to have been harvested for this purpose. The reliefs along the wall were dedicated to those Arcadio thought of as Santa Orisha's siblings, people like Kisin, or Teotl, or Viracocha, and all depicted these remarkable people in positions of strength and power.

Santa Orisha herself stood in front of the altar, her hands clasped and waiting for her new Servitors. Arcadio had been near her on some of her visits to Tawa, though it was a thrill to be with her at the seat of her power. The slight breeze from the door rustled her robes, and she sounded like soft summer leaves. She had the sharp, clean, and powerful scent of a lightning strike. Her body, though small and soft by his standards, seemed larger than it was. The air shifted around her at odd angles, individual gusts vanishing in one place to reappear in another. When she moved her hands, the clicking of her bracelets sounded like bone dice.

Some of the bakru fell to their knees instantly, but Arcadio knew that such displays were not what the goddess wanted. She had recruited strength; she would want to see strength. He had walked to the front of the altar, bowed, and took his place by the front of the pew, concentrating on every breath of wind, knowing where everything was in the room. He was vindicated when she quickly gestured at the kneeling bakru to rise, and he was overjoyed when she returned his bow with the slight incline of her head.

The doors, visible now from his vantage, were armored. They felt wooden, complemented by a heavy iron bar that could easily barricade them shut. A door behind the altar led into the rest of the church, and later Arcadio learned that a secret door in the rooms went into her subterranean home. The church was a fortress, and now one filled with a highly trained warrior race, led by a goddess incarnate. Arcadio could not imagine a force able to threaten them.

The ceremony had been a welcoming one, like attending church, only instead of a mere priest, it was the goddess herself. At the culmination, she brought them forward one at a time and gave them each a new name to protect them from the other gods that walked Axalik. Arcadio was the first to get his name, and after that moment favored it over the one with which he was born. He closed his senses to anything but Santa Orisha as he knelt before the goddess, felt the soft kiss of her fingers upon his forehead, and heard the whispered name, and he knew he was finally complete.

His job was patrol. He and a collection of other bakru, all clothed in their jaguar shapes, flowed into the jungles around the Hounfour each morning. For the first several years, Arcadio was alert to any movement in the jungle. He tracked every sound to its source, inevitably frightening some poor animal. He returned to the bakru barracks in the evening: little more than a small plaza open to what sky peeked through the jungle cover, and a surrounding breezeway. The bakru lounged in human or jaguar form as they preferred, and those who had day shifts passed the time until the sun rose again. There were services at the church several times a week, most presided over by the elder bakru and some by the goddess herself, and Arcadio was there faithfully.

After one long day of patrolling the jungle with nothing to show for it, he joined a group of his fellow recruits. They had coalesced around Eugenia, an older bakru who had served for several decades. Arcadio settled down next to them in the plaza, finding a place where the sun could touch his skin.

Diego, one of the other recruits regarded him. "Anything?"

"Oh yes," Eugenia laughed. "Can't you smell the blood on his claws?"

Arcadio shed his jaguar form in favor of the human. "Nothing," he said. "Well, other than a monkey pleasuring himself."

"Sometimes I wonder how they find time to do anything else," Eugenia said.

"Tomorrow," Diego said. "There's always tomorrow."

"And the day after. And the day after that, on and on, until the world ends in fire."

Arcadio frowned. "What do you mean?"

"You'll know," Eugenia said, a smug cinnamon glint to her scent. "Eventually, you'll know."

It was a week after that the first alarm sounded. The portal opened in front of Arcadio's face, no bigger than an apple. An insect, almost like a butterfly, emerged, and the flap of its diaphanous wings carried the sound of Santa Orisha's voice. "Help."

They had protocols in the event of the warning, and Arcadio followed his to the letter. He made a beeline back to the compound and scaled a tree as soon as he felt the slight currents flowing up and over the wall. He reached out with his senses into the central square, but there was no breeze coming from intruders. No breath, no movement. The soldiers who kept the goddess safe had taken up their defensive positions, from simply finding cover behind buildings to manning the bunkers cunningly hidden into the wall itself. The bakru were all around in the trees, ready to pounce in a crushing counterattack. The church was closed up tight, and he had no doubt Santa Orisha was inside with her elite cadre. Safe.

Arcadio had no idea how long he waited in that tree, probing the stillness for signs of whatever had summoned the entire force through the jungle. He found nothing. He realized he must not be looking hard enough and mentally scolded himself for failing the goddess in her hour of need.

At some point that seemed like hours later, the church doors opened, and Silva, the human head of security, stepped out, and with a single wave of his hand, informed the gathered force that whatever had caused the signal had been resolved. Arcadio returned to his patrol, nerves stuttering for the rest of the day.

It happened a few days later. And again a week after that. And again. And again.

The signal was always the same, as was the result. Each time it came, Arcadio was a half-step slower to respond. The crack widened every time he was summoned and there was no attack on the Hounfour. Religious faith only took him so far. It was possible it had only been as strong as it was because he had never met his goddess. Now that she was solid and living, her flaws were laid bare. He wasn't the only one. Though Diego never wavered, the source of Eugenia's amusement had become apparent. What had once been the goddess in danger slowly turned into the cries of a woman frightened of stillness. Ash Wednesday—Arcadio no longer thought of him as the Thousand Man—was not coming. He was never coming.

Santa Orisha rarely emerged from her lair. Even with the compound safely locked down in the remote forest, she was a prisoner. What was worse was that she was a self-incarcerated prisoner. Whatever danger Wednesday and the others represented, it was not equal to the danger in her mind. Though he responded to her calls, he no longer rushed to her side, and no longer waited for the enemy to reveal himself from the trees. Arcadio waited until the all clear was signaled, and then he would slip off into the trees to search for something else that wasn't there.

She left the Hounfour only to visit the nearest sunchamber within *el Labertino*. She habitually took the bulk of her force with her, despite the fact that the caverns were ostensibly safe, patrolled only by those loyal to the Priestess. The trip was a short one as well; the Hounfour was intended to be right by Santa Orisha's seat of power. Eugenia explained that the sun—the nexus, that was the term—was as close as it could be without undermining the bedrock upon which the Hounfour sat. Had it been possible to place it in the church itself, Santa Orisha would have done it.

Arcadio was often part of the vanguard of the descent into the Labyrinth. The caverns angled down into the freezing caves where pockets of air sat stale with nothing to stir it. The denizens of the caves, both animal and otherwise, made sounds, but they echoed through the endless caverns. The first time he had gone in, he understood the human word, "blind." He concentrated on the way the party moved the air, the currents hitting the walls and coming back. It was dim, but there was nothing to distract him from anything advancing. It would stand out like a beacon.

There were a few men left behind in the Hounfour, alert in case of an attack. They would not be expected to fight, but to blow up the whole place. Arcadio had felt the bombs wired to every building. He hadn't known what they were until he'd asked one of the humans, who laughed and made an explosion sound. When Arcadio kept waiting for an explanation, the human expounded. The bang was supposed to be loud enough that Orisha would be warned even if she was in the sunchamber deep underground.

After the warning, they would flee. They had a route planned, though Arcadio had never walked it. Even the escape plan was too dangerous to drill, as Santa Orisha neither wanted to be that far from the Hounfour or without her guards. They had to make do with maps. Arcadio knew those were practically useless. The Labyrinth was aptly named, deliberately built and rebuilt to baffle anyone who went into it in search of the sunchambers. The maps were a hopeless tangle of carved ruts, with routes marked first to the Condor's Nest, then to Ezcalli, Itzcoatl's fortress beneath Tenochtitlan. They would not be expected to go the whole way; the Priestess's men would come to them, called by Orisha in the same manner she called her men for help.

The tunnel wound downward into the earth. It was a relatively straight trip by the standards of the Labyrinth, with the side tunnels being present though not quite as large as the central one. Arcadio and Eugenia were in front, and they could easily walk side-by-side with room for several more. Arcadio was alert, though he did not expect danger.

Finding the sunchamber was not difficult underground, at least from the Hounfour. There was no sun in the sky, no warmth. So when it began to bloom ahead, in the deeper earth, they knew they were close. It was a strange warmth, as it was not precisely the revitalizing comfort of Axalik's one sun nor Tawa's three. It had a gritty, glassy quality, as though the heat itself were ready to shatter.

The sun blazed in the chamber, some thirty meters from every side of it. Arcadio had been in awe the first time he beheld it: he had felt these creations before on Tawa, known they were the work of the Priestess, but he had not seen one quite so large. It threw off light and heat in such force, the bakru instinctively quailed from it. Santa Orisha entered the chamber alone to be greeted by the Luminous Ones within. *Los Luminosos* were the only beings who could live in such close proximity, and they had been changed by it. They wore the shape of humans, though they were somehow brighter. Even though Arcadio had no idea what the word "bright" meant, it seemed to apply to these people. They gave way when Santa Orisha stood beneath the nexus and siphoned its power. It came in rings of blazing plasma, flooding her body and provoking the rapturous shuddering of the penitent.

When she was finished, her body fully charged, the expedition returned to the surface and she would retreat to her church. No matter that she was powerful enough to summon anything she liked from the sweep of worlds, Santa Orisha went to her chamber and locked herself in.

Arcadio still had a germ of his old faith stubbornly lingering after every test. He still believed that maybe, just maybe, there was something he was not understanding. He wasn't the naïve believer like Diego, who refused to even recognize any intimation of fault in the goddess. Arcadio was not yet ready to embrace the wry atheism of Eugenia. Not until Saltamontes.

The warning came when Arcadio was on patrol, as usual. When the insect flapped its wings, the call for help was far more desperate this time. The spike that went through him felt like the first time she had called. He knew that, no matter what had happened in the past, this time was real. This time, she was in danger.

Arcadio leapt off the branch where he had been watching the jungle. His wooden muscles bunched up, and shot him across the jungle floor in a powerful run. Every loping step flung him farther than any animal could have managed, and soon he could feel the wall encircling the Hounfour. There was no pop of automatic weapons, no screams, no shouts and cursing, no eldritch words.

In itself, this didn't mean anything. It was possible the attack had come as a surprise, the assassins having killed all of those outside before going in to finish off the goddess. Arcadio barely paused, leaping up to the top of the wall as easily as a cat, then down into the compound so he would not present too tempting a target. In the cool space between the wall of the church and the wall of the compound, where the ferns grew thick on the ground, he took stock.

The soldiers were going about their business. They had broken up and returned to their postings, some of them shaking their heads sadly. Arcadio couldn't help himself. He assumed human form, concentrated on altering his skin to give the appearance of clothes—humans could be very squeamish about that—and strode from the corner. One of the guards, a grizzled man named Zamora, looked up from his cigarette, blinking away the cottony threads of smoke. "Arcadio," he said by way of greeting.

"What was this? What happened?"

Zamora shook his head. "Saltamontes."

Arcadio knew the name. Saltamontes was one of their own, one of the Priestess's Familiars. In Arcadio's understanding of the power structure, this placed Saltamontes beneath Santa Orisha, though it was not a perfect division. His powers made him a scout, spy, and occasional messenger.

Arcadio knew instantly what had happened. Saltamontes had appeared somewhere within the compound and Santa Orisha raised the alarm. For one of her own people.

"I feel the same way," Zamora said.

Arcadio realized his features were running in frustration. "I... I..."

Zamora touched his shoulder, unusual as the humans tended to find the cool smoothness of bakru flesh disturbing. "I know, kid." Zamora stubbed his smoke out on the heel of his boot and went back to patrol.

Arcadio learned later that Saltamontes had appeared to announce the creation of a new Familiar, to replace the fallen Huracan. Orisha had turned the news of reinforcements—the news of strength—into a spiral of terror. When that happened,

Arcadio knew for a fact that the danger would never come. Before, he had thought there was nothing waiting in the jungle. After six years, he knew.

And on this particular day, he was set on appreciating the touch of this alien world that had become his home. If he was going to exist at the behest of a brittle madwoman, he might as well enjoy himself. Most of the bakru were back at the church at one of the ceremonies that now seemed meaningless to him. Usually, they alternated between missing the services in exchange for guard duty, or else it was used as a punitive measure. Arcadio volunteered for them.

"You found it finally," Eugenia remarked after he had raised a hand for the duty.

"Apparently, I did," he said.

Eugenia still went to the services, and Arcadio never had to ask her why. He knew she was not one to draw attention to herself.

That day, he was out in the woods with eight others, including poor, faithful Diego. No punishment in his case; the assignment had come about honestly. It was Diego's turn. He was one sector over, probably creeping through the undergrowth and tracking down every last monkey and bird that had the misfortune to rustle a leaf within a mile of the Hounfour, the whole time cursing the fate that kept him from honoring the goddess for the third time in a week.

Arcadio spent his time with his mind wandering. There had to be a way home. There was the obvious—getting Santa Orisha to open a portal and send him back to Tawa. That was unrealistic. She wouldn't give up one of her guards for no gain. She already believed she needed more than she had. No, the only way out would be to arrange some kind of transfer. There were other bakru through the Priestess's organization, attached to various members or floating as discrete units. One of these could be perfect. He could continue to serve the larger armature that had helped his people and not directly under the madwoman who jumped at emptiness.

Arcadio had not realized he'd wandered from his sector until he ran into the massive root structure of one of the largest trees in the area. He recognized it as being near the edge of the next sector over. Diego's. He turned to go, not in any particular hurry to do so. The worst thing that would happen would be Diego catching him patrolling the wrong place, and from there, hopeful exile to somewhere beyond the Amazon.

A sound stopped him. It was a sudden *chok*: a single hit and nothing beyond. Arcadio turned, every fiber in his body straining to feel the wind. He waited, listening in the soft cacophony of the jungle, but nothing came. He nearly dismissed the first sound, but something stopped him.

There was no insect coming through the portal with a whisper of help on its wings.

He paused again. Diego catching him would almost be worth it. Maybe this was his excuse.

Arcadio had a fairly good idea of where the sound came from, his skin getting the vibrations in ways an animal's never could. He zeroed in on it, slinking beneath the densest undergrowth, keeping a layer of papery leaves between him and the blankness of the sky. The source of the sound was farther away than it had initially seemed; noises had a way of doing that in the jungle.

Diego's body was lying at the foot of a tree, already losing coherence. Soon, he would be nothing but a fallen log. He was still identifiable, though the distinguishing marks were fading into cracked wood by the second. The wound was a chip through the center of the back, as though he had been speared right through the middle. His heartwood had been severed in two, and no bakru would live through that.

There was still no call from Orisha. No alarm.

Arcadio moved quicker now, staying in the undergrowth, straight for the Hounfour. Every ten meters or so he would pause and wait, concentrating on the feel of sounds against his skin. He grew closer and closer to the wall, until he saw them by the currents of air caressing their forms: a group of men crouched by the base of the wall, armed with machine guns. They had three thraxians with them, their lithe exoskeletons producing strange eddies in the vapor. The agile creatures made it up and over the wall with difficulty, attesting to how good a barrier it truly was.

Arcadio had to sound the alarm, but he couldn't do it. It wasn't fear that stopped him: it was responsibility. He had to know what they were doing before he could stop it. He put a trunk between him and the hit squad and quickly scaled the tree. From that vantage, he felt the thraxians alight into the courtyard. They killed five men without a sound, their insectile limbs concealing the still corpses in the undergrowth.

There were only a few men in the courtyard, all of whom were still unaware of the incursion, and now the hit squad outnumbered them. The bakru were out in the forest on patrol or else they were in the church with Santa Orisha, singing her praises. The thraxians returned to the wall, and reached down, pulling the first man over. A second followed, and then a third and fourth. The men dropped packs and fished out bricks of plastic explosive, which they began to affix to the church. It was a crude attack, but it would work. Kill or cripple everyone inside, which included Santa Orisha. Then the thraxians could make short work of whatever survived.

Arcadio could wait no longer. He climbed up to a higher branch, then ran along the surface. He no longer cared about making noise. He only needed to make the jump.

He heard popping sounds, felt the spray of wood from the branch below. The men outside the wall had seen him and were firing. He broke cover and leapt.

The wall was impossibly far, but he made it, his wooden body clacking off the stone. The force knocked him off the top and threw him into the bushes behind the church. He heard shouting, this time in Spanish. That was the sounds of his allies spotting the enemy. He hoped his men would last.

One of the soldiers, who had been kneeling, placing a bomb against one of the corners of the church, whirled around with his gun. Arcadio pounced on him and tore the front of his throat away with a single bite. He willed the change, and was only halfway turned when he ripped the bomb off the building and flung it over the wall as far as he could.

He turned, ready to get the next bomb. He found one of the soldiers in his way. The man was huge. He got off a couple shots, the silenced weapon making distant cracks, and Arcadio felt each one, chipping away at his flesh. Nothing important there. He got his hands on the soldier, and that was all he needed. A moment later, the man's corpse fell into the dirt.

Arcadio took his jaguar form again, loping around the back of the church to the other bomb. He ran into the other two soldiers first, and killed both with swipes of his claws. The bomb was similarly flung into the jungle. The men screamed, and this time, there was thunder. The trees cracked and a shower of dirt and rock came raining down on the compound from beyond the wall. The bakru felt it through his body, a crack that wanted to throw him to the dirt and keep him there.

Arcadio didn't care. He flung himself at the first thraxian he felt. What he knew of them was academic; he had never actually faced one. The files had said they were fast, but he was not prepared for the alien grace the creature had as it scuttled aside from the first attack and hit him across the body with a flick of its claws. It was incredibly strong, sending him tumbling across the dirt to slam into the rock wall. Arcadio got to his feet and bared his teeth. The thraxian smiled, licking its strange, almost human teeth.

Arcadio braced for the thing's charge, but the attack came from the wall. One of the other thraxians pounced, batting him around like a toy. Arcadio tried to give as good as he got, but it was a losing battle. He managed to get his mouth around the hand and he felt something snap, tasted the caustic blood, but even that was short lived as he was thrown aside into the wall of the church. Getting up was more difficult this time. His body felt soft. The thraxian's barbed tail flicked, as though challenging him to attack.

He snarled. He was on his feet, though far from stable, and his flesh was covered in horrible rents from bullets and claws. The raw wood of his body was showing through.

The church doors boomed open. A new chorus of automatic weapons erupted, and both thraxians Arcadio could see whipped their masklike heads around to see what had arrived. Arcadio didn't bother to look. He saw only an opening.

He bounded forward. He felt like he was running through thick mud. His body wanted nothing more than to give up. He refused that temptation, launching himself at the distracted thraxian. He bore it to the ground, getting his mouth around the neck, and sinking his teeth in. The creature thrashed and squealed, its claws and bladed tail opening up new wounds on the bakru. Arcadio barely felt these, concentrating only on crushing the creature's throat.

He heard Santa Orisha's voice, and it thrummed through his body like it had not since the first time he had heard her speak. It carried more power than the explosion. She was speaking arcane words, and Arcadio felt them inside and out, echoing through this place and something far away. He felt more creatures around him, heard more screams and hoots, sounds both human and alien. He did not bother to concentrate on them, reducing his world to just one other. He would crush this creature's throat.

He felt a hand on his back.

"Bakru." It was the goddess herself. Her hand was soft, and unmistakably warm. The touch was light, but the hand was heavy with power. She was utterly calm in this moment. No quaver marred her voice, and he felt nothing else around him. She had already mercilessly eliminated all of those who stood against her, as a goddess should. "Arcadio," she said. "Kill him."

He obeyed, more from the shock of hearing her say his name. He had not ever expected her to remember, let alone to tell one jaguar from another. He did not know where the strength came from, whether it was a gift from her touch or merely the inspiration of obedience to a goddess returned. His jaws snapped shut like a trap, and with a loud crack, the thraxian's head came loose. The creature was still, its blood sizzling in the soil. Only then did Arcadio allow himself to collapse.

The move took place a week later. The location in the Amazon was known to the Twins, and thus was no longer of any use. Orisha remarked, one day deep in the Labyrinth, that they had been lucky. The hit squad was probably little more than a scouting party. Diego had likely spotted them and they had been forced to kill him. Knowing that once he was discovered, the Hounfour would be moved, they had gone in with what they had. "Not enough," she had said with a smile, as she touched Arcadio's shoulder.

Arcadio was still wounded, but he could scarcely feel it. Not when he was by Orisha's side. After his heroism at the defense of the Hounfour, he had been elevated to part of her personal guard. He was the youngest member, but he had some measure of respect. It wasn't every bakru who could lay claim to saving the mistress and killing a thraxian all in the same day.

After a week of travel, they emerged from the Labyrinth into the blinding sun. When Kisin had found them on the second day, he helped move them along on waves of rock. Another god for Arcadio to marvel over, though he was plainly lesser than the goddess.

The Atacama Desert stretched out on three sides, with the Pacific on the third. The wind whipped inland, tracing the contours of the sand. Arcadio could feel the world for miles in every direction. "Here," said Santa Orisha, shading her eyes with her hand. "This will do."

Kisin, sighed. "Very well."

And with a whisper and a word, he pulled a new Hounfour from the bedrock.

Arcadio never left his goddess's side. Her fear had been justified, and he was the fool for doubting her. Never again. The Thousand Man would come again, and when he did, Arcadio would be ready.

Until There Was Nothing Left

THERE WAS NO SKY IN the underworld, though one could be forgiven for thinking there was. The roiling sooty clouds occasionally parted enough to glimpses of something that might be a ceiling, though it certainly was no sky. Anansi hardly looked up anymore, not after the years he spent learning to enter, navigate, and eventually master this place. Even if this were the first time, if he was utterly unfamiliar with the mysteries of the deadlands, he would not have taken the time to so much as glance. Because he was going home.

Before he had changed, before he had been forged by the Lion and tempered by the Butterfly, he would have traveled by air, most likely. Packed into a plane for the long series of flights from Japan to the southern tip of Africa. Even that was slower than a walk through the underworld, for those who knew how to traverse it. He fought the urge to call it *Diyu*, as the Butterfly had. He was away from her and it was time to reassert himself once again. He would use his word for it, and eventually it would feel natural.

He appeared to be walking along a dirt path. The sand at his feet would be thick, black, and coarse, as though from a volcanic beach. It was hard-packed; his feet never sinking more than an inch or so. On either side, there was darkness. It was not the dark of a closed eye, but the dark of absolute void, to all appearances as though the world fell away on either side of him. The winding trail he walked was a pathway through this nothing, supported by nothing, coming from nothing, going toward nothing.

He knew there was a way to descend deeper into the underworld. Sometimes, the path would turn into stairs, descending into the black. Down there, the underworld grew stranger still, as the human concepts of mind and memory were burned away into the more primal stuff of the beyond. It was a useful place to go for power, but not for simple travel. Staying near the caul was best.

Every fifteen to twenty paces, the path branched, and when it did, the destination would reveal itself as though emerging from a black fog. The ground would change, not all at once but gradually, as though formed out of the same material, compacted and molded into a recognizable shape. In this case, the coarse sand had become a hillside. The grass was green, but it was muted and washed out until it looked to be under a thin coating of ash. The trees as well, even though the leaves on them promised a heathy and robust plant. Headstones moved out in orderly rows, and if Anansi were to stop, he could easily read the inscriptions. The stones themselves were among the most solid objects in the underworld, as they existed on both sides.

The shadows that walked between the rows, that paused in front of the graves, to genuflect with the placement of offerings—those were people. More accurately, they were souls, barely glimpsed as they passed through a place of death. Far more solid were the souls who had made their homes there. When he passed, they saw him, and after a moment to understand what he was, fled into hiding, either back into their graves, or into the black mausoleums dotting the surface. The changes in those buildings on this side were apparent: the doors that appeared as mouths, the grasping hands along the eaves, the bones inlaid along the surfaces, these were how dead and living alike saw them in their dreams.

Anansi ignored the maggot-white ghosts scattering from him. He had no use for them, at least at the moment. He merely wanted to continue his journey unmolested. He kept to the border of the cemetery, and soon the ground turned back into volcanic sand, and the graveyard was engulfed in the black mists of the underworld once again.

The next thing he saw along the path was a light up ahead. The shadows swirled about it like living things. As Anansi grew closer and the fog parted to reveal a small room, opened by violence. It looked like a wall had been sliced by a gargantuan blade, a bare bulb illuminating a scene of horror. The ghost, its skin dripping in sticky webs of ectoplasm was on its knees and begging in an otherwise empty room. The shadow behind it was stabbing, and black blood splashed on the walls, ceiling, and floor. The ghost was by definition dead, but likely it did not know that, even if the murder took place years ago. Thinking was difficult without a brain, and ghosts had left theirs behind with the rest of their bodies. For this ghost, there was only the murder, and it would be trapped in the moment of its trauma, for as long as there was any memory linking the act to the surface world. Then it would fall deeper into the underworld and find a new existence as a creature of pure death.

Anansi turned around the base of the building, scarcely paying attention to where the wood and plaster walls gave way to a grooved material not unlike an insect's exoskeleton. He passed along the border of this moment of death, and found the path once again. The light was swallowed up, and the Necromancer continued.

He passed through the underworld like this, from cemeteries, and crime scenes, and battlefields, all the places where death had scarred the underworld. Some of the places were crystal clear, the atrocities either recent or so awful that they persisted for years in an untouched state. Others were being reclaimed by the sand, falling apart and sinking into the black.

There was a time when all Anansi could do was gape at the stark beauty he found on the other side. Now, it was nothing. He was going home, but home was not a place.

Pretoria was where he was born, where he lived until the Lion came for him and offered power. He was returning to Pretoria, but that was not home. Not precisely. Home was a person.

He had left her behind when he went with the Lion, returning to her too infrequently. But after he left Khem for Shi Jie, he had not spoken to her and he couldn't ask his family to do it. They didn't know about her.

They knew who she was; she was their maid, after all. They just had no idea the heart of their youngest son belonged to her. They would have reacted with horror to find out their son loved a *kaffir*. He winced at the mere thought of the word. He had used it without thought in his younger days, but now he saw its thorns. Now, years had passed and they had not spoken. Aside from the mundane concerns of his parents, there was the real power over him he would have given the Butterfly had she known of his attachment to a mortal. He guessed than many of the others, Apprentice, Familiar, and Magus alike had someone hidden away. Immortality would be lonely otherwise.

Before he had gone, Zara Iblisa, the Lion's heir, had explained to him the rules. Her Afrikaans was flawless, but her accent, as it was with many of the elders, was a muddle. There was a time when Anansi would have looked down upon her for being native African, but his eyes had been opened, and he hung on every word. She told him to never reveal his name, which was something not even she knew. Only the Lion himself did, a failsafe against Anansi ever betraying him. And then, Zara had paused.

She pursed her lips, considering carefully. "And if there is someone, a mortal, whom you love, you mustn't speak of her either." Her eyes, almond in shape and color, searched his. He felt the meaning behind it, knew she spoke from experience.

He nodded. "I'll keep quiet."

He had. While he had expected the interrogations to be obvious, they were not. Not a single one of the Butterfly's minions ever sat him down and demanded to know. Instead they made him feel safe, helped him drop his guard, and probed with the kinds of harmless questions any friends would. Her gambler, Wei Lai, had done the most in this regard, keeping up a constant chatter during their games of mahjongg. As Wei spoke of his own experiences, Anansi listened, realizing they were probably all made up. He, in turn, offered nothing.

He kept his love safe.

Anansi was, after all, a danger to the Butterfly now. Trained in Necromancy, he would be in a prime position to replace her in the League should she ever be killed. And yet, she still trained him. It was an odd arrangement the Magi of the League had. The treaties, the agreements, the unofficial power the mentor gained, all of these things made the arrangement worth it. A potential ally in a rival camp, a source of information, even something so prosaic as a friend. They would not want to admit it, but the tie between mentor and student could be stronger than that between Magus and Apprentice. The Lion and the Butterfly were the most ancient of allies too, their association born hundreds of years ago in the Shadow War, so when the Lion sent Anansi to be trained as a Necromancer, the Butterfly was happy to oblige.

And now he was returning to his love, to Nkosazana, a name that once sounded alien that had turned to music. He could take her away from South Africa, settle someplace farther north in Khem: Morocco, maybe. Egypt. Somewhere where they could live as man and wife. He would give her enough of his magic to arrest her aging, and they would be together.

This, too, was forbidden. Not because she was black and he was white: the League was above those petty concerns. He was an Apprentice, and making a Familiar, no matter the motive, was against the rules. If he were a Magus, it would be different. Children were also against the rules, though he planned to disobey that as well. The fact was, Anansi could not live without Nkosazana. Not only was he at peace with that fact, he celebrated it.

He moved past the scenes of death, each one looking more and more like home in the bits of architecture that remained unchanged by the pervasive brush of the underworld. He knew the way to Pretoria even though he had never walked it. The Butterfly had taught him to follow the signs in the bleeding places, and he did that now, finding comfort and familiarity in death.

He had changed during his long absence, it was not just that he was far more powerful. His body had become altered. It was impossible to become a conduit for magic without the physical form reacting in some way. He had been frightened at first when his hair fell out and his already pale skin grayed. He had always been thin, but now he was little more than skin and bones. He knew that his newfound appearance wouldn't stop Nkosazana from loving him, though a tiny voice kept insisting it might. It was the one thing that tied his stomach up in knots and kept him from running the whole way through the underworld. If she would reject him—she wouldn't, she couldn't—he wanted to live in the beautiful world in which she loved him for as long as he could.

It wasn't his face that made her love him. If anything, the mere fact that he was white was a bigger barrier to their love than any subsequent change. She had probably seen him as merely that: a color, in much the same way as he had not seen her at all. She had to get a glimpse inside to see anything worth her time.

He was still Johannes Voorhoeve in those days, and she was Nkosazana Mbeki. He had taken the name Anansi when the Lion took him as an Apprentice, and Nkosazana would need a name as well. He smiled at the thought. Her name would become his alone to know, and she would be the only one to speak his. A secret for them, and them alone.

The Voorhoeve family were well-to-do, with a beautiful house on a hill in the affluent suburb of Waterkloof. Johannes was the only one of the boys still living at home. He probably should have already moved on, but he told his parents he was trying to figure out what he wanted to do. The truth was he knew already. He wanted to be a painter. His father was not going to accept that, and so Johannes was stuck in a form of stasis. All three of his elder brothers were doing the family proud, moving into law and business. Johannes was the young one. The fragile one. The strange one.

His father used friends and acquaintances to get his odd son jobs, and Johannes would go for a time before inevitably losing interest. He never quit; he just stopped showing up. Though he didn't know it at the time, the only reason the behavior was tolerated was because he was a Voorhoeve. Ironic, then, how much he wanted to be someone else.

Whenever he could, he sneaked off to the cemeteries around town, and spent his time walking the rows. When he found a name he liked, a stone with an interesting offering, an inscription that caught his eye, there he would settle. He would take his sketchbook from the pocket of his jacket and get to drawing. He drew a picture of the person as he imagined they appeared in life. Sometimes these were happy scenes surrounded by loved ones, other times they were depictions of the person's final days. In the early days, he always lined them up with the quality of the stone: a rich grave got a nice picture, a poor grave the opposite. Later, he started exploring the irony between these, and he found the truth. After all, he was wealthy but wasn't particularly happy and was definitely unsatisfied. When he was finished, he would tear the page from the notebook, and put a rubbing of a portion of the stone behind the picture. He had no idea what he was going to do with them. He knew only that he had the irresistible compulsion to keep making them. He imagined, at some point, that he would wake up and be done, wrap them all up and put them aside. The project would tell him when it was finished and he could find something new. Yet no matter how many he made, there was no decrease in the desire; if anything, each one made him want to do exponentially more.

He had reams upon reams of them, hidden behind his bookcase, away from the judgment of his family. His father would find it a waste of time, his mother would be shocked by the morbidity. His brothers probably would just laugh and destroy them. He lived with a gnawing dread that someone would find them, see them, and mock him. Call them stupid, shallow, any number of things. He was an idiot, wasting his time with fake eulogies for the dead. They grew to hold the titillating thrill of pornography, even if they were anything but.

It was with an intense horror that he came into his room one afternoon to find the housekeeper staring at them. He didn't know her name, merely that she was relatively new, and much younger than Benya, who had retired a few months ago. Her head was wrapped up in a scarf and she wore the white costume Johannes's mother preferred the help to wear. At that moment, Johannes saw nothing more than the white clothes and brown skin of the woman.

"What are you doing?"

She jumped, put a hand to her heart. The fear might have abated. He was the white man here, and in scaring the young woman—she looked to be no older than nineteen—he had asserted his dominance. He didn't feel dominant. In fact, he felt weaker than ever, the fear consuming him raw. As for the girl, he didn't see much beyond the eyes that had been perusing his work. He searched them for some sign of amusement. He couldn't imagine another reaction. "Mr. Johannes, I'm sorry. I was dusting," she gestured at the feather duster sitting on a shelf, forgotten until that moment. "I saw the papers. I didn't want them to be bent."

Johannes felt the heat in his cheeks. He could barely look at the woman, the author of his shame, and instead snatched the papers from her hand. "Who told you to look at them?"

"No one, sir." She was silent, and if she had remained so, she might never have revealed herself. "I was going to put them aside, but I saw the name on the one on the top. Liwa."

Johannes looked at the papers in his hand. They had been shuffled through, that much was plain. One of the older ones was on top now. Liwa's picture wasn't immediately visible, but he remembered it. He had drawn it yesterday.

"Liwa," she repeated. "It's a Xhosa name."

"A what?" He was momentarily baffled, forcing him to look at her. Her face was downcast. She was frightened still, but there was an undercurrent of wonder. She was pretty. No, that wasn't enough. She was beautiful. He blinked, wondering how many times he had seen her without noticing her face.

"Xhosa," she said. "African. Black African."

"He was buried in the black cemetery," he managed.

"You went to the black cemetery?"

He nodded. Of course. He was running out of people who were close by. "Why did you look at them?"

"The name," she said. "And then I looked at them because they were beautiful."

He swallowed. "Beautiful?"

She looked up then. Her eyes were large and brown, delicately slanted. "Yes."

"You liked them?"

"Very much. Why did you hide them?"

"So no one would look at them." He chuckled then, and she stifled a laugh of her own.

"I'm sorry, sir. I won't do it again."

"Johannes."

"What?"

"My name, it's Johannes."

"I know. Mr. Johannes."

"No. No 'mister.'" He stood there, not certain what to say to her. Not certain if there was anything to say. She was in his room. She had just seen the most private thing he had ever put down. It was though she had leafed through his soul. And she had found it beautiful. He would have been tempted to call it flattery, yet he heard no lie in her voice.

He swallowed, and turned to go. Then he realized he was still holding the sheaf of paper in his hand. He held them out to the young woman, the most lovely he had ever seen close up. "Would you put these back?"

She accepted them reverently. But it was not a respect born of fear, but rather the respect of the objects themselves. In another situation, Johannes might have read her differently, but in that moment, there was nothing at all between them. He could see into her, and she could see into him.

"May I look at them? The others, I mean?"

"Um. Yes. If you like."

"Thank you."

He swallowed again, thinking it was time to go. "What's your name?"

"Nkosazana."

It took him several weeks to say it properly. He loved the sounds of it, the pleasing exoticism of the syllables. Most importantly, he loved it because it belonged to her. Was her. He knew the power of the name before the Lion explained it to him, because of the power of her name.

The romance started slowly. Her seeking him out and shyly asking if she could see the newest ones. As time went on, he left them out for her to find. She was beautiful, she loved his drawings, but she was black. He knew, from his years of education, from the things his parents and teachers said, from the institutions of government, that blacks were not truly people. He couldn't feel anything for her. And, the doubting voices whispered back, there was no way she felt anything for him.

Yet she was never far from his mind. He found himself wondering what she would think of a figure as he sketched it. He felt the butterflies in his stomach when he set out a new one for her to find. He felt no greater pleasure than the smile she gave him after looking.

He didn't clearly remember the kiss until he was already in the midst of it. In some recollections, he leaned in first. In others, it was her. She had just seen a new one, another name he had gotten from the black cemetery, and her face lit up. She didn't smile exactly; it was more an expression of wonder. In her face, he saw what he had drawn. It had given her happiness, but it was tinged with sadness and wonder. And then, he was kissing her, and her him. He felt her hand, warm and dry, on his cheek, her mouth soft and insistent. When they parted, only for an instant, close enough so that he only breathed the air that had been within her moments ago, he knew his life as he envisioned it was at an end.

And he could not have been happier.

The romance continued in secret. Stolen moments whenever they could be managed. To make up for her lost labor, Johannes helped her with the housework, hiding his participation from his parents. This worked well until he overheard his mother complaining about Nkosazana's sudden inability to clean the bathroom. It was the hardest he'd worked in his life, and apparently a lot harder to meet his mother's standards in this arena than he thought. He joked later with Nkosazana that at least his mother was consistent: she was judgmental about everything. Nkosazana covered her mouth when she laughed, her eyes glittering. The work was worth every moment he could be with his love. He wished they could be outside together, but to do so would have endangered her, and he could not be so selfish.

He showed her one of his recent works, and she smiled, though it was not the smile he had become accustomed to.

"What is it?"

"It's that… you don't have the reality to draw a black person."

"I thought you liked them."

"I do. I was surprised at first that you would have any empathy at all. I saw that you meant to draw it well and honestly, but your ignorance got in the way."

"Ignorance?" he teased her.

She giggled. "You heard me."

"Then teach me."

She did. She told him stories. Her own, her family's, her friends'. He pestered her for details and as he got them, he listened and understood in growing horror what he had been a part of for so many years. The injustice. The cruelty. The evil. Nkosazana showed him the world beyond the walls of his house, and she did it not to lecture, but to make him a better man.

He had to marry her. He even proposed, though the ring was purely hypothetical at that point. She turned him down with frustrated tears. They couldn't live in Pretoria or anywhere else in South Africa, and getting out would be hell. There was no way, even for the son of a prominent family. They were trapped.

This changed when the Lion found him. Johannes was grateful to Nkosazana for the lessons, as the old Johannes might have dismissed the Lion as a mere *kaffir*. Might have missed the aura of power, as no black man could have such. The Lion might have immolated him then in a sheet of flames at the slightest sign of disrespect, and in Johannes's mind, he would have deserved no less.

The Lion appeared in his life without warning. Finding Johannes scribbling at the newest rubbing in the black cemetery, trying to use what Nkosazana had taught him about reality, the Lion had spoken. He had heard about the young white man who frequented the graveyards and was curious. Johannes, emboldened by the praise Nkosazana had given, did something he never would have otherwise. He handed over the piece of paper to the large man speaking to him in a foreign accent.

The Lion looked it over, nodded, and returned the paper. Then he offered Johannes power. Johannes might have laughed, but the Lion was serious, and the man seemed as solid, as constant, as a mountain. This was what Johannes had been hoping for without knowing it had been there to hope for. This was what he needed to make his life with Nkosazana real. He nodded. And when the other man walked away, noticed that in his footprints were nuggets of gold.

Johannes started his training in the basics, the Lion meeting him in the black cemetery and then traveling beyond. Johannes told Nkosazana about it every day. She thought he was teasing her at first, until he showed her the few minor tricks he had learned. The affair continued through all of this, and Johannes remembered why he was doing it. It was for her. It was all for her.

Then came the day he was ready to depart for Japan. He found her in the living room, cleaning the windows that looked out over the grove of jacaranda trees. He explained that he had to leave soon.

"Why?"

"Because... What I'm learning isn't taught here. It's in Japan... They call it Shi Jie. That whole area, Shi Jie."

"You can't learn it here?"

He shook his head.

She went to him then, unafraid, even though his mother was in the house. She was wearing rubber gloves, and he felt them on the back of his neck when she wrapped her arms around him. "Then go. Learn. And come back to me."

"I'll never be apart from you."

"Romantic fool," she said, and kissed him.

"When I come back, we'll leave. Anywhere in Khem... in Africa you want. Somewhere far away where we can be together."

"As man and wife."

He kissed her. "As man and wife," he said the words so soft he heard them only as a breath. They stayed together as long as they dared, the tears on their cheeks joining into a single stream.

Leaving that day was the hardest thing he had ever had to do. And now, after years of study, he was returning. He was returning in a way that he could never have imagined, through the underworld, passing by the reflections of places kissed by death, toward a home he would barely recognize, and a woman he could never forget. He had sacrificed for her, but he had grown to love the power in its own right. He hoped he had not changed too much. He would know soon.

He paused at one of the scenes. The rocky ground, the trees, they looked more or less correct. The corner of the shanty, with the panels that looked like human skin stretched taut had the sting of familiarity. The faceless men in armor swarming a fallen and frightened man reminded Anansi of a story Nkosazana had once told him. He stepped over the ghost, cowering beneath his attackers.

The ghost hissed, and a chattering came from its teeth. Anansi turned, cocking his head at this development. The ghost had been a man at one time, and the injuries he had suffered in death were apparent across his bloodless flesh. He was ivory white in places, and in others, he was more grayish, like burned paper. The features, from what Anansi could see beneath the wounds, were African.

Ghosts did not quite speak as they no longer had minds to make words. The soul was pure feeling; it was the brain that focused the desire into higher thought. When he first learned to talk to ghosts, he was frightened of the raw emotion and the alien way they had. But soon he learned to translate the body language, the environmental effects, and the context of the haunting. Now, he almost heard them speak.

The ghost crawled forward, its form stuttering against the shadows of its attackers. It gnashed suddenly sharp teeth and stared at Anansi with black eyes. *Stranger. You don't belong here and yet you are here.*

"I am a Necromancer," Anansi said. He spoke another word, and with a wave of his hand, the attackers dissolved into wisps of oily smoke.

The ghost's eyes widened. It chattered its teeth and moved away. *Help me, stranger. I need vengeance before I can rest.*

"If it's a deal you want to make, ghost, I'll hear it. But not yet. I'll return for you, and when the time comes, we'll talk."

No! Stranger, you must—

Anansi ignored the howling spirit. There was nothing it could do to harm him. He stepped through the wall of the shanty, and emerged into the bright light of the world.

Anansi winced and pulled his hood farther down his face, and put on his pair of dark sunglasses. He wrapped the long coat around himself—regardless of the temperature, he was always a

little cold now—and walked out into the slum. He was a strange
sight: a pale man in black stalking between the shacks, but he was
not bothered. Those who approached soon hesitated and ran off.
Anansi never lifted a finger, never made a threat. He didn't have
to. He was grateful for this: there was no joy to be had in hurting
someone who could not defend himself.

He found his way to the edge of the slum, and began the long
walk home. He spoke to no one along the way. The magic that
had changed him, that deadened his nerves, cooled his blood,
and prolonged his life, had also taken the fatigue from him. The
walk that would have been impossible in his mortal days was now
merely an inconvenience. He probably could have found a place
of death even closer, but he wanted the time to think of what he
would tell his love.

After the hours and hours of walking, he had no ideas beyond,
"I'm home."

As his footsteps crushed a carpet of fallen purple flowers, he
knew he was nearly there. A nearly solid canopy of jacaranda trees
enfolded him, and he could see the house on the hill peeking
between the boughs every now and again. His steps quickened.
He should have kept his head down, though he had grown thinner,
paler, and he no longer had hair or eyebrows to speak of, he was
more recognizable here than anywhere else on earth. There were
still people who knew Johannes Voorhoeve, the strange graveyard-
obsessed black sheep who had left suddenly and never written or
called. That name, and those who knew it, were dangerous. He
could not lower his head, as there was a chance, no matter how
slim, of catching sight of Nkosazana. His old house, a Spanish-
style manor the color of baked clay, gave nothing up. She would be
inside somewhere, maybe even cleaning his room and wondering
when he would be back. He felt another twinge—he wished he
could have written her, but it would have been too dangerous. He

now had the rest of his eternal life to make certain she never felt unsafe or unloved again.

The trees thinned a bit as he neared the crest of the hill. The front door opened. A woman came out, and Anansi's heart actually hurt in his chest. All he saw was the smooth, chocolate brown skin and the white maid's uniform. He started to run, and it wasn't until he was up and over the outside wall of his home that he realized this woman was not Nkosazana. She was shorter, rounder. She had none of Nkosazana's delicate beauty.

The woman turned to see him coming up the pathway. She opened her mouth to scream, but her body had other plans. She fainted dead away on the stoop. Anansi caught her only barely, setting her down gently on the front steps, keeping her head from cracking open on the stones. He peered at her face. He'd never seen this woman before.

He stepped inside the house. The foyer was as he remembered it, with the umbrella stand and the coatrack, waiting for the Voorhoeves as they went outside. His mother's coat was there, and he could already smell her perfume. It felt like a hug. He hadn't missed his mother while he had been away, yet now, smelling her, he did. He looked through the other coats, for Nkosazana's. It was beige, and the nicest thing she owned, bought as a Christmas gift a year before Anansi left. His mother had gotten it, she said to be nice, but Anansi knew it was so that there wouldn't be a threadbare eyesore on the hooks by the front door.

The coat was not there.

Had she been fired? His mind spun helplessly at the imagined crimes that could have cost Nkosazana her job. Or had they hired more help? Seemed like the kind of frivolous waste of money his father never would have tolerated. It was possible she had a different coat, but he couldn't imagine her affording one nor of his parents getting her another while the first was in decent shape. Anansi stalked through his former home, searching for Nkosazana.

He stepped into the living room and found his mother, sitting in her chair, reading by the light from the window. She shivered, pulling the afghan from the back of the chair and wrapping it around her shoulders. The motion made her look up and she saw Anansi in the doorway. She looked older than he remembered. Shrunken and pale.

She choked off the scream, her hands going to her mouth. Her eyes searched him, and the slow relief of recognition bled into her features. "Johannes?" she whispered. The name burned through him with an electric charge.

"Hello, mother."

She stood up, ready to cross the room and embrace him, but something stopped her. She wrapped the afghan around her closer. "What... happened?"

He had told them he was leaving the country to study in France. The Lion had been good enough to provide him with enough fake documentation to prove he was anywhere he liked. "I'm fine," he said.

"You look... Are you all right?" His mother was still stunned. He knew that snapping her out of it would be impossible as long as he strung her along. She was as fragile a woman as Anansi's father had made her.

"Nkosazana," he said.

She frowned, momentarily forgetting his odd appearance. "What?"

"Nkosazana Mbeki. The maid. The old maid... The *previous* maid. The one when I was here."

"What about her?"

"Where is she? Did you fire her?"

"Why do you care?"

"Mother, please. Where is she?"

"She's just a—"

"Mother!"

His mother flinched, the hand once again going to her mouth. She wasn't used to being talked to like that, least of all by her shy youngest son. The one they thought was weak. She straightened up, and defiantly, "She's dead."

"Dead?"

"Murdered," his mother said. He didn't miss the spark of cruelty in her eyes when she said the word. She seemed to have gone whiter too, the blood leaving her cheeks until she was as pale as flour.

He repeated what she said, horrified and breathless.

The moment had passed, the vicious glint in his mother's eyes faded away, and it would have been easy to believe he had imagined it in the first place. When she spoke again, it was softly, gently. "Johannes, what's the matter? It was a tragedy, but you know how they are. She was going home..."

Johannes barely heard what his mother was saying, his brain taking the salient points and filling in the gaps that politesse left. Nkosazana had been attacked, probably by white men. Raped. Murdered. Thrown away like garbage. He could only imagine the barest edge of her pain and fear and would have cut any part of him off to spare her that. No one was caught. No one was punished. Not yet.

"Johannes, are you all right?"

He looked up, and his mother was blurry. He blinked, and felt icy tears on his cheeks. "What?"

"Are you all right? You weren't... *fond* of the girl, were you?"

"I was in love with her. I *am* in love with her."

His mother gasped again, but Anansi no longer cared. Her last connection to him was gone. There was nothing for him in the house, but there was something in the cemetery. She was waiting for him. He would keep her consigned to the underworld not one second longer than necessary. He didn't want to think of how many times she had been forced to relive the attack. How much pain she had endured. That thought put wind at his back. He sprinted to the cemetery, never once pausing to catch breath he barely needed anymore.

The black cemetery was little more than a hillside a short way from the shanties. Had he known, he could have skipped the trip home entirely. Had he known, he never would have left. Except that she was killed doing what she did every day. In leaving, he had been given the tools to undo the harm. He could not have prevented the attack, but he could heal it.

A few people walked the irregular rows looking at the markers. Most of those were wood and scrap, carved or painted with the cheapest of materials. As Anansi passed, the people exchanged frightened looks and moved off, though whether it was because Anansi was a white man or whether the price of magic was that apparent, he would never know. He barely paid attention, hunting through the names on the markers for the one that mattered most.

He saw several that he had found before, old subjects of his drawings. He gave those the barest of a nod, in thanks for their assistance to the understanding of death. Without them, he might not have ever been given the power that he would now use to save his love.

As he hunted for her name, he tried to stamp out the persistent gnaw of fear in his belly. The Butterfly had taught him how to summon ghosts from the other side; it was one of the most basic aspects of the Art they shared. She had impressed upon him that ghosts were born from unfinished business. Others could be brought over, but they tended to fade away, bit by bit. Spirits were desire incarnate, and without that, they went on to a place where they could no longer be touched.

Nkosazana would have unfinished business. She would have lingering desire. Love. She would want him, would be waiting for him to return. He could summon her, anchor her with an object, and she would be beside him forever. And the best part was that there was nothing to stop him having a Servitor the way there was for a Familiar. Apprentices were expected to create and maintain creatures like this. A ghost at his side would be the epitome of normality to someone like him. They would live as man and wife after all.

He moved through the rows, reading the names off the wood in the dying light of the day. The cemetery emptied out, but no one ever tried to tell him to move with it. As the sky turned red, then faded to blue, he continued his hunt. Until he found her.

At the very edge, near the crest of the hill, he found a wooden marker in the shape of a cross and hung with a few flowers. She had been buried beside other members of her clan. NKOSAZANA MBEKI 1947–1968. She had died the year after he left. All that time he had spent thinking about her, wishing he had called, and she was already cold and dead in the ground. He knelt, touching the reddish earth with the palm of his gray hand. The sorrow welled up and he knew he'd soon be helplessly wracked with sobs. He fought it.

Grief was for those who did not have mastery over death.

He straightened and he spoke the words the Butterfly had taught him. They fell from his mouth like spiderwebs, sinking into the dirt where Nkosazana's bones waited. Her soul would still be connected to those bones until they turned to dust, and would form a conduit between this place and the next. The words, soft as a caress but strong as steel chains, pulled the spirit from the other side. He felt her at the end of his will, somewhere out in the black. He wished he could add other words, other tones, to comfort her. He knew she was likely reliving her torment, and now being pulled to parts unknown. She wouldn't know it was him until she saw him, and until then, was probably frightened. He could alter nothing. Necromancy was power, not subtlety.

Nkosazana was beautiful even in death. Most of those killed by violence bore the scars of the act upon their souls. The cause of death was right there, the poor devil never able to escape it. Nkosazana was unblemished. Her skin had darkened to a deep ebony, and her eyes glittered like onyx. She wore a long gown of purest white. She looked, to Anansi, like a goddess.

"Nkosazana?" he whispered.

She floated, the fluttering edges of her gown drifting into wisps of white smoke. She did not precisely speak, but he felt the recognition and love flooding from the specter. Her voice sounded like wind rustling the jacaranda trees of his home. *Johannes.*

"I'm so sorry, my love. I wish I could have saved you."

I know. I love you. I am at peace.

"You don't have to be. I'm here now. I can bring you across. You can be with me."

No, my love. I need to be dead, so the pain will go away. I will wait for you on this side, and we can be together some day.

"You don't understand. I don't age anymore. I won't die until someone kills me."

I was killed.

"I know. I'm sorry. But I'm not human anymore. Not really. A human who tried to kill me... he might as well try to kill death itself. I won't die soon."

I will wait.

"That's too long!" He peered at the ghost, floating before him, shedding the fitful light of death. He saw that it wasn't just her gown, but her flesh also faded away into smoke. It was as though she had been drawn in charcoal by a great artist, and then a finger had been smeared over her edges. She was fading away.

I will wait.

"You're at peace?" he asked. The tears were back now, and through that lens, she had faded even more.

Death is gentle.

She was at peace. The love, the desire to be with him, was not strong enough to keep her in reality. She was not a ghost, she was a soul at rest, ready to move on. She was fading away before his eyes and nothing he could do, not all of the secrets he learned at the feet of the Butterfly would keep Nkosazana in the world with him forever.

But he could keep her for a time.

He removed a piece of paper from his coat, and sketched her shape as she appeared to him, floating above her grave.

He rubbed her name and dates behind the drawing, and kissed it once. Then, gazing into the gentle eyes of the spirit of his love, he spoke a few more words. The syllables wrapped around Nkosazana's soul and drew her into the paper. He kissed it again, and put it in his coat.

She would stay with him. Until there was nothing left.

Masu Station

MUST BE NICE MISSING SOMEONE that much. One look at this corpse I'm wearing and this guy was a blubbering mess. If I told him to jump out the window, he probably would do it. I wouldn't do that, though. I'm not a monster.

Well, all right, so I am. But I'm not that kind of monster.

I was supposed to be playing a role here, so I should probably focus. Specifically this poor Prodigal's dead girlfriend Yumi. It was her meat I was walking around in. Watching him sob in front of me, and it was almost enough to forget he was the one who killed her, using some weird Prodigal combination of Sorcery-Alchemy-Thaumaturgy. That was the problem with Prodigals. They couldn't even practice one Art and leave it there. Oh no, they always seemed to cobble together some warped understanding of the world.

"Please, Yumi, forgive me! I didn't know!" he wailed, and I did my best not to roll my eyes. I mean, I could have told him that death wasn't the end. Not even close. I could probably go look Yumi up, considering how odd her death had been. The stranger the death, the more likely to spit out some offspring. Just like sex, really.

This Prodigal wasn't much to look at. Some kind of harajuku fashion reject from a nameless subculture that would be absorbed tomorrow. To me, he looked a little like what would happen if a pop star decided to be a hillbilly somewhere in America, then got an anime makeover from a drunk raccoon. He was in so many bright colors, it was hard to look at him without squinting, and I was looking through eyes that had already gone a bit milky.

The fucking freezers in the local morgues, I swear. Raise them half a degree. The world isn't going to end any quicker.

"I need you to leave the kami be, and then I can rest," I said, using my best "ghost girlfriend" voice, and the sad truth of it was, I had developed one. I hadn't been a ghost for too long—only a couple years—but this was pretty far from my first one of these.

When I first started, I wondered why my mistress, that's the Butterfly, didn't have these Prodigals killed. Then I asked her heir, Tōriki Satoru, a guy so creepy he gives ghosts the willies. He grinned at me in that way that said he could read my ectoplasm like a book, and told me why. It was because she would rather wait until they were needed, then have them killed and turned into ghosts or zombies or one of her other Servitors. They were easier to control that way. I shuddered, and he laughed and laughed at me.

I should mention that he's basically my boss now. I used to work for another Apprentice, a fellow named Wei Lai, but he went and got himself shot. Didn't see it coming. Okay, that's only funny if you know him. Knew. Whatever, doesn't matter. I worked for Tōriki, but on this job I was backed up with some of Oni's men who were waiting for me outside. If this Prodigal realized he was getting played, we would go to plan B, which was replacing his vital organs with lead.

So I was really there on a humanitarian mission.

"I will, I'll leave the kami alone! I'll never call them again! As long as you forgive me!"

So I forgave him. If he didn't cut it out, the spies would report it, and he'd be dead, so really he was going to stop one way or the other. At least I wouldn't be the one to kill him. Not that I minded killing people. After you learn death isn't the end, it's pretty easy to force someone in that transition. It's just that after all the crying and so on, I felt like we'd shared a little something.

I left him in his tiny apartment to think about what he'd done to the nice lady whose rotting skin I was wearing, and went down to the curb. My backup was loitering outside, and maybe it's me, but ex-yakuza made me nervous. Haven't always, but once one of them murders you, it kind of sours you on the whole thing. It wasn't like I could avoid them, either. About a quarter of the Butterfly's soldiers came from their ranks, and they didn't really leave the lifestyle behind. They were the flashiest soldiers in the bunch, with their shiny suits, ornate tattoos, expensive sunglasses, and glittering jewelry. Waiting for me on that nighttime corner in Tokyo, flashing like nickel-plated guns, were two men I knew as Sato Masuyo and Yamashita Kitano.

Sato fancied himself a thinker, leaning his wiry frame on a Toyota modified VIP style, while he flipped a butterfly knife open and closed. He wore a mustache and goatee that made me think he was trying to look like a bad guy from American TV. Yamashita was his opposite, standing on the sidewalk, arms folded, feet apart. He always stood like he thought someone was going to try to knock him down. His shaved head was as shiny as his suit. Yamashita was practically a legend for being one of the few soldiers who ever killed a Familiar.

I walked out to join them, the body's stiffening joints starting to give me a little trouble. She was far from the worst body I'd ever ridden, but she was seriously making me consider writing a strongly-worded letter to the Tokyo city morgue.

"How did it go?" Sato asked, the knife clicking as he flipped it shut again.

"I think his magicking days are over."

"Good work, Kaeru." Yamashita's voice was gruff, but from him that was rapturous praise indeed.

I got in the back while the two soldiers rode up front. Sato insisted on driving, and I don't think it bothered Yamashita. He was the kind of man who didn't want anything to get in the way of his ability to kill.

"So you want us to take you to a station, or do you want to come out to the club with us?" Sato asked.

I blinked my borrowed eyes. I wasn't expecting that. Soldiers, even the experienced ones, usually wanted to get as far away from ghosts as they could. Unless Sato was thinking of me as a conversation piece or oddity. Still, didn't seem like him. If he was inviting me out, there was either an angle he was playing, or he wanted my company. Teasing, bullying, or party tricks wouldn't factor in.

"Sure, I'll go with you." I was intrigued enough, and I was pretty sure the body's taste buds hadn't gone yet.

The club had a neon sign out front, blazing down on the line of people waiting to get in. The crowd were like larval forms of Sato and Yamashita, like they might somehow turn into those two someday. They probably thought that the yakuza were the pinnacle of aspiration, without ever considering there was a far more powerful organization beyond. Whatever the case, the doormen knew the Butterfly's men, or else knew their attitudes were not put on, and waved us by. Probably thought I was a gangster's girl. That was enough to put a wry smile on my face, and when one of the doormen saw it, he shuddered noticeably. That made me grin even wider.

Some salaryman was onstage crooning "Don't Cry Out Loud." He was clearly drunk and exhausted, but the weird part was, he wasn't half bad. I'm sure his English was crap. He didn't have my advantage of growing up with American action movies to teach him, I guess. I swear, it's incredible I don't speak English with an Austrian accent. Small miracles.

Yamashita led the way through the crowd, his fire hydrant of a body moving people aside without even trying like a destroyer through the ocean. Sato followed in his wake, and I came along behind. My left knee—well *Yumi's* left knee if you want to be pedantic, but she wasn't using it—was locking up every third step. Inexperienced ghosts always thought it was rigor, but the truth is, rigor mortis comes and goes. After that it's all vigor mortis, and believe me that always gets a laugh. Well, to the ghosts who speak English anyway. No, it's from the collection of fluids and it comes from our friend gravity. It meant I had to help circulate it with my own ectoplasm, and that's like walking, chewing gum, and juggling chainsaws at the same time.

The salaryman onstage was really getting into it. His forehead was glistening with sweat as he belted Melissa Manchester into that microphone. And like I said, I don't think he spoke English, so he was singing from memory. When he was done, he was going to get a drink bought for him by a ghost.

I was so distracted that I ran right into Sato's back. He had stopped, and when I collided with him, he turned, his hand already reaching for the butterfly knife in his jacket. He saw it was me and grinned. "And you're not even drunk yet."

"You try rotting."

Sato's grin brightened. I smiled back, but that died as soon as I saw who was at the table. I would have shit, but Yumi already had the last one of those she ever would. One of the guys I didn't recognize, and barely saw anyway. The one I did see was younger than the others, maybe a full decade in some cases. He still looked like a teenager, especially with that bleached blond hair. Anyone looking at the group would have been much more frightened of any of the others, but they didn't know this animal like I did.

"And who is this little lady?" The speaker was the man I had barely noticed. I took the time to look at him now. He looked like a goddamn movie star, like some kind of Japanese Brad Pitt. He knew it too, with a confident smirk on his lips and a white rose on his lapel.

"It's a he," Sato said, "and the body is dead, Yoshiro."

The handsome man shrugged. "Still moving, though."

The others laughed at that.

"Meet Osugi Yoshiro and Watanabe Takashi. Gentlemen, this is Kaeru," Sato said.

Watanabe. That was an alias. He had a real name. Maeda. I wasn't going to forget that. They nodded to me, and I was too stunned to nod back at them.

I started to sputter while my thoughts were struggling to catch up. I only knew that I couldn't be anywhere near Maeda or whatever the fuck he was being called now. I had to get out of there, get away from these soldiers. I didn't breathe for any reason than to get air to talk, but I was having the distinctly human sensation of being unable to get a breath in my useless lungs. The crowd pressed around me too close, and the man on stage seemed to be singing directly to me now, telling me not to cry out loud, telling me to be quiet, while I tried to scream.

"You okay, Kaeru?" Maeda—Watanabe—asked me.

"I... I have to go... I forgot..."

Sato smirked, and then saved me without even knowing. "Just wants to get to a masu station."

"Yeah, I just remembered I needed..."

"Masu... what?" Watanabe asked.

"You'll find out. Once you've been around a little longer."

The raucous laughter from Yamashita and Osugi chased me out the door. I knew it was for Sato's comment, for the implication about we ghosts, but it felt like they were mocking my cowardice. Maybe they were. They couldn't know, right? Unless they were recruited at the same time. Maybe they knew the story, had heard it around some club table after a hundred drinks. But they couldn't know me at least, couldn't know I was the one it happened to. I wasn't born being called Kaeru. I didn't get that name until the Butterfly brought me into her service. I didn't have a face to recognize. But what if? What if?

Ironic to have a ghost haunted by anything, but there it was. Those thoughts ran through my borrowed gray matter while I staggered through the Tokyo night on a knee that wanted nothing more than to lock up. Maybe Sato was on to something. A masu station would take my mind off it. Mind, right. I didn't really have one of those. I was thinking through someone else's brain that was rapidly turning into useless jelly, but that didn't stop me from having memories. It was as though the mind didn't actually store memories, but kept them from hurting too badly. Now there was no buffer, and all I could see was Maeda's face on my last day as a flesh and blood man.

No one would have known the masu station just by looking at it. I could have sensed it from miles away. Ghosts are like that; we can smell each other better than dogs. Anyone passing would assume it was an apartment building, and not a good one either. It was the kind of place for the lost and the desperate, which was perfect for a bunch of dead people. I went inside, hoping to leave the looming memories of Maeda outside and knowing I could not.

The front room looked like the lobby of a ratty hotel. Pretty accurate. The woman behind the counter was dead. She was a zombie, the other side of the coin from ghosts. We're souls without bodies, and they're bodies without souls. The Butterfly used them for menial tasks and shock attacks. Anything that didn't require any imagination. This woman was in good shape, and if she had any wounds, they would have been under the dress that hung off her like a sail. Her flesh was grayish and her eyes just the tiniest bit milky. She could pass for human, but just barely. Any mortal who wandered in would have a creepy story to tell.

"Name, please?" the zombie asked.

"Kaeru."

She consulted a ledger in front of her. It was encoded, and understanding that code probably took what imagination she had left. Finally she located my name and made a mark. "The usual then?"

"Please."

"Follow me."

The zombie shambled away from the desk. A closet opened behind her and another zombie emerged, this one a man, and took the first one's place. I wondered how many were around, just waiting. The first zombie led me to the first door, which was metal and locked up tight. She opened it, and the wall of freezing air kissed us with looping tendrils of ice. I stepped inside. It was much like a morgue, with trays and trays of bodies inside each one. The zombie selected a tray and opened it up. I nearly laughed when the body was revealed. He was medium height and pretty fit, with a bullet hole through his heart. He was also covered in yakuza tattoos.

"This one should be perfect," the zombie said.

"You have no idea," I said, and left Yumi's corpse. It was an odd feeling, becoming liquid smoke, and oozing from her nose and mouth. I had gotten somewhat used to that light sensation as I left a borrowed body behind. Stranger still was the way my thoughts went from neat and ordered, an internal monologue to make a private eye proud, and turned into the chaotic scratching of my ghost thoughts. With everything stripped away, there was only my desire. Usually it was for sex, images of breasts and asses and pussies and cocks pounding in at me with the screeching chords of my need, but this time... well, yes, that was there. But they kept getting interrupted with images of Maeda leveling that gun at my head, and the sound of my blubbering for mercy. Then the shot, bigger than my life.

And then I was inside the dead yakuza, my ectoplasm forcing the heart to work again and I could think like a person. The zombie had opened an empty tray and I helped him put Yumi on it. It was a good idea to save her. Never know if that Prodigal would forget our little visit and decide to start his bullshit again. They'd preserve her body too, secret techniques probably gained from an Alchemist Apprentice long since dead. Yumi would be even fresher the next time they needed her meat.

There were freezers like this all over Shi Jie, and truth be told in every other domain save one. Bodies the Butterfly's servants bought or stole from crematoria, cemeteries, mortuaries, and morgues. The dead people didn't need them and families were just as happy scattering wood ash or burying empty coffins. Some were sent to the masu stations to help entertain us. Others were used for more official business. It was tough to argue with both the logic and the generosity of it. The Butterfly ensured that her children were well cared for.

My body was in one of them.

I knew that because that was how they found me. I was murdered, and that made for a good ghost. I mean, someone dying at ninety, surrounded by kids, and grandkids, and great grandkids, and what the hell, a couple ex-wives, they did everything they needed to do. They didn't have these crazy needs that kept them going. Someone gets shot in the head by a loanshark? Well, that fellow has demons.

Apparently my murder wasn't solved either. What with my murderer, you know, not in prison. That was the kind of thing that kept ghosts up nights. I shook my head. I was at a masu station. I should try to enjoy myself.

The masu stations were also scattered around Shi Jie, and unlike the simple freezers didn't have franchise locations outside of the Butterfly's borders. They were a little difficult to hide, especially when any Magus would do their level best to shut them down. The stations rather elegantly addressed a pretty simple problem: how do you get a ghost to do what you want?

Any Necromancer could compel obedience. I knew that from experience. The Butterfly was better than that. More powerful and a lot more subtle. She knew that ghosts were pure souls, nothing but desire, and no outlet. Every ghost has two things motivating them. The first is unfinished business, usually revolving around how we died. Once that's solved it's useless as a leash, and any ghost that lasts more than a few decades will inevitably get that wrapped up one way or another. The other is the desire, that one thing we miss from our breathing days. The worst part is that this desire, whatever it is, just gets worse and worse the older we get. It's like food, water, air, shelter, all those things that make a living person tick, rolled into a single pungent substance.

Inevitably, our tastes get a bit jaded. And we need more.

The doors along the way were left open. Careless. Also, safe. We were among our own in here. A house for ghosts, staffed by zombies. All undead from top to bottom. It was a good thing because we ghosts could lose control in here, and no one would die. Well, no one else anyway. Someone wandering in would get a nice close look at Hell before we tore him apart, and then, what do you know, a death violent and weird enough that we just made a new ghost.

As I passed by the doors, I couldn't help peeking. I saw a corpse set in front of a feast, and he was gorging himself. Gravy and chocolate ran in rivers down from his mouth. The body had been fat, but the ghost was eating so much the belly was distending. He would eat until he burst. I knew that for a fact,

MASU STATION // 289

even as the zombies brought him another plate of sushi and a full rump roast.

In another room a possessed corpse hung from the ceiling, massive fishhooks through his flesh. The zombies in here weren't preppy waiters, but were dressed in leather costumes, the studs glinting in the dim light. The masked women beat the body with cat o' nine tails, the barbed lashes mortifying the flesh with thick cuts that looked like the wounds from a wild animal.

In another room, a nude woman knelt in the middle. She was covered in blood, just like the room. Pieces of bodies were scattered apart, torn to shreds in a rage.

We all had things we had to do, and everything was on the menu. The Butterfly didn't care, and the zombies couldn't, so we were indulged in every way we needed. The zombie opened up a room for me. The two girls on the bed were dressed in school uniforms—well, school uniforms as reimagined for someone like me. They were holding hands, and staring at the door. They were hot, too. These two were well-preserved, and barely looked like they had a wound on them. I don't know how they got bodies so perfect, but someone was happy with my service if I was going to get them. The room was decorated like some high school girl's boudoir, and they were just waiting for me to get home.

"Enjoy yourself," the zombie receptionist said.

I tried, I really did. Normally a couple hot-to-trot zombies is exactly what I need to unwind. And if I needed a little help, they were always willing to get started on each other. They didn't really care one way or the other. No soul, no desire. While I preferred enthusiastic partners, it was a bit harder to get laid when your meatsuit was sweating off your body. I usually provided enough enthusiasm for all of us. Hell, I've been so enthusiastic I've completely ruined not only whatever body I was wearing but the zombies tasked with helping me out.

But I could not stop thinking about Maeda.

That's the last thing I want to be thinking about normally. Unless I get a hankering for a guy, which while not exactly rare is definitely less common. And I didn't want to fuck Maeda.

Watanabe.

Watanabe Takashi.

Get used to the name, I told myself. That's how I'd find him. If I started hunting "Maeda" the best I'd come up with were rumors. He vanished, but someone's cousin saw him in Tokyo with some new crew with a heavy rep. Watanabe. Watanabe.

I hated that it bothered me. It didn't matter. Or, in a perfect world, it shouldn't. If you're a ghost, you have a murderer. It's like having a father you know for a fact hates you. Watanabe was mine, and that's where it should have ended.

I pushed the girls away, disgusted with myself. If I couldn't get focused for these two, what the hell was wrong with me? They took it the wrong way and started to put on a little show for me. Normally that would have triggered something, but all I saw was Maeda holding that gun and hearing the sharp report and then I'm a ghost.

I cursed on the way out.

I left the body right there. No need. I turned to smoke and reformed on the other side. Let the schoolgirl zombies clean up the body where it collapsed onto the floor. My thoughts went haywire immediately, and I was down to the chaos of images. The need, what propelled me, was no longer images of wet, engorged genitalia. All I could see was Watanabe. I saw him screaming, blood running through those stupid blond locks of his. Saw his eyes distended, his mouth opened in a scream.

I crawled out of that place, my mind going in circles. I barely recognized my path, just traveling along by instinct. The path was floored in black sand, winding away into the impenetrable dark of Diyu, the underworld. I could have climbed down the craggy walls into the next level, but I had no wish to go there. I had a destination in mind, and it was here, at the place closest to the surface.

I passed the massive Torii that marked this place as part of the Butterfly's dark empire. Other Necromancers had staked out corners, Anansi in the reflection of Khem, Tumudurere in Thawun, and the domains of all the others who had long since passed into the next realm. Those places sank beneath the volcanic sand only to emerge on lower and lower levels of the underworld. The black basalt necropoli of the Crocodile could still be found if you went deep enough. And didn't mind dealing with packs of wild and mad ghosts.

Two Pale Lords stood watch by the Butterfly's Torii, their forms gigantic in Diyu. One was old, the other young, but both had gained power in this place, and were two of the Butterfly's most dangerous Servitors. The first was Akehara. He had grown strong enough to incarnate his ornate samurai armor, though it was only in shades of gray. He held his severed head under one arm, and his belly was split open, revealing the mutilated tentacles of his intestines. I had seen Akehara grab ghosts that annoyed him with his entrails and squeeze them until the ectoplasm dripped down to water the black soil. On the other side was Kiko. She was possibly nude or possibly clad in some diaphanous tatters of cloth. There was no clear definition where her body ended and the garment began. There was no real distinction anyway; it was all the plasm of her soul. She was skeletally thin, her thinning hair falling to her shoulders. Mouths covered her body, obliterating any other features she might have.

The two Pale Lords didn't acknowledge me as I passed, but neither did they stop me. I had no rank comparable to them, but even my lowly position had its privileges. Instead I crawled along, my fingers and toes digging into the sand, and finding just a bit of the hard stone beneath it. I barely saw what I passed through, and in this state, I didn't need to. Not really. Humans who came to Diyu needed landmarks, but I wasn't human anymore. I was a piece of a human, turned into something both greater and lesser when my body and mind had been stripped away. Only a Necromancer could have stopped me from finding my destination, and even then only for a little while.

I passed through crime scenes, barely conscious of the reflections going through the endless passion plays of their deaths. I could have been locked in that form. I couldn't think of it in those terms, not without a mind, but when I did I felt a sense of regret and relief that almost overpowered me. It wasn't compassion. Couldn't afford to start crying ectoplasm for every ghost caught in a loop. I'd never get anything done.

My destination was well-hidden. Chances are even experienced necronauts would pass it by. It wasn't like the garish fresh crime scenes, or those places that had become such indelible homes of pain, death, and madness. Only one crime happened there, and it was a couple years ago, and really it wasn't so bad in the scheme of things. My soul wasn't there, powering my grief and fear, either. I'd moved on to bigger and better things, namely stealing dead bodies at the behest of an immortal in some never-ending mob war. You know, job security. That didn't mean that the crime scene was gone. No, it was still there. It was at the end of a winding path that had narrowed to the barest spit of basalt, and every step sent more sand tumbling into the deep dark below. I saw the room, lit by a bulb that should have been changed had it existed as more than an imprint of trauma. When I was pulled out of the loop before I'd had a chance to decay, I left behind a reflection. A faded version of myself, and this was what I looked at now. It was a ghostly image—no pun intended—of a human shape kneeling on the ground. The killer was gone entirely, so it looked like whoever it was was begging to thin air. And then the shape shuddered, threw up its hands, and collapsed, and white liquid, like milk, growing in a pool around its head. Wait a minute or two, and the whole show could start again.

The violence still marked it as a portal. In a couple years, maybe not so much, but now I could still affect the shift over. All it took was wanting, and if there's one thing we ghosts could do, it was want. So then I was in the skinlands, on the floor of my old apartment.

It was dark in here. It looked like someone had rented the place. Someone who really liked *Trigun* judging by the art on the walls. He probably had some problem with strange sounds out here in the living room from time to time, but he had no idea how lucky he was. Without my soul powering things, the manifestations would just get weaker. And then, nothing. Just like every other place.

Except not anymore. Because I was there now, and the crime came back into me. There was no filter, nothing to stop the raw memories from blasting through my entire body. And there I was, kneeling again in the center of the room, crying like a baby and hating that I was doing that. Maeda—Watanabe now, serving my mistress—had his gun to the back of my head telling me it was about his money. I shouldn't have stolen. And I was telling him I didn't, because I didn't. I was a gambler, yeah. I had debts, sure. But I always surfed them, paying one off with the loans from the next to make sure something like this never ever happened, and here it was, and I was crying and begging and burning with shame that when the bullet finally came it was almost a relief.

I collapsed on the floor, my ectoplasm bleeding out over the wooden surface. I couldn't stop it if I had tried. The memory, my death, had me. Until the show was over, I wasn't breaking out of the loop. All I could do was mime the begging, my teeth chattering in place of words my mindless soul could never make, and take the phantom bullet.

It wasn't until I was done that I heard the scream. I turned and found the occupant, a tubby thirtyish woman in her underpants, staring in horror at me and the place on the floor where I had died. I felt like apologizing to her—or at least I had a sudden rush of guilt—but there were no corpses to possess. Good thing too, since in my mindless state, I would have just done it, and not figured out the problem until I was halfway through the apology and the poor lady was shitting herself listening to a dead guy say he was sorry. My only option was to wish myself back into Diyu, and there I was. I was still technically in the apartment for the time it took to skitter out of there, since it existed in both places. At least I was out of that woman's life.

I needed to do something with what had happened. It was not a plan, or even a voiced desire. It was a need, a pain shooting from my head where the ghost bullet had split my skull. I was rushing to alleviate that agony, and I knew the place to start.

I found the freezer without much trouble. I didn't even have to backtrack to the Torii where Akehara and Kiko waited as representations of the Butterfly's power. Like I said, there were freezers everywhere, and Tokyo was one of her most important cities. The ghosts got to be dead in style.

I emerged in the freezer room, and the zombie manning it, though he had blue skin from the cold and eyes entirely milked over, instantly opened up a tray. It was some middle-aged guy, and I guessed he had probably worked himself to death. I got the image of the salaryman singing "Don't Cry Out Loud," and took it as a good luck sign. Yeah, I was a gambler. Still was, I guess.

I entered his body, and then I could think. Perfectly preserved, this one. The Butterfly's people probably had him before he even hit the ground, and the alchemical processes had kept him spic and span. He was the very picture of health! Other than being dead, I mean. Nobody's perfect.

I hopped off the slab and the zombie closed it behind me. I went into the locker room and went through the racks of clothing, looking for something that would fit this body's form and not draw too much attention. A cheap suit would be perfect. A punk outfit and nipple rings would be pushing my luck. A zombie came in as I was going through the racks. There was a time I would have covered up in shame in front of such a pretty girl, but I was dead and the body wasn't even mine.

"Name please?" she said to me in a monotone.

"Kaeru."

She checked the ledger in her hand, and found my name amongst the list.

"Are you on assignment?"

"No. I need a body for the masu station."

"Why not use one of theirs?"

"Because I have rather... specific needs, and unfortunately nothing they have there is quite right."

"Understood. Enjoy your new flesh, Mr. Kaeru, and if possible, return it undamaged."

"I'll do my best, but you know masu stations. Am I right?"

She didn't have a sense of humor about that. She didn't have a sense of humor about anything. Poor dear. She was nice enough, though.

I went out into the streets, and it took some time, but I found him. He was coming out of a club with a girl under each arm. I would have spotted that blond hair anywhere. And I stuck out here, amongst the young and beautiful in my salaryman skin and cheap suit, but not enough for him to see. He wasn't even looking for me. It's so easy to tail someone when you can switch bodies, and this one wasn't even getting gamey.

I was already grinning as I followed him to the hourly hotel. Even though I had a brain to think through, something to sort of focus that grinning slurry of madness, I hadn't really thought of a plan. I knew what I was going to do, but then I was just going to wing it. Why? Because I hadn't haunted anyone in awhile. Other than the other night, which I wasn't even trying to do. I was going to throw a lot of stuff at the wall and see what stuck.

I stashed the body in a closet, and hoped no one would find it. Then again, I would have liked to have seen the look some maid's face who found a dead guy next to her mops. I crawled over to Watanabe's room, judging that he probably was already in the throes of passion. Call it payback for fucking up my trip to the masu station. And no, just because he liked girls and I liked girls didn't make me think there was some kinship. This asshole killed me. I didn't care if we were twins. I was going to make him shit out his own kidneys before his heart finally gave up.

I slunk under the door, easy to do when you're dead, and climbed the wall. I wasn't really thinking anymore. The anger was back, the insistent memory of this fucker who got to be alive putting a fucking bullet in my brain. It was black, and red, and it was dripping through my body. I wanted to get him. I wanted to tear him apart, starting with the parts of him he could never ever put back together. I saw him in the dark, and now he would see me.

I don't remember what I did in that room. I got isolated images, sure. Once I got going, I really got going. It's not something we ghosts can help. Our rage is like one of those cartoon snowballs, and mine was rolling at a pretty good clip. Because of what we do, a lot of people think our power comes from the fear we siphon from hauntings. It doesn't. It comes from the anger we experience when we unleash it. Anger begets anger begets anger. And there's no filter telling me to back it off. To calm down. No, this was me with my murderer trapped in a room. The powerful ghosts, the Pale Lords, know how to call on anger like it's the pizza man. Me, I'm a pretty cheerful guy most days. I need inspiration.

Watanabe gave me that.

I know that I made the walls bleed. Not dripping, either. Later I found actual brain matter that pushed through the wallpaper like fungus, weeping with gore. I know the door was locked, too. One of the girls died there, scratching her nails to the bone trying to get out. I felt a little bad about her. She hadn't deserved that, but I could apologize once I mentioned a couple potential recruits to Tōriki or someone else. The floor was covered in stinking standing water, and unidentifiable things flopped around in there. I still don't know what that's about, but that's what happens when your subconscious gets the wheel.

I only came back to consciousness wearing the skin of the other girl now sadly dead, a pair of scissors plunged through her heart. My ectoplasm pumped around that, jury-rigging her heart to do its job now that the blades skewered it. Watanabe cowered on the bed, wearing only underwear he had thoughtfully filled with shit. The bed was alive with centipedes, and Watanabe was weeping.

I blinked. I had no idea what brought me out of the red haze. The kid was begging for his life, sure. I wasn't seeing the kinship there, really just the whole justice angle still. I stood there, getting ready to leave the dead girl's body—and I apologized to her again—and get to work on the real asshole here. It wasn't until the blubbering took a turn, and then I realized it. He must have said it, and in my ghostly state I had somehow understood and needed him to get an answer.

"Please! Why are you doing this?"

I smiled. *Why are you doing this?* It was almost funny. Only one of the Butterfly's people would ask that. Only those who understood ghosts. He did have a right to know, or, more accurately, I had to tell him.

"My name is Kanke Hiromichi, you asshole. You killed me. Now I'm going to return the favor, and believe me it's going to take a little longer than you took with me."

Watanabe blinked in terrorized confusion. "Kanke?" Even as he said my name, I felt the ripple of power through my diaphanous tissues. "Wait… wait… I know you."

"You do! Or you did, when you put a bullet through my head."

"It was nothing personal! I swear!"

I pulled the scissors out of the girl's chest, followed by a gout of turgid blood. "It doesn't get more personal than murder. But look on the bright side, it's like that movie with the lions. You kill me, I kill you, it's the circle of life."

"No! I only killed you because you stole from me!"

"I never stole from you. Never once. I knew who you were. I knew you were trouble. It's why I borrowed money from a lot of guys but never from you."

"You stole! You stole from me, and if I didn't answer then it was going to be the bullet in my head! I had to kill you, don't you understand?"

"Who told you I stole?"

"Horikawa Ryo! He told me!" Watanabe kept screaming, but I couldn't hear him. Horikawa Ryo. My friend. My best friend, in point of fact. The one person I had never even dreamed of being involved. Why would he even do it? I let the girl's body tumble to the floor and I got out of there. I was too stunned even to pick the dead guy up in the closet. More memories, flashing through me, unfettered by flesh to put any kind of brake on them.

Horikawa Ryo. My partner. When I needed a player on the other end of the table to chew up some tourists, he was the one I went to. Sure, we fed each other's bad behavior. He drank more when he was around me, and I chased more skirt, but we were friends. Inseparable even. What passed through me were images of us together, drinking, laughing, whoring, gambling, but while the memories had once held the shine of friendship, now they were jaundiced. Every one of his expressions looked fake, brittle. He was wearing a mask of his own face.

I didn't start thinking straight until I found a brain to think through. When I came through in the freezer room and the zombie in there—a different one—opened a tray, I opened another, using my rage to do it for me. On any other day, I wouldn't have picked this body. After all, it helps to have a brain to think with, and this one was practically obliterated. My ectoplasm would repair it and even spackle some false flesh over the ruined forehead. I didn't even realize what I'd done until I stood up.

I was wearing my old body.

I stumbled out of there to the locker room, and quickly found a hat I could put over the hole in my forehead. I guessed no one had thought to use some putty to maybe patch that. It was a little late to complain in any case. I was half dressed when the zombie came in.

"Name please?"

"Kank..." I faltered. "Kaeru. My name is Kaeru."

"Are you on assignment?"

"Masu station."

"Our records show that you were just at a masu station, Mr. Kaeru."

"Yeah... that last body didn't work out."

"This one has a hole in the head."

"Works everywhere else."

The zombie marked his tablet. "Very well. Watch the time."

I nodded, and the remainder of my frozen brains nearly tipped out of my head. I focused on the ectoplasm keeping them in place. I wasn't going to pass even the most casual inspection, but I didn't need to leave a trail of braincrumbs for people to follow. That was bad for business.

As for my destination, I could find it as easily as my own murder site. Although unlike then, when I trusted in my new, death-born senses, here I could trust my memory. I had been there countless times. Picking him up, decompressing after marathon games, or sometimes just watching a little TV with a beer. He wouldn't have moved, either. Ryo was a creature of habit, and it had only been a couple years.

I had doubts. I wasn't completely sold. I didn't see a lie in Watanabe, but that didn't mean it wasn't there. It was an unlikely lie at best. Horikawa Ryo wasn't a name he was picking out of a hat. If I were him, I'd send me after someone in the yakuza he hated and always wanted gone. And Ryo did owe money, just like I did. Only he wasn't as careful about who he borrowed it from. Give him a drink or two and he'd take cash from a boss, promise to pay it back the next day, and piss it all away.

The ring of truth was more than a little troubling.

But that's what I was doing. I wasn't running off half-cocked. I wasn't turning into the enraged ghost, ready to kill anyone and everyone. I wasn't wild. As dead people went, I was pretty well-adjusted. So I was going to find out who was really responsible, and if it was Watanabe, I'd give it to him even worse.

And if it was Ryo...

Well, I could hope it was Watanabe.

I broke into Ryo's apartment using the spare key he hid on the light in the hallway. It burned my fingers, but I barely felt it. My stomach wasn't in knots; I felt the unbearable tension as a humming through the liquid smoke of my body.

It was the same old place. Cramped, cluttered, and with a week's worth of empty food and beer containers on the table. I sat down on his couch and waited. Time was, I would have been bored. But with death had come patience. I could sit there happily all night, and knowing Ryo, that's what I was going to do. I focused on the facts, ran through them again, and hoped to find deception.

Ryo came through the door at the same time as the sun. His clothes, still in a style a couple years too young for him, were rumpled. Bags weighed his eyes down. He hadn't shaved in a couple days. And I swear it's not just vanity saying this, but he smelled worse than I did.

"Hello, Ryo."

He jumped right out of his skin when he saw me sitting there on the couch.

"Who—?"

"You know who it is," I told him.

He did. After a little bit, anyway. He stopped in the doorway, unsure if he should just sprint down the hall and hope for the best. I didn't move, and that gave him some confidence. I took off the hat and set it aside. He could have a look at my face. The bullet fucked it up some, especially in the forehead area. My milky white ectoplasm helped somewhat with the identification.

Ryo blinked at me. Then, with dawning horror: "Hiro?"

I buzzed with the name being spoken out loud. It felt wrong. Even after only three or so years of being Kaeru, my name had taken on a nearly religious significance.

"That's my name," I said.

"I heard... I thought... you were dead."

"Do you not see the hole in my fucking face? You think I lived through that?"

"Medical technology being what it is..."

"Unless they perfected brain transplants, no."

"You're... dead?" Even though he was still my friend, I have to admit I enjoyed the horror in his voice. I felt like I was some English Gothic novel.

"Oh, very dead. Gangster put a bullet through my head." I tapped the side of the entry wound in the back of my head, feeling the sharp edges of my broken skull, then the blasted open forehead. The ectoplasm was slick but not wet, feeling like a thin plastic bag filled with water beneath my fingers.

"God... but how are you..."

"I'm a ghost, Ryo. I'm wearing my own body, which is a little confusing, I guess, but I'm a ghost."

"I'm sorry. I'm so sorry," he said.

I tried not to let the reaction show on my face. Was he sorry because that was just what you say to a dead friend, or because he'd done something to cause it? I stayed quiet. Let him fill the silence between him and his dead friend.

"Maeda. It was Maeda."

I nodded.

"I didn't know. When I told him you stole from him, I was scared, Hiro. I didn't know what else to say. He had a gun."

"I remember the gun."

"He pointed it at me, and I told him, I told him you took the money."

"I didn't take any money."

"I know, I know." He dropped to his knees. "It was me, Hiro. I stole from him, and then I lied about it. I'm so sorry. I can't sleep, I can't eat..."

I wanted to snap back, *Me neither,* but I kept that in too. Watanabe hadn't been the one lying. My old "friend" had me killed and now he wanted my forgiveness. The worst part was I was going to have to give it to him. I was going to have to pretend.

I stood up and he quailed in front of me. He was guilty, but still valued his skin enough to be scared of death. Good to know. I reached out to him and he cowered from my dead hand. "You're forgiven, Ryo."

The light and his eyes might have been funny if it hadn't been so pathetic. "Really?"

"Sure. It's done. I'm dead, and bullets through the head don't really hurt. It's like turning out the lights. But, I do need you to come somewhere with me. Briefly. Then I can pass along."

"Yeah, of course. Anything for you. Anything."

I picked up the cap and pulled it low over the wound. I felt like it should hurt when it scraped over the bloodless rind of my flesh, but it just kind of scratched a little. Ryo followed me, not as close as he used to. There was still some of the instinctive revulsion the living had for the dead in him. I was his friend, but the act of dying also made me the other. *Well, if you don't like it, maybe don't have your friend killed next time?*

He was quiet for the first couple blocks. He looked exhausted, and the sun was coming up over the city which always made it worse. The night's sweat dried on the skin, the night's food was a lead ball in the belly, the night's booze was a sick feeling in the back of the throat. I liked the sun. I didn't get much of it in Diyu, and I was seeing it with my own eyes for the first time in years. Granted, the left one didn't work so well after that bit of skull took half the eyeball, but it was still nice to see. Just made it look like I was watching through a dirty car window sometimes.

He finally started talking when we were a block or two from our destination, and he probably should have kept his mouth shut. "What's it like being dead?"

"Oh, it's a nonstop party."

"Really?"

"Oh, yeah. I hung out with an old friend, then I did karaoke the other night, then I was in a hotel room with a couple of chicks and things got a little messy."

"Is that... is that Heaven?"

"Does that sound like Heaven?"

"The two chicks part does. Don't know about the karaoke."

"That wasn't so much fun for me either. Well, here we are."

The cemetery was on a gentle hill cramped amongst the high rise apartment buildings. The rows of stones, like pillars had the brush of familiarity. Not for their shape in this place, but for Diyu's tendency to warp everything until it looked like the marks of the dead.

"A graveyard?" he asked, his voice small.

I went in without answering. His guilt, or whatever it was, would keep him on his leash. And follow he did. I acted like I wanted a specific stone, and he probably thought I was looking for a relative or someone. No, I just wanted to get into the middle of this place of power. I felt it as a churning in my liquid guts, and I had to clamp down on my ectoplasm. It wanted to burst from the wound in my face, swirl around on the floor until I could take my true form.

The memories were coming, and I was glad for what little brain I had left. I placed it between them and me, but I still saw it. The gun, the apartment, the blood. Only this time, it wasn't Watanabe holding the gun. It was my friend, Horikawa Ryo.

I stopped in the middle and turned. Ryo stopped, almost running into me. "Here we are," I said.

"Where?"

I grabbed him. I wasn't especially quick. I didn't have to be. He wasn't expecting me to lash out like that. I brought the memory back as strong as I could, really experiencing the moment of my death, the fear and shame, and turned it through the bright lens of need. The bullet blazed my trail the first time, and I followed its reflection in my mind, grabbing the hot lead as it burned into the underworld.

Ryo was screaming. I could hardly blame him. The first trip could be jarring, and even the quietest cemeteries were haunted. I glanced around. For the most part, the ghosts were mere echoes, doing ghost things. Either weeping on their own graves for the more self-absorbed or re-enacting their own murders for those who had a shaky understanding of location. They didn't react to us, as there was either not enough of them left to perceive us, or they were too locked into their internal dramas.

I grinned. Ryo punched me.

I fell on my ass, laughing.

"Where the fuck are we?"

"Diyu."

He gaped, probably expecting another answer. "What?"

"Diyu. It's a Chinese word. Probably a holdover from the last Steward of Shi Jie."

"Shi..."

"More Chinese. Don't worry about it." I stood up, reflexively checking my mouth for blood. Even though his fist had ripped the inside of my lip open on my teeth, there was no blood. "Westerners would call it the underworld, or Hell, or Sheol... I've heard a lot of terms for it, really. It's where the dead go."

"Why did you bring me here?"

"You wanted to know what it was like to be dead. Thought I'd show you. Well, look around."

"What are those?"

"Those are ghosts."

He yelped.

"Yeah, I'd keep quiet if I were you. If they sense you're human, well... actually I have no idea what will happen. I've never brought anyone over. Wasn't sure I could."

The front of the cemetery still had the gateway that led in from the sidewalk, but here, it had grown taller, spikier, the gates themselves looking like a carnivorous metal mouth. Beyond, the pathway extended into the darkness. I couldn't really see it, only glimmers off the shiny sand against the matte of the walls. To him it probably looked like we were on some strange island in the night sky.

"Where?"

"Come on," I said.

As we got closer, the pathway revealed itself. A few steps away, and it apparently dropped into nothing, but each step revealed more as it snaked into the darkness of the gargantuan cave. I wished for the sight I had as a ghost, but I needed to stay thinking. If I dropped the body, the rage and the memories would take over and Ryo would be destroyed. I wanted him to see what I saw. And it was a walk to get where I wanted to go.

"You said you forgave me!"

"Is this not what you had in mind?"

"Taking me to Hell?"

"You could call it Heaven if you wanted. It's all the same place. I mean, maybe. There is a way to pass on somewhere else, but it's not like anyone ever comes back. It's possible they just stop."

"Why are we here then?"

The path swooped and bent, like a rollercoaster. Someone should build one of those through this place if only so we didn't have to walk the whole way. I should ask the Butterfly. The path opened up and revealed a place of dying. People strapped to beds while spiny fingered monsters stuck and prodded them. All around were screens that said the same things over and over again: death. The building was broken in the side, and we could have climbed right in to be among those suffering.

"What the hell is that place? A prison? A torture chamber?"

"A hospital."

"Which one?" He asked like he wanted to avoid such a horrible place.

"Doesn't matter. Lots of people die in hospitals, you know.

And a lot of them die in pain. Enough of that, and you have this. Here. We could go back to earth through there."

He shrank away from it. "Is there anywhere else?"

"Oh, of course." I didn't want him to ask to go through there. I didn't want him seeing my cards yet. Poor guy.

I led him past other places where the violence had bled through and marked this place. Some places were fading while other places were brand new. I almost took him to my apartment, but I didn't want to scare that one woman again. Besides, I had a better plan.

I guided him to the Torii, where the two Pale Lords stood sentry. He gasped, staggering back at the sight of their terrible grandeur. "Holy shit."

"Yeah, they're something, right?"

"They... they..."

"Come on, stay with me. They're ghosts, just like—"

I didn't get a chance to finish the thought. Akehara's intestines had snaked out and wrapped around both of us, drawing us in to the air. I'd gotten his attention this time. That's what happened when you took flesh into the underworld, I suppose.

The intestines held me up for inspection, the rubbery white serpents constricting the both of us. Akehara held his severed head outward to really have a look at what he'd caught. His face had become the model of samurai pugnaciousness, the sort of thing seen on old artwork. It was likely not what he looked like in life, but the way his soul had always wanted to look. He inspected us with the pure black eyes of a ghost while ectoplasm dripped sullenly from his neck.

Ryo was screaming, and I probably should have been. It was the closest I had been to a Pale Lord. I nearly did scream when Kiko leaned in to regard us with the mouths she had in place of eyes. The teeth gnashed and her tongues writhed like maggots.

"What do you have?" When Kiko spoke, it was out of all of her mouths. They talked over each other, echoing her words before and after the main chorus of the meaning, and when she was quiet, some of her orifices were still whispering.

"Humans," Akehara said. "Outsiders."

"Ghost, actually," I told him.

"Who are you?" Kiko asked.

"Kaeru. I serve the Butterfly."

Kiko nodded. "I know the name." I'm not ashamed to admit I was flattered. Even though it was her job to know these things.

"Why did you bring a human?"

"He was the one who killed me."

The Pale Lords set me down. "Sincerest apologies, Kaeru, for obstructing your path," Akehara said.

"May your vengeance be bloody," whispered Kiko.

I bowed to them, hoping it was the right thing to do. The one thing every ghost understood was revenge. We didn't really have laws other than that one, and it was more of a commandment. I had been betting the Pale Lords would understand, and they had. Akehara inclined his head slightly, and Kiko offered a terrifying curtsy, holding the tattered tail of what might be a gown and might be flayed flesh.

"What was that? Vengeance?" Ryo yelped.

"Calm down and shut up. I had to tell them something."

"What the hell are those?"

"Pale Lords."

"What the hell is a Pale Lord?"

"This is just going to go in circles." I led him through the Torii, with him sputtered behind me, demanding to know more. The truth was, he'd know everything he needed to know soon enough. It was difficult to understand a Pale Lord anyway, not without knowing the chaotic hierarchy of the afterlife. I had no desire to explain it to him, not when the end was so close I could taste it like bloody milk.

Beyond the Torii was a castle. It didn't look like that from the other side, but those of us who loved it had sculpted the form without trying on this side of the veil. I took him inside, and we were only in the antechamber. It was decorated here, with the horrible art of the dead subconscious. The vilest pornography, the most decadent foods, the goriest torture, all on display for the visitors to this place. Masks sculpted from the same black basalt as the underworld, grinned at us with empty eyes from the walls. On the other side, in the skinlands, it was just a ratty old apartment building.

"What is this place?"

"A masu station," I said, grabbing him once again and stepping through.

We were in the hallway and I heard them, the ghosts losing control all around, slaking their every unholy desire. Fucking, eating, injecting, killing, all around us, making sounds no human throat could attempt without tearing itself to ribbons.

"What's that?" he asked, his eyes white with terror.

"That would be my forgiveness," I said.

The doors burst open. Some of the bodies were streaked with blood, some were spilling entrails, some were covered in streams of gore and gravy. Ryo got a chance to scream before they were upon him, ripping, fucking, eating. He couldn't make sounds after a moment or two, but he was still alive. I could tell by the terror in his eye before it was sucked from his skull.

I turned to the zombie who had come into the hall to investigate the disturbance. "Kaeru," I said, "returning a body. I don't need it anymore."

I dropped the body and scuttled away, not bothering to look as Ryo's soul materialized into its new home.

Appendix

THE TWINS

Magus
- The Twins, Faith and Hope, Mistresses of Diablerie, Stewards of Pemhakamik

Apprentices
- Ash Wednesday, Diabolist, Heir to the Twins, man of blood
- Rose Cross, Theurgist, trained by the Monk, spymaster, right hand of the Twins
- The Machinist, Enchantress, trained by the Artisan, retro-futurist
- Grandmother Coyote, Physurgist, trained by the Lion, deceased (killer still unknown)

Familiars
- Blackthorn, dryad, cheerful killer
- Shahmeran, wyrm, the snake goddess
- Ghostwalker, hellhound, the huntsman
- Coldheart, wendigo, newly created

Servitors
- Gnomes, ghoulish workers
- Orrerites, small living solar systems
      The Keeper of the Menagerie
- Thraxians, demonic warriors
      Zeryss, part of Rose Cross's security detail
- Vree-ka-vree, urban hunters
- Sadhvi Deva, Ash Wednesday's right hand

Soldiers
- Michael Barnes, head of security for Rose Cross

THE TWINS cont'd

Locations
- Northwind, extra-dimensional manor house
- The Menagerie, collection of wondrous creatures
- Chevalier Tower, lair of Ash Wednesday
- Bellamente, manor of Rose Cross
- The Machine Shop, workshop of the Machinist
- Darius Island, meeting place for emissaries of the Twins and the Lion

THE PRIESTESS

Magus
- The Priestess, Mistress of Sorcery, Steward of Cemanahuatl

Apprentices
- Itzcoatl, Sorcerer, Heir to the Priestess, ancient right hand to power
- Kisin, Physurgist, trained by the Lion, haunted enforcer
- Santa Orisha, Diabolist, trained by the Twins, paranoid cult leader

Familiars
- Teotl, fist of the Priestess, human battery
- Viracocha, indestructible immortal
- Saltamontes, teleporting messenger
- Huracan, telekinetic assassin (deceased, killed by Coldheart)

Servitors
- Bakru, wooden shapeshifters
    Arcadio, bodyguard to Santa Orisha
- Los Luminosos

Soldiers
- The 400 Sons, intelligence arm of the Priestess
    El Conjeo y La Luna, Quetzalcoatls

Locations
- The Condor's Nest, Manor of the Priestess, Andean temple complex
- El Labertino, artificial ley lines and nexii underground
- Ezcalli, lair of Itzcoatl and headquarters of the 400 Sons
- The Hounfor, mobile lair of Santa Orisha
- Santa Rosa de Lima, island home of Teotl

THE SERPENT

Magus
- The Serpent

Familiars
- Sotek, fire-breathing hobgoblin

Servitors
- Mimics, humanoid shapeshifters

THE LION

Magus
- The Lion, Master of Physurgy, Steward of Khem

Apprentices
- Zara Iblisa, Physurgist, Heir to the Lion
- Anansi, Necromancer, trained by the Butterfly, dark diplomat

Familiars
- Edunara, master of lightning
- Oorun, miniature sun

THE ARTISAN

Magus
- The Artisan, Master of Enchantment, Steward of Ki

Apprentices
- Jibreel al-Jannah, Sorcerer, trained by the Priestess, young Apprentice

Familiars
- Jihaz, the Artisan's finest weapon of war

Servitors
- Rajol Hadidi, the Clockwork Men

Soldiers
- Faisal al-Jarallah, covert agent

THE WOLF

Magus
- The Wolf, Master of Theurgy

Familiars
- Koshmar, the nightmare

THE BUTTERFLY

Magus
- The Butterfly, Mistress of Necromancy, Steward of Shi Jie

Apprentices
- Tōriki Satoru, Necromancer, Heir to the Butterfly, gothic zombie master
- Wei Lai, Prophet, trained by the Hermit, blind gambler

Familiars
- Jiangshi, soulless and nearly indestructible walking corpse
- Oni, soul-render

Servitors
- Ghosts
    Akehara, Pale Lord, samurai martyr
    Kiko, Pale Lord, starved model
    Kaeru, murdered gambler
- Zombies

Soldiers
- Captain Zhu Baolin, former People's Liberation Army, head of security for Wei Lai
- Corporal Wang Pingtou, former People's Liberation Army, bodyguard to Wei Lai
- Osugi Yoshiro, ex-yakuza, bodyguard to Oni
- Sato Masuyo, ex-yakuza, bodyguard to Oni
- Watanabe Takashi, ex-yakuza, bodyguard to Oni
- Yamashita Kitano, ex-yakuza, bodyguard to Oni

Locations
- Diyu, the Underworld
- Fantan Tower, lair of Wei Lai

THE HERMIT

Magus
- The Hermit, Master of Prophecy, Steward of Thawun

Apprentices
- Tumudurere, Necromancer

Familiars
- Kabur, prisoner of time

PRODIGALS

- Rahsan Ashar, brittle guru
- Olga Pineda, elderly witch
- Domingo Rey, Nahual hermit

SCIONS

- Father Typhon, son of Shahmeran, High Priest of the Cult of the Snake

Acknowledgments

To say that none of this could have been done without my wife is an understatement. Not only has she been the portrait of support that every writer dreams of, but she copyedited and laid out the book you just finished reading. She gave up nights and weekends to do this, and I could not be more grateful. Still, I'm going to try.

My two readers on this project, Penny Gronbeck and Leila Vandiver, were both invaluable in making sure what I was putting in here made sense as stories, and weren't the fevered ranting of a madman. More so than usual, at least.

Lastly, I want to thank all of you. If you just finished reading this, that means you. Don't bother to look around to see if I'm there. I've already vanished into the ether. The fact is, I could not write anything really without the loyal fans that make it possible. Thank you. All of you.

About the Author

PHOTO © LEORA SAUL

Much like film noir, Justin Robinson was born and raised in Los Angeles. He splits his time between editing comic books, writing prose, and wondering what that disgusting smell is. Degrees in Anthropology and History prepared him for unemployment, but an obsession with horror fiction and a laundry list of phobias provided a more attractive option. He is the author of more than 10 novels in a variety of genres including detective, humor, urban fantasy, and horror. Most of them are pretty good.

He and his wife reside in Los Angeles with an old cat, an idiot cat, and extensive book, comic, and DVD collections.

Books by
Justin Robinson

Daughters of Arkham (with David A. Rodriguez)
The Dollmaker
Everyman
Nerve Zero
Undead on Arrival

The Ahriman Cycle
The Last Son of Ahriman
The Dark Price of Ahriman

City of Devils Series
City of Devils
Fifty Feet of Trouble

Fill in the _____ Series
Mr Blank
Get Blank

League of Magi Series
Coldheart
The Daughter Gambit